Pandemonium

Pandemonium

MARYANNE COLEMAN

www.blkdogpublishing.com

For Taliesin, the Singer ....

With Love.

Other titles by Maryanne Coleman:

Goblin Market

No Faff, No Fuss, Just Food

Preface

Previously in Goblin Market . . .

Titania is Queen of Faerie. She knows that. Oberon knows that – which is only right and proper, because he is the King. The Goblins (Freckles, Tiny, Thydney and the gang) behind the skirting board know that . . . But, as she drags her weary self back from working at shelf-filling, it seems to Titania that they are the only ones that really believe in Faeries.

But a Faerie Queen can only take so much – she decides to rally what is left of her Folk and if they can't rise again, at least they can go out with a bang, not a whimper. They soon find Puck (doing a milk round in Woodford Green), Mab (making herself generally unpopular with practical jokes, since her Music Hall career went into decline), Cobweb (still looking after changelings when she can find one) and, with Oberon's help, the Goblin numbers are on the up.

The trouble is there is so much competition out there, these days. Television. Internet, Mobile phones. It's a hard job for anyone, especially Faeries who can't read or write.

Counting is a bit rudimentary as well, which was why Titania wasn't missed too much at the supermarket. What they need is someone to help . . . it's a bit scary, but they decide to get in touch with the Unseelie, the bad guys of Faerie. They used to stick north of Hadrian's Wall, but now they are everywhere. And that really does mean everywhere. Benedict (as he likes to call himself), their Lord, isn't just at home with technology. He invented it. Think fire and go on from there.

Benedict is a whizz in the city, making a mint wherever he clicks his mouse. Leanne is a theatrical agent – her days of Leannan-Sidhe, lurking at cottage eaves and luring young men to their doom are behind her . . . mostly. Benedict's butler, James, is usually fairly well scrubbed, thus hiding his bogle beginnings. He's all for the Return of Faerie as soon as he experiences the gentle touches of the lovely Titania in all the places dogs are ticklish – although in some cases, many of those are places no-one would want to scratch.

Add wizard-turned-lecturer Gwyddion, Black Annis, now a bag lady with a taste for (very) fresh pigeon, a tree-spirit with ideas above his station, a sprinkling of taxi-drivers, a studio floor manager on the verge of a breakdown and essentially you have it: a perfect recipe for the Return of Faerie – 'wiv knobs on,' to quote the porcine, but very lovable when you get to know him, Freckles.

They're back – but so is Someone Else . . . Enjoy Pandemonium, before it starts enjoying you!

'Good lack, the Spring is back, and Pan is on the road.'

Spring in Vermont, Rudyard Kipling

Chapter One

Titania lay back on her heather mattress, her eyes closed, ears attuned to every rustle, breathing in the soft scent of petals, honey and – she breathed in more deeply – yes, a faint, lingering undernote of Oberon's musky perfume.

New every morning she spent a few moments luxuriating in being herself, being where she was, and what she was. She was Queen of Faerie, supreme again in the world she so nearly had lost. Under her thoughts she knew that not all her Folk had chosen the Old Way; but enough of them had come with her to her glade in the wood to make her little world seem complete, so that was alright.

At last she could spend all day, every day, just being beautiful. No more having to tone down to be acceptable in a workaday world. Her hair could twine where it would, be any colour, all together if that was how her fancy took her. She could dress to her own taste, which tended to be sparkly and frilly. Or slinky and velvety. Or all at once. She sighed with pleasure. She was her own Faerie.

She turned over slowly and reached for the tiny silver bell which hung beside her bed. Almost before her fingers reached it, Freckles was there, grinning in his usual disconcerting way. Since his decision to join his Mistress rather than his Master he had tried to clean up his act. Not so much gambling, not so much staying out in rather smelly swampy places and not so much . . . Titania would rather not know about his really private pursuits. It was enough for her that he wasn't doing it so much. His green Mohican haircut was smarmed down with something glutinous and his eponymous complexion was polished to a gleam.

'Mistress?'

'Ah', she opened her eyes, but slowly. Cleaned up he may be, but he still took some adjusting to, first thing. 'Freckles. A bit of breakfast, not too much. Perhaps some dew and honey. Something like that.' She sniffed. 'Have you been eating bacon again? I don't know how you can; it seems so . . . so . . .'

What she wanted to say was 'cannibalistic', but the goblins didn't like being reminded of their porcine past, so she just let her sentence fall away into a queenly smile. She patted him on the shoulder.

'Sorry, Mistress. It was Puck started us on vat. We keep a bit in, in case he pops by. We have to watch ve sell-by dates – well, you know all about that.'

She shuddered. She had put her supermarket days in a little mental compartment marked 'Ugghh', but she couldn't forget them entirely.

'Isn't he about due for a visit?' she asked. She knew that Puck had his own agenda, out and about in the world now he had his speed back. But she missed him and wished he would come more often. Oberon kept him busy, of course, but, even so, surely it had been a long time. She had lost the knack, if she'd ever had it, of keeping mortal time, but still, it had been . . . weeks? A month even.

'What month is this?' she asked Freckles.

He looked at her in confusion. He raised his little shoulders up around his ears and shook his head. 'I dunno, do I? Winter, is all I know. January, do vey call it? Feb'ry?'

She set her lips in a little pout of annoyance. 'It has been a bit long since we saw him, Freckles. Have we heard from your Master at all?'

'Thydney was down the ovver day, Mistress. He says the Lord is busy, busy, busy.'

Titania and Freckles shared a quiet moment. That phrase from Thydney's lips must have been a wet one indeed.

'Is he still doing his programme?' Titania had disapproved of Oberon's rise to media fame. But she knew there was no stopping him, and she supposed it did keep Faerie exposure high. She was all too aware of how easily they could be forgotten. If people forgot them when the only entertainment available was music hall and lantern slides, how much more likely it would be with the bombardment of modern living – television, radio, CDs, DVDs, X boxes, Playstations, Internet; she didn't know what most of them were, but she was wary of them nonetheless.

Except for the Unseelie, now safely ensconced again North of Hadrian's Wall, Faerie didn't really mix too well with gadgets on even the most basic level. High in his penthouse flat, sub-let from Benedict when he moved back to his Highland castle, Oberon had struggled for a while with the electronic curtains, voice-activated clocks and phones in every corner. It was a battle he lost with good grace and now he lived the life of a technophobe, lights and television being his one concession to the electronic age. He put up with the lift some days, but when he was feeling flighty he would swoop up the outside of the building, hovering effortlessly outside the picture window, entering at a click of the fingers. Some of his neighbours on the floors below had learned to cope with it; he was, after all, a celebrity. Others would never get used to it – they were for the most part in their villas in Mustique or a safe, secure place where pretty girls in white coats looked after them, speaking in quiet, comforting voices and giving them pills.

Oberon had taken a while to settle in. He missed Titania more than he was prepared to let her know, and his visits, though brief, were frequent enough. In fact he had discovered it suited them very well. Even so, he was due for a few days R&R. He'd go down for a bit while he was waiting for Puck to get back. Rather like the Old Days, he stayed just long enough for the arguing to begin, then went back to what he did so well – charming people. Only now, to his delight, he could do it on a grand scale. His Saturday evening chat show was prescribed viewing for almost everyone, with the repeats late night on satellite picking up the insomniac remainder. He was rather like a bar of chocolate; you plan to only eat one square, but before you know it, the whole thing is gone and the hunt is on for another. So with Oberon – once seen, always addicted. And he *loved* it.

Like Titania, he had his own style. But his was never sparkly and frilly. His was always slinky and velvety. As far as he could see, the only worthwhile colour was black, although a touch of deep forest green was occasionally rather smart. As long as it was a green so deep that everyone thought it was black.

He tossed his raven curls and called to Thydney. 'Thyd, we're going down to visit your Mistress. Tell the others to take messages if they have to.' Oberon wasn't convinced that his goblins were very good at that sort of thing, but the odd sheep still in residence gave it their best shot. Anyway, if anyone wanted him, they would always get back to him later. Missed messages, Oberon found, only happened to other people. He had also discovered that Benedict had had staff, a concept he had embraced willingly, and sometimes literally. They, being Benedict's people, could be relied upon when the goblins couldn't. He held open his coat. 'Jump up, Thydney.' The little creature jumped into Oberon's arms and buried himself in his elegantly styled silk shirt. 'Thydney?'

He poked his head out. 'Yeth?'

Oberon wiped the spit from his coat lining. 'What were you doing when I called you?'

'Wathing up. I don't like that machine thing.'

'Well, dry your tr . . . hands, please. You're all damp.'

'Thorry, Thire.' He obediently jumped down and trotted into the kitchen. Oberon could hear muted conversation as Thydney said goodbye to his current squeeze, an ex-rabbit called, rather wetly, Thumper.

He scurried back, hopped into place and they were away.

Naturally, Puck kept the whole show going. Oberon was supposed to choose his own guests, but, as he would perhaps be the first to admit, since when had Oberon taken any notice of anyone but himself. Jeanne was his agent. The easiest job in the world, since every programmer wanted a piece of the Faerie King action. He had his rules of course. No gratuitous flying. No magic – he had people to do that for him. No couples – men and women both fell gladly under his glamour, but a couple was more difficult. He never knew which one to target and sometimes there was ricochet. It could cause endless trouble. He looked back with a shudder on the never-broadcast Affleck/Lopez interview. That had really put the cat among the pigeons, though to be fair to them, they'd not blamed him.

So, Puck was his talent scout. He was also in his element, keeping his ear to the ground, sniffing out gossip, who was hot and who was not. Looking as he did, like a nineteen-year-old, had never been a problem for Puck. For a start, few nineteen-year olds were as truly gorgeous as he was – a spot had clearly never invaded that perfect skin. And then, should anyone be in doubt, a look into his steady eyes was enough to confirm the truth. This was one elf that had been around for a long, long time.

He got to go to some great parties, and he was looking forward to his first Oscar night like Black Annis looked forward to Hallowe'en. But occasionally, among the transatlantic stuff – no Concorde for him, it was far too slow – he spared a thought for Titania. He had to assume she was happy. If he couldn't believe that, he knew his love and conscience would have him back down in her glade full time, bored, miserable, doing his duty. And it was true that his visits were pleasant times. They recharged his batteries, got him grounded. It was an odd thought that a woodland glade, staffed by goblins, tree sprites, elves, pixies and the odd shimmery thing would keep him grounded, but that was perhaps more a reflection on showbiz than Faerie.

He turned lazily in mid air, flying back to Oberon after a quick sift through the new talent in California. He was ahead on the list; the female Oscar judges had been easily persuaded to tell him a few little secrets – strictly between themselves, naturally – so he had already booked the winners for the show following the ceremony. He chuckled to himself as he flew. He would pop down to see the Queen; it had been a while and he missed her. He flipped one last roll and sped off. Another twenty minutes should easily do it.

Chapter Two

Titania was taking her time to get up. She always took her time. The two goblins summoned by Freckles to hold up her looking glass were beginning to feel the cold. Why, they asked themselves, couldn't she just use glass like everyone else? It didn't have to be *new* glass; it didn't have to be magnifying, lit by neon, nothing *modern*. It could be just a bit of glass they might find somewhere. But no, not the Mistress. It had to be a bit of ice, cut fresh each morning from a still pond on the edge of their territory. In their opinion, they thought, as they stood there, hatted and gloved for the purpose, in their opinion, she was taking this back to nature stuff *a bit too far*.

She read their tiny minds. She smiled at them, and they felt a bit warmer. 'Sorry to take so long, lads,' she said. 'Let me just get this bit of hair right, and you can go.' The hair twirled itself into an even more beautiful tendril and she patted the nearest one on the arm. Or wing. Whatever 'Thanks, Bill,' she whispered. 'You're so patient.'

Grinning like idiots, they hopped down from her dressing table and went outside. The card school was hard at it under a huge, bare-branched oak tree across the glade and they hurried to join it. Without Oberon's cheating ways, card games were much more predictable, but much less fun.

Titania stretched and reached again for her bell. She fancied a bit of a ride in the woods and for that, she needed ponies. Tiny had turned out to be a dab hand at ostling, if that was the word, and she had never had such obedient mounts as these. He did have a habit of calling them things like Dobbin and Cloppy, rather than Swift-foot and – she automatically turned her head and spat – Shadowfax, but they were well-behaved and to some of her Rade, the names were a small price to pay.

Before she could touch it, however, there was an ear-splitting crash and an awful lot of cursing out in the clearing. The silence which always follows such a row was filled after a few seconds with running feet and concerned twitterings. She ran to the door and looked out, astonished. Then, she burst out laughing.

In the middle of the glade was a tangle of arms and legs that could only represent Oberon and Puck. Plus, yes, a spray of spit and a tiny bent trotter that could only be Thydney. Oberon's voice was the first to become coherent.

'Puck! For crying out loud! How much sky do you want?'

Puck spat out a mouthful of leaf mould. 'It wasn't so much the sky that was in short supply, Sire, if you don't mind my saying so,' he retorted. 'More a case of the ground. Couldn't you see me just about to land?'

'I wasn't watching,' Oberon said grandly, standing up and brushing himself down. Why do you always make yourself so small when you're flying? You were *very* difficult to spot, even if I chose to look about me. *You* should be looking out for *me*.'

'What with?' Puck squared up to the King. 'The eyes in the back of my head? The eyes, I might add, which you would have poked into the middle of next week with your goblin, if I had any.'

'Don't you speak to me like that!' Oberon was reduced to platitudes.

'Why not, you great clumsy thing?' Puck muttered, straightening his jerkin

'Boys, boys,' laughed Titania. 'Don't fight. No harm done, I'm sure. Except for Thydney, possibly. He looks a bit bent.'

Oberon squatted down anxiously. 'Are you all right, Thyd, old son?' he asked, patting him vaguely all over his little body.

Thydney gave himself a cautious shake and, one at a time, extended his legs and arms, checking for breakages. Everything seemed to be in working order, so he said, 'I'm fine, Thire, thankth.' He bowed to the Queen, 'Mithtreth,' he said, bending low and thus saving her a shower.

Oberon patted him on the head, 'Run along, old chap,' he said, in an avuncular way. 'I'll give you a call if I want you.' He watched the little creature hop and skip over to the oak tree, where he and his friends bounced up and down with pleasure.

He sighed. 'It always seems a shame to break up the little guys, but they've all made their choices.' He brightened up and turned to Titania, who by now was locked in an embrace with Puck.

'Excuse me,' he rumbled. They ignored him. 'Hello.' He coughed.

Titania broke away and said, 'Dearest, you're back for a while. How funny you should decide to come down just as Puck is here for a visit.'

Oberon looked at them with one eyebrow raised. 'Perhaps just as well,' he remarked, and strode off to the bower next to Titania's private apartments. Titania gave Puck's hand a squeeze and they followed him. She clicked her fingers behind her head as they walked and soon a stream of faerie of all types and sizes were lining up in a shimmering line to deliver food and sweet drinks to the three.

They sipped and chewed while the food and drinks kept coming until, with a small belch, Oberon rolled on his back and waved the rest of the horde away. Puck looked over his shoulder and caught Freckles' eye. He nodded and mimed eating a bacon sandwich and put his trotter up in confirmation. The mime was so graphic, Puck could almost smell his favourite snack. Later, he thought, and tried to stop his mouth from watering. His Lady was so strict about Faerie food

'Well, Lord. Puck,' Titania inclined her head to both in turn. 'To what do we owe this pleasure?'

Puck spoke first. 'I have a bit of time spare, Mistress,' he said. 'I have lined up the guests for the show for some weeks in advance, so I can have a break.'

Oberon almost spoiled a tender moment. He leaned forward with interest to hear his guest list, just as Titania reached forward to stroke his hair 'Who've we got, Puck?' he asked eagerly.

'That would be telling, Sire,' said Puck, placing a finger alongside his nose.

Oberon fell back and collided with Titania's hand. 'Ow.'

'Serves you right,' she muttered, but still turned it into a stroke. His hair was as soft the softest down and black as a so raven's wing. Unless, of course, he happened to be with a mortal woman who preferred blonds. In which case, it was spun like dwarf gold and soft as baby hair.

'I've just come for a visit because . . .' his voice fell . . . 'I missed you.' His look this time was directly into her eyes, opening a path into his heart. She gazed back at him and knew it was true. Puck had to glance away; it was a private moment between his King and Queen and, no matter how she loved him, Titania would never look at him like that.

She broke the lock of the look and clapped her hands. 'It's so lovely to have you both here. Quite like old times.'

'You mean Old Times?' asked Puck.

'No, just old times,' she smiled. 'The house, the plan, all that.'

Oberon wasn't too good at hearing subtleties like capital letters, so was by this time very confused, but smiled benignly anyway.

'I was planning a ride,' Titania said. 'Do you want to come?'

'A ride?' Oberon asked. 'Why? Where to? What for? Who's coming?'

Titania looked a little crestfallen. No-one liked riding like she did. She couldn't understand it. What she couldn't see was that she had the best mount, the long golden dress in perfect folds over its rump, its (temporarily) silver-shod hooves tripping lightly over the moss. The rest of them had whatever Tiny could conjure up from the Forest ponies, hairy, unkempt, clumsy as all get out and usually nasty-tempered. But they loved her, so they went along with it, saddle-sores and all.

Puck made peace as usual. 'We've been travelling, Lady. May we rest awhile and then,' he shot a glare at Oberon, 'we'd be happy to. Wouldn't we, Sire?' He poked him in the ribs for good measure.

''Spect so,' grunted Oberon. Never do anything with good grace when you can sulk, that was one of Oberon's many mottoes. 'I could do with a sleep, personally.' With that, he turned over and closed his eyes.

Titania and Puck talked in whispers over the King's shoulder.

'How is it going, Mistress?' Puck asked.

'It?' she asked, somewhat frostily.

He shrugged. 'You know, It? Faerieland and all.'

'It's going well,' she said. 'Oberon keeps the mortals up to speed, being out there all the while. Leanne, I'm sure, keeps his profile up. There are still feral goblins about, dwarves tunnelling all over the shop. Freckles fell down one of their holes the other day and could have hurt himself quite badly. They're a bit of a nuisance, to tell the truth. They don't want to be with us as such, but they won't quite go away.' She sighed, but happily. 'Our area is small, but we like it.'

Puck patted her arm. She grabbed his hand and kissed it lightly. Her eyes said what she daren't – come without him, next time. Puck, who could see the King's expression, pulled his hand away with a wry smile. 'So you've just this glade then?' he asked, in a conversational tone, hoping to put Oberon off.

'Well, when we Ride, it sort of comes with us. Otherwise, yes. It's too much work for one to make it any bigger,' she said, with an acid look at the back of Oberon's head.

Puck nodded, thoughtfully. He hadn't been for a stroll in a wild wood for ages. Although he wasn't expecting this one to be Wild in the old sense, it would be nice to get back to Nature, proper, un-messed-with Nature, for a bit. 'May I go for a walk, Mistress?' he asked.

She made to rise, and he stopped her. 'Perhaps you ought to be with Lord Oberon for a while, on your own.' He laughed a little laugh. 'You don't always want me knocking about.' She reached out her hand to stop him. "No, no. Don't worry, I won't be long.'

He jumped to his feet and made off across the glade, six inches off the ground. He stopped at the card table, and she saw him bend down to speak to Freckles. Something changed hands, but she couldn't quite see what it was. Puck was happy with it, anyway. He turned a somersault, which made him cough. After some vigorous back-slapping, he set off again and was soon lost to sight amongst the trees.

Chapter Three

Puck sang softly to himself as he skimmed lightly over the frozen ground between the trees. He wasn't much of a singer; whenever his Lady had needed entertainment in the Old Days, it had indeed been Puck who got the call. But only so that he could fetch a singer. Or harpist. Whatever. But, even so, he sang as he skimmed along.

'February brings the snow, makes our feet and fingers glow . . .'

And there were small pockets of snow, nestling still in the mossy pockets of the ground, under the ancient trees. There were even snowdrops, carpets of them where the weak sun could reach. Their heads, too large for their slender stems, nodded in an almost imperceptible breeze. Some had sent up their green spears clean through a dead leaf, which hung now, suspended, halfway up the stem, a frilly collar out of place on that frigid simplicity.

Puck's breath smoked on the air as he hummed the rest of the jingle. He smiled as he flew, enjoying the crisp clean air. In the months since the faerie had Come Back, he had been busy. Sometimes if, when he woke up, it was dark, he had a heart-stopping millisecond of wondering whether the comeback had all been a dream, or whether it had really happened. Did he have to go and deliver milk, or could he lie in and doze until the sun through the curtains woke him properly. And every day the answer had been; wait for the sun. It was all real.

In the Old Days, February had been something which happened to other people. When you can put a girdle round the earth in forty minutes, seasons are a matter of personal taste. Puck's had tended towards pearly spring days, with a faint breath of summer on the air, or, for a change, those early autumn mornings, with mist in the sunbeams like the dust from a moth's wing. Since that heyday, he had delivered milk in the most filthy weather the seasons could throw. Snow, frost, slush, wind and rain; in Puck's book these were only a bit worse than sticky summer mornings, with mosquitoes fresh from a night's fast massed around the float waiting to breakfast on him. That they found he tasted . . . different . . . didn't seem to dissuade the next cloud. Mosquitoes have very short memories, and don't tend to pass things on.

Now that Faerie was Back, Puck could have his choice of season again and yet, perhaps perversely, he had decided to stick to the one everyone else was having. He was enjoying having a foot in both camps; indeed, using mortal time was essential, to help him keep track of what was going on.

So, despite the cold, he sang on as he skimmed the frozen ground. He was quickly brought up short by a clump of primroses, poking through the dead, rime-edged bracken. Global warming, eh? He said to himself, but flew on with his mind rather more focussed. At the edge of his vision, movement caught his eye, and he now saw the primroses bursting from the ground in their dozens. Bluebells joined them, then, at head height, dog roses began to scent the freezing air. The breeze that blew was warm and scented with new mown hay. Brambles, loaded with blackberries, clutched at Puck's jerkin as he spun three somersaults. He was back at Titania's bower in the flick of a mayfly's eyelid. She wasn't on the bank outside. Nor was Oberon. Usually, Puck would be far too discreet to do the unforgivable. But he was in a bit of a state and he burst into her bedroom anyway.

A tousled Oberon gave him a lazy look from sleepy eyes. The eyes held a challenge; the challenge of one lovely male to another. It was the look of the cat that had definitely got the cream. Puck shook his head and turned to Titania. This wasn't the time for locking horns and stamping.

'Mistress!' He was ever so slightly out of breath. She shot up out of the bed, clothing herself in a mossy green as she did so. The flash of creamy skin had no effect on Puck. This alone made her see the seriousness of the situation.

'Puck? Whatever is the matter?' she said.

He took a deep breath to steady himself. There was no easy way to tell this news. 'He's waking, Mistress,' he said. 'He's turning in his sleep. There are primroses out there, bluebells. The season's gone all to buggery. He is waking.'

Oberon leapt up too, without bothering about the clothes. The sudden movement dislodged Titania and she landed on the floor in a heap. With as much dignity as she could muster, she got to her feet. Puck rushed to dust her down.

'Global warming?' she said, hopefully.

'That would be nice, Mistress. But I think not.'

'He's been asleep for . . . ages. What can have woken him up?'

'How about the return of Faerie? With knobs on?' Puck ventured.

'Surely not.'

'I think he's right,' Oberon said slowly. He wasn't the brightest glow-worm in Faerie, but he understood what was happening perhaps more than any of them. And he had the most reason to fear it.

'What can we do?' she said, stepping forward and grabbing both of Puck's hands in hers. She gazed up into his eyes, her lips parted, moist and pink.

He shook her off gently. 'No need for all that, Lady,' he said, turning for the door. 'I'll do it anyway. Now he's awake, none of us will have any peace. Call your Rade together. When we've met, Oberon and I will get back to London. Leanne can help us to contact the others. We've got to find him, for a start. Can anybody remember where we buried him?'

The glade was almost full of the motley crew that was Faerie.

At the front, as always, were the goblins, their excited little eyes gleaming, Tiny was hopping up and down, from trotter to trotter and this had infected the more rabbity who were running round in ever decreasing circles and almost disappearing where the sun don't shine, as Freckles would doubtless have said.

'Stop that,' Freckles said to one of them, putting a friendly hand on his sloping shoulder. 'Or you'll disappear where the sun don't shine.'

This was no comfort to the goblin, who now had something else to worry about.

The dwarves were sulking out on the edge of the glade. In their tunnels beneath the soil they were always aware of general goings on, but they couldn't grasp the detail. Hence, they had heard lots of running about, muffled shouting and mild hysteria from the sheep-goblins. Now, too proud to ask, they just leaned on trees, trying to look macho and failing, because Lofty, the tallest, was only thirty inches high.

The flower fairies had clustered on the nearest flower, a piece of gorse, always in season. The first ones there had a good seat – the others were just being very, very careful. As the most mobile of Faerie, they tended to come and go – a bit like bees, Puck always thought – clustering where the flowers were blooming. They of all Faerie were now very confused. The bluebell fairy was all of a lather. She hadn't expected to be working until May, April at the earliest, and she hadn't darned her dress. In their world where everything was so tiny and a mortal breath was like a hurricane, they were unaware that even the biggest tear or darn was invisible. Some of the grumpier ones – and, ounce for ounce, some of them were very grumpy indeed – couldn't see the problem. Their flowers might be more plentiful, always in season, easier to find. Less work, in short. But, mostly, they were worried.

Slowly, the crowd grew until the glade could hold no more. Those who could flew up and hovered over the others' heads. The dwarves naturally took this as a heightist slur, but everyone knew there was no pleasing them, so they were ignored, as usual. When the buzz of wings and conversation had levelled out, Oberon stood and raised his hands for calm and silence.

Puck and Titania had to allow – the King was good at this sort of thing. He arose, a column of flowing black, sparks flying in his hair. His eyes searched the crowd and every one of the gathered Faerie knew he knew their name. He managed to hide the fact that, some mornings, he hardly could remember his own.

He spoke. His tone was so finely judged that he hardly needed words. Beware, the voice said. A frightening time may come, but, with me at your head, we will survive. Triumph. We did it before and we'll do it again. The words he used were fewer.

'Pan is waking.'

He took one step back and waited for the mixed clucking, baaing and general whimpering to die down.

'We subdued him before. We'll do it again.'

Thousands of eyes turned to look on their King and Queen. Such naked trust could almost be felt as the wave of it struck them, Puck, Titania and Oberon as they stood on the bank outside the Queen's Bower.

Oberon smiled at them all. 'Trust us,' he purred, like something crouched on the Serengeti. 'If we all pull together, we'll be all right.'

Even the dwarves were listening. They were One Nation. They would be all right. The king said so.

Tiny – well-meaning as ever – opened his mouth and stepped right in.

'Er . . . Sire. Sires. Sires and Mistress. I wasn't made when you put him under his hill.'

Titania beamed at him. Dear little creature. So new, in the scheme of things.

'So I don't know where that is,' he continued.

Titania looked encouraging. Puck tugged her sleeve, but she ignored him. He leaned forward to Tiny. 'Can we discuss this later?' he hissed out of the corner of his mouth, but Titania's elbow in his ribs made it sound more like 'nnnnhhh!'

'So, what I was wondering,' Tiny was unstoppable now, like a runaway train, never going back. One way on a one-way track. 'What I was wondering, was . . . Well, where is he?'

The silence was so thick it almost had a colour. Puck stepped back, a hand over his eyes. Titania mumbled and turned away. Oberon chuckled in the rather half-hearted way that even Kings of Faerie do when caught out good and proper.

'Tiny, old chap,' he blustered. 'No need for you to bother your little head over that, is there, now. We're on the case. Soon be sorted, eh?'

Tiny looked up at him. He was bright, but in a focussed way that took no hints. Freckles was trying to hush him, but not so anyone would see him. He didn't want to see Tiny disappear in a cloud of dust, but, if he did, he could do it by himself.

'But we're supposed to be helping, Sire. You said so. How can we help if we don't know where he is?'

Oberon glared at him.

Tiny tried to continue, but he suddenly found his mouth was full of toffee and nothing he said came out right. Oberon was basically kind, and very fond of his goblins. Titania was looking fiercer. She'd have dematerialised the little twerp.

But the damage was done. The crowd was mutinous and coming their way. Titania stepped forward, beautiful as the day and sparkling for all she was worth. She gave a tinkling laugh, which held them momentarily.

'Faerie,' she said and paused, holding them in her luminous gaze. 'At the moment, we are trying hard not to let the god . . .' she made a mime of zipping her lips, '. . . you-know-who hear too much. Yes, we buried him in charms and magic webs, under his hill, many years ago. But he can still turn in his sleep and we think that may be all he is doing now. If he hears his name too much, though, he may waken properly. That would be serious for us. Some of you,' her eyes raked the crowd, 'may remember what it was like before.'

There were nods and murmurs of 'too right' and 'no peace night nor day' 'bloody flute all the time', with just the odd, much quieter, mutter of 'good bloke' 'good laugh', quickly suppressed.

'So,' she finished. 'Puck and the King are on the case, and

so, although you must be ready, it would be best if you went about your business and didn't say the p word too often.' Another dazzling smile. 'Ok?'

Silence.

'People. After all we've been through? Hmm?'

After a microsecond of silence, there was a buzz that sounded as if they might agree. The crowd began to thin, and soon the three were more or less alone.

'Well,' Oberon said, rubbing his hands together. 'That didn't go too badly.'

Puck looked at him in amazement. 'Are you mad?' he demanded. 'It could scarcely have gone worse. They're worried to death. They'll talk about him all the time. He'll hear it and grow every day and we still don't,' he dropped his voice to a whisper, 'know where we buried him!'

Titania smiled calmly. 'Benedict will remember,' she said. 'He has that kind of memory.'

'Oh, yes,' Oberon sneered. 'Mr Computer. Where on the Internet will he find that piece of information, I wonder?' He stamped off, flinging aside the gossamer curtain and disappeared into Titania's bower.

'Oh, dear,' she sighed. 'Still as jealous as ever.'

'It's not as bad as he tries to make out, Lady,' said Puck, laying a gentle hand on her arm. 'They speak sometimes.'

She looked alarmed. 'Not on the phone, surely?' she said.

'No, no, of course not. Well, in a way. Leanne got a bit tired of Oberon never being in touch, so she concocted this web thing, that she and Benedict had been working on.'

'Yes,' the Queen said. 'The web. The worldwideweb. I know about that.' She paused and gave a beautiful pout. 'Know about it, but I don't understand it.'

'You don't have to worry about that sort of thing, Lady,' smiled Puck. 'But I'm not talking about the Internet. I'm talking about this.' He whistled and there was a scrabbling from behind the Bower. Titania turned round and immediately leapt behind Puck with a shriek that could strip paint.

The creature standing there in the full glare of her terror was not the most beautiful creation, perhaps, but it had feelings. Puck rushed over to comfort it. Some of its eyes were filling with tears.

He turned to the Queen. 'Quick, say something nice. It doesn't work so well if it's upset.'

Her eyes were wide with shock and her mouth was hanging open in a way which, on anyone else, mortal or Faerie, would be hideous. She came to, blinked once or twice, closed her mouth and licked her lips nervously. 'Hello,' she croaked.

The Isp, as it had amused Benedict and Leanne to call their creature, blinked all its eyes and smiled a shy little smile. It bounced once or twice on its many legs and, with its main foreleg, reached up to tap Puck on the shoulder. He looked down at it and it motioned him nearer. He bent down so his ear was near its mouth. It whispered something.

He spoke to it, nudging it in a matey way.

'The Isp wants to say something to you, Mistress, but is very shy,' he said to the Queen, but keeping eye contact with the arachnoid. He spoke directly to it again. 'Go on, she won't bite.'

Titania wondered to which of them he was telling that piece of news.

A tiny voice, more like many voices speaking in unison, but all very far away, came from the creature. 'I have heard so much about you, Mistress,' it began. It looked up at Puck with all its eyes, a gesture it would be better avoiding, Titania thought. 'And you are just as lovely as I was told.' It smiled.

What a sweet creature, Titania thought, despite herself. She stepped forward to pat it, but stopped herself. She wasn't sure what bit of its body was pattable. You heard such tales!

The Isp continued. 'What message do you wish to send, Mistress?'

'Message? How can you take a message? Can you, perhaps, run very fast?'

The sound the creature made had to be a chuckle. The Isp bounced up and down and wiped an eye with a leg.

'No, Mistress,' its many distant voices said. 'A scuttle is more my line. No, I . . . send messages.'

'Who to?'

'Who do you want to send to?'

Puck broke in. Titania was looking puzzled and the explanation could take all day. 'I don't really know how it works, Mistress.'

'Yes, you do,' broke in the Isp.

'Yes, all right,' Puck kicked it lightly and it moved away, offended. 'All I know is, that there are loads of these Isps about, but they are all actually one. So, if you tell it something, they all know it and the one nearest the person the message is for, can tell whoever . . .' The sentence had no end that Puck could see.

Titania held up a finger, the finger of a Queen of Faerie who had suddenly got it. She smiled at the Isp. 'You have . . . bits of yourself, all over,' she said.

'That's right,' said all the Isps.

Titania looked at Puck. 'What's so hard about that,' she said. 'I do that all the time. Don't I?'

'Indeed I do,' replied the Queen leaning against a tree at the far side of the glade.

'Me too,' said the Queen, peeping round the curtain to the Bower.

There was a soft pop, as they all flowed together again. 'Except that you,' she pointed at the Isp, 'are like it all the time.'

The Isp giggled and bounced. It beamed up at Puck. Suddenly, it didn't feel so alone. The Queen could do it too! Puck knew when he was beaten and wandered off, in search of Oberon.

'So,' the Queen said, crouching down and looking into the spider's ruby eyes, 'if I want to ask, say, for example, Benedict something, I just ask you, and the bit of you near him asks him. And then, when he answers it, you tell me.'

'Got it!' said the Isp excitedly and its main foreleg came up to give the Queen a high five.

She stood up, hurriedly. The Isp sagged down a little. It had gone too far. In many tiny voices it said, 'What is your question, Mistress?'

'Benedict,' said the Queen, loudly and clearly.

'I'm not, deaf, Mistress,' said the Isp, a little peevishly.

'Sorry,' said Titania. 'Benedict,' she continued in her normal voice. 'Where did we bury Pan?'

After a short pause, filled with a strange hissing static from the Isp, came a voice, Benedict's, but a metallic, soulless version, the Scots accent rather more pronounced than when she had heard him last.

'Buggered if I know.' It sounded as though the message was ended, then, with a sigh, 'I'll ask James. He has a rather unhealthy interest in buried things. I'll get back to ye.' The hissing stopped and the Isp turned to go.

Titania stopped it. 'Can I send a message to more people?'

'Yes, Mistress.'

'Same message, then, to everyone with an Isp. Where did we bury Pan?'

The Isp crossed its many eyes and waited, holding its breath. After a few minutes, it looked up at the Queen.

'How do you want the answers?' it asked.

'Can you give me the gist?' she asked.

'Yes.'

'Gist it is, then.'

'Buggered if we know,' all the Isps said together.

Chapter Four

Puck gave a cursory look inside Titania's bower, but he knew Oberon wouldn't have stayed in there – altogether too girly. He was worried, Puck knew, and so had to be found. His connection with Pan had been the strongest in Faerie – his ablest pupil, some might say, and still applying the old techniques. Oberon knew that when Pan woke, reached for his pipes and stretched one muscled goat leg after another, cracking his knuckles, ready for the chase, he knew that he, Oberon, would be the one the god would look for first. And he wasn't sure he would be able to cope, after years of soft living.

Puck was worried too. Not so much worried, as scared to death, if that had only been possible. He had been made in Pan's image and sometimes, in his dreams, he still had goat feet and a tendency to whistle. Pan had been so certain that Puck and Oberon would always be his that he had taken his eye off the ball. Life with the great god had been a bit rough at times and Puck and Oberon had not fought too hard when Titania and the Faerie liberals, backed by Benedict and his northern crew, had persuaded the two that Pan needed to be . . . well, toned down.

So, one night, one cold and frosty winter's night when he lay asleep, his shaggy legs rimed with sparkling white, his snores shaking the trees, the wine barrel, last of many, still spinning slowly at his feet where he had dropped it, they had summoned all of their powers and buried him, roped down with enchantment, under a Faerie-made hill. Then, they had run as fast as they could, putting as many leagues between themselves and it as they could.

Afterwards, the subject just didn't seem to come up. If life was more boring, it wasn't so scary. Everyone was reasonably sure of waking up the shape they went to sleep in. Titania had a temper, but it was nothing like Pan's. And, anyway, you could always apologise to her and stand chance of forgiveness. So, very soon, Pan's Hill was forgotten, except perhaps for a little niggle hidden in the hindbrain. The kind of niggle that makes even Faeries jump just as they drop off to sleep, making them kick and start awake.

But, essentially, Pan's Hill was forgotten.

The locals had avoided the suddenly sprouted hill for years. Odd things happened if you slept on its slopes. No sheep grazed it. No rabbits burrowed there, no spiders' webs were spun between tall blades of grass. Any living thing that accidentally walked on it soon jumped aside. It felt, they would say, as if the hill was . . . breathing. Then, with a shake and a nervous laugh, they would skirt the hill, though it took them half a mile out of their way. No railway engineer thought it would be just the route he needed. No motorway cut through, or even near it. The Hill just sat there, breathing its long, shallow breaths, silently in sun, wind and rain.

And slowly, the trees, small and stunted, crept up to its margins. Brambles twined around the trees and gorse sprang up on the edges of the copse. Birds sang in the branches only briefly, before flying off, feeling, in their tiny feather brains, that they had been singing flat.

And eventually, Mortal brains being what they were, grounded in the visible, the plausible, the everyday, everyone had accepted the place. Hardly thinking why they did it, men erected a marker. But soon, it became part of the landscape and everyone forgot it had once been Pan's Hill.

But where was it? Landmarks were different then. Titania

couldn't even swear as to what country they had been in at the time. There was a lot of wine around, but, that was Pan for you. There always seemed to be wine about when he was nearby. So, she supposed, he could be buried in . . . another country. Geography had never been her strong point. She was, basically, a people person. She furrowed her lovely brow. People! That was the clue. Who was around when they . . . she didn't even like remembering what they did, in case it woke him up in some way. When they did what they did.

Oberon, obviously. Puck. Mab, Cobweb, Mustardseed, all the usual gang, although going by different names way back then. Cobweb and Mustardseed were gone now, of course. Mab she could find easily enough – she kept an alternative therapy and craft shop in the nearest town and popped in from time to time for supplies. Otherwise . . . was Phoebe there? If so, she'd be no help, she had been Pan's Faerie through and through and had been very half-hearted about the whole thing. Any mortals? Tam Lin? No, he was from the north and anyway much later than the whole business. That knight? The rather depressed one who loitered around all the time? What was his name? Dead, anyway, so why brood.

She stamped her foot. Freckles came running.

'Yes, Mistress?'

'Hmm?' She looked down at him. She had been miles away.

'Do you want something, Mistress?'

'Yes,' she sighed.

'A nice drink of dew?' He looked into her face. Was that a tiny line forming between her eyebrows?

She looked down at him and heaved another huge sigh.

'Got any gin?' she asked.

Puck found Oberon halfway up a tree, a few yards outside the glade. He was perched on a branch, back to the trunk, curled in what would be called a foetal position, had he only been mortal. The foetal position held no place on Oberon's memory.

Puck stood below the tree and called softly. 'Sire? Sire?'

A mumbled 'What?' made its way from under Oberon's folded arms.

'Come down, Sire,' Puck wheedled. 'We've got to talk things over.'

Oberon raised his head and looked down at Puck.

'Shan't.'

'Please, Sire. I'm getting a crick in my neck.'

'Come up, then,' Oberon sulked.

Puck gave a little hop and landed lightly on a lower branch.

His head was a few feet lower than the King's. Oberon liked that sort of thoughtful gesture.

'Why won't you come down, Sire? You'll have to eventually, you know.'

Oberon shook his head emphatically, making his curls fly. 'I shall fly everywhere and hover when I have to.'

'You'll be exhausted.'

'Possibly. But it's better than touching the ground.' He lowered his voice. 'He can *feel* me through the ground. I've got a sort of buzzing in my feet.'

'I think that's just a nervous reaction, Sire. If he wanted to feel for you, then he could do it through this tree.'

'Don't be ridiculous.'

'The tree is touching the ground, isn't it?' Puck asked, reasonably. 'In fact, it's more than just *touching* the ground. It's growing in it.'

Oberon gave a little cry and leapt off the branch. He was only inches above the ground before he got control of himself and stayed there, slightly dishevelled, hovering uncertainly.

Puck joined him but landed firmly on his feet and gave his monarch an impatient little tug. 'I know you'd rather hide, Sire, but it's no answer, is it? Not in the long term, anyway. We've got to remember where we put him, find him, bind him with more magic and get on with the next couple of thousand years before he stirs again.'

Oberon flopped down on the ground and looked up at Puck. 'I know,' he said. 'But I don't know where to begin. Can you remember where we were that night?'

Puck shrugged his shoulders. 'In a field?'

'Everywhere was a field, then, more or less. Or a wood.'

'It would have been hard to find him then, but not now,' said Puck, an idea taking shape.

'How so?'

'Well, I can't be sure, but I'd hazard a bet that nothing has been built on that Hill. Even after so long, the magic must be quite strong, or he would have woken before now. In the early days, anything walking on that ground would come off it a different shape. Stories like that linger. So, what we're looking for is a bit of ground, possibly in the middle of a built-up area, with nothing on it. It could be any shape, but it should still be raised.'

Oberon jumped up. 'We can arrange a fly over. Get everything with wings, quarter up the country and – huzzah! – we've got him. The Queen, you, me . . .'

'Benedict.'

"Yes, I suppose so. Benedict, we'll all go there, renew the magic and the old goat's tied down again. And *this* time, we'll make sure we mark the place!'

'Brilliant plan, Sire,' Puck cried. This was too important to start arguing over whose plan it was. It was a good one, and that was enough.

Chapter Five

James was worried. Since their return to their old haunts he hadn't seen his master like this. He was pacing up and down, hands behind his back, eyes to the floor, muttering to himself, livery now and again he would suddenly stop, cry 'Ah!' raising his finger in the air. This would instantly be followed by a disappointed 'Uh!' and the pacing would continue.

Earlier, when that horrible Isp thing had come and found him, he had started this weird behaviour. And if James found it weird, it was weird. But before he had begun pacing, the Master had put a friendly arm around James' shoulders, only flinching a bit as matted hair met the armpit of his Saville Row suit.

'James, old man,' he had said. James immediately began to feel uncomfortable. 'James, you and I go back a long way, don't we?'

'Right back, master,' said the butler. 'Back to . . .' he let his small, doggy mind wander. A cave. A silhouette against the fire. 'Right back, yes.'

'Yes, indeed,' said Benedict, adding a pat on James' back to his friendly gesture. 'So, you no doubt remember a great deal.'

James wasn't stupid. Well, he was stupid, but he wasn't *that* stupid. He shrugged off the arm and stood, a model of butlerish decorum, a little way away. He wasn't going to take the blame. He drew himself up, then stopped, because it hurt.

'I'm sorry, Sire,' he said, with a sniff. 'I'm afraid I don't remember.'

'Remember what?' Benedict snapped. 'Have you been listening to my mails again?'

"No, I have not,' James snarled. 'I don't have to listen and eavesdrop. You speak loudly enough, and this one made you shout to bring down the castle walls.'

'All right, then, clever dick,' hissed Benedict. 'Remember what?'

'Where we buried . . . him,' yelled James.

'You were there!' countered his master.

'So were you! And that hoity-toity lot from Down There. And Annis. And Leanne. Everyone who could get there was there. Why don't you ask them?'

'You helped dig the hole!'

James bared his teeth. 'Of course I helped dig the hole. I was a dog, at the time, if you recall,' he said nastily. 'That's what dogs do.'

'You could always be a dog again, you know,' Benedict spat, and turned his back.

James stood by the door, eyes filling with tears. He loved his Master, as only a dog knows how. He wanted to please him, but he really didn't know the answer. At the time, the only place he knew was Here; the only time Now. It was only in the years since that he had sometimes looked back on the whole episode and wondered if they had tied him tightly enough. He remembered the tiptoeing, the magic glistening in the air, the soft, drunken snoring of the god, the way his eyes flew open and bored into him as he realised, too late, what his People were doing. He remembered the digging, he with his paws, the others with claws, spades, magic. He remembered the Hill that was left, clothed immediately in Faerie grass and flowers. He remembered trying to forget what he had seen. But, in all the remembering, he couldn't remember where.

Benedict, without turning, said, in a thick voice. 'James?'

'Yes, Sire?'

'I'm sorry.' The voice was small, the words unfamiliar,

but, for a faithful hound, they were more than enough. James knew better than to acknowledge them and quietly, claws clicking on the stones, he left the room and quietly shut the door.

Leanne hit the speed dial and waited, fingernails tapping on the desk. Finally, the number answered. 'James? Is that you?'
'Yes.'
'Is Benedict there?'
'Yes.'
'I know you don't like phones, James, but could you try saying more than one word at a time?'
'Yes, Mistress.'
'Oh, ha. Could I speak to Benedict, please?'
'Yes.' The phone was put down in the draughty, echoing hall.
'It's a cordless!' she screamed into her mobile. 'That means *it* can go to *him*, you imbecile!'
The phone was picked up. 'Leanne?'
His voice sounded different. 'Benedict? Are you all right?'
'At the moment.'
Her heart, such as it was, stopped beating. 'So it's true, then?'
''Fraid so.'
'Can you be sure?'
'Where are you?'
'What?'
'Are you inside? No, wait a minute, you must be. You're always inside. Well, peep out of your window. What do you see?'
'Sky.'
'Look down.'
'Traffic.'
'Alright, then. Look out, into the sky.'
'Few pigeons.' She pressed her nose disbelievingly against the glass. 'Swallows?'
'I rest my case.'

'Well, we've . . . we've just got to stop him, surely. We can't let it be like it was before. Mortals have been very understanding. Oberon's show is going a storm. We're well in line for an award, even if they have to invent a category. But . . . I don't think they'll stand for it. Not all of the . . . well, the way he used to . . .'

In his Highland fastness Benedict closed his eyes and let his shoulders sag. 'I don't think I need Technicolor, Leanne. Just let's say it would be . . . politically incorrect, these days and leave it at that, shall we?'

Leanne was off with the fairies, so to speak. Pan's attention span was mercifully short, but when the beam of that attention was focussed on you, it was more than a Mortal could stand. And, back then, just before they dealt with it, he was rather struck on nice warm Mortals. And Benedict was right. They just wouldn't stand for it, not these days. And she was enjoying her life too much to let some goat legged idiot with his brain in his crotch spoil it all. She shuddered and came back to earth.

'Leanne? Are you there?'

'Going into a tunnel,' she said, automatically, and switched off.

'A tunnel?' echoed Benedict, looking at the buzzing phone in his hand. One. Four. Seven. One. Three. The phone rang and Leanne's answerphone switched in.

'Hello. Leanne can't take your call at the moment. If your call is in connection with bookings for "An Evening with Oberon", press one now. If it is in connection with . . .'

'Shit, I haven't got time for this,' Benedict threw down the phone in disgust. 'James!' he yelled.

The butler materialised in his usual uncanny way at his elbow. 'Yes, Sire?'

'Fetch the Isp,' Benedict demanded.

'Here, Sire,' whispered the Isp's many voices.

'Message to Oberon, copy Leanne . . . make that global copies. Message begins.'

'Sorry, Sire,' echoed the Isps. "Not recognized.'

'Oh, right. New message.'

'That's better.'

'Meeting essential. Stop.' In his excitement, Benedict was back in the days of telegraphy, his first and favourite communication invention. 'Pan must be stopped and . . .'

The Isp was tugging on his trouserleg. 'Have you read your messages, Sire?'

"No. get off my clothing, you . . . thing, you. Look what you've done to my crease.'

'Only . . . I think you should read your messages first.'

'Are you supposed to think of things for yourself?'

'I don't know, Sire.'

'I'm sure we just meant for you to do as you are told.'

'Probably, Sire.'

'So, do as you're told, then. Take a message.'

'Sire, really . . ."

'Do. It.'

The Isp shut its mouth tight and closed its eyes, one by one, the ruby glow winking out along the rows. It sagged down on its many jointed legs until its furry belly touched the cold floor. With a little squeak, it pulled up just a touch. The Isp had gone down.

'Oh, all right,' Benedict said with a sigh. 'What are my messages?'

'Précis? Or verbatim?' asked the Isp, complacently.

'Précis.'

'Everyone has been agreeing that a. Pan is at least turning over in his sleep; b. Puck's idea sounds good and who has a map? and c . . . oh, no, that's just junk mail.'

'Puck's idea?'

'From: Puck@faerieserve.co.uk   "Everyone. I think that Pan's Hill will still be visible from the air. All fliers get back to me asap, and we'll divide up the likely areas for a detailed flyover. I'm at Titania's at present, get me there or on this address. If you do phones, phone Leanne or Benedict. Cheers, Puck." Any reply?'

Benedict patted it, grudgingly and swiftly. 'Well done. I could have looked a bit . . . behind the times there.'

'You're welcome.'

'I'd better get down there.'

'You don't need to, Sire,' said the Isp, a little peevishly.

'You can do everything through me.'

Benedict looked down at it. He loved his technology dearly, but sometimes it got a bit above itself.

'What did Annis do to her Isp?' he asked, sarcastically.

The poor creature shuddered and several of its eyes flickered alarmingly.

'Quite,' he said. 'You're not the answer for everyone, you must agree. Call James.'

Its lights started to flash.

'No. Just *call* him. He's only just down the corridor. When you've done that, mail Leanne. Tell her we'll be with her as soon as we can. About ten minutes, if the wind is in the right direction. You might also say, that if she hangs up on me again, she'll wish she'd never been . . . well, whatever.' Rubbing his hands together, he ran up the stairs, two at a time. Back in action. Against Pan. There were scores to settle – if only the invention of the bagpipes!

Chapter Six

Benedict hovered lightly outside Leanne's bedroom window. She was always in there, titivating or, he had to admit, doing things he'd rather not dwell on. But today, she was just on the other side of the glass, waiting for him. She opened the window and in he flew. He touched down, light as a dandelion clock, in the middle of the acres of carpet. Leanne knew how to live, alright.

The touch of his Unseelie toe on the rug was soundless, but even had it not have been, the racket as James hit the window and slithered down it, tongue trailing drool and claws trailing an unearthly screech, would have drowned it out.

Leanne rushed to the window and threw it open again, hauling James up from where he clung to the ledge.

'Benedict!' she said crossly, as she brushed James down and smoothed his dishevelled pelt, 'You might have said he was with you.'

Benedict shrugged. 'Why? He's always with me.'

James gave himself a shake and went and lay on the foot of the bed.

'Down!' snapped Leanne, then, quickly, 'Oh, James, I'm sorry. Gut reaction. You know how it is.'

He rolled his eyes at her and slunk off onto the floor. She patted him absentmindedly and turned back to Benedict.

'That was quick,' she smiled brightly.

He had flung himself onto an easy chair in the corner. He

looked at her appraisingly. She was nervous, and with reason. When they and the world were young, she and her sisters had been very close to Pan. With her kind all gone, she would have to bear the brunt alone, and Pan could be tiring, Benedict had to admit that. Party, party, party, that was the old goat's motto.

'We've got no time to waste,' he said. 'I checked the weather reports as I flew and the forecasters are a little confused. At the moment, global warming is still taking the blame, but if things get much worse, they'll start blaming us.'

'And they'd be right, in a way, wouldn't they,' growled James. His nose hurt and he was fed up. All this talk of digging – he knew who would be first in line when the wussy faeries gave up because their little hands hurt. He subsided in a muttering heap.

'I mean,' said Benedict in a threatening way, 'I mean, blaming us for the weather, not because we didn't dig a deep enough hole all those years ago.'

'How long will the warming thing hold?' Leanne asked.

'I don't know. Not long. I've got my boys working on some new sites with other theories, to keep them busy. But, you know what it's like. Scientists . . . all that nonsense . . .' His voice trailed away. Scientists were his fault too, to some extent. He hadn't noticed that the alchemists had got better at their jobs until it was way too late.

'Anyway,' he jumped up, clapping his hands, 'We'd better be off to Titania's place. I expect that's where everyone is, is it?'

'Mostly. Oberon lives in your old place, of course.' She blushed and he pretended to ignore it. 'Puck is here and there, Mab has moved out of the glade, but only to the nearest town. She likes people. I mean, people, rather than People, if you see what I mean.'

Benedict nodded. 'And their goblins?'

'Mostly with the Queen, I think.'

'Can his lot fly? I can never remember.'

"No, they can't, but they hitch lifts and they're quite . . .' She was stuck for the right word. Bright? No, hardly. Shrewd, yes, that was it. Street wise. '. . . canny,' was the word she settled for. It was the right one and would make Benedict feel at home.

'As opposed to uncanny?' Benedict asked.

'That as well,' she sighed. She could always tell when he was nervous. The puns came thick and fast.

'Shall we go, then?'

'What, now?'

'Why not?'

'Well . . . I don't know. I'm out of the habit of dashing about in the air. Oberon's show is a full-time job and . . .'

'You can't get out of this one, Leanne, much as you might like to. We need to get our heads together as quick as we can. Otherwise . . .'

She'd never seen him shudder quite that way before and it made up her mind for her.

'I'll get my coat.'

James hauled himself to his feet, still rubbing his nose.

'You great pansy,' Benedict said, turning to his butler. 'Pull yourself together. What sort of bogle will they take you for down in Dingly Dell if you whine all the time?'

That was true. He had a reputation to keep up. Plus, there were all those sheep-like creatures that Oberon had conjured up. It made James' paws itch just to think of it. He shook himself again and his Master was rewarded with a fine spray of spit and hair.

Leanne came back into the room. More than coat-getting had taken place. She looked gorgeous, translucent skin and slightly pointed teeth, topped with her amber hair would soon have Titania's glade in a twitter. Benedict closed his eyes and sighed. What way was this for the King of Unseelie to travel; with a moulting pooch and a nymphomaniac vampire theatrical agent? Never mind, needs must when the Lord of Misrule drives.

She opened the window and they all swooped out into the damp air. The warmth so soon after the frost and cold had created a light, swirling mist and the cuckoo they could hear in the distance sounded muffled by the gloom. They flew higher to get their bearings, pointed southwest and were away.

Puck had finally got his Master and Mistress together, both ready to go and pointing in vaguely the right direction. Oberon's flying was rustier than he cared to admit and shrinking down to Titania's favoured flying size of a rather well-grown bumble bee sat ill on the shoulders of an A list celeb. But they had a long way to go and should be steady.

Oberon smiled condescendingly at Puck. 'OK,' he said, rubbing his tiny hands together, 'which way is it, then?'

Puck, even after so many millennia at his Lord's side, could still be caught off balance. 'North,' he said, trying to keep the mild despair from his voice.

Oberon smiled brightly. 'Yes,' he said. 'But which way?'

Puck sagged in the air. He pointed, over the trees, away from the glittering sea at his back. 'That way,' he sighed. 'Up.'

'Oh, up. You should have said.' And the King was away, looping the loop and divebombing sleeping goblins down in the glade.

'He seems very cheerful, Puck,' Titania said, hopefully.

'Just a cover, Mistress,' Puck told her. 'He's almost as worried as he should be.'

'How worried is that?' she asked, a tiny wrinkle between her perfect eyes.

'To death.'

'But we can't die . . .'

Puck raised one eyebrow at her and swooped away, before Oberon was out of sight and halfway to America.

She trod air for a moment. Her heart beating like a trapped moth against a windowpane. Her throat was dry, her palms were damp. She was afraid and didn't like it. In the distance, she saw a small commotion as Puck guided Oberon onto the proper route to the Highlands. Pinning a smile on her face, in case she passed any Folk on her way, she set off after them, but her heart was so heavy, it was a wonder she made headway at all.

Finally flying together, they watched the land whizz by beneath their feet. The further north they flew, the more obvious the Pan effect became. Heather cast a purple haze over fells and moors which should have been under snow. Skeins of geese flew aimlessly back and forth, their confused honking making Titania almost jump out of her skin on more than one occasion. In one stand of trees, they saw autumn colours, full leaf and bare branches on one schizophrenic looking oak and lakes steamed quietly in the warming air.

There wasn't much conversation. Only Puck knew exactly where Fincastle Mill was – Totania had been there, it was true, but her visit was brief, clandestine and a secret from Oberon, so she tried not to think of it, in case he picked up on what had happened there. Oberon had also been there, with Leanne, but with him, it wouldn't have mattered if it had been in daylight with an accompanying Ordnance Survey map to guide him, he still wouldn't have known how to get there again. Sometimes, he couldn't find his new penthouse home in the City and had to fly around until he spotted Thydney's anxious little face in a window.

Eventually, Puck shouted.

'Look! Down there!' He pointed at the dark, crouching shape of Benedict's home, lurking next to a stagnant looking lake, hiding in the shade of the overhanging pines. One light burned in an upper window, like the glint on the eye of a hunting beast as it prowls in the undergrowth.

'Eeughh,' Titania shuddered. "Not very homely, is it?'

'What did you expect,' snapped Oberon. 'White turrets and flying pennants, silver armoured knights at tourney?'

'There's no need for sarcasm, Oberon,' she said. Her fondness for pale lads in polished steel, her favour at their elbow was a longstanding quibble between them.

Puck spun round in the air and hovered in front of them like a miffed gnat.

'Lord. Lady. I know I speak out of turn when I say SHUT UP. We're fighting for the world's survival, here. For mankind as well as faerie.'

Oberon shrugged and looked away.

'Don't sulk,' Puck said sharply. 'We must put our differences to one side. Benedict and Leanne will be waiting down there, and I dare say even they will have done something mildly hospitable. Please don't let's argue amongst ourselves. We need to put our shoulders to the wheel here and find Pan. And quickly. As I recall, he wasn't a very quick waker-up, but he won't just turn in his sleep for long. Let's get down there to the castle now and brainstorm.'

He met Titania's eye and regretted the choice of word.

'All right then, have a think, as best we can.'

He and Titania dropped in air and touched down in the castle's dank yard.

Oberon landed beside them. 'I have too got a brain,' he said.

'Yes, Lord, of course you have,' Puck said, patting him as he brushed past him to knock on the thick oak door, with its hidden faces in the knotholes of the wood.

'Of course you have, beloved,' said Titania, patting the other arm. 'You just don't always have it with you.'

Puck knocked again, the knocker so heavy that he could hardly lift it. The sound echoed through the halls, bouncing off crumbling damp stone in James' lair in the kitchen, gliding off the brushed metal in Benedict's study. What it didn't bounce off was anything living – even allowing for Benedict's rather wide definition of that word. He'd given the staff the afternoon off. He loved to play the laird.

Puck turned to his Lord and Lady. 'There's no one at home,' he said, puzzled.

'What do you mean?' Benedict was shouting at a cowering goblin at precisely that moment. 'What do you mean, there's no one at home?'

The poor little rabbity thing gulped and squeezed its eyes shut to stave off the tears which were welling up. 'I mean,' it whispered, 'they've all gone out. The Lord and Lady and Puck have flown somewhere. The f-f-f-faeries are in the woods, checking on the weather. Some of their flowers are out that shouldn't be and they're a bit flummoxed.' A little hiccoughing sob escaped, and it hurried on with its tale. Leanne was looking a bit . . . foxy. 'They left me to watch out for a bit.'

Leanne sneered down at it. 'Good choice,' she hissed. 'You've got me scared, I can tell you.'

The goblin drew itself up. 'We don't do scary,' it announced. 'We leave that to you.'

Leanne's eyes flashed and her talons flexed. James drooled a little more in anticipation. Benedict stopped them both with a raised hand.

'OK,' he said, wearily. 'I suppose you mean by flown somewhere, that they have gone to my castle?'

The goblin gulped and nodded. It made him cough and Benedict gently patted his back. 'Yes, Lord,' it said.

Benedict straightened up and shut his eyes. 'What now, I wonder?' he said.

'Well, Sire . . .' James began.

'Rhetorical, James, rhetorical. If we stay here, they'll stay there. If we fly back, they'll fly back. We could be batting . . .' he flexed his leathern wings very slightly, "back and forth for ever, while Pan wakes up and takes over the world for the few seconds he'll have it before he blows the whole boiling up.' He fixed the goblin with a baleful eye. 'Does Puck have a phone with him?'

The goblin twitched and looked hopefully from Leanne to James in hope of extra clues.

'Does Titania have her Isp with her?'

A slightly hysterical laugh was the nearest to an answer this time.

Leanne broke in. 'Oberon has a mobile, but hardly ever carries it. Titania obviously doesn't have any such thing and I imagine she has tucked up her Isp in a little soft nest with a spot of nectar on the side. Puck . . . who knows? It's no good relying on technology with those three. Why don't you stay here and I'll go back to the castle and see if they're there. I'll ring you when I get there and we can lease.'

Benedict tapped his fingernails against his teeth. James always wished he would keep them long, like in the Old Days, but it interfered with his keyboard skills and so they were trimmed and neat.

'OK,' he said, and with no further ado, curled himself up against the roots of a tree, closed his eyes and went to sleep. James watched for a moment and then, when the first faint snore was heard, made a tiny, clandestine movement towards the goblin, who froze in terror, eyes wide.

'James!' said his Master. 'Heel!' and with a whine, the bogle slunk to the Unseelie Lord's side.

The goblin gambolled away, leaving a tiny pile of currant-like droppings behind, as proof of how scary it had been.

Above them, Leanne spiralled away, heading North. Benedict slept, uneasy dreams chasing through his head. James slept too, his dreams mostly of rabbits, wearing little jackets and jumping happily into his drooling jaws.

Pan turned once more in his sleep and a little flock of bluebirds flew from the crest of his forgotten hill.

Chapter Seven

Leanne circled over the castle, wheeling high in the realms of the eagles. She could see three figures down in the castle yard. She knew who they were, because, even from this distance, she could tell that one was twinkling softly, one was in quiet despair and the other was throwing a tantrum. She spun lazily off her warm up-draught and plummeted down to the ground.

Puck looked up at possibly the worst time in the process. He saw what many a cottager walking late, had seen, the difference being that Puck was going to live to tell the tale. By the time she landed, Leanne was looking a little more like her usual (as opposed to her Old) self and Oberon came out of his sulk to simper at her. Titania barely repressed her snort and the toss of her head, though small, was unmissable.

Leanne smiled around the little company. 'So,' she said, vinegar lacing every word. 'Everything much as usual, then?'

Puck nodded ruefully. 'Where's Benedict? He doesn't seem to be in. And that dratted bogle isn't answering the door.'

'That's because,' Leanne said, slowly and carefully, as though speaking to a backward brownie, 'Benedict and James are waiting for you in Titania's glade.'

The queen spun round. 'James? In my glade? Is Benedict mad?'

'Mad, as in insane? Well, naturally he is. Mad as in really,

really annoyed.' Leanne tapped her flawless cheek with a talon. 'Well, naturally he is. Couldn't you have waited five minutes for us to get there? You sent a mail.' She stopped and turned to Titania, her most patronising smile firmly glued in place. 'Well done on that, by the way, Lady. I must admit, I was surprised you grasped that so fast.'

Titania dimpled condescendingly back. 'No problem. The thing is just a spider, after all. I'm quite comfortable with spiders.'

Leanne couldn't help herself. 'Where is your Isp now?'

'Tucked up, poor little thing, in a web in my bower. It seemed so lonely.'

The vampire grinned to herself, showing her wicked eye teeth. Leanne one, Benedict nil.

'Anyway,' Titania said, wrapping herself in her cloak. 'James is rampaging through my glade and we're just standing here. Come on.' And she flew, straight as an arrow, due south.

Oberon was caught on the hop, still smiling soppily at Leanne. Puck was off in hot pursuit, Leanne on his heels before Oberon even realised Titania had gone. Hitching up his goblin, he jumped once or twice, and then was also airborne, flying what he always considered to be downhill, down to the south, hovering through the fog and filthy air.

❦❦❦❦

Benedict was waiting, with a disgruntled James by his side. There was no solid reason, thought the bogle, why he should be prevented from chasing the rabbity looking goblins. After all, there were so very many of them and he hardly ever actually caught anything. Well, not caught to eat. Well, not eat *all* of, at any rate.

Benedict was thoroughly fed up as well, because he hadn't slept outside for hundreds of years and the snooze in Titania's glade had left him with a crick in his neck and leaves in his hair. The fact that a flower fairy, deranged by the strange weather, had seen fit to sprinkle him with rose petals had done nothing to improve his temper.

'At last,' he snapped, as the four landed with various degrees of grace in front of him. 'Perhaps we can get started now.'

'That petal looks pretty,' Titania observed brightly, pointing.

He brushed it off, as if it were poison. 'Everyone's crazy down here. Haven't you got any control, woman?'

The glade stood still. Woman? Benedict had been on his own too long.

Titania smiled, with a smile cold enough to bring the February weather back at a stroke. 'I do not control, Lord,' she hissed. 'My folk follow me because they want to, not because they are afraid of me.'

A nervous laugh from behind her underlined the optimism in her words, but the sentiment was more or less accurate and even Tiny decided to let that one go. The silence was replaced with mildly hysterical chit-chat, which subsided when Oberon raised a hand.

He gazed over his People, gathered in tight, anxious knots all over the glade. It wasn't as warm as it had been earlier, and a few flowers had wilted. He decided to make the most of it. 'Judging by the more seasonal nip in the air,' he said, 'it is possible that P . . .' Leanne's hand clamped over his mouth in a flash. He shook her off. 'It is possible that Someone We All Know is dropping back off to sleep. Even if that is the case, I think we should still put on our thinking caps,' Leanne nudged Puck and mouthed, 'Bless,' at him, 'and try to remember where he is. This is a warning, People. Don't let's ignore it.'

The whole crowd was impressed. That sounded pretty much like sense to them. And sense was not Oberon's usual style. Still, they all thought, he was closest to P . . . Someone, in the Old Days and so he should know. Accordingly, they all shuffled their feet, hooves, trotters and what-have-you so as to face the King more squarely.

But their Lord had shot his bolt. Benedict opened his mouth to speak, but Puck was in there first.

'Perhaps it would be best,' the People's Elf said, 'if you all just got on with the usual stuff you do. You know, flitting about, cards etc. Then, I think you'd agree, thoughts might just pop into your heads.' The heads in question nodded around him. He was quite right. How many times had they remembered things while just buzzing around. Still muttering and nodding, the crowd dispersed.

'Oh, good,' said Oberon brightly. 'Carry on as normal, eh?'

'Of course not,' snapped Benedict. 'If I understand Puck correctly, he was just doing a bit of general reassurance and crowd dispersal. Am I right?'

Puck nodded. He was also trying to put a bit of space between James and the smaller Folk, who were beginning to get very nervous, as well as less numerous. 'I think,' he said, 'that we all ought to get our heads together and swap what memories we have. After so long, there will be inconsistencies and I think that talking them through might get us to a consensus.' He looked at the King. 'We've remembered different things and we need to sort it out.' Oberon raised a happy finger and smiled.

'So,' Titania looked around. 'Who's going first?'

The silence was deafening.

Benedict broke it. 'I'll go first,' he said, and subsided onto a tree stump, which immediately started to rot. He gave a small cough and began . . . .

✹✹✹✹

'I remember . . .' Benedict said, his voice reaching into everyone's brains, weaving its fingers around every cell, conjuring up his memories, making them their own.

He is buried in the border country, way up to the North. Where the land is so wet it is almost water, the water so brown with peat it is almost land.

He is buried where the Romans built their futile walls, still patrolled by their ghosts, dreaming of the warm and fragrant breezes of Roma, Napoli, Firenze, feeling only the sharp chill of Cumbria in their spectral bones, smelling only the smell of tourists; chips, orange squash and wet mac.

He is buried where the Vikings strode, raping, pillaging,

leaving only their place names and red hair behind.

He is buried where the Reivers rode, widowing women, orphaning children, stealing cattle and valuables, only to lose everything in the revenge raids the next week.

He is buried where the mountains seem to meld and move, each turn of the road shifting the view until no one can be sure of their way.

The night he was buried was like this, hissed Benedict's mind in their minds. It was warm – it was always warm when Pan was out and about. The Lords of Unseelie – without number then, like stars in the heaven, not trammelled with the petty squabbles which they later learned from men – they decided that enough was enough. Mankind was not as yet very sophisticated, it was true, but they were beginning to build their little settlements to last. They weren't forever chasing game, upping sticks, moving on. They wanted to be safe and secure in their little houses, happy to till their fields, warm themselves by their peat fires, have the same number, by and large, in their family in the morning as when they went to bed.

They were tired of their daughters going missing, coming back exhausted, with grass in their hair and a grin on their lips. Most of all, they were tired when, nine months later, a little dark baby was born, mischievous, the pride and the heartbreak of the house. So, the men, one dark and stormy night, had come to Benedict, where he sat in his hall, not much bigger than theirs but lit always with flickering torches, as befitted the Lord of Unseelie. He was lounging on his throne, his feet on a small pink elephant . . .

Benedict broke off his memories and spoke out loud.

'O . . . O . . . Oberon! Do you have a problem with this?'

Oberon looked outraged. 'Me? What have I done?' he looked appealingly around the group, eyes and hands wide.

'You're trying to distract me.' Benedict snapped. 'As you well know, there were no small pink elephants in my Court.'

'Yes, Oberon,' Titania fixed him with a beady eye. 'Let him get on with it. And,' she glared at Benedict, 'while we're on the subject, keep to the facts, will you? There's no need for all this . . . poetry.'

Puck looked wistful. 'I was rather enjoying it. It helps me imagine. It might help us to remember.'

Benedict inclined his head gracefully at the elf. 'Thank you, Robin.'

Puck went pink under his light green sheen. He'd always been rather fond of his nickname and didn't hear it much these days. Then, his heart contracted and clenched in his chest. He looked around. Suddenly, everyone seemed a little more . . . Faerie than they had a while ago. He looked down at his own hand. Had the nails been that long before? Had the skin been quite so green?

But Benedict was continuing.

The men had come to him in a body. Pan had to be controlled. Some of the men, farriers and farmers, had a method.

They were carrying with them cruel looking pincers, hammers and knives. Benedict felt quite squeamish even in his own head and drew a bit of a blank over that bit, but the others got the picture.

To save Pan from that ignominious fate, he had agreed to do something. He had gathered his lords, ladies, goblins, bogles and the rest and they had decided that the best thing would be to tie him, under a hill. The wizards went out and looked for the hair of a maiden to truss him with. Due to Pan's proclivities, this took a fair bit of time, maidens being a bit thin on the ground, and getting rarer with every night Pan was loose. They found enough hair eventually, from the heads of the daughters of one family. Their father had, apparently, an ambition to capture a unicorn and guarded his daughters extra carefully, against the day when one turned up in his courtyard.

So, they wove a cord, light yet strong. Unseelie smiths forged rings of platinum, the hardest metal earth had then, and some itinerant dwarves bedded them in rocks. The rocks were carried by bogles to a pit dug at the foot of a hill by any night creature with talons that Benedict could gather together. This had taken some time and the men with the pincers were growing testy.

Titania's smug glow engulfed Benedict's memories. *Your lot always were hard to control*, said her voice in their heads.

Do you mind? his brain-voice growled. Where was I?

Maidens, said Oberon.

Digging, purred Leanne.

The rocks were carried by bogles to a pit dug at the foot of a hill by any night creature with talons that you could gather together. This had taken some time and the men with the pincers were growing testy, said Puck.

I'm glad someone was listening, Benedict thought. Right. Eventually, it was all ready and the lovely daughters of the unicorn hunter were sent to Pan, who couldn't believe his luck. He perched himself on a rock and played his pipes to them, making them think very unmaidenly thoughts. They had strong liquor with them, and he drank it all. Finally, with a lovely woman twining round each limb, his brain fuzzy with the peaty Uisbeagh, we all fell on him and carried him, roaring, bellowing, flexing his mighty muscles, to the pit, chained him, and sat with him, until he fell asleep.

Then, our most powerful magicians bound him with spells and there he has lain until just now.

The voice in their heads stopped and they all drew a great breath and sat up, stretching and yawning. 'So, where is he then?' Puck said.

Benedict looked at him, shrugged his shoulders and said, 'Buggered if I know.'

Chapter Eight

'Well, I don't know!' But Benedict was talking to empty air. He sat disconsolately on his rotting log as everyone else stumped off into Titania's bower. He could hear muffled voices from in there, broken every now and again by Oberon's yell.

'The most useful bit was the pink elephants!'

He picked moodily at a primrose which had unwisely bloomed at his feet.

'Sire?' James put rather more doggy whine into his voice than was usual. His Master liked that.

'What?'

The butler added a bit of cringe. 'Sire, I wonder if you got it quite right, there? Um.'

'Are you questioning . . .'

'Of course not, Sire. I just . . . remember a bit more, that's all. Something else . . .'

'Everyone,' called Benedict and the glade was suddenly packed to the edge. "No, no,' he flapped his hands at them all. 'Not everyone as in everyone. I mean your Lord and Lady and Puck and Leanne.'

The muttering from the crowd had a mutinous edge, which turned to ragged cheering as Oberon and Titania came out from her bower.

'Yes, People,' said Oberon, King to his finger ends. 'Still thinking, eh?' He tapped his head meaningfully and waved.

The goblins cheered again. No harm in humouring the person who kept you in existence, they always felt. The dwarves refused to cheer and some of them mimed zipping their lips. But in a few minutes, the six of them were alone, by and large. Tiny had settled himself in Oberon's lap and managed to blend in with his clothing, although anyone looking closely might have got a surprise.

Benedict told the others what James had said.

'Excellent,' said Titania briskly. 'OK then, James. Let's hear it.'

James stayed where he was and looked at Benedict pointedly. 'Yes, old chap,' said Benedict. 'Off you go.'

'I want to sit on the stump,' said James. 'That's where you sat to tell your bit.'

'Oh for P . . .' Benedict stopped himself in time. He looked around the others for support. He found none. With a sigh, he levered himself up and sat grudgingly on the ground. The only small pleasure in this was that he finally managed to finish off that dratted primrose.

James wriggled to get comfortable and began. But after only a few seconds, Leanne spoke.

'I'm sorry, James,' she said, wrinkling her lovely nose. 'I think you'll have to speak out loud. There are . . . other thoughts in there that perhaps you don't want us to experience.'

James blushed under his hair. It was true that Titania was looking a little unwell and Puck was even greener than usual. 'Sorry,' he said. 'I don't get the practice.'

'No harm done,' Oberon said. 'But let's get on with it, shall we? What's different in your version?'

'Not a lot,' said James. 'But what is different is important, I think. We didn't bury him in our own country.'

'Typical,' snorted Oberon.

'We were going to, but we just weren't sure it would work and those men were getting really, *really* annoyed. And there was always so much upheaval, local squabbles and everything and we were rather afraid that some mad tribe of Mac-whatsits might dig him up to get back at their second cousins twice removed.'

Benedict nodded. 'That's true. I remember now.'

'So, as I remember it,' James went on, 'we brought him further south.'

Titania sat up straighter suddenly, with eyes shining. 'I'm beginning to remember myself, now,' she said. 'Those maidens, the unicorn bait ones, they didn't have enough hair. You borrowed some from some of my girls. Not my Faerie, of course, that wouldn't work. But from some of my village girls who used to help with the . . .'

'Don't be embarrassed, Lady,' Puck said. 'We've always known about the changelings.'

Titania blushed. Oberon looked at her. 'I didn't know,' he said.

'Well,' she hung her head. 'It was before we were married, and . . ."

'Can't we discuss this later?' Leanne snapped. 'This group thing seems to be working. Don't lose the flow.'

'She's right,' said Puck. 'Keep going, everyone.'

'You were there,' Benedict said to him. 'Don't you remember anything?'

Puck laughed nervously. "Not there as such,' he said.

'Where, then?' asked Leanne.

'I was . . . pretty much Someone's to command, as you may know,' he said. 'It's not something I'm proud of, but there it is. When I saw the way things were going I . . . ran away. Well,' he laughed nervously again, 'flew, naturally.'

'Alone?' Titania dripped vinegar again as she spoke.

'No.' Puck's answer was so quiet it wouldn't have woken a sleeping changeling.

'Sorry?'

'No.' he jumped to his feet. "No, all right. I went with Phoebe. We knocked around in Hellas for a while. The Greeks always liked Phoebe.'

'No accounting for taste,' Titania snarled.

'Anyway, when I came back, Lord Oberon was in charge and so I sort of . . . hung around until he couldn't do without me.'

'Don't flatter yourself,' Oberon said, automatically.

James had been looking increasingly miffed and now, having tried the doggy things like dragging his bum along the ground and scratching behind his ear coughed discreetly and said, 'If I may . . .?'

'Sorry, old chap,' Benedict spoke for everyone. 'Do go on.'

'Well,' the bogle continued, sitting back on the stump, 'I don't know where exactly we put him. Now that the Queen comes to mention it, I do remember some help from that quarter.'

She inclined her head graciously and James allowed his tongue to loll, just a little.

'But the other thing I remember is that we marked the hill.'

'You mark everything, James.'

'Not like that, Sire,' James said. His feelings were hurt. 'I mean that some of the Faerie marked the hill. With . . . I can't remember though.'

'Probably with web and bower, thyme and honeysuckle, thorn and briar,' said Titania brightly.

"No,' James shook his head. 'No, none of that.'

'Come on,' Leanne fetched him a clip round the side of the head. 'Remember, you stupid bogle.'

'Oy,' James rubbed his ear with a great paw. "No need for you to get hoity-toity. You hung around with . . . Someone . . . even more than Puck did.'

'I did not!'

'Did.'

'Didn't.'

'Did.'

'Oh, please,' said Titania. She reached out to pat Oberon's leg for wifely reassurance and gave a small yelp. She looked down to see Tiny's unnerving grin focussed on her from the King's lap. 'Stop bickering. We all know that Leanne will . . . well, with anyone in trousers. And anyone who can't wear trousers for physical reasons is even more likely to enjoy her company.'

'Oberon!' exploded Leanne. 'Are you going to let her talk to me like that?'

'Well, *Oberon*?' Titania purred. '*Are* you?'

The King looked from one to the other and knew what he

must do. With a flash of glitter, he disappeared.

'Typical!' said the Vampire and the Queen, for once of one mind.

Benedict and Puck sighed and turned to James. Titania and Leanne were squaring up to each other and that might go on till dawn. Meanwhile, James had some information, buried as it was in his canine, no, further back, lupine brain.

'Shall we go for a walk, eh boy?' Benedict said to the bogle. James leapt up and ran in excited circles around the two.

'He doesn't wear a lead, does he?' Puck asked in horrified tones.

'No, no,' Benedict said. 'But he likes to let the dog out now and again. It does him good.'

So, leaving the spitting cloud of gossamer and venom which had enveloped Leanne and Titania, the three mooched out of the glade, and took the primrose path through the wood.

Chapter Nine

The primrose path was now much, much more. It was a tangle of roses, vines – with grapes of every colour including, rather unnervingly, bright blue – orchids and some plants which even Puck, forest dweller from Way, Way Back couldn't begin to identify.

'What's going on, Puck?' Benedict asked, bowing to superior knowledge. Nothing much had ever grown in his natural habitat, except perhaps a few stalactites and the odd bat.

Puck looked around, at the lush growth rustling with hidden fauna, which he hoped he'd recognise, when the time came. 'I'm not sure,' he said slowly, "but I think he must be dreaming. Stirring in his sleep, you know, and dreaming so . . . *loudly* . . . that it's spilling out. I think we have as little as a Mortal day to fix this.'

Benedict chewed his lip. He looked around and called for his butler. A strangled yelping from the undergrowth was his only answer. He extended a hand and a small lightning bolt parted the vines into a wisp of acrid smoke and a tangle of scorched, twisted stems. In the middle of it was James, pinned to the ground with what looked like an enormous squirrel.

'Wll y gt ths sqrrl 'ff me.'

'What?' Benedict asked.

James shook his head and the squirrel, taken by surprise, lost its grip.

'Will you get this squirrel off me? Please. Sire.'

'Sorry, old chap. I was a bit . . . are you sure it's a squirrel? It's pretty big.'

'Of course I'm a squirrel,' said the squirrel, nastily. 'And don't think I like being this size. The wife has cleared off and you have no idea how many nuts you have to eat to keep going when you're as big as this.' It let go and James sprang back to his Master's side.

Benedict adopted an Oberon-like pose, both hands behind his back and a mirthless smile across his face. 'Have you been like this long?' he asked in a condescending tone.

'Since I woke up this morning,' the squirrel answered. 'And if it's your fault, I would like to get back to normal as soon as possible, please. It appears to be the mating season, judging by the weather, although goodness knows we should all be asleep, and the wife'll be off with the next likely-looking squirrel that passes by if I know her.' It stood there, looking expectant.

'I'm afraid it's not us that did this,' Puck said. 'It's . . . someone else.'

'Well, I'm sorry,' sniffed the squirrel. 'It's only since you Faerie types arrived here that all this has been going on. I'm afraid most of us blame you.'

'Well,' Benedict said crossly, straightening up from checking James for nibbled bits, 'it isn't us, or rather, I would rather say, them. Puck is quite right, it is someone else and we're dealing with it, OK.' This last was said in the voice he used when telling someone that his people would talk to their people. 'And anyway, since when could squirrels talk?'

The squirrel drew itself up. Six foot tall was an imposing height for any animal, but the teeth and tail that made squirrels cute at eight inches long were more than a little threatening at that height. Benedict and Puck stepped behind James.

He looked up at them by rolling his eyes, not moving his head. 'Don't hide behind me,' he whined. 'It's bit me already and you don't want to know where.'

The squirrel leaned forward and said, quietly, threateningly, 'Don't ask stupid questions. Just *do* something. There's animals in this wood you don't want to know about. Wolves.

Bears. Striped things, spotted and everything. Things what eat even six-foot squirrels.'

Puck raised his head and opened his mouth as if to speak.

'Six foot *talking* squirrels, yes, smartarse. So. Get. It. Sorted. Or you'll be sorry.' The squirrel turned and with a fluid movement breathtakingly beautiful from so large a creature, it flowed in a river of amber and gold up the nearest tree. Then, it crashed down to the ground as the branches broke one by one under its weight.

The silence following its fall was complete. Nothing moved. No-one spoke as it gathered its tail haughtily over its arm and stomped off to disappear among the trees.

In the hush of the wood, the trilling of Benedict's mobile phone was harsh and unreal. He reached into an inside pocket and flipped the thing open.

'Yes. Yes. No. What time have I had? Alright, I'll check.'

Puck raised an eyebrow. 'Problems?'

Benedict and James looked at him uncomprehendingly. 'Problems? *Problems*? Of course, problems. You've just been talking to a six foot squirrel, and you ask me if there are problems.'

'I mean,' Puck gestured at the phone, 'other problems.'

'Yes, yes,' Benedict sighed and tucked the phone back in his pocket. 'As I suspected, Mortals are blaming us . . . you. Global warming can't quite cut the mustard any more. This phenomenon . . .'

'Good word, Master,' muttered James at his most sycophantic.

'. . . has only reached these islands so far. Even Ireland is fairly unscathed.'

'Hmph,' snorted James. 'That stuck up lot never had much to do with Pan. They were all islands and water nymphs and mooning about at full moon, gazing at each other across loughs. Never could see the fun in it.'

Benedict waited for the disgruntled bogle to stop, and then continued. 'As I thought would happen, someone has linked the weather to our return and things are looking ugly. It's the men with the pincers and pitchforks all over again. Only bigger.'

'And singing,' James was continuing, almost under his breath. 'Singing all the time.'

'Yes, yes,' Benedict said soothingly. 'I must just check on the Web, Puck, if you'll excuse me.' He opened his coat and his Isp popped out, ruby eyes flashing on and off frantically.

Its metallic, distant, echoing voices said in unison, 'You've got mail.'

'And fiddling.'

'James! If you can't shut up, you can just go back to Titania.'

In a flash, the hound was gone. As he crashed through the undergrowth, they could just hear him say, 'And drums. All for the craic.'

With a patient sigh, Benedict turned back to the Isp. 'Can you read the messages to me please?'

Incorrect password.'

'Don't mess me about,' hissed Benedict. 'Just let me know what my mails say.'

The Isp cleared its many throats and began. After the first few, the messages weren't worth listening to, as they were all the same.

'Just précis, please,' said Benedict, wearily.

'Same old same old,' chorused the Isp. 'What's going on? Where are you? Most of the Mortals are talking about suing, selling shares or . . .'

'What?'

'You don't want to know.'

The old memory of pincers and knives swept through Benedict's hindbrain. He went pale. Paler.

'Global message,' said Benedict. The Isp raised itself up on its many legs and was all attention. 'We are dealing with the problem, which should be considered to be a little local difficulty. We will be on track . . ." He paused and looked expectantly at Puck, who shrugged his shoulders and shook his head, ". . . shortly. I will be away from my desk for the next few days and so messages may not be answered immediately. For urgent matters, please contact me on my mobile. Thank you.'

He smiled benignly at the Isp, watching as it closed its eyes one by one and clenched its little jaws as it concentrated on sending the message. While it wasn't looking, Benedict, gesturing Puck to follow, crept away around a tree. Then, he reached into his inside pocket, took out the mobile and threw it into the bushes.

Puck was staggered. He had never known Benedict willingly parted from his technology before. The Unseelie King smiled at him, a wolfish, canine-rich smile that took Puck Back to the days when the Lord of Misrule was still out and about. Puck's shudder was a mix of trepidation and delight.

The game was afoot. The goat-foot was their quarry. And all they had to do was find him. At that moment, Puck felt that that was no trouble at all. Easy peasy.

Chapter Ten

Back in the glade, Titania and Leanne had decided to set their differences aside. Or rather, Titania had stopped struggling and Leanne realised that there could be no glory in biting the Queen when surrounded by her Court. Plus, Oberon had come back to watch. He had always rather enjoyed seeing women fight over him. His ego had no limits.

So, when James had come bounding out of the wood without the other two, Titania had rushed over to him at once, glad to have something to do except adjust her clothing and try to look serene. James had immediately rolled over to have his tummy tickled and was only saved from complete ignominy by a swift kick in the ribs from Leanne. He had got up and dusted himself down before resuming his place on the stump to bring them up to speed, suitably adjusting the size of the squirrel – 'Nine feet, nine feet if he was an inch.'

'Is that tall, dearest?' Titania had turned huge innocent eyes to Oberon.

Leanne snorted. 'Whatever are you asking him for?' she asked, quite reasonably.

Puck and Benedict arrived just in time to prevent another spat and they all turned to face them. Benedict was still wired from his decision to dump technology and rely on instinct. He walked up to James and pushed him off the log. James fought down his instinct, since instinct was scenting the air, to bite the hand that had fed him down the millennia and lay down quietly to listen.

'I've picked up my e mails for the last time,' said Benedict. Leanne nearly fainted. Oberon and Titania couldn't quite see what the fuss was about. Puck waited. He'd heard the plan already and, though it needed work, it was good.

'I've thrown away my mobile phone.' This time, Leanne did

faint, and had to be brought round by Oberon.

Titania gave him a slap. 'She doesn't need the kiss of life,' she said nastily.

Benedict waited patiently on his stump, which by now was so rotten that only its willpower was keeping it together. 'I've nearly got it worked out,' he said. 'I don't want any interruptions. No pink elephants. No fainting. Just listen.'

And so he began. Pan had been buried, more or less under the circumstances they had already worked out. Facts undisputed were that a) he was bound, but mostly by magic. If that had worn out the hair and whatnot wouldn't hold him. b) the site had been marked in some way, but they didn't know how. He suspected something not written, obviously, but some kind of picture, or shape to show the place. Or perhaps, though less likely, a name, so that Mortals would also understand, c) though no one present could remember, there must be somebody still around who could. And he had had a thought that it might well be the person who had put the spell on in the first place. Therefore, they should look for Druids, witches, that kind of thing. And finally, d) . . .

'I don't think we had a "d", did we, Sire?' Puck said.

'Surely?'

"No, no d. But I think we have plenty to be getting on with. And bearing in mind the state of things in the wood, we ought to be quick about it.'

Oberon stood up, with his glamour on in full measure. 'I'll go and check on the maidens, I think.'

Titania stood up alongside him, sparking with annoyance. There was only so much a Queen could stand. 'Sit down, Lord,' she hissed. 'The maidens aren't at issue. But if I may say so, you are getting very . . ."

'Horny,' said Leanne.

'Is that any of your business?' Titania whirled round in a cloud of petals and sparks.

"No,' Leanne pointed at Oberon's head. 'I mean, he's got horns. Look. Little ones in his hair.'

They all turned to look at the King and, indeed, within his ebony curls there were just two tiny horn-buds, soft with velvet like on a new-born deer. He re-arranged his hair to hide them, but they knew that the little things were another sign.

Puck felt tentatively on the top of his head. Nothing yet. He looked covertly at his feet. Still quite normal, nothing hoof-like about them. He would wait until he got some privacy before he peeked down his trousers, to check his legs but, so far as he could tell, his knees still bent in the conventional way.

Benedict gently cleared his throat. 'I think we should divide in order to conquer,' he said. 'The best fliers should go out and see if they can spot anything that might represent P . . . Someone's resting place. A tor, say, or cairn or something similar. The ones who can read – that's my lot, by and large – should see if they can get a few maps between them and see if there are any place names that seem to suggest that the goat-foot is buried there. Leanne – do you still have Gwyddion as a client?'

'Yes, but he hardly does any telly these days. He's gone very native.'

'Even so, he's probably the brightest of the wizards, even if he has gone a bit Tolkien.' They all spat solemnly, and small flowers grew up where the saliva landed. Benedict's little hellebore died as it bloomed. 'Get him here, if you can.'

Leanne wrapped herself in her cloak and was off into the blue, hot sky which burned above the mists.

'Mab has a shop in town,' Titania said. 'She could bring a few maps – she must know where to get them. Or,' she smiled in his direction, 'perhaps you could do it on your web thing, Benedict?'

"No,' he held out a hand in front of him, as if to ward her off. 'No more technology for me. Or,' his voice faltered, 'at least not until this is sorted out.'

'Well done,' Titania leaned forward and patted his knee. 'Maps it is, then. Puck, perhaps you'd like to nip down and see her?'

'Consider it done,' and he was off.

Oberon stepped forward. 'I think I have something I can do,' he said. He had been obstructive long enough. The horns, and his unruly thoughts had scared him and it was hard to shake the feeling off that when, not if, the Lord of Misrule was back, he, Oberon, Lord of Faerie and, now, prime time television star, make that megastar, would be no more.

'What's that?' Titania said, not unkindly.

'I could go for a bit of a fly with the lads. More heads and eyes watching and remembering might come in useful. Tiny, as you know,' the goblin in question peeped out from the King's coat with what he fondly believed to be a winning smile, 'is pretty bright, as goblins go. He'll spot the place in no time.' And, a tiny inner voice told him, they weren't around then, so might not be quite so influenced. And it was true, they seemed interested rather than nervous, unlike the rest, most of whom could remember, not clearly, but too well.

'What a good idea,' Benedict said, incredulously. 'Off you go, then.'

With a slightly suspicious look, Oberon whistled up his goblins and tucked as many as he could about his person. He only had one rule. 'No chickens,' he said, sternly. Bill's little beak drooped as he turned away. 'Oh, all right then, but only Bill Not the rest.' He looked at Titania and Benedict, who were watching with interest. 'The clucking,' he explained. 'It gets on my nerves,' and away he flew, after a preliminary wriggle, to distribute his load.

'You seemed keen to get rid of him,' Titania turned on Benedict.

'Yes, I was, in fact,' the Lord of Unseelie answered. 'I think he might be attracting attention from You Know Who. He's giving out signals an earthworm could recognise.'

He didn't even look down at the slight movement at his feet and after a second, the ground was still.

'You see,' he continued. 'Everything is so . . . alive here. And if you'd seen that squirrel! Poor James. He had quite a turn.'

Titania absentmindedly stroked the bogle's back and he chuckled quietly.

'What are we going to do?' the Queen asked.

'I suggest you get the others together and split them into teams, depending on their various talents if any. Then, when everyone gets back, we'll be ready to start work.'

The queen stood and raised her arms and suddenly the glade was full of a murmuring crowd. Benedict wished he hadn't thrown away his phone. He was too proud to ask for a loan of Titania's Isp. So he had no choice but to go for a flyover and find his Horde as best he could.

He stood up, flexed his wings and was gone. The stump mouldered into dust, but no one noticed.

Chapter Eleven

Titania had often thought, in the dark days when she was filling shelves, before the return of Faerie, that a better career for her would have been that of Teacher. Her only stumbling block there had been a total lack of aptitude for even a single R, let alone all three. But apart from that, a tiny voice had dreamed in her head, apart from that, she would have made a great teacher. And, in fact, she wasn't far wrong.

In a twinkling of an eye, she had her Folk in ordered groups, not so small as to stop the ideas flowing, not so large that arguments would break out. In some cases, that meant a group as few as one. The Mr Dobies could have been put in a group of infinity squared and the ideas would have flowed like treacle. But, generally, she knew her People and had achieved optimum effectiveness, minimum bloodshed. All they had to do now was wait for the first of her scouts to return.

She sat on the threshold of her bower, head lolling in the weak rays of warm sun that were managing to pierce the mist which swirled above their heads. She was letting her mind wander to the Old Days, when she and Oberon had just got together. He was a bit of a demon, she recalled. Bit of a lad. She sighed. He still was, she supposed. You could bind Pan with silken ropes, bury him where no one knew, forget about him, except in those dreams that would come now and again, and leave even Faerie drenched in sweat. But what you couldn't do was drive out that last bit of Pan out of a Faerie like Oberon. It was buried deep, but was as essential as his bones. She knew why he was behaving like a boor. It was because he was afraid that, without Pan being in existence, that if, with their advanced skills since last time, Mortals could this time kill Pan, then he, Oberon, would also cease to be. She sighed again and opened her eyes.

The sight that met them was unbelievable. Puck and Mab, flying for their lives, landing in a heap in the middle of the glade. Behind them, screeching to a halt just in time before her carefully assembled throng, was a huge car, with metal bars on its front and angry men hanging out of the windows.

'Mistress, Mistress,' Puck was at her side, with Mab a close second. 'Talk to them, will you. They won't listen to us.'

The Queen stepped forward, her glamour laid on with a trowel.

'Don't look at her,' one of the men shouted to the others. 'She'll put a spell on you. She'll turn you into something horrible.'

Frankly, thought Titania, there's nothing much more horrible than you are already, but she pinned on a smile and walked towards the men.

'What is the matter?' she purred. 'Is there some kind of problem, gentlemen?'

With his hand shielding his eyes and his head turned away the ringleader said, 'You're damned right there's something the matter. Look at the weather, for a start. It's February, for goodness sake, and the temperatures wouldn't disgrace July.'

Titania tutted prettily. 'English weather, eh?' she said, smiling.

A few of the men made 'told you' noises and started to back away but the leader spoke again. 'English weather be buggered,' he said. 'It's you lot, messing about with the seasons. Not warm enough for you as it was, I expect. Something like that. I said no good would come of it. And look who's here, lads,' he shouted, pointing at Mab, who hid behind Puck. 'It's her from the health food shop. Health food! Heathen food, more likely. My missus has been a changed woman since she started going in there. All sorts of demands, she's been making.'

The sound of the chorus changed slightly. The men were looking at each other and Puck's superior hearing could hear what they were asking each other. He blushed under the green. Mab smiled secretly to herself.

The group of men had started to drift away. Their leader was getting hot under the collar, spluttering in the middle of a suddenly very empty glade. Titania slid towards him, using her best Leanne-style walk. Before she reached him, he broke and ran for the Land Rover. As he reversed frantically out of the clearing, he waved his fist out of the window and shouted, 'We'll be back.'

Cries of 'Speak for yourself, Mick,' and 'Drop me at home, I've got to have a word with the wife,' grew fainter as the men left the wood and eventually everything was quiet again. The groups reassembled, more or less, in the glade and Titania went back to Puck and Mab on its edge.

Titania and Mab air kissed as they had seen Mortals do. It was a habit of Oberon's, learned in the world of television and Titania preferred him to do that to all and sundry rather than his usual alternative.

'Well, Mab,' said Titania brightly. 'It sounds as if the shop is a success.'

Mab grew a little defensive. 'I only give them what they want,' she said. 'They ask for it, they get it. Sometimes I . . . ginger it up a bit. It depends.' She looked sulky.

Puck put his arm round the Faerie shoulders. A look from Titania soon made him release Mab and another look made him release the Queen.

'Maps?' Titania said.

'Pardon, Mistress.'

'Maps, I said. Not Mab.'

'Sorry. Yes, here they are.' Mab picked up a bag labelled 'Mab's Medicaments. Good For What Ails You' and from it brought out a pile of atlases. Those were put aside for when Benedict got back with his readers, one to be assigned to each team. Meanwhile, Hazel and a few of his less irritating friends were plucked from the hedgerow and made a start.

After a brief silence, save for the turning of pages, he was back.

'Excuse me, Mistress. One finds oneself sadly devoid of any means by which to annotate one's thoughts as they occur to one, in perusing the geographical material with which one has been provided.'

'What?' snapped Mab. Hazel could really get on your wick.

'He needs a pencil,' translated Puck. 'To write things down.'

'Ahh,' cried Hazel, closing his eyes and clasping his twiggy hands together in pleasure. 'One is always so glad when you are around, Puck. Straight to the nub and gist, as always.'

'Do you have a pencil?' Puck asked the Queen.

She looked at him in her regal way. 'Do I look like the sort of Queen of Faerie who would have a pencil?' she asked him.

Puck had to concede she did not. A thought suddenly struck him. He called to James, who had been snoozing under the eaves of Titania's bower.

'Yes,' said the bogle, wiping sleep out of his eyes.

'You know when you had that problem with the squirrel,' he said.

'James had a problem with a squirrel?' asked Mab in amazement. 'You've gone soft, James!'

"Nine foot, he was. Nine foot if he was an inch.'

'Don't start,' said Puck. 'Well, go back there and gather some of the burnt wood from there. Hazel can write with that.'

'Burnt wood!' Hazel's voice was a shriek. 'Burnt wood! What are you thinking?'

'Yes, I'm sorry.' Puck did understand Hazel's natural squeamishness. 'But I don't see any option. Run along, James.'

The bogle loped off, but looking round constantly for the squirrel or similar unnaturally large and bad-tempered rodents. Hazel bridled with hurt solidarity with the burnt tree but was consoled by some light stroking from the Queen.

Soon James was back, holding some lengths of charcoal and Hazel, with evident distaste, took them in his hand and distributed them among the tree spirits, to cries of 'I say' and

'Was it anyone we knew?'

Puck turned his back on the glade of bent heads of all sizes and drew a breath to speak.

Mistress? Master Puck?'

'What now?'

'Now one has the means to write, Mistress, one finds one has no material upon which to make annotations. Could it be that, within your dwelling, you might have some such materi-al?'

'What?'

'Paper,' sighed Puck. 'Do you have any paper?'

'Don't be difficult, Hazel.' Mab turned to face him. 'As the Faerie who forked out hard earned cash for those maps, I happen to know they have plain paper at the back for notes.'

'Yes,' Titania said. 'Please try not to waste time, Hazel.'

'Sorry, Mistress. Puck. Miss.' With a necessarily stiff bow, Hazel went back to his teams.

'Right,' said Puck, turning to the two, 'When the oth . . .'

'Mistress? Could one crave a miniscule amount of your majesty's extremely valuable and royal time?'

Puck's teeth were clenched. 'What is it now, Hazel?'

'What are we looking for?' It was an extremely short sentence for him. It even contained a grammatical error and Mab was quick to take advantage.

'Surely, Hazel,' she said sweetly. 'That should be "for what are we looking?"'

'Don't start, Mab,' Puck snapped. 'Time is short enough as it is, without you making things worse.' He turned to Hazel. 'I thought you knew,' he said.

'Well, in principle, certainly. We are looking for place names that might imply that . . . the god . . . is buried there. But what, for example?'

'Well, go on, Puck,' said Mab. 'Off you go and tell him.' She smiled and crossed her arms.

'Well,' Puck played for time. 'Well, there's . . .'

'We're waiting,' Mab sneered.

Hazel looked alert and expectant. Puck felt a small rivulet of un-Faerielike sweat trickle down his back.

A small voice lower down said, 'Anything with "pan" in

the word. There's loads of those. Also, places like "Wappen-bury", things like that.'

They all looked down. Standing there, in all his modest glory, was Mr Dobie, quiz-watcher, crossword-doer extraordinaire. He smiled a tentative smile. The Queen forgot herself so far as to plant a kiss on his little bald head, making him blush and pluck at the front of his long, dun-coloured coat in embarrassment.

Puck looked Hazel in the eye. 'Yes. What he said.'

'That was all one required,' said Hazel, coldly and strode away, making sure he grabbed a group with a Mr Dobie in it. His clear tones rang out across the glade, with instructions that sounded new minted from his very own pith. Soon, every head was bowed and little cries of discovery rose and fell over the otherwise silent glade.

'What were you trying to say, Puck, before all that?' asked Titania.

'I can't remember,' sighed Puck. 'I think I'll join a group. See how they're getting on. Which one has the most Mr Dobies and the least tree spirits?'

Mab pointed one out.

'I'll have that one, then,' said Puck and picked his way across the grass.

Chapter Twelve

Gwyddion lay back on a grassy bank and drank in the birdsong. He wasn't too worried about the unseasonal weather, although a little, ignored thought was tugging on the hem of his subconscious and trying to tell him that this wasn't right. But Gwyddion was used to things being not quite right. His role, rediscovered and relished, as Head Druid here in the Western fastness of Wales involved various substances that Faerie in general and the Unseelie in particular were glad humans hadn't discovered. The colours. The sounds. The three-foot diameter spiders.

The spider in question cleared its many throats. No response, just a happy smile. It tried a rather larger clear, this one sounding like all the throats in the world being cleared in a metal tunnel thousands of miles away. Still nothing. So, the Isp tried the last weapon in its armoury. It waited until Gwyddion had forgotten he had ever seen it. This involved a wait of a few seconds. Then, it stroked, as gently as a whisper, one clawed foot across the Druid's face.

'Aaggghhhhhhhhhh.' Gwyddion sat up, screaming and flailing his hands. He inhaled a length of beard and started to cough. The Isp gingerly patted his back but, as it knew it must, this only made him worse. Eventually, wiping the tears from his eyes, the Druid sat up and took notice.

'Hello,' said the Isp, in a friendly tone, bending its eight knees and squatting beside him. 'You have mail.'

'What?'

'Mail. You have mail.'

This time the Druid just stared. The Isp sighed. He knew that Benedict and Leanne had never meant it to be like this. A web, the world over – well, the Faerie world over – with none of the problems of the Web of the Mortal world. And Benedict should know – he had created both the Web and its problems. But they had forgotten just one thing. That most of the Faerie, Titania's or Benedict's courts, had a concentration span as long as a gnat's. You teach them one minute how to use a nice simple system like the Isps. Next minute, they're spitting and choking just because one of them gets mail.

It tried again. 'Leanne has sent you a message. It's important. You needn't bother with your password or username or anything,' it added helpfully.

'Oh, good,' said Gwyddion, nodding as if he knew what the horrible thing was talking about. He got to his feet with a sigh. 'Where is this message then?'

'Here,' said the Isp. 'I have it.'

'Where?' The Druid looked a little uncertainly at the Isp's hairy little body. There was nowhere he could see where any message might be hidden.

As the Isp spoke, its eyes flickered with foreknowledge. 'It's inside me.'

Gwyddion grabbed a stick and raised it above his head and the Isp hurriedly said, "No, no, not like that. I mean I know what it is. I can tell you.'

'So, I don't need the stick?'

"No. A password would be nice, but I don't expect miracles. And she did say it was urgent.'

'All right, then. Spit it out, boy.' Like Benedict, Gwyddion's accent had grown stronger since his race had Come Back.

The Isp raised itself up on its toes and its rows of eyes flickered. 'Gwyddion, you idiot.'

He raised the stick again and the Isp hurriedly interrupted itself. 'I'm quoting here. This is Leanne speaking, really, only it sounds like me.'

The Druid looked doubtful but lowered the stick.

'Why don't you answer your phone? We need you urgently in Titania's glade. I can't really tell you over the web but someone is waking up and giving us trouble. Haven't you noticed the weather? I expect it's stopped raining, has it? Isn't that rather odd for Wales? Anyway, just get here. And for goodness sake, make sure you haven't been smoking anything, or eating anything. Whatever it is you lot do. Just get here.' The Isps eyes flickered out and it sagged down a little.

Gwyddion gave it a poke with his toe. 'Anything else?'

'Sorry,' said the Isp. 'I can only say what I'm told.'

'But you know more?'

The creature lowered its rows of eyes modestly. 'I pick up a bit, here and there.'

'What, then?' Gwyddion was gathering up his bits and pieces, sickle, herbs and things which no self-respecting Druid travelled without.

'Well, I've only been around a few months, of course, so I don't have the memories that you lot have. But somebody is waking up, is what I gather.'

'Well, yes. I do believe I know that now I've heard the message. What else, you stupid arachnid?'

'I have a large on-board dictionary,' said the Isp smugly, 'and so I am not offended.'

'Who is waking up?' But the cold feeling in the pit of his stomach was already answer enough for Gwyddion. The flowers. The birds. The sun. and, as Leanne had pointed out, the distinct lack of rain. It could only be Pan.

The echo of his thoughts from the Isp was spoken to empty air, as Gwyddion, grasping his sickle for dear life, spun round on the spot until, in a haze of smoke, he disappeared.

The Isp, inhaling at that moment, suddenly crossed all its eyes and dropped onto the bank, trying rather disastrously to cross some of its legs. 'Hey, man,' it said to the sky. 'You've got mail.'

Benedict flew ponderously on his tattered leather wings. He didn't like flying in daylight. For one thing, he could hear the little shrieks from below and, while it was gratifying to know he hadn't lost his touch, it was still irritating. It was ironic that Mortals reacted like that, when he had been running their lives for centuries, starting with . . . well, fire. He could have shrunk himself down, as the Faerie did, but there were certain standards that the Lord of Unseelie had to maintain. And leather wings was just one.

It wasn't long before he spotted his first target and he spiralled down with a cry he liked to consider pretty eldritch, bearing in mind he didn't get the practice. Annis hardly turned her head.

'Hello, Annis.'

'Lord.' She hardly bothered to nod her head. Things had been a bit cool between them since she had rotted all the fabric and tarnished all the metal in his apartment before the Return.

'Nice day,' he said, brightly.

'Too nice,' she spat. She was sitting on what used to be a park bench, picking the remains of her breakfast – a pigeon, with heart still beating, her favourite – out of her tooth with one of the bird's ex-feathers.

'As you say. Perhaps a little too nice.'

'He's waking.'

She spun her head round to stare at him from her one functioning eye. Even so, its focus missed him by a decent margin. 'What're you lot and that hoity toity madam doing about it?'

'We're planning at the moment.' He gave a nervous laugh. 'That's why I'm here, in fact.'

Suddenly, a beautiful woman, clothed only in flowing golden hair was in Annis' place. "Not for the pleasure of my company, then?' she asked, inclining her head coquettishly.

'Er, well, naturally that as well,' Benedict stammered. Annis could be so unpredictable and he knew what lay beneath that beautiful skin. But she was in no mood for games today and the real Annis was back with a pop and a smell of ancient marshes which made even Benedict gag slightly.

'Pan.'

Benedict looked round frantically.

'Don't worry, Lord,' she said sarcastically. 'There's never anyone near enough to me to overhear.' She gave a phlegmy chuckle. 'I can't imagine why.'

'Well, you're right anyway, we think,' he said.

'You think! You mean you haven't been to check, haven't strengthened the spells, tightened the bonds that bind him. You've all gone soft. It's this mixing with Mortals. I said no good would come of it.'

Benedict didn't remember her saying anything of the kind, but he let it go.

'You've woken him up, ye daft things. Her, her Ladyship Hoity Toity flying around sparkling all over the shop. Him, on the telly all the time, never off he isn't. You and your business interests.' She spat and just missed his shoe. 'Ye've woken him up, haven't you?'

Benedict had the grace to look ashamed.

'Well,' she started to gather her bags together and clucking to various unknown life forms foraging in the shadow under her bench. 'You'll have to give me a lift. I don't travel so fast, as you know. It's time somebody with some sense started making some of these plans.'

Benedict clenched his teeth and held out his arms to her. Chuckling, she climbed up, winding her legs around his waist and resting her cheek against his. Her various pets clung to whatever they could and Benedict took to the air.

'Just like the old days,' Annis murmured. 'Although I suppose I've let myself go a bit. Nothing a brush and comb wouldn't put right, though.'

Benedict smiled and nodded, teeth still firmly clenched to stop the bile that was rising in his throat. As they flew over Hampshire, a thought came to him and he managed to ask, 'You asked if we had visited his burial. Er, where would that be, then?'

The good people of Winchester, going about their daily lives, heard above their heads as the strange couple flew by, could just hear, from the quiet of the Cathedral Close, an unearthly scream that could have been laughter. The ones with good hearing also heard a harsh voice cackle.

'I'm buggered if I know.'

Chapter Thirteen

Oberon was also his normal size. None of this shrinking down for him. He had his public to consider. Besides, keeping the goblins small when they were on board took a great deal of concentration. Since a nasty incident in which a plummeting Thydney, suddenly life-size, nearly crushed a courting couple in some sand dimes one Sunday afternoon when Oberon and the lads were out for a bit of a fly, he tended to not bother with his size. Size just didn't matter, he thought to himself.

As might be expected, his flight was more erratic than the Unseelies' had been. Leanne had gone straight to her office and, ignoring her secretary's list of calls to make, she had got straight on to Gwyddion. She was so efficient, that she rewarded herself with a private interview with the next big thing in young actors. Benedict had delivered Annis and flown off again immediately. Titania thought, watching him fondly as the sound of his beating wings, like thunderclaps, died away, that he was off to find more Unseelie. And so he was, but only after a bath and change of clothing. He'd borrow some of Oberon's. It wasn't that he thought he wouldn't mind – he would of course be furious – but bits of Annis tended to cling, and he couldn't bear it any longer. But otherwise, he was pretty focussed.

The goblins had, in the end, got quite firm with Oberon. After the fifth stop to sign autographs, it was Tiny who had grasped the King by the horns, as it were.

'Sire,' he said, as they flew away from the waving crowd. 'We really must do this job, you know.'

'Hmmm,' said Oberon, still wiggling starry fingers at his fans.

Tiny clambered up the King's back and flicked one of the horn buds with a trotter. There was no need for words.

'Sorry, lads,' said Oberon.

'We underthtand, Thire,' said Thydney. 'Your fanth need you.'

'Yes, indeed, Thyd,' sighed the King. He didn't know whether to be angry or frightened. He settled for a bit of both. For this to happen just after he had Come Back. And what a Come Back it had been. And then – the old goat waking up like that! It was so unfair! Had he not been two hundred feet in the air, Oberon would have stamped his foot.

Bill tried a diversionary tactic. He pecked Oberon lightly under the chin and pointed with his huge forefinger at the ground. Oberon nearly dropped all his goblins in his excitement.

'Look, look lads! That must be it.'

They all looked down and it seemed he might be right. Carved into the hillside below was a gigantic man, stark white chalk against the green grass. He carried a club. But that wasn't why Bill had pointed the figure out.

'Look at the size of that!' Oberon gasped. 'Only . . . he . . . is built like that! That must be the place we put him.'

The goblins made their appropriate sounds of agreement; clucks, oinks and a kind of soft susurration, made by the rabbity one. Only Tiny was silent.

'And what's your problem?' asked Oberon, coming out of a victory roll which made the rabbit cover its mouth with its paws.

Tiny was ill at ease. When his Lord made up his mind, which wasn't often, it wasn't healthy to disagree. 'I just think it might be a bit . . . obvious, Sire.'

'Obvious?'

'Well, perhaps it's just me, but I thought that the sign might be a bit more . . . subtle, Sire. A sort of symbol, rather than a picture of a man with a huge . . .'He glanced at the rabbit. It was already looking offended, so he stopped and let the silence speak.

'I don't see how subtle would help. You need to let people know,'

'Yes, but as the bogle said, someone might have dug him up to use in battle. So a great big carving that might as well say "we've buried . . . someone here and so if you want you can dig him up" would be a bit pointless. So, I think . . ."

'Oh, you think, you think. Well, I think Bill was very clever to point it out.'

Bill clucked with pleasure and did a little light clawing of Oberon's chest.

'Ow. And so we're back to the glade in a twinkling and get the chaps. We'll dig him up and bury him again and everything will be all right by nightfall and I can get back to my show and . . ."

Tiny sighed and burrowed down in Oberon's coat lining. He knew, in his own mind, that he was right. In fact, between autograph signing three and autograph signing four, he had seen, out of the corner of his eye, a huge mound with a big column on top that had seemed to call to him. It wasn't just the shape, which was just what he was looking for, but something in the air around it which had caught his attention. It was useless trying to tell the King, so he just put a picture of it in his mind, ready for Puck or someone sensible to lift out and identify when the little scouting party landed in the glade.

Puck was sitting at the sharp end of a queue snaking round and round the clearing. The noise was almost unprecedented in any Faerie gathering. Everyone seemed to be shouting at once and Titania had given up and gone into her bower, where a peace always reigned, a silence slightly muffled by the thicker air that held sway in there. In vain did Puck shout for quiet. In fact, when he had raised his voice, all that had happened was that everyone else had shouted louder, to drown out the idiot shouting at them. So, he just sat there, and listened to the litany of names and suggestions being thrown at him.

Hazel stood by his side, looking inscrutable. Puck beckoned him lower and the spirit grudgingly bent in the middle.

'Why are they all queuing up?' Puck yelled.

'They don't trust the scribes,' Hazel shouted back. 'Since Benedict's goblins arrived, they think there's a sort of plot. So they all want to tell you themselves.'

Puck shook his head, squared his shoulders and smiled weakly at the first creature in the queue. It was a goblin, of the rabbity design. It was clearly speaking, because he could see its lips moving, but its quiet voice was no match for the cacophony.

'What?' Puck yelled.

The little creature wrinkled its nose and tried again.

'Panshanger.' He just managed to make it out.

'Where is that?'

This time he couldn't even begin to hear what the goblin said, but nodded and pretended he knew. The goblin backed away, wreathed in smiles. Soon, it was gambolling randomly on the edge of the crowd, the last half hour gone from its tiny brain.

So the time went. Some places sounded as if the god might be buried there. Some were the names of places where barrows were, or mounds of some kind. None had that jolt of recognition which Puck felt he should feel. His heart was heavy, and he could almost feel the goat-legs developing beneath his makeshift desk. The only slightly exciting moment was when a crowd of flower fairies, banded together to give their voices volume got to the front of the queue.

'Pandy,' the yelled in unison.

'Where?' he said, sitting up to attention.

'Wales.'

'Wales? Where the Druids come from?'

'Yes.'

His heart soared and he almost dismissed the rest of the queue but didn't want to start a riot. Then, the next one in the line, a Mr Dobie, grinning broadly, said triumphantly, 'Pant-y-dwr.'

'Wales?'

Happy nodding.

Twenty more Welsh pants and Puck was no longer a happy elf. When Gwyddion suddenly appeared at his elbow, he nearly got a beardful of fist, until Puck remembered his manners.

'Hello, Gwyddion. Leanne's not back yet.'

'Don't worry. I know why I'm here. And, before you ask, I remember what we did but not where. Although . . .'

'Yes?'

'It wasn't in Wales. That much I do remember.'

'Yes, I think I'd already worked that out.'

'I think it was in the West, though.'

'You mean really West. Like the Lizard, or something like that?'

"No. Just . . . West.' Gwyddion snapped. 'Look, Puck, how long ago was this?'

'Look into my eyes.'

Gwyddion did so. 'And?'

'How old are they? What have they seen?'

The Druid sighed. 'Yes. I know. There's been no more room in my head for the last three hundred years. I have to kick stuff out to remember where I've left my sandwiches.'

'Precisely. We're all in the same boat.' He turned to the queue, which still seemed unreasonably long. 'Pull up . . . something. There, that sheep will do. No offence. Help me with this lot.'

And so the time passed.

'Goatacre.'

'Painswick.'

'Gravelly Hill.'

'Penstone.'

A crash and a muffled curse told him, without looking up, that Oberon was back.

The line broke and gathered round the King. He held up his hands and spoke to the crowd.

"No need to worry,' he declaimed. Titania came to the door of her bower and gazed adoringly on the Lord of Faerie. 'I have found the place.'

Puck and Gwyddion were on their feet in an instant. Puck stepped forward and immediately fell over Tiny, who was holding onto his leg. The goblin was rolling its eyes madly and gesturing, drawing a trotter across its throat and pointing at its temple in a meaningful way. Puck shook it off and went over to the King.

Oberon was continuing. 'I have found. Ow.' Bill was pecking his foot. 'Bill and I have found the place. It is a hill with a huge man carved on it.' He looked over the upturned faces and realised that a large percentage were female and adapted what he was going to say. 'Various features, well one feature at least, makes me think it represents . . . the person we're looking for.' He gave Puck and Gwyddion a meaningful look.

Gwyddion turned to Puck and raised his eyebrow.

'I think he means it's got a big . . .'

'Puck!' Mab and Titania were at his elbow. 'I don't think we need a picture.' Titania swept forward and tucked herself under Oberon's arm, smiling up at him, radiating glamour till it bounced off the trees.

'Puck.' The voice was down near his waist. He looked down into the earnest features of Tiny.

He bent down. 'You're persistent. What's the problem?'

'He's got it wrong. It's not the place. I've seen a much better place.'

'Well, where it is, then?'

'I don't know.'

'Gwyddion,' said Puck, turning to go. 'Turn Tiny into something unpleasant, would you, please? More unpleasant, I mean, of course.'

Gwyddion raised his arms.

'No, no.' Tiny ran round the Druid, whose spell fell on a rather inoffensive brownie, who turned into a lizard, but only briefly. Gwyddion wasn't concentrating. 'Please listen. I've been remembering it all the way back. Come into my head and see if you recognise it.'

'Eurgghh.'

'Please, Puck. He's wasted so much time. We can't do another flyover. It may be our last chance. I'll keep all my other stuff out of the way.'

'Oh, all right then. Hold still.'

Puck found himself in a strangely tidy little head. There were even labels on some stuff, but he didn't look too closely. Because there, in the middle, was a faithful rendition of a mound, a top-of-the-egg shaped hump, topped with a spike of stone. All round it a path wound and, when he looked closely, the air around it seemed to shimmer. A town was nearby, but no buildings were on its slopes. The grass was short, but that was the only vegetation. Puck knew that this was The Place.

All they had to do was find it by retracing Oberon's flight path. Get some spades. More bogles who could dig. Trolls were big, they could help. And dwarves, of course. Digging was their thing, after all. A wizard to redo the spell. Maidens . . . hmmm, perhaps another spell would be enough. And then it was done and DONE.

Puck spun round, his face glowing. Ah, but first he would have to persuade Oberon. Not an easy job, but he was the elf to do it. He elbowed his way into the crowd surrounding the Royal couple and tapped Oberon on the shoulder.

'Sire?' he said. 'A word?'

Chapter Fourteen

Oberon was still sulking. He couldn't be made to see the logic in Puck and Tiny's argument. Everyone was ganging up on him. He was the King, after all. He could command that they dig where he said. Then they'd see.

'But, Lord,' Puck had said. 'The hill you suggest is too big. It can't be a cairn built in one night. And everything we remember suggests that we made a hill where it had been flat before. Your carving – although very persuasive in many ways – is on landscape. Tiny's idea; well, we just feel it's right.'

'Do we know where it is, Puck?' Titania asked, patting Oberon's arm absentmindedly as she spoke.

'No, but when Benedict gets back, we think he might be of some help. He knows geography much better than we do.'

Titania drew herself up. 'I don't think so, Puck,' she said, rancid honey dripping from her lips. 'No one knows my kingdom like I do.'

Leanne, who had returned looking like the cat that got the cream, snorted.

Titania glared at her and folded her arms. 'I'm sorry?' she said to the vampire. 'Are you suggesting that I don't know this country? I could fly its length and breadth in a single blink.'

Leanne smiled, showing her pointed teeth. 'We all know

you could, Lady,' she said. 'But do you? In fact, if you had been flying your kingdom, would we be in this mess now?'

Puck stepped between them, hands outstretched. 'This has got to stop. We don't have the time.'

Titania and Leanne subsided, but only as volcanoes do when not actually erupting.

Then bickering Faerie were as nothing. Benedict had touched down in the glade, to much capering from James and a scream which could curdle milk from Oberon.

'Hello,' he said, a little too brightly. 'How are things?'

'You're wearing my coat!' hissed Oberon.

'Found anything, have we?' Benedict advanced, rubbing his hands together with a papery hiss.

'And my trousers! And look. They're covered in dog hair, now.'

'Benedict,' said Titania sternly. 'Why are you wearing Oberon's clothes?'

Benedict looked down, amazed. 'Are these yours?' he said.

'Don't give me that. You've pinched my clothes!' Oberon sniffed the air. 'Obsession for Men! You're wearing my cologne.'

'Let's not make a fuss,' suggested Benedict.

'Yes, let's not,' said Puck. 'I'm sure there's an explanation. But can you get it later, Sire? We need the Lord of Unseelie's help on this one, remember?'

Oberon glowered, but stepped back. He gave a little start when he saw his shoes gleaming out from below the well-turned trouser-cuff also half-inched by Benedict, but otherwise was quiet.

Puck described the site from Tiny's head to the dark Lord.

'Hmmm,' he said. 'I recognise it. Now, let me see. Tor.'

'You saw it on a tour?' Leanne suggested, helpfully.

"No, no, woman. Whisht.' Benedict became very Scottish when he was thinking hard. 'It is a Tor.'

'Where?'

Hazel stepped forward. 'Should one muster one's colleagues, Master, Mistress, Master Puck, Mistress Leanne, and reperuse the geographical material thus far examined and attempt to . . .'

Benedict struck himself smartly on the forehead and stepped back. 'Got it!' he said.

The entire clearing was silent, even at the back, where the dwarves were usually something of a bad influence. The little crowd immediately around Benedict leaned forward, their mouths open in encouragement, but he just stood there, smiling. Suddenly, a carrier bag filled with something indescribable sang through the air and caught him a nasty one on the side of the head.

Everyone stepped back a pace to avoid the fallout.

'My coat!' wailed Oberon.

'Get on wi' it, you nelly,' cried Annis. 'we've got work to do, even if you haven't.'

Benedict picked a sticky feather from his lip before speaking. 'Glastonbury,' he said. 'It's Glastonbury Tor, that's where he is. It's all coming back to me now.'

Everyone who'd been there looked around them, nodding, but saying nothing. That terrible night was flooding back in all its horror. The thunder. The lightning. The screaming, wrenching god pinned down by maidens' hair. The sweat. The heat. The crying. The digging. And now, they had to do it all again. If they were quick, he'd still be sleeping and they could sneak up on him, take him unawares. With any luck, it wouldn't be anything like as hard this time.

The crowd was all at once in a scurry. Goblins, who weren't there, but were well aware who'd be digging this time, were doing their thing; jumping up and down with excitement, milling around in an aimless mass, leaving piles of nervousness around for the unwary to tread in or, in Tiny's case at least, looking horribly smug.

Oberon strode through the crowd. As he did so, he caught the little goblin on the back of the head with his hand.

'Oh, sorry, Tine old man,' he said, jovially. 'Didn't see you there.'

Tiny rubbed his head and watched the King's retreating back. He sighed. It would be a long time before he rode in the Royal waistcoat pocket again, he couldn't help feeling. But, never mind. At last he had found his place in song and story, as Tiny, The Goblin Who Saved The World From The Return Of Pan And Inevitable Anarchy. He liked the way that rolled off the tongue. He wasn't much of a reader, but he'd heard a lot about this Jeffrey Archer lately. Perhaps he would be the Bard to write his story. With a happy sigh, Tiny went off to find a spade.

Chapter Fifteen

'We can't take everyone, Mistress,' Puck explained patiently. 'Not enough of them can fly. Remember how long it took them to travel when we Returned? Well, we didn't have long even then. But this time, I don't think we have longer than . . . well, until dawn tomorrow.'

'And that's pushing it.' Leanne was lounging against the wall of Titania's bower, smoking a cigarette. Puck had never seen her do that before and he realised it was the only sign of stress that she was allowing herself. Gwyddion was standing near to the vampire; this was not because she was his agent, It was, however, the only way he could get to inhale her smoke. He'd forgotten where he'd put his tobacco pouch.

'Well, who can we take, then?' Titania asked.

'Let's make a list,' said Hazel, brightly.

'Let's not and say we did,' Mab snapped. 'It's obvious, isn't it. Gwyddion, for the spells. Tiny, to guide us. You, Lord,' she nodded at Oberon, 'to chat up any Mortal who gets in the way. Leanne, to keep . . . him busy. My Lady, for the same reason but, obviously, not in quite the same way.' She stopped, embarrassed.

Leanne blew a smoke ring. 'Chat wasn't his strong point,' she said, 'as I recall.' She pushed herself upright and threw down the cigarette, grinding it out on the threshold of the bower. Titania, for neatness sake, turned the ash into a smear of glitter.

'Puck, of course,' Mab went on.

'Why of course?' Puck appeared around the corner of the bower. 'I wasn't there when you buried him. What use can I possibly be?' he sounded hopeful, rather than convinced.

'Because you weren't there,' Mab sneered, 'is why you're definitely going to be there this time. Digging, with your hands, if needs be.' She continued with her list. 'Benedict. James.'

'Oh yes.' The bogle got up from his position at Titania's feet. She found his devotion rather annoying. She had fallen over him twice already. 'Got a bit of digging to do. Let's get the dog to do it.'

'Don't be sulky,' Leanne poked him playfully in the ribs and nearly drew blood. 'You're essential. You were there before.'

James shook himself and turned his back. He'd show her sulky.

'Some goblins. Ask the dwarves if there is a Glastonbury Chapter and if they're in touch. That would be helpful. Ummm . . .'

'You.' Puck couldn't resist.

'Me? What could I do?'

'I'm sure the Lord of Misrule could find some use for such an apt pupil. Perhaps we could tie you down there too, for some company.'

'Mistress . . .'

'He's joking, Mab, I'm sure. But why shouldn't you be there? You were there before, just like us.'

'Yes, but,' her brow puckered in thought. Eureka! 'You'll need someone here, Mistress. To co-ordinate.'

'Mab,' Leanne hissed. 'You couldn't co-ordinate your way out a of a paper bag. You're coming with us, Faerie. Make no mistake.' She took up the list making. 'Annis.'

'I'm not carrying her.'

'Me neither.'

For once, Puck and Mab were in agreement.

'Honestly. I'll carry her.'

They all looked up to see Benedict walking towards them.

'You will, Lord?' Puck asked, in amazement.

'Why not?' Oberon's bitter voice came from the branch of a tree above their heads. He still suspected that he was safer from Pan's influence if he was off the ground. 'He's wearing my clothes. What's he got to lose?'

'That's got nothing to do with it. I merely offer because my goblins are weightless, so I can carry any number and still have room for a passenger. Your . . . things are bigger and so you can't carry so many. James doesn't do carrying. Not since . . .' he gave James a significant look, 'that time, eh, James?'

The butler looked at the sky and tried to whistle.

Unsurprisingly, it didn't work.

'What happened?' Titania couldn't bear not to know.

Benedict raised an eyebrow at James. 'Started off with three, arrived with one,' he said, briefly.

'Ah.'

'Leanne can do co-ordination, but from the Tor. She still has her phone and Isp.'

Leanne patted her pockets and Oberon nearly fell out of his tree.

'Puck can carry any tools we might need. Gwyddion will be carrying his gear – the spell has to be really strong this time. We've given up the search for maidens' hair. We wouldn't be able to find enough to tether a gnat at this notice. Mab and you, Lady,' he nodded at Titania, 'can just grab what's left.'

Oberon hopped down from his branch. He looked uneasy. 'Tell you what, though,' he said. 'I don't feel at all well, if you all know what I mean. Time is short. Really short. I think we should be off.' He put his fingers to his mouth and blew. The ultrasound brought goblins from all corners and he stowed Tiny, Thydney and Bill in their favourite pockets. Bill was very excited and was swiftly turfed out again. 'None of that!' Oberon told him. 'How many times do I have to tell you?'

'Sorry,' clucked Bill and hopped back in again.

A clamour of goblins of every size clambered up their king and soon he had a full load stowed. Freckles, last up, fell out of his chosen pocket, which was already full. He hopped up and down in frustration, tears in his little eyes.

Titania smiled and clapped her hands to him, opening her arms. Freckles nearly passed out with joy. That he was something of a favourite, he already knew. But to ride with the queen – what an honour! He jumped up and burrowed down, keeping his trotters and similar sharp bits well tucked in.

Oberon gave a final pat to his payload. 'Sorry, lads and lasses,' he said to the rest. 'We'll be back soon. Be patient goblins and keep thinking of us. It can only do us good.' He ruffled a few crests here, a few soft ears there and they drifted away, consoling each other and reaching for their packs of cards.

Titania and the others dispersed over the glade. Black Annis was waiting for Benedict and hopped on board with no preamble. Gwyddion finally managed to remember where everything was and had it safely tied or otherwise attached about his person. Puck had a word with the dwarves, emphasising the damage to the collective that was Faerie that Pan was doing and so a message was sent via their tunnels to the dwarves in Glastonbury. Their fastest tapper was sent down to tap out 'Brothers stop help needed stop gather at tor stop help posh gits dig stop stop pan stop'

When all was ready, the fliers met in the middle of the glade. They stood in a Faerie ring and held hands. They bowed their heads and silence fell, except for distant crashes, such as those possibly made by a six-foot squirrel falling out of a tree. The flower fairies landed on their shoulders, not stinging or complaining for once, but murmuring like a million tiny bees, singing their encouragement in the language of flowers.

Titania raised her head. She raised her arms. Tiny took up his position as route finder on Oberon's shoulder and they were off.

In the silence they left behind, it was almost possible to feel the thoughts of the Faerie. They stood or hovered, faces upturned to the darkening sky, watching as the motley crew grew smaller and smaller as they gained height. Soon, it wasn't possible to tell one from the other, Benedict's leather wings and his noisome burden being the same small dot, flickering in and out of vision, as Titania, lovely as day and scintillating in her own special light.

Soon, even the dots were gone and all they could do was hope.

In the dark, flowers bloomed and died; clouds of butterflies rose out of the damp grass and flew for a few beautiful seconds before crumbling to dust; snow fell, melted and was gone in a minute; dolphins swam in village duckponds and, far from any zoo, lions roared. Women stirred uneasily and looked over their shoulders, feeling hot breath on the back of their necks; men felt their hackles rise and old instincts, long buried, rose in their brains.

Pan was turning in his sleep.

Pan was dreaming.

Pan was awake.

Chapter Sixteen

Up ahead, by the light of a harvest moon which, to the astonishment of astronomers should by rights have been just a sliver of light in the velvet sky, Tiny was having trouble.

'I'm sorry, Sire,' he said. 'We didn't come this way before.'

'It's the exact same route,' Oberon snapped.

'No.' Thydney stuck his head out of Oberon's collar, and spoke in his ear. 'We had a few stopth for autographth, if you remember, Thire.'

'Oh, those.' Oberon dismissed the stops and Thydney with a shake of his head and a wipe of the cheek. 'But, apart from those, it is the same route.'

'I'm not sure,' said Tiny, scanning the horizon, shielding his eyes theatrically with his trotter. 'I think we are too far west.'

'Problems?' Benedict came alongside on a waft of Annis, mercifully somewhat thinned out by the altitude and a following wind.

'I think we're too far west,' Tiny said.

'I think so too,' Benedict agreed. 'We've just flown over the Isle of Man ferry. Come on.' He swooped away with a crack of his wings and a smell of old cellars, 'follow me.'

The string of fliers and their various burdens flew across the moon, heading east. It was almost possible to forget, in the crisp, high air and the pearly light that washed the sky that they were flying to their doom. There was even a background of light chatter, with Titania's clear laugh ringing out, making Mortals out walking the dog, clandestine lovers and burglars look up at the sky and feel unaccountably glad.

The mood lasted until they heard Tiny cry out. 'There it is! Down there.'

They spiralled lower. Through the light cloud streaming by in the breeze, they saw it and the memory of that night exploded in their heads. Oberon held his temples between his palms, jack-knifing in the air. He howled with pain as the horn-buds on his crown grew an infinitesimal but scalp-tearing amount. Puck bucked in his flight, fighting with all his might against the goat-legs trying to gain ascendancy. He put his fists in his pockets to brace against the pain that ran down his spine and found, to his horror, a set of pipes already there.

Somehow, they all reached the ground. Puck and his King stood, teeth clenched against the song in their heads. Gwyddion was gathering his magic requirements and trying to look important. The goblins, who had jumped out of Oberon's suddenly very disturbing orbit as soon as his feet touched ground, were terrified by the most scary thing they had experienced in their lives – Titania, Leanne and Mab all holding hands. Benedict seemed strangely reluctant to let go of Annis. He also seemed slow to fold his wings, which he usually put away with a snap as soon as he touched earth. He looked ready for the off.

Titania tried a silvery laugh. There was something tarnished about the way it came out and she opted for silence. Eventually, Puck said, slowly, 'Well, this won't help, will it? Standing around. Let's start digging.'

'Ah,' said Oberon, with the air of someone who has managed to wriggle out of a dental appointment from hell, 'We'd better wait for the dwarves. They're the diggers in this operation.'

'We've been here ages,' said a disgruntled voice from near his knee. 'Where have you been?'

'At a cocktail party, prob'ly. Hur hur,' said another voice in the shadow.

'Where shall we dig?' asked James, pawing the ground ruminatively.

'Where is he buried?' Leanne asked a question by way of reply.

Gwyddion whipped out a forked twig from the recesses of his robe. 'I will dowse for him,' he announced. 'Quickest way,' and he grasped the twig with a short fork in either palm. In a winking of an eye, the twig began to turn, gathering speed so quickly that it was a blur and he had to move fast to stop it winding his beard in. He turned this way, then that, twisting as if on a turntable. Then he was off at the gallop, pulled by the madly turning twig, his feet sometimes on the ground, sometimes trailing behind, like a bizarre and low-flying comet.

The others ran, flew, toddled behind, gathering magic items that rained from his pockets in his flight. He seemed to be following the spiral path up the mound and Puck soon decided to cut out the middle man and sliced across the grass, toes trailing and so met a startled Gwyddion once every turn, as the Druid sped up until not just his stick, but his body was a blur.

When he reached the top, the stick stopped, trembling like a stopped clock, before spinning madly round, but this time, widdershins. The chasing Faerie crowd cannoned into one another as they reached the wizard, who, eyes wild and speech dopplering with the speed, flew past them again, down the spiral path.

'What is he doing?' Oberon asked, plunging back in hot pursuit.

'Hanging onto his stick, if he's as wise as he says,' cackled Annis, riding on Benedict's back like a terrible jockey. 'Otherwise, he'll do himself a serious mischief.'

They heard the horrible cry, followed by a crash, followed by the sound of a heavy body falling down a hillside before they made the turn. Of Gwyddion there was no sign. But there, in the moonlight, quivering in the ground, was the stick.

Mab leaned over the edge of the path and called down into the dark. 'It's OK, Gwyddion! We've got your stick.'

'Oh, hurrah,' the Druid's voice called from below. They heard his dragging footsteps making their way back up the path.

Strung out across the track, the Faerie made a pool of dark shadow in the light of the moon.

'That's queer,' said Puck. 'I wonder why the twig did that?'

Titania stepped forward, and with gentle hands parted the group into two. Where the moonlight fell in the gap between was illuminated the most horrible sight they had ever seen in all their millennia on earth.

It was a hole.

And the hole was empty.

Chapter Seventeen

Oberon pushed his way to the front. Like the others, he could only gape at the hole, dark and threatening in the, bleaching moonlight. The edges were piled up, with clods of earth scattered yards away, where they had rolled down the slope as the hole was dug from the inside out. Different strata from the centuries were tumbled together, undisturbed for the first time since the original burial. Oberon opened his mouth to speak, but Titania grabbed his arm and said, 'Ssshhh. Listen.'

Everyone held their breath. Sure enough, there was a laboured breathing, there on the edge of hearing. It sounded like – well, it sounded like someone would sound who had dug themselves out of a hole they had been in for many hundreds of years. It contained a suspicion of whimper, there in the background.

Mab's soft heart got the better of her. 'Oh, listen!' she cried. 'He doesn't sound at all well.'

Puck was suspicious. His memories of the Lord of Misrule didn't include any signs of fragile health and, he reasoned, the chaos he had been causing when still asleep didn't suggest any frailty now, either. He crept off down the path, keeping in the shadow as far as possible and skimming the ground lightly, so as to give no clue to anyone with razor sharp hearing by cracking twig or feather soft footfall that he was approaching.

He tuned out of his hearing the whispered exchange higher up the hill.

'Be quiet, Mab,' he heard Leanne hiss.

'You daft besom,' Annis didn't bother with niceties, at this, or any other time. 'He doesn't need your sympathy. But if he senses it, well . . . brace yourself, Faerie!'

'Yes, Mab, dear,' Titania added. 'I don't think he will need any help from us.' She sighed. 'In fact, far from it.'

Oberon was getting frantic. 'My head, my head,' he moaned. 'Please do something. I don't do pain.' His voice was strained with the effort of speaking through gritted teeth. 'I am . . . a celebrity. Ow.'

'Sorry,' said Benedict crisply. 'That last one was me. Stop being such a luvvie, and do us all a favour.'

Oberon rubbed his head, fingers lingering over his little horns, which felt huge, like a teenager's spot before her first hot date.

Puck listened. Yes, there it was again. A groan, heavy breathing, rustling clothing. The elf gathered himself together to spring. This might be the last thing he did. Even Immortals could die – cease to be, rather. They had no comfort like Mortals had, no Heaven, no Nirvana, no Valhalla to look forward to. Just the fact that they once had been and now were not. He edged nearer and then, muscles at screaming point, he let go and flew through the air, focussed on the source of the noise.

His coiled body landed on something soft and floaty, over-laying something soft and flabby. In the second before it fell down the hill, tumbling head over heels, with a small, but somehow unsurprised whimper at every bounce, he knew it was Gwyddion.

He leant over the edge and whispered into the moon washed dark, 'Sorry.'

He met the others on the bend of the path.

'What was that?' said Leanne, softly.

'I've just knocked the Druid back down the hill,' Puck whispered back.

A snort at the back told everyone that Freckles had not lost his sense of humour. That snort proved to be infectious. The stress of the flight, the relief at finding the place, the unadulterated, bowel-loosening fright at finding the hole and no god in it all got together in their heads and exploded in laughter, all the more diaphragm-wrenching for having to be quiet. Eventually, it subsided. They were still wiping their eyes and fighting for breath when they heard Gwyddion approaching again up the path. At least, they had to hope it was Gwyddion.

It was a tattered Druid that hove into view. His robes were torn and dirty. His beard was full of all sorts of things he didn't want to think about. Not too much dog shit, he was pleased to note, although any could be said to be too much, when it is in your beard. He stood there, a picture of dejection, looking from face to face. He cocked one eyebrow, interrogatively. No one moved or spoke. He pushed his hair back from his brow and tried the eyebrow again.

Oberon gestured with his thumb over his shoulder.

Gwyddion pushed his way through and saw the earthwork. He turned to them, his eyes gleaming wide in the pale light. He licked his lips, dry with the shock, as well as his many falls.

'He's gone,' he croaked.

Cynical mutters swept over the crowd, the dwarves enjoying the proof, if proof were needed, that the nobs might swan around in fancy gear, but they were dumb as all get out.

'We thought you might be able to tell where he's gone, dear,' said Titania, condescendingly.

'Whyever did you think that?' the Druid asked, amazed.

'Well, you always seem so intelligent.' The Queen was disappointed. The Druid had been a Professor before the Return and had retained his aura of arcane knowledge, honed to perfection in front of the laser glare of students.

'Also,' Annis pushed herself belligerently to the front, 'He was bound by one of your spells. I suppose Her Majesty thought you might be able to track it in some way.' She leant down further and sniffed the ground in a way which made the others shudder. Especially those of them who were small and would go well with apple sauce or possibly a touch of sage and onion.

Gwyddion frowned. 'You might be right,' he said. 'Has

anyone been down the hole?' He looked round at their stricken faces. "No. No, well, perhaps not.' He went to the edge and looked in. 'Hmmm,' he said, fingers twined behind his back. Usually, when thinking, he toyed with his beard, but that was no longer a real option.

'Oh, stop messing about,' said Annis and, with a well placed boot in the small of his back, sent him flying into the darkness.

Gwyddion was by now used to the bouncing downhill sensation, but even so, couldn't help a few small whimpers. His voice, when he had gathered his breath enough to make a noise, was echoing and distant. 'It smells in here,' he said, plaintively, 'of goat.'

'Well, yes, it would,' Oberon roared down the tunnel. 'It's had a goat in there for,' he cast around for a timescale, 'a really long time.'

'There's a kind of bed thing, all kicked to pieces. And four rings set in great big boulders.'

'Any hair?'

'Hare?'

'Yes, hair.'

'No hares down here. No animals at all, in fact.'

The little group looked at one another. Oberon shrugged, and, down in the town, sleeping women smiled slyly.

'What've animals got to do wiv it?' Freckles muttered to Tiny.

'I don't know.'

'What've animals got to do with it?' Titania shouted, testily.

'Hares are animals, aren't they?'

Benedict twigged. 'Oh, hares. No, we mean hair.'

There was a long silence while the Druid worked it out.

'Oh, *hair*! No, no hair.'

'Where did that go, then?' Mab asked. 'As I recall, there was a lot of it. I helped weave the rope.'

'Huh.' Annis could say more in one syllable than most Faerie, Unseelie or not, could say in an hour. 'Human hair, wasn't it? Rotted, hasn't it? Rotted clean away.'

'Of course,' said Puck, trying and failing as usual to click his fingers. 'It had to rot away sooner or later and then the spell was broken. That's how he woke up and got free. As usual, Mortals are the weak link in the chain.'

'That doesn't sound like you,' Titania said, surprised. 'You've always been such a big fan of Mortals.'

Puck looked thoughtful. 'True,' he said, and nipped round the corner for a quick leg check. Still normal, as far as shape went and no hairier than was acceptable.

He went back to the group, who were still crowding round the hole, straining for any news from Gwyddion.

'It wasn't the hair that held him,' came the Druid's disembodied voice. 'There's no sign of it. It must have been gone for centuries. Something else failed.'

'The spell,' snorted Leanne. 'That must have been it.'

"Nothing wrong with my bit of the spell,' Gwyddion was quick off the mark, passing the buck wherever it might fall.

'What do you mean? Your bit?' called Titania.

'Ow,' yelled Oberon, holding his head. He looked round plaintively at Titania. 'My head still hurts. Why do people keep shouting?'

'You're the only one shouting, dearest,' she said, patting him on the shoulder, as one might pat a dog. James felt quite jealous.

'Will you just talk one at a time?' called Gwyddion. 'It's hard enough as it is, down here.'

'Sorry.'

'Sorry.'

'Sorry.'

'Sorry.'

'Sorry.'

'S . . .'

'Shut up, will you!'

'S . . .'

'Yes. I know. You're sorry. I mean, we all clubbed together. I represented the Druids, and the people of the West. Taliesin did the words. He never was much of a hands-on Druid. I think there was some talk of a mistletoe allergy, or something. Anyway, we tied him down with spells and incantations.' He paused, thinking. 'I think some totemic animals were involved, somewhere along the line. Anyway, that was our bit and I've never known it fail.'

'Huh.'

'I heard that. She needn't be so smug. It was one of the Unseelie witches that put another spell on. It involved blood and shirts and bits of dead Mortal I don't want to talk about. It was all very unpleasant.'

Benedict turned to Annis. 'Who was that? Do you re-member?'

She spat. 'I certainly do.'

He smiled, archly. 'And it was . . .?'

'It was a Glaistig, if memory serves,' Annis said, turning her back and edging to the back of the group. The goblins, lurking at the back as their natural habitat, in their turn edged nearer the front.

'Glaistig?' boomed the Druid's voice from below. 'Are you sure?'

'Uh-huh.' Annis subsided into a rancid heap and closed her eyes. Benedict sighed. They'd get no more help from her.

Titania suddenly raised a remembering finger. 'Niamh,' she cried.

'Who?' asked Leanne.

'Niamh of the Golden Hair. Very active she was for a while, around then. Her father is . . . oh, you know, thing, what's his name?'

'Finvarra.'

'Thank you, Puck. I knew you'd know.' She threw him a dazzling smile, but he hardly noticed it. Something about the Glaistig was worrying in the back of his head and he couldn't shake it off.

'Do you think her spell was all right?' Oberon asked. 'Her dad is King of the Dead, after all.'

'Yes,' said Benedict, in the voice of one who has already checked. 'I already checked. He's still tucked up tight as you please under Knockma Hill.'

'Oh.' Oberon flopped down, alongside Annis and jumped up again, brushing himself down.

'Who represented you lot?' Leanne asked Titania.

'We were never ones for spells and such,' she prevaricated.

'There must have been someone.'

'We wove the hair,' said Mab.

'And?'

'And what? It took ages.'

'And he is buried . . . was buried in Our Lands.' Titania could speak in upper case better than any other Faerie.

'So.' Benedict stood up the Hill a little way, so they could all see him. 'What we have is this. Gwyddion put a spell on Pan . . .'

'Ssshhhh,' cried Oberon, flapping his hands. 'Keep it down.'

'Why?' said Benedict. 'He's awake and out. How much worse can it get?'

Oberon looked down, his little horns catching the moonlight. 'He might find where I am,' he muttered. Titania put her arms round him. Her Lord had never been so vulnerable. She loved him all the more.

'Yes, there is that,' Benedict said callously. 'Where was I?'

'I put a spell on him,' came the voice of Gwyddion from the hole.

"Yes. And a Glaistig put another. Niamh put another and You Lot,' Benedict could do capitals as well, 'wove the hair.'

'And did the digging, I dare say,' called out a disgruntled dwarf.

'I did that as well,' said James, truculently.

'Yes, yes, we all did that. But You Lot must have done more than weave the hair. I mean to say! Weave the hair?'

Oberon pushed through the crowd and up the slope. 'Yes,' he said. 'Yes, we did do more than weave the hair. I put a spell on him too. Mine was the final binding. And that's why I know he's after me. I was his favourite. We did everything together. And now, he's out to get me. He doesn't care about an old Glaistig. Or Niamh. She's dead all these years anyway. She married a Mortal, or have you forgotten. And Gwyddion got education and anyway, we all know a Druid'll do anything for money. But me. He's out to get me.'

Puck suddenly remembered. He whispered to the Queen, who rushed forward to join Oberon. She linked her arm through his. 'He is out to get you, dearest Lord,' she said.

'You were his trusted henchman and you helped to tie him down. But it was the Glaistig's spell which had . . . Benedict, you know. That thing you've been telling me about. It's a thing you make.'

Benedict looked confused. 'What thing?'

'You know. It's what that ghost thing makes.'

Puck knew. 'Built-in obsolescence, Mistress?'

'That's the thing.'

'Ghost?' asked Leanne.

'Deus ex machina. Ghost in the machine,' Puck said, in an aside.

'Ah.'

'Why the Glaistig?' asked Mab. 'She always seemed quite nice, considering.'

'Puck has just remembered her most . . . shall we say, striking feature.'

Oberon wrinkled his brow. 'Quite well set-up, as I recall,' he said. 'Always wore a green dress. Never took it off.' He blushed.

'It's what was under it we should have remembered,' Puck said. 'I don't know why you let her get involved, considering.'

'Oh, Puck, stop messing us about,' Mab said, clipping him round a pointed ear. 'What did she have up her dress? And you stupid lot can stop sniggering,' she said, without turning round. The dwarves and the goblins tried to look innocent and failed miserably.

'Ask Annis,' said Puck. 'She knows.'

They all turned to look at the Hag, not something they usually did willingly.

'Well?' Mab asked her.

Chapter Eighteen

The hag rose to her feet, using several unwilling dwarves as climbing posts. They had no choice but to help her – a fistful of talons in your shoulder is a great persuader. She looked around the company, faces turned towards her in touching trust. She made her way slowly to the front and, leaning on the dwarves and dragged bodily by James and Benedict, she climbed the slope. Her good eye swivelled back and forth. She sighed. It was a disappointment to her that one of her own had let the side down. But, as she recalled it now, standing on this hill, under that unnatural moon, with nature all to buggery, she knew she had no choice but to rat on a colleague. She should have known that the Glaistig was too close to the goat-foot to be trusted. She also knew that, if and ever she got her fingers round the stupid Glaistig's throat, she would throttle her, but long, slow, painful. Her hands clenched with anticipation and the dwarves yelped.

The sound brought her to the here and now. She cleared her throat and the company flinched, as one Faerie.

'Moira.'

'She had a moira up her dreth?' asked Thydney, confused already.

'Idiot goblin! Her name was Moira. She was the strongest of the Glaistig. We thought one of them would be best. We had earth, represented by Oberon, who lived in the woods.

We had water, Niamh, water-nymph from the peat-bogs. We had Gwyddion and Taliesin, airy-fairy as even their best friends would agree.'

'Hmmph.' The sound was accompanied by falling gravel as the Druid tried to clamber out of the hole.

'But we were stuck for fire. As you all know, we don't really have much to do with it. Too much trouble and we've always been able to keep warm by other means.'

Benedict threw a small lightning bolt above their heads, just to be flash.

'Exactly, you big-headed fool. So, we thought that perhaps someone who was fiery by temperament would do the job. As you mincing Southern Lot might think, most Unseelie are bad-tempered, but the Glaistig were the worst of all. And Moira – well, you should have seen her in a paddy.'

'I thought she was Scottish?' said one of the dwarves.

She looked down at him and flexed her fingers. 'When I want my walking sticks to talk, I'll let you know.' She continued. 'She went out of her way to frighten Mortals, always leaping out at them on country roads and following them home, now visible, now invisible. Yes,' she gave a reminiscent sigh, 'She was a scary one, was Moira.'

Mab, who knew a bad temper when she was in one, said, 'But what did she have up her dress?'

Annis looked surprised. 'You really don't know?'

Puck said, 'I know.'

The hag chuckled. 'And so you should, my lad, so you should.'

Mab turned on him as being nearer and not so unpleasant to touch. 'Well, Puck. We're dying to know.'

'Possibly,' muttered Oberon.

'Goat legs.' Puck said, simply. 'A Glaistig is goat from the waist down.'

Mab exploded. 'And we . . . you let her cast a spell?'

'Well,' said Oberon, trying for a defence at this late stage, 'She didn't do too badly, did she? It's been . . . ages . . . he's been bound. If she'd really meant to fool us, he's have been up and about the next day, with a bit of a hangover.'

There was a scrabble and a flop as Gwyddion struggled

out of the hole. He stood up, brushing himself down, but remained a travesty of his usual Druidic splendour. Titania looked him up and down, and her glance was enough magic to spruce him up, to Faerie taste; in other words, clean, white, but perhaps a bit sparkly for the average Druid. In a rare moment of compassion, Benedict toned the look down a little. Gwyddion elbowed his way to the front.

'Don't try and make it sound better than it was, Sire,' he said.

'It was only because our spells held that he has been Down for so long. Hers probably broke within the first few years. I flatter myself that our spells have been the last to unravel. After all . . .'

'Rubbish!" Titania broke in. 'It is obviously Oberon's spells that lasted. He laid spells by wood and leaf, by growing things. They can't fail.'

'Mmmph.'

Titania looked round for the source of the noise. 'What was that?'

'It's poor ol' Tine,' Freckles called out. 'He's got bindweed growing all over him. Here, somebody, help me unravel 'im. 'E'll choke in a minute.'

Leanne extended one languid talon and sliced through the strangling cords in seconds. Tiny fell out of their hold and lay on the ground, more frightened than hurt.

Benedict raised a cynical brow. 'Too right, Majesty,' he said. 'But perhaps, like Moira, your Lord was a little too in tune with Pan. Made his bed a little too comfy, perhaps.' He turned to speak to Oberon over his shoulder. 'A little half-hearted, perhaps.'

Oberon blustered. "No, not at all. I meant those spells I laid.'

Puck came to his defence. 'To be fair, Sire,' he gave a little bow to Benedict, 'I think the fact that the Lord of Misrule is playing havoc with the weather and such shows that the spell was strong. I think that it was the last one to hold, and he is using its remnants, until he reaches his full strength.'

'But I didn't play about with the seasons,' Oberon objected.

'Oh, really?' Benedict snorted.

'Well, obviously a bit, to make it more comfortable. I don't really enjoy rain and for Titania at flying size it's a disaster. Isn't it, sweetness?' Oberon turned to his Queen, making the most of her sudden affection. She nodded. 'But, not so as to affect any Mortal or anything.'

'Well, I suppose not,' Benedict conceded. It was no good squabbling, although he knew they would continue to do so. It was the Faerie way.

Gwyddion couldn't resist blowing his own trumpet. In fact, he had made it a major part of Druid lore. He fished it out from under his robe and blew a blast.

'What the . . .?'

'Aagghh!'

'Do that again, you Welsh idiot and I'll shove it down yer throat.'

Titania reached out a hand to restrain him. She was unsurprised to see it was trembling. 'Don't do that, Gwyddion,' she gasped. 'There's a dear.'

'Deer?'

'Don't start that again,' snapped Titania, her nerves twanging. 'What is it with you and animals?'

'I assume you blew that stupid thing for a reason?' Benedict snapped.

Gwyddion nodded, pompously. 'I merely feel,' he said, 'that the part of the Druids has been underestimated. Have you forgotten the six-foot squirrel?'

'Nine foot,' muttered James, mutinously. 'If it was an inch.'

'Your point being?' asked Leanne, tapping her foot. Gwyddion might be her client – a small voice suggested to her that he might be an ex-client when all this was done – but he really was such a prima donna.

'Well, our spells were fauna based.'

'You're not lecturing now,' Oberon said. 'Don't use fancy words with us.'

Light cheering from the dwarves was acknowledged by a Kingly bow. The light cheering became boos. There was no pleasing them.

'The spells we laid and the poems and incantations Taliesin spoke over the hill were based on our animal lore. So earth, air, fire and water was reinforced by animal, vegetable and mineral.'

'But fire didn't count.' Puck was thinking aloud.

'No.'

'So, to rebind him, all we need is earth, air and water. Animal, vegetable and mineral.'

'Yes.'

'Have we got those?'

'In a way. But not represented by the same Faerie as before.' Gwyddion said.

'By which you mean?' Titania asked, archly. Sometimes, she felt, the rest had to be reminded who was Queen around here. She sighed for her little glade.

'Well, I could do earth. I also deal in growing things. Lord Benedict could do water. He was saying earlier that his land is as much water as earth. Lord Oberon could still do vegetable . . .'

Mab snorted behind her hand and was rewarded by her Lord with a brief moment of lizard-hood, but his heart wasn't in it. She popped back in a second, chastened but able to see behind her without moving her head. This unsettling attribute also faded fast, but hardly fast enough for the goblins' peace of mind. It was quite unpleasant to watch.

'. . . with the help of the Queen.' He paused.

'Mineral?' Leanne prompted.

'Yes, I was getting to that. Are you strong enough, Leanne, to do mineral'?

'Why shouldn't I be?' the agent bridled. 'And on the other hand, why mineral?'

Mab smiled sweetly. 'Because you're as hard as nails?' she asked.

"No,' the Druid took her question at face value. 'Because she is very much of the Mortal world, very grounded in brick and stone and . . . well, I can say this as her client, in gold.'

'OK,' said Leanne. 'Why not. Yes, put me down for mineral.'

'Animal,' said the Queen.

'Pardon?' Gwyddion was startled. He couldn't see that he'd done anything to deserve that.

'Animal. Who's going to do animal?'

Everyone looked around. Several answers sprang to mind, but no-one spoke. Those who had immediately thought of Annis smothered the idea with particular speed.

There was a sigh. Puck stepped forward and said, 'Yes, yes, all right.' He dropped his trousers to reveal a pair perfect goat legs, their sleek for gleaming in the moonlight. 'Yes, I'll do the animal.'

Chapter Nineteen

Puck had felt the goat legs take over while the others were bickering. He had been fighting it for most of the flight and the wait on the hill, but it had become too strong for him. Mab put out a tentative finger and stroked his thigh. 'It feels like skin,' she said. 'Not fur at all.' Leanne didn't mess around with just one finger. She ran her hand down his leg and lingered at the knee. 'Do you know,' she said. 'She's right. It feels like skin and looks like fur. It's an optical illusion.'

'Oh,' laughed Puck, mirthlessly. 'Is that all? Well, that's all right then. It only looks like I've got goat's legs. Why worry?'

Benedict pushed forward but stopped short at feeling Puck's leg. 'If it only looks like something, then it means that deep down, you aren't changed. For our purposes, that's excellent. Because, if you really had goat's legs, we'd have had to test you . . .'

'. . . to destruction,' purred Leanne, licking her lips, '. . . to make sure we weren't making the whole Moira mistake all over again.'

'That's true,' said Oberon, joining the discussion. He felt a bit more chipper now that someone else seemed to be in Pan's firing line. 'But this is Puck, everybody. It doesn't matter what he looks like, surely? We know we can trust him.'

The silence was thick and seemed to crawl along the ground. Oberon made encouraging hand gestures and eventually Titania said, possibly a little too brightly, 'Of course we can trust him.' She stepped nearer to Puck and gave him a Queenly peck on the cheek.

By degrees, the others made various sounds of approval. Thydney was suddenly overcome with the emotion of the moment and leapt at the elf, wrapping his legs around his waist

and burying his little porcine face in Puck's neck.

'Er . . . thanks, Thyd,' Puck said, prying him loose. 'Thanks everyone. I knew I could count on your support.'

'Actually,' purred Leanne. 'Since your legs are only an optical illusion, do you think perhaps you ought to put your trousers back on. If I really concentrate, I can see beneath Pan's glamour.' She made a growling sound in her throat and Puck hurriedly resumed his britches.

Benedict muttered to Annis, bending low towards where, in anyone else, her ear would be, 'Does this mean what I think it means?'

'Dunno. What do you think it means?'

'Don't be obtuse. I think it means he's near.'

She shrugged. Things moved which shouldn't have done, and they continued moving for too long. Benedict flinched. "Not necessarily. He probably isn't in control yet. I think what we've had so far're his memories. Y'know. And dreams.'

'Dreams?' Benedict didn't dream. He left that to James, twitching on the rug of an evening.

'Well,' she whispered, 'sometimes, dreams can be very real. I sometimes go to sleep hungry and when I wake up, I'm full and I've got feathers round my mouth. Get the picture?'

He stood up sharply, and looked down into her one glaucous eye, peering up from her matted hair. 'Hmm,' he said and swallowed hard. He knew Leanne's habits. He knew what James liked to do to relax, but he himself had always erred on the side of fastidious.

Meanwhile, the conversation, or, to describe it better, argument, had moved on.

'Air. Who's doing air?'

'Well,' said Mab, desperate to be more important, 'any one of Us could do air. We all fly.'

'We don't,' said Tiny.

"Nor us,' the dwarves chimed in.

'I thought you were here to dig?' Mab said.

"Not just to dig, surely?' said Tiny, his little lip trembling.

'We're on overtime,' said the spokesdwarf. 'We ain't paid to stand around while you lot rabbit. We're off. Come on, lads.' And, to faint sounds of rather off-key singing, they disappeared round the curve of the hill. Then the singing got louder, and they passed the group of Faerie again, going downhill this time. Everyone waited until they could be heard no longer.

Leanne was the first to speak. 'Is it just me,' she asked, 'Or does anyone else find them annoying little f . . .?'

'Ah ah ah, Leanne,' said Benedict. 'They may be annoying, but we may need them again, so let's not be hasty.'

'And what will we need them for? I don't snack between meals.'

Titania was optimistic. Ever since her Return against all the odds, there was nothing she didn't believe in. She even had her own flock of flying pigs – as long as someone gave them a hand. 'For digging. When we find Pan and rebind him.'

Leanne turned away with a little hiss. 'Bless!' she said under her breath.

Puck patted his Queen's arm and got a sharp look from Oberon.

'So. Air?' Oberon asked.

'Like I said.' Mab was being stubborn.

'No,' said Puck thoughtfully. 'We need to spread the load. It will need more than just one faerie, I think. These spells need to be really strong.'

'Well, all right then, Mr I've-Got-Goat-Legs-But-Not-Really. Lots of us, all working together.'

'Oh, yes. Har har. You work so well in a team!'

'Mistress! Tell him . . ."

'He's quite right, Mab. You aren't a team player. None of us are, if we told the truth. And that's why we nearly disappeared. Think about that for a moment.' The Queen sighed. She was about to do something she had tried to avoid. 'There is one person who I always think of when the wind is blowing. Someone who always smelt of fresh air in the Old Days. She could blow the cobwebs away.'

'Cobweb's dead,' Mab said, flatly.

'I wasn't thinking of Cobweb. Was I, Puck?'

'No, Mistress.'

'Who were you thinking of, then?' Mab asked, crossly. She wasn't sorry not to be doing the binding. She had never dealt well with responsibility. And this was responsibility with a capital . . . whatever.

Titania smiled at Puck and inclined her head, encouragingly.

'Phoebe.'

'What!' Mab and Leanne exploded.

'She and Pan were very close for a while, just as he and I were. She wasn't here when he was bound, any more than I was, so she will perhaps have a few fresh ideas. And, as the Queen says, she was always light and air in the Old Days. She seemed to carry the sunshine with her and a fresh breeze from the West.'

'Very sunny she was last time we saw her,' said Mab. 'Whinging and moping about in that house with that miserable vicar. And she's got a couple of Mortal children.' She folded her arms and looked triumphant. 'She won't come.'

Annis pushed herself forward. 'It's because of those Mortal children that she'll help,' she said. 'I've watched them. Lives over in a wink, worrying about the world they'll leave for their stupid offspring. When you live as short a time as they do, you have to worry about the next generation, or you wouldn't worry at all. No. I reckon she'll come.'

'Right then.' Oberon, despite the pain in his head and a steadily growing feeling that he ought to be out, carousing and having a bit of wine, women and song, decided to take charge. He was the King of Faerie, after all. 'We'll just recap. Earth?'

'That's me,' said Gwyddion.

'Need any help?'

'I think not, but if I do, Taliesin's verse is available in all good bookshops.'

'What? Still?'

"No, not really. I was trying to be clever.' Gwyddion was crestfallen. 'I just happen to have a copy, here.' He pulled it from his sleeve.

'All right then. And, guys,' Oberon looked around, best Personality personality firmly in place. 'Don't let's be too clever, eh? Let's just get on with it. My head hurts. Air?'

'Phoebe,' said Titania. 'I'll go and find her.'

'You, Mistress?' Puck said, amazed.

"Yes. I am the Queen – her Queen. She'll come for me, I'm sure.'

'If you say so, Mistress.' Puck was unconvinced.

'Fire we're not bothering with this time. Right,' Oberon counted on his fingers. 'Water?'

'Yo.'

'Yo?'

'I was trying to create a martial atmosphere,' said Benedict.

'Please don't,' said Leanne. 'It's quite upsetting.'

'Oh, OK. I thought you were supposed to be a bit theatrical.'

'No. I just control the luvvies. I don't want to have one for a King.'

'Sorry. Yes, I'm water,' said the Unseelie Lord.

'That's better. Right, what's next?'

'Animal. That's me,' said Puck.

Oberon looked around. 'Is everyone agreed on that? Even when his legs are only a . . . an . . .'

'Optical illusion, Sire.'

'Yes. That.'

'James can help me. And the goblins. Animals are well-represented here, by and large.' The goblins nestled closer. They were so proud.

'I'm so proud,' whispered Tiny and Bill gave a smug little cluck in agreement.

'Right then. Vegetable?'

There was no answer.

'Come on now, don't be shy. Vegetable?'

Puck whispered in his ear.

'Oh, is it? Yes, of course it is.' Oberon gave a little laugh. 'That's me, of course.'

'I rest my case,' muttered Mab.

'I must admit,' said Oberon, humility seeping from every arrogant pore, 'I'll be grateful for help.'

'We're here for you, Lord,' said Mab, mechanically.

Oberon swung his searchlight smile in her direction and the effects were felt for miles around. Mab wasn't quite as immune as she thought she was and hung her head coquettishly.

Titania gave Oberon a slap. 'There's no need for that,' she said. 'I'm sure everyone will pitch in, anyway.'

'Sorry. Right. Who've I left out? Mineral?'

'Me,' said Leanne.

'Right. Yes. Do you have any . . . spells, or anything?'

'Of course not. I'm a vampire, remember? We don't do spells. We bite people.'

'Hmm. Perhaps you can ask someone to help.'

'I'll do that,' grated Annis. 'Be pleased to be of assistance, dearie.' She stood next to Leanne and took her hand. A piece of the designer trim fell off Leanne's couturier suit and fell, sizzling, to the ground. 'I think we make a nice pair.'

Leanne gritted her teeth. Several goblins whimpered with fear. 'Yes, Lord,' she said. 'I will be fine. And if I need help, then Annis will be the first to know.' Secretly, she wasn't too sorry. The old hag would be easy to shake off. She couldn't even fly on her own.

'Don't think of shaking me off, my Lady,' wheezed Annis. 'I can't fly, but I can hold on real tight.'

Oberon gathered Titania under his arm and smiled regally over the company. 'Off you go, everyone,' he declaimed, spreading his spare arm in a wide gesture. 'Off you go, and do your duty.'

No one moved.

'Go on. Clear off. We've got work to do. It's nearly dawn and, oh, my heads hurts.'

'Sit down, dearest Lord,' said Titania. 'I'll make sure everyone gets off.'

Oberon curled in a ball, holding his head in his arms.

Mab, kindly in her heart, bent over him and bathed his poor little horns with the newly formed dew. Titania gestured for a huddle and she whispered to them all, 'Get your helpers together and come to my glade when you are ready. We'll work from there. Not only do we have to get the spells worked out, we have to find Pan. We can't bind what we don't have captive, do we?'

'No, Mistress. But we mustn't find him too soon. Otherwise, how will we hold him while we work on the spells?'

Titania wanted to curl up like Oberon and rock back and forth. This was really hard. But she lifted her chin and let a little glamour dust the group. It made her feel better and even Annis looked a little more acceptable that way. 'Get your helpers, if you need them. I will get Phoebe. First one back to the glade start mobilising anyone who can look for him. Flower faeries, dwarves, goblins, tree spirits, anyone. This will have to be a miracle of timing. And we can do it! Everyone say Aye!'

'Aye!' It rang down the hill. It echoed in the land around. It fell on the ear of bird and beast and Mortal. It fell on the ear of one crouching low in the reed beds, fingering his pipe. He lifted his head and smiled. It was going to be Fun.

'We can do it, can't we, Puck?' Titania asked anxiously as the others flew away, in twos and threes.

He looked into her eyes and held out his arms. In his warm embrace, she could feel safe, if only for a moment. And he felt better for it, too. He rubbed his green-tinged cheek against hers, smooth and scented as a new-burst rose petal.

'Aye,' he whispered. 'Aye.'

Chapter Twenty

An overview of the company as they left the Tor would have been of a silent scene. Everyone was wrapped up in their own thoughts. Leanne had managed to inveigle Benedict into carrying Annis. After all, he didn't seem to mind, and his clothes – Oberon's clothes – were ruined anyway.

Mab was heading back to the glade. Lucky me, she sulked, getting those knowall twigs, the cross-grained flower faeries, a horde of Mr Dobies and the occasional elf mobilised to hunt for Pan, Lord of Confusion, Shape-shifter extraordinaire. Whoopee, she thought, lucky, lucky, lucky. A tiny black cloud formed over her head. She looked up, frowning. Don't even think about it, she thought at it, and it disappeared.

Gwyddion was still feeling a bit giddy. His method of takeoff was rather random and he had flown in circles for some while, before heading off into the West. The rising sun behind him threw his shadow on the ground, huge and misshapen, like an approaching storm. He never stayed miserable for long and soon he was swooping through the air, scattering the odd sacred object here and there as he flew. He was mulling over whether to try and flush out a bit of help. Despite the triumphant Return, Druids had remained close to Mortals and the ones with true Power were few. Taliesin, as far as he knew, hadn't been seen for centuries. Myrddion, as Merlin had rather pretentiously renamed himself, had cleared off with a nymph and on his rare appearances still had a rather faraway look in his eye and tended to talk about the 'little woman' in the mock chauvinist way of a man totally under beauty's thumb. Gwyddion doubted he would be allowed out for long enough to be of any help.

So, he was on his own. He did a victory roll. He could do this thing. He would gather his lore books together and plan his spells with care. He would wander again in the groves of Avalon, the groves of Academe. He would gather leaf and twig, bulb and corm, a drop of nectar fresh culled by a golden bee, a stoup of water from the highest mountain stream. He would pound and crush in his crystal mortar a paste that would bind Pan for eternity. He rubbed his hands together. A small bewildered owl flew out and perched in his hair. He brushed it off. Merlin had been the owl guy. He, Gwyddion, was more a raven sort of chap. But the owl was persistent and perched on his shoulder. With a sigh, Gwyddion let it stay and, together, they continued into the West.

Oberon was glad to have the goblins, hanging out of every pocket, enjoying the dawn air as it whistled through their various approximations to hair. They were keeping him on the straight and narrow, off to plan his spells. They were preventing him from doing what every cell in his body was screaming at him to do – head off down to the town, sneak across as many bedroom windowsills as he could and take the never-unwilling woman as she woke. If she had a bottle of wine about her person, that would be even better. Then, a few practical jokes, a tune or two and sleep the day through until night fell like a blanket over the land and Mortals hid from the Lord of Misrule and his Rout.

Oberon stopped himself short and a goblin fell from his pocket.

'Sire,' screamed Tiny, his voice like a steam-whistle cutting through Oberon's aching head. 'You've dropped Bill.'

The King dived through the air, like an arrow, and caught Bill as he reached the tops of the trees. His feathers were all ruffled and he kept opening and closing his beak in a frenzied gape.

'He'th hythterical,' said Thydney. 'Thlap him, thome-body.'

Bill gave a little shake, putting his plumage in order and then tucked himself away, well away, in Oberon's most inside of inside pockets. The cold spray had brought him round.

Oberon sighed and trod air, while his goblins risked patting him, for their own comfort as much as his.

'Thanks, guys,' he said, mournfully. ''Preciate it.'

The goblins looked at Tiny, nodding their heads, encouraging him to speak. He cleared his little throat.

'Sire?'

'What, Tiny, old friend?'

Oh dear, maudlin. It usually took quite a bit of drink to get him to this.

'It's just, Sire, I, well, the lads, well, us, we want to say we're right behind you, Sire. We won't leave you . . . whatever happens.'

It was meant to be a comfort. Somehow, it was not. But Oberon knew they meant well. 'Boys. Lads. That's . . . well, that's very good of you.' He gave them all a little pat. Looking down, their trusting little faces pierced his heart. For once, he had to tell them the unadulterated truth. He landed, light as thistledown, on the topmost branch of a tree and encouraged them to hop out and sit opposite him, in a row.

He leaned forward with his elbows on his knees and looked at each of them in turn. He realised something. He loved these little creatures. And, unless he did this job well, they might cease to be. Harried and hunted by Pan, for whom no joke was too big, too small, too horrible, too cruel. He swallowed hard.

'Tiny, Thydney, Freckles, Bill. I know you mean it, when

you say you'll never leave me. But, you have to promise me, that if I . . . change; if I become, well, like him, you will run. Run like the wind.'

"No.' Freckles stood up and fell off the branch. Oberon caught him just in time, and he decided he could speak just as well sitting down. 'We'll never leave you. I dunno about the ovvers, but,' a fat tear rolled, in a rather circuitous route, down his bristly cheek, 'but wivout you, we wouldn't want to go on.'

'Couldn't, probably,' added Tiny, pragmatic as always.

'We'll go down fighting,' said Thydney. 'It'th the leatht we can do, Thire.'

Bill gently pecked his King's foot, but it spoke volumes.

'But . . . I might change shape.'

'So?' With so much diversity, even among the old guard, what was the odd extra tail or fang to them?

'I might . . . behave oddly.'

How would they tell?

'I might . . . be dangerous.'

Dangerous sounded like fun. They continued to look up at him, with their trusting, if unsettling, little faces. Bill swept his quiff back and Oberon watched it spring into place, just like always. Tiny looked bright and eager, the goblin equivalent of a boy scout. Freckles looked truculent, ready to rumble. Thydney looked enthusiastic, a word it was to be hoped he would never attempt to say.

Their Lord rose to his feet, his toes, the air. They jumped aboard just in time and he spiralled into the hot, blue sky. They hoped he had understood. They loved him and wouldn't ever leave. If they had peeped from their pockets his expression would have told them. He understood. He wasn't alone.

And so, Oberon and the Boys flew off, to who knew what. But at least, they would be doing it together.

Puck and Titania flew away together, hand in hand. Without words, each knew the fear in the other's heart. Titania was grieving in advance for something she knew might never happen. But she loved Oberon despite everything, and the thought of watching him being taken into Pan's world, lost to her forever, made tears course down her cheeks. Puck knew better than to try and comfort her, except by being beside her. Any words he spoke would ring hollow. He had felt the pull of the goat-foot. He knew that Oberon had it bad. They all might have only hours left. It concentrated his mind.

'Mistress,' he said, when the dull hum of the town the Queen thought she had left for ever came into the lower parts of hearing. It was like having a bee caught in your hair, she thought. A half-heard, almost soporific drone, the sound made by cars, vans, alarm clocks, Mortal voices, life waking for the next day, hundreds of feet below. Above it rang the occasional dog's bark, a warning car horn. Even Mortals could hear those.

Also in the mix, for Faerie ears only, was the squeak of a knife through toast, the whisper of bedclothes as the liers-in turned over, the parting of lips as a mother kissed her child awake. 'Mistress, I must leave you here.'

She grabbed his tiny, flying-size arm. 'Don't go, Puck,' she begged him, her earlier confidence gone. 'Please come with me. Phoebe likes you. She'll listen to you.'

'And to you, Mistress,' said Puck, prising her fingers loose. 'I must go and work out a binding spell. I must do it quickly, before Confusion gets me.'

'He won't get you.' She spoke firmly, but without real conviction.

'My legs are proof enough that I might fall under his spell. Before I do, I must have something in place that someone else can use.'

'You have help?'

'Yes. James is waiting for me at the glade, I hope. I suppose animal was a good one to be given. James has plans which I may have to change. He tends to the gizzardy sort of spell. I am hoping to go more in the direction of Gwyddion's totemic ideas. As the earth element in this, I think he will be helping the King and Leanne as well as me. We all come under his blanket, as it were.'

Titania gave a small laugh. 'A comfort blanket?'

'No. There is no comfort in any of this, Mistress, except of our own making. However,' he tugged down his jacket, gave a little twirl and did a somersault, 'don't let's be downhearted, eh? Off you go and persuade Phoebe that we need her. It won't be easy.'

'Can I use magic?'

'You're asking me?'

'Well, would it be . . . ethical?'

'Hmmm, let me see. The Lord of Misrule is out and loose. The seasons are so mixed up that apparently they had six inches of snow in thirty seconds in Central London yesterday. This was doubly inconvenient, as the cold killed the giant vine which had encircled Nelson's Column earlier in the day. As happens in nature, as you know well, Your Majesty, nothing happens in isolation. The baboon colony which had taken up residence . . .'

'Baboons?'

'Don't ask . . . got the hump and presently are holding staff at bay in the National Gallery, where they decided to take refuge. This in turn has dislodged the vampire bats which . . .'

'Yes, yes. I know. It's important. It's urgent. I'm going.'

The queen barrelled off through the air and her tiny voice stayed in Puck's ears as she flew. 'It's important. It's urgent. Off you go, Titania. Sort it out, Titania. Fetch Phoebe. Hah!'

He shook his head and smiled. She was angry now. Angry got things done when miserable and frightened were still hiding behind a tree. He clapped his hands and set out to put a girdle if not round the world, at least across the Home Counties in forty minutes. Or preferably less. Much, much less.

Chapter Twenty One

What was he doing, the great god Pan, down in the reeds by the river? Spreading ruin and scattering ban, splashing and paddling with hoofs of a goat, and breaking the golden lilies afloat, with the dragonfly on the river.

Pan had never read Robert Browning. He had never even heard of Robert Browning. He had never been set to learn at least twenty lines of any of his poems for homework. He had never searched under his bed for rats having read The Pied Piper. He had never giggled with his friends over the poet's rather unusual understanding of the English language, never more clearly demonstrated than in his use of the word 'twats', meaning, in Browning-speak only, a nun's habit.

And the reason for this lack in Pan's education was that he had been stuck under a Somerset hill while the great man flourished. In fact, he had been stuck under a hill in Somerset while civilisation in general had flowered to its current state. And this, as Pan hunkered down in the reed beds where he felt at home, was pissing him off very seriously.

He didn't know, of course, just how long he'd been down there. In fact, if truth be told, it had felt just like a really good night's sleep. Not that he often slept at night. Forget not, the night is for hunting, as Kipling, another poet he had missed, had said, remember the day is for sleep. But who goes for a good night's sleep in a frowsty hole, covered up with rocks and boulders, halfway up a hill. Pan had woken up in some pretty weird places – that is, weird even by his own rather peculiar standards – but never one as weird as that.

And then there were the buildings. Many and big. Really, really big. With so many lights on. And rushing noises. And music, nowhere near as good as his . . . he blew a few notes on his pipe to cheer himself up . . . coming from everywhere. And the air was full of the rustle of Mortals, Mortals Pan could not begin to number. He could hear them breathing, moving, talking all around him.

There weren't the animals, either. Where were the boars, the wolves? Where were the birds, thick in the air? The night-ingales? Nightjars? Owls? Sometimes, you had hardly been able to think for the noise of the birds at night. He had dug himself out of that horrible hole and not heard a note from a bird. Just Mortal din.

He stuck a sulky hoof into the water. Where were the wa-ter rats, the otters, the beavers, the trout, salmon, bream? The hundred kinds of frog, toad, newt? The water seemed empty and had a smell and feel that he hated and made him wrinkle his nose.

No. Time had passed. A *lot* of time.

The god jumped to his feet. He was waking up after a long sleep, peppered in its last hours with dreams of such intensity he couldn't quite shake them off. He had been a bit melan-choly. Certainly lonely – he couldn't remember the last time he had been by himself and he didn't like it. He had thoughts swimming like goldfish in the recesses of his brain which he couldn't seem to control. He was hungry. He was thirsty. He wanted bread and olives, a haunch of some animal which hadn't been an acquaintance, roasted over an apple-wood fire. He wanted wine, lots of it. He wanted women, lots of them. He wanted companionship, singing old songs round the fire. He wanted Fun. He wanted Games. He wanted Oberon and Puck.

He lifted his shaggy head and sniffed the breeze. Eeurghh.

What was that smell? Metallic and harsh, it burned his nostrils. He sniffed again, tuning his scent receptors to find what he wanted. He wanted Faerie Folk. He wanted Unseelie, even, although they were never so much fun. He cast his head from side to side, triangulating on the tiny fragments of smell on the breeze. He found what he wanted and stood up to check his direction.

The fisherman came to in Accident and Emergency. The first thing he saw was the anxious face of the admitting doctor, a harmless-looking youth fresh out of medical school. Nonetheless, the fisherman smothered a scream and scrabbled back up the bed, knuckles to his mouth, in an attempt to hide behind the pillows.

The nurse standing at the head of the bed restrained him gently.

'Come on now,' she said, in professionally calming tones. 'We need to calm down, don't we?'

'Do we?' the fisherman asked, wild eyed. 'Did you see it as well, then?'

'See what?' The houseman leaned forward, light masking his eyes behind his spectacles.

'Him. It. That twelve-foot man. Goat. Well, goat with a man's body. Man with a goat's legs.'

The nurse and doctor looked significantly at each other.

'We're just going to give you a little something to calm you down,' the nurse soothed. 'Just a little prick.'

'No, no,' screamed the fisherman. 'That's just it. It must have been two feet long. If it was an inch.'

Pan had not really taken much notice of the fisherman at first. He was just a Mortal, like any other. But then he looked more closely. The clothes the man was wearing were strange. Layer after layer of very fine material, with strange metal bits all over. There was a small oblong box which, when Pan had picked it up from the man's side, had made his fingers burn, although it wasn't heat that hurt him, but some magical field. The man had hardly any hair, and none at all on his face. Pan took his head in his great hand and thought of breaking the man's neck, just for Fun, but decided against it. He was in strange times. He should study more before he started having a good time and anyway, he didn't want the stench of death to overwhelm the slight hint of Faerie he had managed to locate. It was on the edge of even his senses and he couldn't take risks.

And why had the stupid Mortal fallen over in a swoon like that. Everybody knew Pan, if only by repute, so what was his trouble? Could he have been a poor wandering madman, Pan wondered. One who had forgotten all he knew? But no. His clothes were costly, Pan was certain, not that money had ever played much of a part in his existence. Paying was for others, not the Lord of Misrule. So, the god worked out, though slowly, the chances were that nobody knew Pan. Poor Pan. He gave himself a moment of unfamiliar self-pity.

He looked down at himself. He was rather striking, he had to admit. Not quite the twelve feet the fisherman had credited him with, but pretty near. His legs were covered in a golden pelt which caught the light and threw it back with hints of butterfly wings. His hoofs were golden too, but golden like the precious metal and were shod with silver, once a year, never missed, by a dwarf blacksmith, deep inside the volcano on Santorini, his favourite spot when the nights drew in in these little islands. His skin was olive, without a blemish, although he chuckled to himself remembering the bites and grazes he got on some wild nights, cavorting over the landscape, with the lads and lasses of his Rout. His fine head, crowned with a mane of tawny hair was set on a neck, strong and muscled, \which rose from a set of shoulders such as were never seen ok Mortal man. He smiled fondly at his best feature. Again, the fisherman was slightly out in his estimation. But only by a whisker.

The god shook himself and stamped his hooves. With regret, he made himself smaller. Smaller. Smaller. He stopped at just over two metres tall – there were limits, even when putting on disguise. He toned down his hair. He stroked the pelt on his goat-legs and dismissed them with a flick of his fingers. He had to admit, their replacements were still pretty magnificent. He patted his best feature and it dwindled – but only so much. He turned in the sun, admiring his handiwork. Hp strolled out onto the riverside path and made his way into the town.

Mrs Wetherspoon came to lying on the sofa in her sitting room. The first thing he saw was the anxious face of her husband, a mild-mannered retired post office clerk, who peered at her through thick spectacles. Nonetheless, she smothered a scream and scrabbled back up the sofa, knuckles to her mouth, in an attempt to hide behind the cushions.

'Mavis,' her husband said gently, 'What happened?'

His wife looked round wildly. 'Where is he?'

'Who, dear?'

'Him. The man.'

Her husband had been dreading this. She had recently taken to locking the front door with several deadbolt locks, chains and gizmos, so that hardly any visitors could be bothered to wait the ten minutes it took to open the door. Spectres of rapists and muggers filled her waking hours; nightmares of axe-wielding maniacs and other low-life filled her nights. Accordingly, he spoke with just a touch of condescension in his voice.

'There was no one there when they found you, dearest,' he said.

'Found me?' She leant forward. 'Tell me the truth, Bernard. I can take it. Have I been . . . interfered with?'

Mr Wetherspoon considered this extremely unlikely, unless the man was unusually persistent.

"No, dear.'

She sagged back on the cushions, unsure whether this was good news or not.

'The police are here, dearest. If I call the officer in, can you give him a description?'

'I certainly can. It was a foot. A foot long, if it was an

inch.'

✸✸✸✸

Pan had examined the woman lying on the footpath only briefly before he heard the running footsteps coming his way. He had never heard of joggers, of course, so assumed some kind of hue and cry was in progress. Accordingly, he had stepped into the undergrowth and watched from hiding.

The runner had almost trodden on the woman. Still running on the spot, he had raised one of the little oblongs to his ear and spoken into it. Pan wondered how he could bear it so near his head, when they hurt so much to pick up, but the man seemed in no pain. Indeed, he put it back in his trouser pocket when he had finished. Pan winced.

What was the matter this time? he wondered. He was the right size, and . . . ah! Clothing. He looked carefully at the man, still jogging up and down on the spot. His clothes were like nothing Pan had ever seen, nothing like the man by the river, nothing like those worn by the woman on the ground. But, in a strange kind of way, Pan quite liked the look of them. He waved an arm down the length of his body and moved stealthily through the undergrowth until he could step out unnoticed onto the path.

It was by this sequence of events that the Lord of Misrule, Chaos and Confusion, the Shapeshifter, Goat-foot, the Great God Pan came to walk down the highways and byways as he sought some Faerie to play with, dressed in a turquoise velveteen track suit, Reebok Hi-top rebound trainers and a sweatband with 'Joggers Are Better By Miles' woven in blue across his forehead.

And yet, as all the female drivers in the worst ever shunt on the A361 said in their police statements, he still made a very arresting sight.

Chapter Twenty Two

Titania hung in the air and watched Puck go. She felt very lonely, there in the lightening sky. She had not had so much contact with Pan as the others had had. She had always held herself rather aloof from that sort of going on. She wouldn't say she hadn't had her moments – but Mortal men were more to her taste. More . . . controllable. Titania liked control.

And this was where the thought of Phoebe was worrying her, more than a little. She had been a free spirit, all sunshine and warm breezes. She had flitted through Titania's Rade, never staying long, always off to somewhere else, which made it seem doubly sad and unexpected to see her so tied now, married to a Mortal, tending her garden, sighing for the Old Days but opting, in the end, to stay with her children. And they were more than slightly Faerie, in Titania's opinion. But, the Queen mused, in her way she had been a rebel to the end, doing the other thing. Not going with the crowd. Well, Titania stamped her tiny foot in mid-air. She was going to come when her Queen called this time! Or else!

'Or else what?'

Titania was stumped. That had been as far as her planning had gone. She had arrived, after only a few false starts, at the vicarage, to find Phoebe in the midst of sandwich-making and homework-finding, sock-pairing and gym-kit-ironing, squabble-stopping and cheek-kissing – in other words, it was a school morning. Titania had looked on, impressed and appalled in equal measure. Despite her fondness for changelings she had never been very hands-on in their day to day care. In fact, as soon as they had got to the crawling, snotty-nosed, awkward stage, they had usually been sent back, pdq, no questions asked.

The children had been impressed, of course. Although she had never gone in for Oberon's media-tartiness, her face had been on the front of every magazine and newspaper there was, until the fashion editors and gossip columnists had realised that she had no interest in clothes beyond the glittery and never did anything they could gossip about. If they could only see her now!

Phoebe finally managed to shepherd them out of the door. Titania had turned to her, glamour sloshing everywhere and asked, simply and from the heart, for her help.

'No.'

Titania had drawn back a step. 'You must.'

'Why?'

This was where the foot stamping had started. 'Because I say so.'

"Not good enough, I'm afraid.' Titania was dealing with one very determined ex-Faerie, whose will had been honed on the grindstone of flower-rotas, WI and children. A mere Queen had hardly a chance.

'Or else . . .'

'Or else what?'

And so, here they stood. Nose to beautiful nose, brows drawn together, lips curled.

They might have stayed like that all day, except that Titania remembered her dignity first and straightened up, pulling her gown straight. She gave a small, deprecatory cough.

'Let's not argue, Phoebe,' she said.

'I'm not arguing,' the vicar's wife said. 'I simply said I couldn't help you. You're the one who is arguing with that simple statement.'

'Don't quibble,' snapped Titania. 'I don't really see how you can refuse. You've seen what's happening to the weather. You garden, I believe.' She managed to make the activity sound mildly risqué.

'Yes, I've seen. Global warming.'

'Don't be naive, Phoebe!' The Queen's retort could have etched glass. 'Global warming doesn't reach this pitch in days. It won't reach this pitch in centuries. How, for example, can global warming explain this?' She took Phoebe's arm and led her to the window. 'Look!'

Phoebe twitched the curtains to one side and peeped out at her garden, secure, she had always felt, behind her wall. It was true that the sight which met her eyes was a tad startling. She had liked to sit out on summer evenings, leaning back against the warm brick, her toes curling and flexing in the camomile lawn, letting her memory wander, back to the days when she had frolicked in the herbs with Puck and her friends, when the world was young and she had no troubles. It would not have been a good idea to try that now. The lawn had become parched and dry, long with sharp blades that could cut like a knife. It waved in a hot, dry wind which only seemed to be happening in her little plot. She couldn't make out any detail at first, in the dark and light bars of sun and ink-black shadow, except a slight movement on the edge of perception. Then, the light and dark bars resolved themselves as a beautiful tiger, lips drawn back in a silent snarl, crept out of the grass and on to the terrace, down on its haunches and moving silent as a thought to where the children's rabbit hopped happily and unconcerned in its hutch.

Phoebe smothered a scream and hammered with her fists on the window. The tiger turned its head to the noise and, opening its mouth, roared a roar so loud the windows rattled. The glass steamed up with its hot breath. The rabbit hopped on, unconcerned. There was nothing in its tiny brain that told it to be afraid of tigers. The beautiful animal loped the length of the garden and leapt to the top of the wall, where it sat, a glorious parody of a domestic pet.

Titania stood back, smugly. As long as Phoebe never found out who had put the tiger there, it was all right. The grass wasn't her though. That definitely was Pan.

Phoebe turned, trembling, back into the room. 'I had no idea it was so bad. I . . . don't go out that much.' She slumped down on the sofa. Titania slid into place alongside her. It was going better, now. The Queen allowed herself a glimmer of hope.

'So, will you help us?'

'I don't understand what's going on.'

'Pan has awoken.'

'Oh, you don't need me, then. I wasn't there when . . .'

'I know. But we're gathering a . . .' what was the collective term? Clump? Crowd? Gang? Benedict had a word, but she could never quite remember it, '. . . tango together.'

'Tango?'

'Isn't that it?'

'Do you mean quango?'

'Don't be silly. That's not even a word.'

'Well, let's just say group, then.'

'All right. A group together to rebind the god.'

'Well,' Phoebe looked happier and jumped to her feet. 'Why didn't you say so. I'll get my coat. If it's just a spell you need, I can be back before the children get home from school.'

'Er . . . it's a bit more than that.'

'In what way?'

'We couldn't remember where we had buried him.'

'Oh.' Phoebe sat down again, hard.

'Then we remembered. Or, at least, worked it out.'

'Excellent.' Phoebe was halfway to the door.

'So we went to the place, last night.'

The Faerie looked expectantly at the Queen.

'We found where he had been buried.'

'*Had* been?'

'Yes.'

'So, you managed to control him, in the short term.'

'Not quite.'

'Because . . .'

'Because he'd gone.' Titania hung her head and looked up through her lashes. Phoebe had gone quite white and was holding onto the edge of the table, her knuckles white.

'He's out there?' her voice was a dry husk, from deep inside her closed throat.

Titania nodded, gnawing her lip ruefully.

'He's out there, and you don't know where?'

Um, yes.'

Phoebe rushed to the door. 'My children! They're out there too. He might get them!'

Titania rushed to her side. 'Well,' she said, refusing to comfort while the Faerie's distress could be to her own advantage, 'he will, perhaps.'

'*What!*'

'If we don't stop him. Don't you see, if you don't come and help us, it will be like the old days. Your daughter, she is very beautiful. In a few years, no matter what you do, he'll hunt her down. You know what he's like. Your boy – a bit mischievous, is he? Like a bit of a laugh?'

Phoebe nodded, her hands knotted and winding, clasped against her stomach.

'Hmm,' said the Queen thoughtfully. 'Just the job for the Lord of Misrule, eh? A nice mischievous boy, all sparkling eyes and laughter.' She dropped her voice and draped a sisterly arm across Phoebe's shoulder. 'What a shame, eh?'

'Shame?'

'The Mortals never survive too long. Of course, your lad, being half Faerie, he might last a bit longer, I suppose. He'll be able to drag himself round for a few more routs. Hide his exhaustion from Confusion himself, until the god gets tired of his flagging footsteps, his less-ready laugh and,' she clicked her fingers, 'snuffs him out. Still,' she stood away from the distraught mother, 'if you can't help, you can't. We might be able to do it without you, I suppose.' She paused to adjust her wings, which she had unfolded ready for flight, preening the iridescent, barely visible shimmer of light which she didn't need but used, as Benedict used his foetid wings, to impress.

Poor Phoebe. Looking at her it was difficult to see the

sprite of sunshine and air. She turned her tear-stained face to Titania and, hardly able to speak for crying, whispered, 'I don't know what to do.'

'Of course you do,' said Titania, sternly. 'You tell your . . . husband – where is he, by the way?'

'He's down at the drop-in centre.'

'Well, we'll drop-in on our way, then. You can tell him that you're going to visit some old friends. That you need a rest.' She looked Phoebe up and down. For a Faerie, she looked pretty dowdy. For a Mortal who, by rights should be knocking forty, she looked amazing. But Titania didn't know that. 'You certainly look as though you need a break. Anyway, he can look after the children and then when we've done our work, you can come back.'

'Mistress.'

Mistress, eh? That was a good sign.

'Mistress,' Phoebe tried a laugh, but only a small one, and laid a hand on the Queen's arm. 'You'll never understand Mortals. I don't always and I've lived with them for many of their lifetimes now. I can't come back. I've stayed a bit too long as it is.'

'Well, I did tell you . . .'

'Don't, Mistress. I told you so is a very annoying phrase. When the children were younger, people used to say how motherhood suited me. Then, when they went to school, they thought I might be the au pair. Then they started thinking my husband was my father and the children were my brother and sister. Soon, good bone structure and skin plus a great hairdresser won't cover it any more.' She sighed. 'It's time I wasn't here.'

'But, the children?'

'Yes,' her mouth crumpled again as the tears started afresh. 'The children.' She collapsed into a chair.

'I know!' the Queen raised a finger. 'They can come with us.'

'I don't really think so! What would their father say?'

'Gets on with them, does he?'

'Um . . . he's often busy.'

'Ah. Close, you two, eh?'

'Um . . . he's often busy.'

'There you are, then.'

'But they're only half . . . you know, half and half.'

'Is that a problem?'

'Well, no, I suppose not. They have always rather taken after me.'

'All the more reason to bring them with us, then. I haven't had a new handmaiden in ages. And Puck would like having someone to do the donkey . . .' that word could still make Titania blush . . . 'dirty work.' She nudged Phoebe in the ribs. 'What about it, eh? Eh, Phoebe? Say yes.'

Phoebe didn't answer. She closed her eyes, looked down and held her breath. Slowly, from her toes to the top of her head, she changed into – almost into – the Faerie Titania remembered from the Old Days. She was bathed in a golden glow and her skin was dusted with sunshine. Her soft hair moved in its own breeze, now this way, now that. She rose on her toes and kept on rising. She shrank to the size of a decently fed bumble bee.

Titania clapped her hands with delight.

'Come on, Mistress,' came Phoebe's tiny voice, as she flew through the gap under the door. For years, it had been the source of an annoying draught. Now, it was her way out, in more ways than one. 'Come on, we've got work to do.'

In a winking, Titania was flying size and hot on Phoebe's heels.

They flew through the walled garden and along the road, Titania pausing only to disembody the tiger, which had been sitting on the wall, taking playful swipes at the heads of passers-by.

As they went, flying low for the fun of it, Titania saw someone she knew. She skidded to a halt in the air and flew back, to make sure. She landed on the woman's shoulder and peered into her face. Yes, it was her! Her neighbour from Before.

'Hello, Mrs Jones,' she said brightly.

The woman gave a whole-body twitch, but otherwise didn't respond.

Titania spoke up a bit; she knew her voice could be a bit

hard to hear, sometimes. 'Hello, Mrs Jones. Do you remember me?'

Mrs Jones closed her eyes and tried to think of something nice, the way her psychiatrist had told her. Her current subject was kittens.

Titania tutted and flew off. Some people could be so rude. And she *did* have work to do.

Mrs Jones, walking along immersed in her vision of two kittens playing with string, walked into a lamppost. Pan would have enjoyed that.

Chapter Twenty Three

Benedict and Leanne flew towards her London apartment. Benedict would have been happier at home, in his Highland castle, and Annis was all for going back there. She hadn't seen the mountains for a while and, anyway, she had some old scores to settle. With that stupid, welching, traitorous Glaistig, for one. She muttered and clenched her fingers.

'Ow. Do you mind?'

She had the grace to look sheepish, although it would be a clever Faerie who could tell. 'Sorry, didn't realise I was doing that. I was just day-dreaming.'

'There you go again,' complained Benedict, 'dreaming. What a waste of time that is.'

Leanne swooped alongside. 'By no means,' she said. 'Sometimes,' a disturbing look came over her face, 'sometimes, I dream that I am skimming over the heather, creeping under the eaves, slipping in through the window. . .'

Benedict flapped his wings extra hard and blew her off course. Annis breathed in appreciatively the smell of rot, mildew, mould and long ago death that enveloped them.

'Y'know,' she said, 'for someone who goes in for all this,' a withered claw waved to take in the wings and their odour, 'you can be pretty squeamish.'

Benedict looked down at her. 'I should hold on, if I were you, with both hands. I could have dropped you, then.'

She looked at him, quizzically. 'But you wouldn't, would you?!

He looked down at her and almost smiled. "No, I don't expect I would,' he said.

'You're a good boy, Benedict,' said the hag, as she hutched in closer, just in case. She smiled her dreadful smile.

'Yes, yes, whatever,' Benedict. 'Just don't push your luck. I am Lord of Unseelie, after all. That makes me more than a bit tricksie.'

Annis smiled to herself, tucked up against her Lord's chest. Benedict, tricksie? How sweet that he saw himself that way. Thank the dark powers he stood for that she was there to help, otherwise they might just as well hand Pan the keys to the kingdom now and skip the hassle. She closed her eyes and went to sleep. A hag needed her sleep, especially at her age. No one knew quite what that was, but there were rocks younger than Annis.

Leanne caught up again. 'All right,' she said, 'Long story cut short, dreams are good. And anyway, if Pan hadn't started dreaming, we'd have had no warning he was waking up.'

'A fat lot of good the warning did us,' Benedict observed. 'He still woke up and cleared off before we got there.'

'Ah, yes,' said Leanne, raising a portentous talon in the air, 'but . . .'

'But?'

'Oh, all right. So we didn't get there in time. He's out there and we don't know where. But we have a Plan.'

'It's a bit vague. What if we all get back together and find we've all unearthed the same old tired incantation?'

'Well, be sensible. How likely is it that you and Gwyddion, say, will have thought of the same thing?'

'I know what he will be doing. He'll be doing some weird thing with mistletoe and widdershins, that kind of thing, dancing about in a dress.'

Leanne snorted and nudged the Unseelie Lord as they flew. He risked a smile himself. 'He is rather camp, isn't he?'

she said. 'Before he moved back to Wales, I always saw him as a kind of Wicked Witch of the Home Counties. So, what are you doing?'

'Puck will do something terribly non-invasive with animals. His spell will involve a milk-white doe, captured by a maiden's song on a dewy morning. I expect cute little bunnies will feature.'

'Well, Madam will hardly let her pet elf hurt things, will she? I have to say, though, that some of those totem animals are quite delicious.' She gave him a more than usually evil look. 'For afterwards, you know. Party food. So, what are you doing?'

'I expect O . . . O . . . the King will be doing something involving a crown of ivy and honeysuckle, woven in a cunning way into his ebon curls, matched by the intricately embroidered border on his silk loincloth, woven especially for the occasion by worms fed on the sacred mulberry tree known only to the Queen. He will sprinkle stars, newly plucked from the Milky Way in his path. He will be attended by the loveliest handmaidens Titania can summon, dressed to match in forest green.' He looked sideways at Leanne. 'Perhaps he can be prevailed upon to provide the salad at your after-show party.'

Leanne spat. 'Ugh. I don't do veg. So, what are you doing?'

'I wonder what Phoebe has in mind? I can't quite place her, you know. Which one was she at the return?'

'Well, you wouldn't have noticed her. She was a mousey little thing. She opened the hall for us. She was the vicar's wife.'

'Oh, her. No, I didn't really notice. Is it really the one?'

'Yes, Puck recognised her at once. I believe they had a bit of a thing going, back in the Old Days. And she was really in thick with Pan.'

'Should we use her, then? Remember Moira.'

'None of us is beyond reproach, really. We all liked a bit of a runaround with the old goat in those days.'

'Speak for yourself. Anyway, I expect her spell will be all Faerie-dust and wings, butterflies, a few of the smaller birds, I shouldn't wonder. It will all be very delicate and probably won't last for more than a few minutes.'

'Perhaps she'll put in a few farts,' came a phlegmy comment from Annis.

'Lovely idea.' Leanne said. 'Go back to sleep. Honestly, Benedict. I don't know how you can. And, while we're on the subject, don't think she's coming in to my flat. She can wait outside on the windowsill.'

Annis's dreadful head snapped back. Benedict waited for the explosion. But that wasn't what happened.

'Pigeons?'

'Any number.'

'Fine. Windowsill it is, then.' She went back to sleep.

'Is it me?' Leanne asked, wonderingly, 'or is she mellowing in her old age.'

'No. I'm not.'

Benedict gave a little shrug. Leanne had got off lightly.

'That's Phoebe, then. So, what are you doing?'

'As for you, I would imagine that the minerals will be gold . . .'

'. . . for daylight . . .'

'. . . silver . . .'

'. . . for moonlight . . .'

'. . . silicon . . .'

'. . . for memory . . .'

'and iron . . .'

'. . . for blood. Spot on. You are a clever old Lord, aren't you?'

'Have I already told you not to push your luck?'

"No,' came a sleepy voice. 'That was me you said that to.'

'Was it?'

'Yes. When you threatened to drop me.'

'Well, it applies to you as well, Leanne. I expect your spell will be woven in the dark. The gold will be from a deep dwarf mine, wrenched from their greedy little hands as they cling for all they're worth.'

'Actually, I was planning just to use an old bracelet, but I like your way better. Go on.'

'The silver will be plucked from the finger of a sleeping

youth, taking an ill-omened rest under the moon. He will be sleeping near the sea, soothed by the foam-flecked breakers, cushioned by the still-sunwarmed sand. A smile will cross his lips as you ease the ring from his finger, kissing his cherub mouth as you do so.'

She fingered her lobes. 'Earrings, in fact, but you spin a wonderful tale, Lord. Go on.'

'The silicon will be stolen by a foul swarm of bats, flowing from their cave at dead of night. Their numbers will be so great they will blot the moon from the sky. Mortals will cower, all speech stilled by the rushing of their wings. The silicon will be taken in one perfect crystal from the roof of a cave, high on a mountain top, big as a cathedral, dark, quiet and cold as a grave.'

'I was going to use an old mobile I've got in the drawer at home. But hey – I like the bats better.' She licked her lips. 'And the blood?'

Benedict shuddered and turned his shoulder, so he couldn't see her face. 'I think I can leave that one to you,' he said.

Leanne laughed a happy peal. He was so, so right. They were in sight of her block now and they started to slow. Annis gathered her scattered wits from sleep and got ready to land on the sill. The pigeons were hunched together on the ledge.

'You can leave me here, then,' she said. 'I think I'll call that one "brunch".' Her cackle was subdued – she hated to have to chase her food. Fear made it taste bitter.

Leanne was counting on her fingers, as they dropped down into the room beyond the glass.

'So,' she said as they landed light as thistledown, 'What are you doing?'

Benedict gave his wings a shake and settled them in neat folds on his back. He meticulously brushed off the lingering bits of Annis. Out of consideration for Leanne, he turned them into innocuous bits of down before they hit her black velvet floor. Naturally, for the Lord of Unseelie, the bits of down were black, the under-feathers from a raven's wing or something very similar.

'Did you hear me?' she asked, shaking his arm. 'What are

you doing?'

Annis chuckled to hear him sigh. She knew what was coming.

'I'm buggered if I know,' he said.

Chapter Twenty Four

Puck arrived back in the glade first, but not by much. Mab was a spiralling dot in the distance as he touched down. He glanced over his shoulder and immediately scurried for cover in the wood He told himself that he did this because he was in charge of the animal bit of the spell and that was where the animals were likely to be. Whilst this was undoubtedly true, his real reason was different; understandable, but different. He wanted to hide from Mab. She had always got on his wick, but at the moment she was something he could do without. It didn't help that he felt a bit sorry for her, demoted, as she saw it, to gofer, running errands and getting no glory. Nor, on the upside, any blame, when the whole thing went pear-shaped.

When he thought he was far enough into the undergrowth, he sat down on a stump and let his head rest on his knees. For good measure, he folded his arms over his head. He tried rocking a little. It helped. It really did. He tried whimpering. No, that &as over the top. But rocking was nice. Very soothing.

A voice just over his shoulder made him jump.

'I wish I could do that,' it said. 'But I can't. My arms are too short.'

He glanced back. 'I think, despite your height, that they still count as forelegs, don't you?'

The squirrel budged him up along the fallen tree and sat down beside him. He curled his tail around them both in a companionable way and slumped forward with a sigh. 'No luck, then?' he asked.

'Well, yes and no,' said Puck.

'Ah, like the good news and the bad news?'

'Yes, I suppose so.'

'All right then. What's the good news?'

Puck thought for a moment, planning a way to make anything sound like good news.

The squirrel, politely trying to keep the conversation going, prompted him gently. 'The bad news, then?'

'Pan's loose.'

The squirrel's tail uncurled and stuck straight up, every hair on end. 'What, you mean, just loose? Wandering about?'

'Yes. Or rather, he must be. He wasn't in his hole.'

The squirrel looked round wildly. Poor thing, hiding wasn't as easy as it had once been. 'Where is he?'

'Well, that's part of the bad news. We're not sure. I'm not sure how to find out, without actually confronting him, and we're not ready for that. Any ideas?'

'There's that thing. The thing I saw when you were here last time. It gives messages.'

Puck furrowed his brow. 'The Isp?'

'Is that a big spidery looking thing?'

'Yes.' Blunt, but true.

'Can you talk to it?'

'Yes. Well, I talk to my one, but it's not here. The Queen has one, but I don't know where it is. She put it to bed somewhere comfy, she says, and that could be anywhere.'

'Can you talk to that one you had yesterday?'

'Yes.' Puck was getting rather tired of the rodent. Its brain didn't seem to have grown proportionately. 'But it isn't here, is it?'

'There's no need to get testy,' sulked the squirrel.

'Well,' Puck whinged. 'If you'd had the night I've had . . .'

The squirrel kept its temper, with difficulty. How, he

thought, how this elf had the nerve, he had no idea. Let him try being twenty times his usual size, see how he likes it. Let him try and gather enough acorns for a decent breakfast. Let him try and explain to his missus that the twenty times thing was just a temporary glitch, especially when, for some reason, you could only speak Mortal and the missus was still stuck in Squirrel. Oh yes. But in fact, he just said, mildly, 'It's over there, Hiding behind that tree.'

Puck jumped up and dashed over to the tree. Anxious to keep in with an animal he might need later, he gave the squirrel's shoulder a cursory pat. The Isp cowered back, its many eyes

flickering uncertainly. It too had had a bad night.

Puck approached it carefully, crouching down, a friendly expression glued firmly on his face. 'Come on,' he cooed. 'There's no need to be frightened.'

The Isp licked its lips nervously and backed away.

'Come on,' Puck said. 'Don't you remember me?'

The Isp's voice came from far, far away. 'The system was not shut down properly,' it said faintly. 'To avoid hearing this message in future, please close the system down correctly, correctly, correctly. The system has performed an illegal action. Closedown. Closedown. Press any leg to continue. The system is busy. Busy. Busy. Bizz. Bizzzzzzzzzzzzzzzzz.' The Isp's eyes flashed once. It raised itself up on all its legs, gave a little scream and collapsed on the mossy floor of the wood.

The squirrel ambled over. He kicked the Isp gently with one enormous back foot. 'Poor little bleeder,' it remarked. 'I tried to talk to it, but it wasn't having any. It kept asking for a password. In the end, it just hunkered down here, muttering to itself. Is it dead?'

Puck was gathering up the Isp's legs into a manageable bundle, to take it back to the glade. 'I don't think they can die, as such. I've never been quite sure what they are. I know Titania treats hers as if it is alive, but Benedict and Leanne don't seem to bother much about theirs. Well,' he held out the Isp's little hairy body for the squirrel's inspection, 'as you can see.'

They had reached the edge of the wood. The squirrel

hung back, shyly. 'I don't think I'll come any further, for the moment, if you don't mind,' he said, diffidently.

"No, come on,' Puck said. 'Perhaps we can shrink you down to your right size.'

'I think that will only happen when you sort all this out,' said the squirrel, encompassing with one sweep of his foreleg the whole world. 'I've got a feeling that, if you shrink me, I'll still be a huge animal made small. I want to be a real small animal, talking Squirrel, full up on one acorn, running aimlessly up trees chasing the missus.'

Puck smiled at him, and, hitching the Isp onto one arm, shook the squirrel's paw. 'I understand,' he said. 'Don't worry. And, if I need you . . .?'

'Then I'm your squirrel,' said the squirrel.

'Thanks,' Puck said, and walked into the sunlight of the glade. Mab stood there, tapping her foot. She hated it when folk hid from her. But as soon as she saw the Isp, her maternal instincts took over.

'Poor little thing,' she cooed. 'What happened to it?'

'I think it had a fright,' Puck said. 'Benedict left it in the wood, and it couldn't cope.'

'Bless it,' Mab murmured. 'Let's take it inside and see if we can sort it out.'

'Do you know anything about this sort of thing?' Puck said. 'Only, if we can't get it working soon, we'll have to leave it. We've got loads to do.'

'But won't this make it easier? We can keep in touch with one of these.'

'Yes. But there should be another one around her somewhere. It was given to the Queen.'

'Yes,' said a passing Mr Dobie. 'It was in her bower.'

Puck grabbed him by the shoulder of his long, dragging mac. 'Was?'

'Still is,' the brownie said mildly. 'But its battery's down.'

'Why?' Puck bent down and glared menacingly into the little creature's eyes.

Mr Dobie gestured with his thumb. Over in the shade of a spreading oak on the edge of the woods, a group of goblins were trying to quietly slip away.

'Oy,' Puck called. 'Over here, you lot. Now.'

The goblins pointed to their own chests, mouthing 'me?', eyebrows lifted in surprise. They were still sidling.

'Yes, you.' Puck pointed to the ground at his feet and, at last, with much shuffling and nudging, the goblins, mostly sheep, but led by a big, pig-based creature, whose name Puck didn't know, were in front of him.

'We didn't do nuthin,' the pig one said, sulkily.

'Did you not?' Puck asked sweetly. 'What, not even a bit of surfing?'

'We ain't near the sea, or nuthin.' The pig looked round at his cronies, but they were silent. One of them had large tears rolling slowly down her large Roman nose and soaking into her woolly chest.

'I mean,' said Puck menacingly. 'You were using the Queen's Isp for personal purposes.'

'Well,' the goblin stuck his chin forward, suddenly full of bravado. 'What if we did? It wasn't being used for anything else. We just done a bit of . . . what did you call it?'

'Surfing.'

'Yeah. Played a few games. Done a bit of shopping.'

'Shopping?'

'Yeah.'

'For crying out loud . . .' the last twenty-four hours rose up in Puck's head and exploded in a firework display to shame Disneyland. The goblins cowered, then ran round in random circles, before regrouping as far from Puck as they could, whilst still being in the familiar world of Titania's glade. Puck raised a finger and brought it down, trembling with effort, to point directly between the goblin's eyes – an extremely small target. The goblin stood its ground. You had to give it credit for that. And that might have been its last action, but for the timely arrival of Oberon, crashing to a halt on the mossy mound just outside Titania's bower.

Puck's attention was diverted for just long enough. The goblin dashed for the cover of his King's coat tails as he strode into the centre of the clearing.

'Problems, Puck?'

'No, sire. Just the usual,' Puck sighed. 'Lord of Misrule

coming this way, very probably. Four seasons in one day. Big animals getting smaller, small animals getting bigger. Dolphins in the water-butt.'

'Worse than that,' Tiny chipped in. 'We saw dolphins swimming in the road, just now.'

'What? Floods already?'

'No. Actually swimming in the road. As if the tarmac was liquid.'

'Yes, yes,' said Oberon. He had almost got used to the strangeness surrounding Pan's return already. Nothing could surprise him now. 'But why were you threatening to disembody my goblin?'

'He's been web-shopping?'

'What?' Oberon roared. 'Where is he? I'll see to him myself.'

He paused and looked back at Puck. 'What is that, exactly? I like to know why I'm destroying my Folk.'

'Never mind, Sire.' Puck smiled at his King. 'What's done is done. Let's go and see Mab. See if she's managed to sort out the Isp. We can perhaps get some news and work out where Pan has got to. Then, we ought to start on the binding spells. Time is pressing.'

'The Lord hath made a thtart,' said Thydney and, fishing in his pocket, he brought out a dishevelled looking flower. 'It'th a love-in-idleneth.'

Puck looked at the King, head on one side. 'Sire? That old trick?'

Oberon looked down, embarrassed. 'Just practicing, Puck. Just practicing.'

'Who on?'

'Oh . . . just some people . . .'

'OK.' Puck turned on his heel. He could hardly trust himself to speak. 'Let's go and see if we can find some news.'

They all trouped towards the bower, where Mab stood in the doorway, cradling a recovering Isp in her arms.

'How many people?' he turned to ask.

Oberon spread his arms. 'Some.'

'Some being . . .?'

'A few bus queues.'

'And?'

'A bank.'

'That should be fun. And?'

'That place in London. Do you remember it? Big place. With a clock?'

Puck chuckled. He risked a nudge. 'Well done, Sire,' he said. 'That was a good one. Parliament, eh?'

Mab watched the news a bit more than the others. So she was the only one who wondered whether anyone would notice.

Chapter Twenty Five

The Isp was feeling tons better. In its tiny, arachnid mind, hidden deep below its chips and silicon synapses, there lay a glimmer of an instinct, that which all creatures of the spider persuasion share – snuggled up in the bosom of a female is its natural habitat.

'It's coming round, bless it,' Mab said, placing the Isp carefully on the ground. It staggered slightly, looking up at the Faerie, just to establish that it might need a bit of a cuddle, later.

Puck bent down to the Isp. 'Can you send a message to Leanne?' he asked it kindly. It had been in a state when he found it and he felt a bit cruel asking it to work so soon, but time was pressing.

The little creature waved a foreleg and winked with a few eyes. 'Password?' it asked hopefully.

Puck looked rueful. 'Sorry.'

The Isp had very high security built in – it was after all, the personal computer of the Lord of Unseelie and it took itself very seriously. 'Secret answer?'

"No idea.'

"No, wait.' Oberon pushed through the crowd. He had been amusing the goblins who were crowding round with a few details of his practicing with the love-in-idleness and they were rolling around with laughter. One of the rabbits had had to be taken away to lie down and it was time he calmed things down a little. He leant down to the Isp and raised his voice, as non-speakers of arcane languages do. 'Hello,' he yelled.

The Isp gave a little scream and jumped back, nuzzling into the shelter of Mab's legs.

'Why did you do that?' Mab asked her King. 'It's very fragile, poor little thing. There's no need to shout.'

Oberon straightened up, affronted. 'I didn't mean to frighten it. I was just speaking clearly.'

'Just use your normal speaking voice, Sire,' said Puck, then thought again. 'Just use a nice quiet speaking voice, Sire.'

The King looked down his nose at the Isp. Speaking as if to an idiot, but very softly, Oberon said, 'One green, one blood red.'

The Isp's eyes blinked in quick succession. 'What is your message?'

Puck was staggered. 'How did you know the answer to his secret question? And, more importantly, what was his secret question?'

Oberon smiled. 'We go back a long, long way, Benedict and I. It's not many people know the colour of his mother's eyes. Yes, we go back a long, long way.' He shook himself. 'But, let's get on with this. What's the message?'

'Just checking in, really,' said Puck. 'Letting him know we are here.' He looked around. 'Except the Queen.'

'And therefore, Phoebe,' said Mab, smugly. 'I knew it wouldn't be that easy.'

'Early days,' said Puck, although a trifle anxiously.

'And Gwyddion,' said Oberon.

'Yes. I hope he gets here soon. As Earth, he should be co-ordinating us, otherwise we could end up going round in circles, duplicating his work.'

The King looked amused. 'I hardly think that he will duplicate anything that I do, Puck, do you think?'

'Hardly, Sire. What was I thinking?' Puck loved this language. You could make it say anything you wanted. He turned to the Isp. 'Message from Puck, to unseel-ielord@blackarts.com. Where are you? Is everything going OK? Most of us are here at the glade, waiting for Titania and Gwyddion. Are you watching the news? Ignore anything about Parliament – just my Lord's little bit of fun.' Puck broke off to look over his shoulder as the goblins fell over again, convulsed anew at the wicked joke. 'We need to see if we can find him. If he's coming this way, we'll have to move. We can't have him get to us before we're ready. Please get back asap.' A nudge nearly knocked him off his feet. 'Oh, James sends his. Cheers, Puck.'

'Cheers?' Mab could hardly contain her amusement. It sounded so unlike him.

He shuffled his feet. 'I never know how to sign off eeee-mails.'

The Isp gave a small cough.

'Oh, sorry. Send.'

'Your message has been sent.'

'Thank you. Now, I want to see a rolling news channel.'

'TV?'

A few Mr Dobies pushed through the crowd. They so missed their television. *Countdown, Fifteen to One, Who Wants to Be A Millionaire*, even *Weakest Link*. Oh, how they missed them.

"No. Something Web. That is usually quicker.'

The Isp turned to Benedict's home page. An image flick-ered into view, projected from somewhere inside the Isp onto the hairy contours of its back. The print wasn't very clear. But, frankly, with Faeries, that made no difference.

Puck turned to the crowd. 'Is Hazel here?'

'Waiting, as ever, to be of any assistance, however small, however miniscule, however minor, be it never so slight or inconsequential, no matter that it be trifling, insignificant, nay, nor even unimportant.'

'Er . . . good. Can you help us with this reading?'

'Although it is true that one is able to discern texts under certain circumstances, Lord,' the spirit gave an elaborate bow in the direction of Oberon, 'One feels it only fair – indeed it is incumbent upon one so to do – to apprise you, indeed, and the company, that in this particular occasion, one can be of little, nay, virtually no practical help.'

'But I was sure you could read, if only a bit.'

'Ah, as one was recently expounding,' Hazel stretched upwards, twiggy fingers enlaced behind his back, eyes closed behind their barky lids, 'One could under other circumstances be of enormous help. But, as things are . . .'

'Oh, get out of my way.' A testy voice came from the back of the crowd, underscored by choruses of 'gerroff' and 'oof' from the smaller denizens of Faerie. Puck's heart sank. An Elder, big-head and pedant of the tree spirit world, with an unpleasant streak a mile wide, was pushing its way to the front. It leant over the Isp and started to read. There was something in its tone that made even a story about a skateboarding duck sound faintly threatening.

Puck leaned over to Hazel and asked, 'Why aren't you doing this?'

Before the spirit could speak, the Elder said, over its shoulder, 'Because he's lost his glasses.'

'Glasses?' mouthed Puck.

'Anno domini, alas, Lord,' said Hazel with a sigh. 'Anno domini.'

'Shh,' said Mab.

'Are you sure you don't want this stuff about Parliament?' the Elder asked. 'It's quite . . .'

'No, thank you,' said Mab firmly. She was taking her co-ordinating role seriously. 'Just the gist.'

'Blah, blah, Global warming. Blah, blah . . . oops "sources close to the Prime Minister . . ."'

'Hur, hur,' gurgled Freckles.

'. . . . mentioned to me in the Terrace Bar that it may be necessary to investigate rumours that the recent Return of Faerie, welcome though it is, may have a bearing on the problems with the weather, as it appears that only those areas under their influence, viz and to wit the British Isles . . .'

'Oops is right,' Puck said quietly. 'I knew this would happen.'

'Hang on,' said the Elder. 'Here's another bit. This is a quote from the *Star*, so I'll paraphrase. "Star babes watch out!

Bonking is on the cards as a flasher with an enormous . . .'"

'Hold on, Elder,' said Puck. 'I thought by paraphrase you would clean it up a bit.'

The Elder looked affronted. 'That is cleaned up, if you don't mind,' he said. 'I could give it to you in the original, if you'd rather.'

Mab held up a hand. 'I don't think we need that. I think we get the message. Did it say where this enormous was seen?'

'Hmmm,' the Elder looked down the page as the Isp obligingly scrolled through the item. "No.'

'It's crucial that we find out whether he is on the move or not,' Puck said. 'And if he is on the move, whether he is heading this way, or wandering randomly.'

'My money's on wandering randomly,' said Oberon. 'As God of Confusion, he always just went wherever his . . .'

'. . . enormous,' piped up Tiny.

'Precisely so,' said the King, 'his enormous led him. He was never much for planning.'

Puck looked thoughtful. 'Not in the Old Days, perhaps, Sire. But he has just woken up, dug himself free, found himself in a strange country and alone. He was never alone before. If it wasn't a woman, it was his drinking pals. If not them, then it was you, Sire, or me. But mostly, all of the above. So, he's not going to behave the way he used to. I think we're going to have to put ourselves in his shoes, if we can.'

'And you,' Mab said, unkindly, 'are better placed than the rest of us to do that, aren't you, goat-boy?'

'Oh, har. We don't really need this kind of carping, do we? We've got a job to do.'

The Elder looked up. 'Am I still doing this?' it asked, waspishly.

'Terribly sorry, old man,' said Oberon, condescendingly. 'We are listening. Any other news?'

"Not as such. The Mortals have definitely decided that this is no way Global Warming.'

'No way? What newspaper are you reading now?' Puck asked, looking over the spirit's shoulder, for all the good it did.

'Er . . .' Elder gestured to the Isp to scroll, '*New Musical Express.*'

'What's it got to do with them?'

'Apparently, there is a new supergroup who have formed to save the environment.'

'Crumbth,' said Thydney, excitedly. 'Whoth in it?'

'Slash.'

'Gunth and Roseth!'

'Michael Stipes.'

'Michael Thtipeth of REM!'

'Sting.'

'Thting. Did you hear that, Freckleth? Thting!'

'And Ringo Starr on drums.'

By now there was a significant fallout zone around Thydney, as his excitement grew, wetly. Puck stepped forward and spoke. 'How did they decide who was going to be in it, I wonder,' he mused, as he shepherded a starstruck Thydney back through the crowd before he could drown everyone. 'Did they have to have names beginning with S?'

The Elder had little or no sense of humour. "No, I believe they are just friends of the planet.'

'With a name like Slash?'

'Well, perhaps they just needed a good axeman,' said Tiny.

'Please,' shuddered Hazel. 'One is already feeling a deep sense of misgiving, deep in one's heart wood. One's xylem and phloem is positively quivering with tension. Talking of slashing and axes does not help.'

'Axe as in guitar, I imagine he means,' said Oberon, comfortingly.

A stunned silence followed. It was not often their King was in a position to put anyone right, let alone Hazel. There was a smattering of applause.

Suddenly, the Isp spoke. 'You have mail,' it intoned.

'What?'

'Password?'

'Milkshake,' said Puck, a little embarrassed. It had seemed rather a clever choice at the time, as all passwords do.

'Hi,' the Isp said, perkily. 'We are at my place. I have plans for my spells and Annis is on the windowsill eating pigeons. Benedict is also planning his spells. Well, he's having a bath . . .'

'And changing into some of his own clothes, I hope,' muttered the King.

'. . . which is water, at least. He has come up with an idea for fire, by the way, if any of you fancy re-instating it. He says James will know where to go to get a salamander. We could keep it handy, just in case.'

Everyone turned round to look at James, who looked puzzled. 'Why should I know where to get a salamander?' he asked. 'I've never eaten one in my life. I don't like spicy food.'

The Isp continued. 'Well, I expect you're all busy. We'll be at the glade some time overnight, I expect. Get the salamander, James. Is Titania back yet? I bet that silly airy faerie won't play ball. Have you seen the news about the naked bloke with the enormous. Apparently, he's heading your way. But that was the Guardian report which said where he was, so he could be anywhere. Anyway, must go. I can hear Annis tapping at the window. If she sees me in here, she'll expect me to let her in. Bye now, Leanne.'

A light voice said, from the back of the crowd, 'So, the airy faerie won't play ball, eh?'

Puck spun round. 'Phoebe!' he said. 'You're here!'

She inclined her head.

'Did you fly?'

A dishevelled Titania followed her into the clearing. She held a child by each hand. 'Well, yes, and no,' she said. 'Yes she can fly, about six inches off the ground. But not when she's carrying either of these kids.' She walked forward and flopped onto Oberon, who caught her, but only just. 'I need a rest. Give them,' she gestured with her thumb to the children, who were standing open mouthed looking round at the crowd of Faerie, 'something to eat. Give them some of your bacon, Freckles and don't bother to argue, I know you've got some. Mab, come and get me ready for bed I'm ready to drop and if one person says I don't have time I will turn them into something I haven't decided what, but they won't like it.' She shoved Oberon in the chest and, head down and determined, she stomped off to her bower. A few dwarves and goblins flew out seconds later and the door slammed shut behind them, if a cunningly wrought device of cobweb and dew can be said to slam.

Oberon gave a husbandly smile and followed her inside. A wifely scream was heard seconds later, and he exited, holding a pillow as if it was the most natural thing in the world.

'Um . . . the Queen is a little tired and emotional,' he said to the crowd. 'So if you could . . .' He made little sod-off gestures with both hands and, with much shushing and ostentatious tiptoeing, the little Faerie microcosm dispersed.

Chapter Twenty Six

The glade was quiet. Evening was coming on, heralded by a beautiful sky, pale blue, overlaid with coral pink streaks, lit from below by the sinking sun. Puck and Phoebe were stretched out on a mossy bank. Her children were off somewhere playing hide and seek with some of the rabbit-based goblins. They had taken to things like ducks to water. The bacon sandwich had been a bit of a bonus; their mother wasn't much of a cook, and without much of an appetite for food. For the elder of the two, the girl, Undine, memories were falling into place. She felt at home here. The boy, Padraig, only five but as bright as a button, didn't care where they were. The funny rabbits, about his height but not at all scary, were running him around and keeping him occupied.

Phoebe looked at the sky. 'Red sky at night, shepherds' delight,' she said, turning her head to smile at Puck.

'Or,' said the elf, 'Red sky at night, the hayrick's alight. It all depends on your point of view.'

She rolled onto one elbow and poked at him with a twig. 'It's not like you to be so negative,' she said. 'Or at least, it wasn't like you. I suppose I shouldn't judge, having only seen you once in the last I don't know how long.'

He smiled back at her. 'You're right. What have I got to be pessimistic about? Pan is loose and looking for us. Our leading players on the spell side are a Druid, who has rediscovered hallucinogens in a big, big way; a Faerie King who has become a media junkie and hasn't cast a spell in anger for hundreds of Mortal years; an Unseelie Lord whose idea of forward planning is to have a bath; a vampire who has the morals of . . .'

'. . . a vampire?'

'Leanne.'

'Of course. Leannan-Sidhe. I remember her from your meeting. I'm surprised she has hung around.'

'Well, like Benedict McAdam, Lord of Unseelie, she had the Mortal world pretty much sewn up. Technology is their toy, Mankind their playground. James, over there, is Benedict's butler.'

Phoebe raised a questioning brow.

'Yes, possibly he doesn't look the part at the moment, but he polishes up quite well. He's not usually far from his master, but as I am the lucky Faerie in charge of getting the animal spell together, we thought he might be helpful.'

'Why are you in charge of animal?'

By way of reply, Puck pulled out the waistband of his trousers and invited her to take a look.

Glancing round to make sure no one was looking, especially Undine and Padraig, she leaned over and took a peep. She blushed. She hadn't quite shaken off the shadow of the Manse. 'Really, Puck!' she said, drawing away. 'I don't know quite what you think of yourself, but there's nothing down there that makes me think immediately of animal.'

Startled, Puck took a peek. No goat-legs to be seen, just the usual suspects. He let his waistband go with a painful twang of elastic.

'I'm terribly sorry,' he blustered. 'When I looked last, I had goat legs.'

Phoebe's eye twinkled. 'I bet you say that to all the Faerie,' she said.

Puck smiled uncertainly. 'Are you sure you're not cross?'

'Of course not,' she said. 'I was just practicing, as a matter of fact. Watch.' She called over a Mr Dobie who was ambling past. He stood uncertainly at her feet. He wasn't used to being noticed. 'Come closer,' she said, crooking her finger. He edged nearer and, when he was about two feet from her face, she blew on him, a gentle breeze that was scented with its passage over summer meadows, high up in a snow-capped mountain range, untouched by Mortal or Faerie alike. Under its breath, the Mr Dobie grew a disconcerting eighteen inches and, briefly, looked like Brad Pitt. Then, as she drew breath again, he was back to a Mr Dobie, but now, a Mr Dobie with memories. He scuttled away.

Puck peeped down his trousers. Yes, goat-legs again. He didn't know whether to be glad or sorry.

Phoebe poked him again with her stick. "Not bad, eh? I've been out of practice for I don't know how long.' She was smiling. Only a ghost of the vicar's wife hung over her now, mostly caused by the grey cardigan she still wore.

Puck lay back, hands behind his head. 'So, tell me how you got here. Did you give the Queen a hard time?'

'Possibly. I don't know, really. How hard was she expecting it to be?'

'She was expecting it to be very hard.'

'Then, no. I was a walkover. I had stayed because of the children,' she said. 'Then, with all that peculiar weather and everything, I began to worry about them, their futures, you know, the planet, rain forests, recycling and stuff.'

'So,' Puck said to himself, 'Annis was right.'

'Annis is here?'

'Not at the moment, but she'll be back. Why?'

'Well, I shall have to watch out for the children,' she said, shuddering. 'You used to hear such stories . . .'

'I think she's more into pigeons, that kind of thing, these days. She doesn't like children, it's true.'

'Why not?' Phoebe's maternal hackles rose.

Puck chuckled. 'They give her indigestion.'

'Yes, well, as I was saying.'

'Sorry.'

'I didn't take that much persuading and even before the Mistress conjured up the tiger – I wasn't supposed to know it was her and I didn't let on – I had made up my mind to come.'

'What about your husband?'

'Ah, yes, poor Thomas. Bearing in mind he spends his life believing in a myth, he is not very open to other people's ideas. He was in the drop-in centre when we found him.'

'Dropped in.'

'The Queen has already done that one. I told him what was happening.'

'And?'

She hung her head. She had chosen him as a partner once, for his lifetime if not for hers. It had been difficult there, in the drop-in centre with its pile of old shoes, old clothes, pot of soup and aura of a million jumble sales to see what she had once seen in that grey, embittered, cold-hearted man. He had been a golden a creature, beautiful enough to be a Fair Sidhe; in fact, for years she had hoped that he would admit to being just such a one. But no; he was just an unusually handsome theology student, who became a moderately nice-looking curate, who, in his turn became a prematurely aged, inward-looking and bitter minister. She had felt as though she was talking to a stranger.

The stranger said, 'Now, then, Phoebe. Pull yourself together and go home. Perhaps your friend here,' he had waved a disinterested arm at Titania, clothed in glamour so thick you could scrape it off with a spoon, 'would make you a nice cup of tea. I'll be home later.'

Phoebe had left the centre in tears. At the children's school, it wasn't difficult to persuade the head teacher that there had been a family crisis, with Phoebe tear-stained and Titania temporarily in the guise of a downtrodden neighbour. As soon as they were round the corner, Titania had clothed herself in Queenly gear again, and had taken to the air, a child under each arm. After a few exploratory hops, Phoebe herself was in the air and, if not exactly soaring, was soon on her way. Thomas had taken much of the wind from beneath her wings.

'And so here I am,' she concluded.

'Here you are, indeed,' said Puck. 'No wonder the Queen was tired. Mortal children are heavy.'

'And she should know,' said Mab, passing by. 'She's borrowed enough in her time. And speaking of time,' she said to

Phoebe, 'isn't it time your two were in bed?'

Phoebe looked at the sky. 'It still seems very early.'

'Don't go by the sky,' Mab told her. 'Time is becoming an optional extra, since Pan woke up. I think what I'm saying is, their yelling is annoying the Queen. I think a nice bird's nest or flower of some kind would be a good idea around about now.'

'They can't sleep in a nest or a flower. They're too big.'

'Oh!' squeaked Mab in mock surprise. 'Are they really? Could that be because they're Mortal children?' She frowned at Phoebe. 'Just put them to bed somewhere, Feeb, I may call you Feeb, may I. We've got to get ready for the Unseelie to return, and you know what that means!' She pulled a fang-face at Phoebe and pranced off, mischief done and done.

She suddenly turned back. 'Oh, Feeb, don'tcha want to know what Feeb is short for?'

'Phoebe?' the air Faerie ventured.

'Well, duh. Yes. But also, I think you'll find,' said Mab, nastily, 'it stands for feeble. Bye.' And off she danced.

Puck and Phoebe stood together, watching as the mischievous Faerie threaded her way through the glade, pausing to whisper here and there to goblin, brownie, elf and sprite.

Puck shuddered.

'Cold?'

'No, not really. Mab just made me think, that's all.'

'What are you thinking?'

'I'm thinking, we don't need to watch the news to see where Pan is. Part of him is already here.'

With a pop audible only on the edges of Faerie hearing, the sun sank below the horizon. Its lingering warmth was soon gone and the night grew cold. In the distance, off to the East, could be heard the slow beat of leather wings. Under the noise as the air was shifted reluctantly aside, was a shrill rendition of the Toreador Song.

Chapter Twenty Seven

Leanne was still on the phone as she touched down. Benedict and Annis made a rather less elegant landing, more of an accidental collision with the ground than anything.

'Uh huh,' Leanne was saying, 'Uh huh. Uh huh. I don't think so.' She snapped the phone closed.

'Anything important?' Benedict asked, mildly. Having dispensed with his own technological trappings, he could afford to condescend to those still in their thrall.

'Double glazing,' she said. 'Hardly top of my agenda right now.'

Phoebe had rounded up her children and had given them into the care of a rather more sprightly than usual Mr Dobie. He shepherded them off; the Mr Dobies knew where all the comfy places were.

Titania popped her head out round the door of her bower. She was always pleased to see Benedict, for whom she had a soft spot. Leanne and Annis she could take or leave, especially Annis, who made her itch. She made her way over. Phoebe was hovering, keeping Annis and Leanne in view and therefore not near her children. Puck and James were already there, and Oberon dropped down from what was fast becoming his favourite branch to complete the set.

'Where's Gwyddion?' Leanne asked, craning her neck in an unsettling way.

"Not back yet,' Puck said. 'I wish he would hurry up. Earth covers all the rest really.'

'Except water,' Benedict cut in.

Puck bowed slightly. 'Except water, naturally, Sire,' he said.

'And vegetable,' Oberon added, sulkily.

'Well, vegetable is really . . .'

'I said' Oberon snarled, 'except vegetable. He's only a Druid. I, after all, am King of Faerie!'

Leanne smirked. 'Of course you are, Lord,' she said. 'But I, as mineral, will have to be under Gwyddion, as it were. It would be nice to have you on the team.'

Oberon oozed over to her side as if reeled in on a string. Titania ground her beautiful teeth but could say nothing. It was, she supposed, marginally possible that Leanne had done it to keep the King on side. Just marginally.

'Well,' Puck said, 'as animal, I am looking forward to his input. Ow.' He looked down, to see James straighten up from taking a nip out of his ankle, 'what was that for?'

'Just reminding you,' said the butler. 'I know you Seelie types, always forgetting the underdog.'

'As it were,' said Puck, acidly. 'I hadn't forgotten you, James. But, be fair, since we got back, all you've done is leer at the rabbits, scratch and sleep.'

'I'm just husbanding my strength,' the bogle said, with a sniff.

'Do I come under Gwyddion?' asked Phoebe, mildly.

'Air? I shouldn't think so,' said Titania. She had decided that Phoebe was one of her Faerie, with a capital whatever Faerie began with. She, the Queen, had found her, all by herself, only going wrong now and again. She felt quite proud.

'We still need him,' Annis said. Everyone had forgotten her. She had wandered away in the dark to lie down on the bank outside Titania's bower. As she got up and hobbled back to the group, her legacy of a withered, Annis-shaped patch of herbs could be seen clearly in the moonlight. 'The stupid Druid has probably eaten a few dodgy mushrooms or something and thinks he's a worm or some such relevant animal. I knew he shouldn't be trusted.'

Leanne felt she should speak up for her erstwhile client. 'He's usually fairly reliable,' she said. 'I can't think what's keeping him.' She flipped open her phone and whistled for Benedict's Isp, taking its ease under a log at the edge of the clearing. 'I'll get a few of our people on the case. They'll find him soon enough.' She spoke into the phone. 'Hello? Is that the Yarthkin residence? Could you put him on, please? Yes. Tell daddy it's Leanne. Yes, that's right. Leanne.' She covered the mouthpiece with one hand. 'Why these creatures let their kids answer the . . . Oh, hi. Yes. It's me. Look, can you get some of the guys and have a bit of a sweep for Gwyddion. Yes. I think . . . yes, at one of my parties. Yes. Tall. White beard. That's the chap. Well, anywhere between Wales and Dorset, really. Sorry, can't be any more specific than that. No! No, ha ha, no, I don't want you to work him over. No, not even a bit. We need him asap. He knows where we are.' She listened intently. "No! I really mean it. I'm not just saying it because people are listening. I really don't want him hurt. Ciao.' She flipped the phone closed and turned back to the others. 'Well, that's that. The yarthkin clan will find him quick as wink. They may not be pretty, but they're excellent when you have a bit of a hue and cry on.'

Titania looked anxious. 'They won't hurt him, will they?'

"No, no, not at all.' Leanne's laugh was hollow. 'I'm pretty sure they won't, anyway.'

Titania turned to Puck. 'Puck, dearest, please get some of our Faerie on to this job as well. I know we aren't as good at geography,' she made it sound somehow obscene,' as Benedict's People, but I'm sure they can find Gwyddion. Preferably,' and she gave a little laugh, 'first.'

Puck turned to face the glade and encircling wood and whistled through his fingers, a whistle up in the ultra-ultra sonic, which even bats couldn't hear. James shook his head and growled. He gave hurried instructions to the buzzing crowd of flower faeries, flying brownies and elves and, in an instant, with a faint noise like a distant finger down a damp windowpane, they were gone.

Leanne got busy eee-mailing with the Isp in a quiet corner. Annis squatted near Titania's bower, looking like a fungus, sprouting unbelievably from the beautiful garden, tended daily by the relevant flower faeries. A rabbit-goblin almost tried a nibble, but the smell drove him away before any harm was done. Benedict and Oberon stood, trying to look regal, in the centre of the glade. Neither realised how hard regality is when the King in question is chewing his fingernails and twirling an errant lock of hair, however ebon and lustrous, round one finger. Titania, Mab and Phoebe were trying to chat girl-chat on a bench down wind from Annis, but the conversation wouldn't flow.

They were all worried about the non-appearing druid. 'I wonder where he is?' said Phoebe, speaking for them all.

'Where am I?' asked Gwyddion, sitting up and holding his head.

'Good question, Druid,' said Pan. 'Most recently, you were on the end of my fist. But before that, I don't know. And where you're going . . . well, perhaps we can go together. That will be fun, won't it?'

Chapter Twenty Eight

'**M**y head really hurts,' whined Gwyddion. 'What happened?' He was still at the stage put there by nature to stop every living thing from going stark raving bonkers. In other words, he was in that wonderful place called Shock. Things would come back to him over the next little while, causing screams and random twitching. But, until then, he wasn't surprised by anything. Even though the rather good-looking stranger in the rather nasty jogging suit looked vaguely familiar. Even though he was huddled with this stranger in a rather smelly bus-shelter somewhere he didn't recognise. Even though he knew he should be doing something, urgently. For now, said Shock, don't you worry about it. It will all be all right, you see.

'I'm still a bit confused,' Gwyddion whined.

The god looked at him. He certainly looked confused, with his hair all over the place and his dress caught up in something at the back. Even so, the Lord of Misrule couldn't help thinking, he was probably the least confused of the two.

'Where am I?' the Druid asked, not for the first time.

'I don't know.'

A small, very small and upset synapse fired at the back of Gwyddion's head. Was it his imagination, or did this jogger have a rather odd accent? Perhaps he was Norwegian, or something. Albanian.

'Where are you from?' he asked, trying to scratch the itch in his skull.

Pan, squatting on his haunches, in his favourite position, looked up at Gwyddion, slumped on the red plastic seat with his head in his hands. He couldn't really say. Just, well, here. In an attempt to show his sheer cosmopolitanism, he spread his arms in an expansive gesture, smiling his wolfish smile.

'I am from everywhere,' he said.

'Ah, a bit of a traveller,' Gwyddion nodded. He'd been around a bit himself. But, still, he couldn't quite scratch that itch. 1 le tried to stand up, but his head just swam round and round. 'Oooh, my head.' He glanced across again at the stranger, who was whistling to himself now, a tune that went nowhere, that had no real melody, but one that nevertheless lodged in his mind and wouldn't get out. Another synapse fired and a small, instinctive chill of fear went up Gwyddion's spine and straight down from there to his bowel, which lurched.

'Why does my head hurt?' he asked the jogger.

Pan looked up at him and stopped whistling. 'It may have been when I hit you,' he said. Then, 'Or it might have been when I pulled you down.'

'Pulled me down?'

'Yes. You were flying. I wanted to talk to you, so I pulled you down.'

'I never fly that low,' Gwyddion pulled his robe tighter about him and looked hurt. 'Two hundred feet or so, that's usually my limit, unless I'm landing.'

'I do not know how high two hundred feet is,' said the god. 'But you were certainly high.'

'Well . . . well . . .' The first of the screams snuck past Shock and Gwyddion bit his knuckles to try and stop it.

'Ah, Druid. You seem to be remembering things.'

'I was flying. I was in a hurry. I had been home to pick up a few things. I was . . . flying . . .'

He had been flying. His cares, if not exactly gone, were at least in a part of his mind where they wouldn't worry him. The wind was clean in his face, his hair was streaming, and every cell felt alive with the electricity, the excitement of what was to come. He felt ready for anything.

He had managed to shake off the owl, which had accompanied him all the way home. In fact, there seemed to be a lot more birds suddenly, flocks of geese, whole, sky-darkening flights of geese, whirling and honking in the cool air. There had been swirls of swallows, darting this way and that, full of the pleasure of flight, of being alive and airborne on such a day. A line of stately heron had made him laugh as they flew by, heads still, bodies moving up and down in time with their slow wing beats. The budgies had been a bit of a surprise. But at least they had prepared him for the flock of parrots which had suddenly enveloped him, disappearing suddenly in a flurry of scarlet and blue feathers.

So, there he was, a Druid with a mission, heading back to the glade and the rest of the Faerie, Seelie and Unseelie, plans spinning in his mind, the song of Taliesin in his head, when a hand had grabbed his ankle and pulled him, pulled him with immense strength down to earth. He had struggled and, for his pains, a fist had caught him a smart one on the jaw and all was quiet, and dark and cool, as he spiralled down into blessed Unconsciousness, into the kind arms of Shock.

Pan had not been having a very good time. Wherever and, he had just come to suspect, whenever, this was, it was certainly no Fun. There was a horrible smell in the air, that metallic twang that made his teeth grit and his skin feel dirty. People wearing funny clothes and rushing about in boxes had stared at him and women had made some gestures that he thought unbecoming to their sex. What had the world come to, when the fish bit back. He loved the chase, and the role of prey did not suit him.

He had caught a slight whiff of Faerie on the wind, low,

under the stink of Mortals and what they had done. He had to keep stopping and finding the trail again and his progress was slow indeed. When, suddenly, something had caught his eye, way overhead, above the flocks of birds he had conjured up to begin the restocking of the denuded skies. He peered closer. A Druid! Druids knew everything, or so they always claimed. And a Druid was close at the top of his memories, memories of his last hours before he had slept and so, it followed, a Druid was the man to ask, just the chap to answer his many questions.

In a flash, quite literally and smelling liberally of sulphur, grapes and musk, Pan was as high as the Druid's flight path. Like elastic stretched to its limit, he was back on the ground in less time than anyone or thing could count, but this time, with a handful of annoyed Druid. A smack in the mouth had sorted his problem in the short term and now the Lord of Misrule, as old as the hills – in fact, older than some – could wait until the memory returned to Gwyddion's addled brain.

🕸🕸🕸🕸

'I was . . . flying.'

Pan's temper was short. He looked up at the Druid. 'Can we just say we both know that,' he said, tersely. 'You were flying. I pulled you down. I hit you. You woke up.'

'Yes.' Another scream was trying to get past Gwyddion's gritted teeth.

"Now, I need a few answers. Only . . .' the god knit his lovely brow, 'I'm not sure I know the questions. I've been . . . asleep, I think. I don't know how long for. I don't know where. I don't know why.'

Gwyddion risked a cynical chuckle. 'Don't know why?'

Pan didn't do cynicism. In fact, when he had last walked the earth, it hadn't been invented. A few of the smarter Mortals were just coming up with some light irony, but he had never really got it. In line with most Faerie, since he preferred a good old prat fall to any amount of smart talking. So he just said, "No.'

'Ah.' Gwyddion didn't really feel it was his place to fill the god in. Oberon would be the one to do that. He was, after all, there for most of it. Or Puck. Benedict had had most of the complaints – he had looked, even then, like a Faerie who could make things happen. Gwyddion had only come in at the end. And then, really, only to help Taliesin do his stuff. He wished he hadn't built up his part, back there on Glastonbury Tor. If he had kept his mouth shut, he wouldn't be in this fix now. He stifled a self-pitying whimper.

Pan gave him a shove. 'I said I didn't know. Don't just sit there, Druid. Tell me what I want to know.' He looked cunning. 'I know you were in a hurry to get somewhere. Well, if you want to be on your way, tell me what I want to know.

Chapter Twenty Nine

The small Yarthkin child stood in the hall, thumb in mouth, staring up at its father. Yarthkin Snr, or Kevin, as he was known down the Dog and Duck since the Return, put a finger to his lips and silently shushed the infant brownie. A brownie is an irritating creature by nature, once reviled by farmers' wives as they nevertheless fed it bread and milk to keep it sweet. Kevin was about to learn a quick lesson on the subject of nature versus nurture.

"Where're y'going, Dad?' the preternaturally plain child slobbered, round its thumb but nonetheless piercingly.

Frantic quietening gestures from its father went unheeded.

'Why're y'putting yer coat on, Dad?'

Mrs Yarthkin, Joyce to her friends, appeared in the kitchen doorway, drying a plate with a cloth decorated, for reasons beyond Kevin's ken, with a picture of Windsor Castle, from which beauty spot it was, apparently, a Present.

'Yes, Kevin,' she said, icily. "Where are you going? Why are you putting your coat on?'

Kevin looked at his only child with something akin to hatred. No, actually, it was hatred. Why, for example, did the child have ginger hair? Not from his side of the family, he was certain. The child leant over and without preamble wiped his nose on Kevin's sleeve.

'Yeurghhh.' He pulled away and only just stopped himself from clipping the horrible little sod round the ear, a large enough target, even a parent had to agree.

'Well?' Joyce was hefting the plate thoughtfully.

'I . . . er . . . got a job on?'

'Bricklaying? At this time of night?'

'It's urgent.'

'Urgent bricklaying?'

'Ummm . . .'

'It was her, wasn't it?'

Kevin attempted innocence. He had the wrong kind of face for anything but low cunning, so it wasn't entirely successful.

'Her?'

'Yes, her. Leanne.'

'Of course not,' said Kevin's voice, but his face said, 'Yes, dear, you've got me there. It was Leanne.'

'I thought so. What does she want this time?'

'Just a little job, that's all. She's lost a Druid.'

'Lost a Druid?'' Joyce was incredulous. 'What a weak story. Next time, you worthless brownie, just make up a decent lie. I'm not stupid, you know.'

Kevin managed to keep his face straight.

'You know I'm going out tonight.'

'Are you?'

'Girls' night out. You knew that. You've got to watch Kevin Jnr.'

Kevin had had enough. He drew himself up. "Now, listen here, Joyce. This is important, Leanne says. I need to find this Druid she's lost. Then I'll come back and watch little Kevin.' He looked down at the child with loathing, and it kicked him painfully on the ankle.

'No, you won't,' said his wife. 'You will take your coat off and watch him, starting now. I'm going out.' She started to untie her apron.

'I have to go. Leanne says . . .'

The unhappy domestic scene gave way to bluebirds, whistling an annoying tune which went into Kevin's brain and lodged there. When the bluebirds got tired of singing, he started to take notice of his surroundings which were, starting with the nearest, a rather gritty carpet, some broken pieces of plate and the appallingly smelly trainers of his child, the snot-bedecked Kevin Jnr.

Kevin Yarthkin closed his eyes and went back to sleep.

Oh, bugger, was his last conscious thought for quite a while.

The motley swarm of faeries and elves spiralled up into the sky and were lost in the encompassing light of the setting sun. They squiggled about for a bit until one faerie, a little more decisive than the others, the daffodil faerie, held up her hand and brought the little crew to a halt.

After a brief pause for them to recover themselves, having cannoned randomly off each other for a while, she said, 'Does anyone have any idea where we are going?'

'We're looking for that Druid,' said the Forgetmenot faerie.

'Well done,' said an elf, nastily. 'I think what Daff means is, where are we going?'

'That's right.'

The forgetmenot faerie's lip trembled. 'I don't know. Puck didn't say.'

The lily of the valley faerie swirled around the group in a cloud of sweet perfume. 'Don't be upset,' she said kindly. 'We're not getting at you. I must admit, I feel a bit confused. We've got to find this Druid, but how? He doesn't smell very much . . .'

'You haven't been downwind of him, obviously,' grumbled an elf.

'Yes, exactly,' chimed in the bluebell faerie. 'And it's not as if his petals are particularly showy.'

'Huh,' sulked the chickweed faerie. 'What's that got to do with it?'

'Girls, girls, please,' the daffodil faerie tried to restore peace. 'We need to have a think. He had gone home, I gathered from what folk were saying. As a daffodil, I must say I always had a bit of a soft spot for the great untidy thing.'

'You're right,' said an elf, brighter and not so tetchy as the rest. 'We need to fly into the sun, and we might meet him. We couldn't miss him. He's so much bigger than we are.'

The daffodil faerie looked impressed. 'Good idea,' she said. 'Let's fan out, then we stand a better chance.'

Twittering with excitement, the little creatures strung themselves out in a long chain across the sky. They set off, into the lowering sun as it stained the horizon a beautiful mauve and cream to rival the sweetpea faerie's dress. The daffodil faerie had the right idea. But when a crowd of very tiny things spread out over a long distance, the gaps between would accommodate an elephant. Or, in this precise instance, a Druid and the great god Pan, hunkered down in their bus shelter, having their little chat.

Chapter Thirty

The lights were dim, except for one spotlight, shining on an empty stage. Off to stage left, someone was rummaging through a coil of leads, mixed up beyond the wildest dreams of any Italian chef.

'Who put these away last time?' a gravelly voice asked.

A voice from the shadow, beyond the spotlight's crisp circle replied, 'Well, that would have been you, I imagine.' The voice was soft and curled round the ankles of the listener like mist on an Autumn day. It carried just a hint of an American accent, a hint so small that it left room for what it overlay. That accent, that base note, was unidentifiable in its own right. But the voice, once heard, was always remembered. It had platinum discs to prove it.

The mess of leads were thrown down and the roadie came into the spotlight, shielding his eyes from the glare. Had James had an ugly brother, then this surely was he. His shoulders were muscled from long years of carrying guitar amps, leads bags, drum kits, mike stands, drunken rhythm sections and worn out groupies; on one memorable occasion after the famous Carnegie Hall gig back in . . . ooh, way back when . . . all at once.

The gravel was being scraped from somewhere deep inside the creature's pelt-covered body. Like all roadies, he had tattoos and piercings, but where they were only he knew. 'I don't leave my stuff like this. And anyway . . .'

'Yes?' sang the voice.

The gravel died away to the soft scrunch of retreating, tip-toeing slippered feet.

'Didn't catch that.'

'I said,' the roadie stood as straight as he ever did, hands on hips, facing the softly plangent dark, 'I said, some of them don't seem to be leads any more.'

There was a soft thud, as the voice and its body jumped down from the stool. The American accent was almost gone and another accent, was it Norwegian, Albanian may be, came more to the fore.

'What are they?' came in a whisper.

'Er . . . they seem to be pythons. Well, the speaker leads are pythons. The mike leads are just addery sort of things, but very dozy. One bit me, though.'

'Are you all right?'

'Yeah. I just bit it back. But it's a bit . . . weird, isn't it?' The question was more than a request for information. It said; tell me it's just the air in here. Tell me it's the booze. Tell me the leads aren't snakes. Tell me he's not awake.

The voice walked into the light. It was housed for now in a pretty package that made the fans go wild. The curly hair, the big brown eyes, the angel's mouth outlined with a little beard fit perfectly with the lyric rhythms of the songs it sang. The guitar was slung across his back in a casual way that would usually make the roadie wince. The singer bowed his head, then stared up, straight into the spotlight.

'So it's true, then. He's awake.'

The roadie cringed as though hit with a whip. Race memory goes deep – it had been years since anyone had flogged him, even if he was a roadie. He lifted his head and howled, a primeval howl that made bowels turn to water, legs ache to run away.

The singer put a gentle hand on the creature's shoulder. He bent down to whisper in its ear. 'It will be all right,' he crooned. 'He can't hurt you. He's got to find you first.'

The bogle clutched his master's legs. 'Don't let him get me,' he whimpered. 'I can't stand all that racing through the forests and such. I can't stand the hunting. The crunching.

The blood.' He preferred Macdonalds now, whatever anyone said.

'Ssshhh,' his master's hand was patting on automatic now, as his mind spun. 'Gwyddion is bound to be on it. I know he's around. I've seen him on TV.'

'Yes,' whined the bogle, looking up and wiping his eyes with a paw, bedecked with rings. 'And he's seen you, I expect. Who hasn't? But he doesn't seem to have recognized you, does he? He hasn't come to you for help, has he? I don't think anyone's doing anything! We're all doomed.'

The singer sighed and clipped the thing a sharp one over the ear. 'Stop that!'

The bogle whimpered a bit more.

The singer, who was not unkind, raised his hand again, but with no intention of using it. 'Oh, come on. Dry your tears. What would the lads say if they saw you crying? You'd never hear the end of it. Eh?'

The bogle sniffed once more and straightened up. 'OK.'

'Right.' He sighed. 'Look, I know where they are . . .'

'They?'

'Titania, Puck and the rest. I'll go and see what's going down.'

The roadie plucked at the singer's shirt. 'You'd do that for me?'

The singer looked at the paw shredding his Tommy Hilfiger. The bogle let go slowly, mesmerised by those extraordinary eyes.

'Sorry.' The gravel was just a tiny creak, like a mouse's front door closing carefully.

'That's OK. Don't do it again. And, no, it's not for you. Not just for you, anyway. I'll have a look, see if they need any help. If not, I'll be straight back.'

The roadie's profession tapped him on the shoulder just in time. 'You'll be back for the gig?'

'What time're we on?'

'Ten.'

'Hmmm. Doubt it. I'll try. If not . . . let the support play our slot. Pay the lads anyway and do a deal with the management. Usual thing.'

The bogle thought for a minute. Pan on the one hand, management and two disgruntled bands plus several thousand disappointed fans on the other. No contest. 'OK.'

'Good lad.' The singer ruffled his hair, and the bogle shrugged him off.

'Watch the extensions,' he said. 'They cost a packet.'

The singer chuckled, deep in his throat, a sound which, properly recorded and mastered, could have earned him another platinum disc, easy. 'That's my boy,' he said. 'I'll be back soon.' He walked out of the spotlight and the rush of wind through the theatre was all that marked his going.

As the singer passed overhead, almost invisible, as he preferred to be offstage, Mortals below heard the sound and looked up. Those with keen vision saw a shimmer in the air, a heat haze over the newly emerging stars. The sound they heard was not a tune, not music at all. It was just the song the stars should sing, if it were possible to hear them hum. The singer shook out his chestnut curls and dived as he saw the clearing below.

'He's here!' said Leanne, stepping forward. 'Where have you . . . You're not Gwyddion.'

'Too true,' the singer said. 'I'm not. Have you lost him, then?'

'Y . . .' but Puck's hand was over her mouth.

'Of course not,' he said quickly. Who knew what shape the god would take, although he suspected it wouldn't be anything as soft and gentle looking as this. 'We were expecting him, that's all. We haven't lost him, as such.'

Titania elbowed her way forward. She was fed up and worried. The Druid hadn't been up to the job. Her flower faeries and half the elves seemed to have gone missing, althhough behind her back they were returning one by one, feeling rather silly. Whoever this was, it wasn't Pan. He didn't smell right, he didn't behave right. Plus, the song he seemed to be singing under his breath, even as he smiled a crooked smile didn't tickle your hindbrain like Pan's tunes did. She held out a languid hand.

'Hello,' she purred. 'I am Titania. Queen of Faerie.'

'Indeed, Mistress,' said the singer. 'You can call me Al.'

Chapter Thirty One

The whole of available Faerie gathered round. Usually, strangers found this rather disconcerting, but this one seemed to have no trouble. In fact, his hand made a gesture with which Oberon at least was very familiar, creeping towards a non-existent breast pocket, as if reaching for an autograph-ready pen. Benedict was watching him from the edge of the crowd, standing with Annis, therefore standing with no jostling. It had its compensations.

A sharp elbow in the hip made him look down.

'Ye're right,' she said, with a cough and a spit. 'You have seen him somewhere before.'

'I think I must have seen him on TV,' Benedict said, thoughtfully. 'Or he may have a website.'

Annis chuckled. 'You were never good with people, lad, were ye?' she said. 'Look again.'

Benedict narrowed his eyes, trying to make out details in the soft glow given off by Titania, Oberon and their crew, plus a little fitful illumination by some off-season glow worms.

'It's no good,' he said, exasperated. 'This faerie light is no good for my eyes.'

'Ach,' said Annis, and spat again. She delved into her noisome bag and threw an indescribable bundle to the floor. In a sulphurous flash, the scene was lit with an unforgiving glare, accompanied by the smell as of a thousand stables burning slow and acrid. Leanne hardly looked round. The others all winced and covered their eyes. Only the singer looked in her direction. He ambled over, in three four time.

'Annis,' he said, keeping his distance. He had to think of his throat.

'Tha's me,' she muttered. 'It's been a while.'

'Weren't you at my Gig in the Park last year?' he asked.

'Might have been.'

'It's just that there was a little corner at the back, where there weren't so many people. I hoped it was you.' He smiled and Benedict was amazed to see the foul old hag blush. At least, the dirt changed colour.

'Annis?' the Unseelie Lord asked in amazement.

She looked up with one horrid eye. The other, hidden deep in her noisome hair, was watching the singer. 'Well,' she said, and sounded suddenly like every rebellious sixteen-year-old in the world rolled into one. 'I like a little music now and then. It makes the night seem shorter.'

'Always glad to meet a fan,' the singer said, and smiled that smile again. A faint melody filled the air, rolling over the crowd and making them grin at each other. A few of the goblins held hands bashfully, looking at their toes and smirking.

'That's clever,' said Oberon, rather crossly.

'What is?' the singer asked.

'That music playing. Nice touch.'

'Oh, that's not me,' the singer said. 'Or rather, that is me, singing. But I'm not making it happen.'

Everyone looked around and finally tracked it down to Freckles, standing to one side, oblivious, a Walkman strapped to his little chest, earphones buried deep in the green hair springing from his ears. His eyes were closed, and he tried, in vain, to snap a trotter in time. Oberon leaned down and spoke.

'Freckles, old chap.'

Nothing, but a mild nod of the head and a tap of a trotter on the mossy floor.

'Freckles!' A little louder this time.

The singer looked on, ready to intervene if he had to. Dire though he knew the situation was, he hoped he'd still need a fan base when all this was over.

Oberon lifted an earphone free of the little creature's ear. 'Freckles!!' he screamed, his breath wafting the goblin's hair.

'Aaaghhhhhh!' The King suddenly had an armful of trembling goblin. 'What? What? What is it? What?' His poor little eyes swivelled this way and that and his arms were tight round the King's neck.

Titania reached out and patted his back. 'Nothing, dear,' she patronised. 'Just the King, trying to attract your attention.'

Freckles' teeth had reached the chattering stage and he couldn't tell her what he thought of his Lord's methods.

Puck reached down and found the CD case on the floor, where Freckles had been sitting. Realisation dawned and he looked again at the singer. The CD was an old one, and the man in the picture had much longer hair, a long brigand moustache and a military jacket, covered in gold braid. But the face was the same.

'So that's who you are,' he said, almost to himself. Phoebe looked over his shoulder briefly, then was elbowed aside by Mab.

'Oh,' they said in unison.

Louder, Puck said, 'I didn't realise you were one of Us.'

'Didn't you?' said the singer. 'Well, as you can see, I am.'

'If you're one of Us,' said Oberon belligerently, 'Why didn't you help us when we Returned?'

'No need,' the singer laughed, and a new song was born. 'You didn't need me, clearly.' He swept an arm around the glade.

'Who are you, exactly?' Titania asked. She wasn't much of a media Faerie.

'I told you,' the singer said. 'You can call me Al.'

'Al being short for . . .?'

Annis pushed forward. She wanted to hear his voice a bit better. She wanted to find out why he was there. She wanted to stand by him, peeking through the lashes of her good – well, best – eye. She wanted his autograph.

'Everyone knows that,' she said, the perfect fan. 'He is known as The Singer. His friends call him Al. Al, short for Tal. Tal short for Taliesin.'

The singer bowed low. You can take the Druid out of the Minstrel, but you can't take the Minstrel out of the Druid.

'She's quite correct,' he said. 'I have been dead. I have been alive. I am Taliesin. Now, are we ready to rock and roll?'

Titania and Oberon, Benedict and Leanne stood back while the goblins, faeries, dwarves, Mr Dobies, lorialets, a couple of starstruck fausseroles, Mab and Annis gathered round. Pan and the peril he represented were banished for a while, while the singer sang his song.

Oberon was rather annoyed. He remembered now that The Singer had refused to go on his chat show. At least now he knew why.

Titania was charmed. She had always had a bit of a thing for good looking young minstrels, often to their lasting disadvantage.

Benedict was just amazed. He thought he knew Annis but there she was, swaying gently to the music, unspeakable things falling from her rags as she moved. A pigeon, surprised and relieved, shook its head as it landed and tiptoed quietly away.

Leanne was thinking. She was thinking ahead. And, like agents everywhere she was thinking; has he got representation? She reached for her card.

Chapter Thirty-Two

Most Faerie, Unseelie, Tuatha de Danaan, slimy things at the bottom of ponds, birds which flew so high and far they didn't need feet, creatures visible only at the point of sleep, things with phosphorescent wings, things with pointed, rending, tearing teeth – things which grew, walked, ran, swam, crawled – in other words, Life, thought of Pan as ratty and impatient. Uncertain temper and Pan were definitely two concepts difficult to think of apart. And yet he seemed to Gwyddion set to squat there for the duration. He had shrugged off the jogging suit some while before and now he was there, in all his, feral glory, the musky scent obliterating Eau de Bus-shelter – wee with a base note of old chips – with ease. He leaned his elbows on his knees, tracing antic runes on the dusty floor, using lolly kicks, dropped change and apple cores to point up anything which he seemed to consider especially important.

In one respect, this made Gwyddion pleased. It saved him having to make a decision. It put off that evil hour when the god would suddenly grab him and, no malice intended, quietly rend him limb from limb. The song which hung in the air around Goat-foot stuck in the Druid's brain and seemed to push coherent thought ahead of it, keeping it just out of reach. He knew he ought to be able to formulate a plan, one in which he could escape from Pan, get to the others in plenty of time to warn them, plan the spells, dig a hole, a nice deep hole, lure Pan into it, fill it in and get on with his nice life – a nice fat roll-up and a mushroom omelette, just the job – in his peaceful grove. Nice. He smiled to himself, just daydreaming. Shock was still taking care of him, rocking him to sleep.

A cunning eye gleamed through the god's golden russet curls. He kept on humming, kept on doodling. Just another second and he would have that stupid Druid. To outwit a Druid – not something he'd ever tried before, but how hard could it be? He saw his moment. A stupid smile was spreading over Gwyddion's face. Pan shifted slightly, hooves tipped with silver scraping on the concrete, tiny sparks leaping as he lifted each foot a tiny, infinitesimally tiny bit off the floor.

Gwyddion looked down beneath his lashes at the god. His daydream had made him bold and he stretched his arms luxuriantly, as if stretching. But he kept on stretching, arms wider and wider. He glanced down and still the god did nothing.

Pan looked down at his doodle. His song grew louder, like bees in heather, like a cat purring, overlaid with a nightingale warbling, underlaid with grass growing. Muscles flexed in his thighs, making the golden pelt glisten like new pressed olive oil, running down the extended throat of a lovely Phoenician girl as she gave in at last after a laughing chase through the sun-warmed hills. The hooves clicked once, twice.

Gwyddion stretched one more inch, his feet left the ground and he soared through the doorway, heading south.

The hooves clicked once more, and the god was straddling the Druid's back, iron-banded fingers on his shoulders, thighs gripping his sides as if they grew there. He leant forward.

'Just fly, Druid,' he hissed, right inside the terrified Gwyddion's head. 'Fly to where you were going when we . . .' a chuckle filled the echoing, terrified spaces between the Druid's ears, 'met.' Pan read what was functioning of Gwyddion's mind. 'But no heroics. No landing with a scream in the middle of them all. Land a way away. I want to surprise them.'

The only thing Gwyddion was certain of was that Pan was Lord of Misrule, God of Confusion – he wasn't looking forward to a civilised cocktail and a few well-chosen canapés. He remembered wine by the gallon and olives, certainly olives, but by the barrel and without those cunning little red bits in. Olive stones were for spitting at passing Faerie, ten points for a brownie, twenty for an elf. Oberon and Puck had been willing henchmen, up for whatever mischief was going. No wonder they were worried. They'd got soft over the years. There was no way they would stand the pace. While they'd been getting civilization, Pan seemed to have been growing in cunning, under his hill. It would take more than a few sprigs of mistletoe and a well turned stanza to tie him down this time. Gwyddion sighed.

'Why the long face, Druid?' Pan asked, in a friendly manner.

'Oh, just stuff, you know.' Gwyddion was suddenly too tired to dissemble.

'Stuff?'

'End of the world as we know it, that sort of thing. It's bound to make anyone a bit fed up.'

Pan sat up sharply and the Druid, centre of gravity all to pot, turned turtle in the air and they plummeted alarmingly towards the ground. As Gwyddion fought to regain height, Pan flattened himself along his back.

'Please, Lord, don't do that again.'

'I'd be much happier travelling on the ground, to be frank. I used to have a chariot, you know, drawn by centaurs.'

'I remember it, Lord.'

The god leered. 'Lady centaurs.'

'That's why I remember it.'

Pan chuckled, then his brow darkened. 'Happy days, eh? But, sorry,' he tasted the word as if he had never used it before, which was probably the case. 'Sorry. You were saying?'

A polite Pan was scaring Gwyddion more than a little, but he could see he was just trying to make him feel at ease. He swallowed hard. 'The end of the world as we know it.'

'Why? What's happening?'

The Druid lurched in the air. 'Well, you are.'

'Me?' Pan sounded genuinely hurt and surprised. 'What have I done then?'

'It's hard to explain. Especially twisting round like this.'

'Land, then. But only for a while. Don't think this changes

anything. But I would dearly love to hear what's going on. You talk about the end of your world. Perhaps I can help you understand that idea better.'

'How so, Lord?'

'Because,' said Pan, jumping down from Gwyddion's back as he landed on a river bank, 'because I think mine has ended.' A golden tear ran down his perfect cheek. 'And, take it from me, Druid. It's not nice. It's not nice at all.'

Very gently, it began to rain.

Chapter Thirty Three

Gwyddion looked on in amazement as the god squatted on his haunches, face turned to the darkened sky. The starlight seemed brighter when he was out in it and it twinkled now off the slick surface of his rain and tear-damp cheeks. He suddenly gave a blokeish sniff and turned to the Druid with a smile, that was only a little forced.

The rain stopped, with as little fuss as it had begun.

'Are you surprised, Druid?' Pan asked.

Gwyddion nodded. The god's sadness had filled the air and the lump in his throat stopped toy thought of speaking.

'I'm right, in my remembering, am I? You were there?'

'There, Lord?'

'There, when they tied me down, piled earth over my head.' He paused, head back, searching his memory. 'I heard singing.'

Gwyddion hung his head. Yes, he had been there. He even used a spade, though a golden sickle was more his usual line in gardening implements. 'Yes,' he whispered. 'I was there, yes.'

'Hmm.' Pan hung his head and the muscles of his great neck rippled.

The Druid flinched, out of habit long-forgotten, soon remembered.

'And him, I suppose?'

'Oberon?'

Pan laughed. 'I know he was there. He never left my side. No, him. The Singer.'

'Yes,' said Gwyddion, always glad to pass the buck. 'Taliesin was there. He wrote the song that bound you.'

'Yes, the Song to my Tune. We duetted well, the shape-shifter and I, back in the old days' He pulled his pipe from . . . well, Gwyddion had to assume it was some sort of pocket. He blew, an exhalation of sweet breath that almost made the sluggish river dance and sparkle, as if it ran over mossy stones, high up in a cool mountain, on the edge of the treeline. He blew again. The stars seemed to wheel. The trees on the bank rustled their leaves, but quietly, so they could hear the music. The grass was alive with small things, come to listen. He blew again.

In the glade, Taliesin raised his head from his guitar. Sudden-ly, his strings seemed slack and out of tune. He looked around and saw that he was the only one who could hear that note, plaintive, clear, yet far away. He bent to the strings again.

'I am Taliesin,' he sang.
'I sing perfect metre,
Which will last till the end of the world.
My patron is Elphin.'

Pan's pipe music, though just notes – he had never been a lyrics man – nonetheless put words into Gwyddion's head, right behind his eyes.

'I know why there is an echo in a hollow,
Why silver gleams; why breath is black,
Why a woman is affectionate.'

189

'Why milk is white,' sang the Singer, 'why holly is green;
Why a kid is bearded; why the cow-parsley is hollow.'
He stood up now, hitching his guitar strap up for comfort.
He raised one foot and a goblin back was there for it to lean
on. The magic grew.

'Why brine is salt,' muttered the pipe. 'Why ale is bitter.'
Gwyddion felt the tastes on his tongue, on the tip and
round the edge. His lips were parched and as he licked them,
he felt the froth from a pint of Extremely Peculiar burst in
millions of bubbles in his moustache.

'Why the linnet is green,' Taliesin sang. 'And berries are red.'
He turned to the north west, still singing, fingers busy on
their own account among the strings.
'Why a cuckoo complains, why it sings.
I know where the cuckoos of summer go in
winter.'

Pan muttered under his breath, 'You do, do you?' and,
stretching up as tall as the trees, he blew down his pipe in
reply.
'I know what beasts there are at the bottom
of the sea;
How many spears in battle.'

'How many drops in a shower,' pianissimo, pianissimo.
'Why fish have scales, why a blackbird has
yellow feet.
I have been a blue salmon,' sang the Singer,
loud and

clear, making the listeners jump.

'A dog, a stag, a roebuck on the mountain.'

'A stock, a spade, an axe in the hand,' sang Taliesin. He knew when he had last had a spade in his hand, and Pan had been there too.

The pipe shrilled until Gwyddion's head swam and he curled up on the ground, fists pushed against his ears.

'I have been a stallion, a bull, a buck,' the pipe was a bassoon, a tuba, the sound of water deep, deep underground.

'A grain,' crooned Taliesin, 'a grain which grew on a hill.
I was reaped and placed in an oven.
I fell to the ground when I was being roasted
And a hen swallowed me.
For nine nights I was in her crop.
I have been dead.
I have been alive.'
The song stopped for one heartbeat, two, three, four. The hand swung and the strings echoed.
'I am Taliesin.'

The crowd were silent. Their hands were poised to clap, but somehow no one could bear to break the silence which took the place of the Singer's voice.

Then, in that silence, they heard a far-off sound. Not pipe now, but a roar like a bull.

'So you may be, Druid.' The voice was near as their skin, far off as the moon. It made even Faerie skin crawl. 'So you may well be. But I am Pan! And I'm on my way.'

Chapter Thirty Four

Gwyddion slowly uncurled. He peeped out from under his tousled hair and saw that Pan was back to his normal size, or at least the size Gwyddion had become used to. He was pacing up and down on the riverbank, hands behind his back, hooves Humping silently on the grass, muttering to himself. The Druid risked a small cough.

Pan's great head swung round. 'Do you have an ague of some sort, Druid?' he asked.

Gwyddion struggled to his feet, tangled momentarily in his robes. After a couple of false starts, he felt ready to dust himself down and speak to the Lord of Misrule, God of Confusion.

'I am fine, Lord, thank you for asking,' he ingratiated. 'But, will you forgive me if I ask a question?'

'Yes.'

'Thank you. I thought you were . . .'

'Another question?'

'Pardon?'

'And another. I only forgave you for the one.'

'Yes, I know. But I haven't asked you anything yet.'

'Yes, you have. You asked if I would forgive you if you asked a question. And I said yes. So that was a question and I have forgiven you. Do you want to ask another?'

'Another what?'

'Ah, I see you do. Well, that one was all right as well.'

Gwyddion shook his head. God of Confusion, and well named, he thought. He tried again. 'I haven't asked a question that is important yet and don't interrupt me please Lord because I can't be the only one who knows that time is short and I can't say that I know what was going on just then because my ears still hurt but what I think happened is that you were duetting again with the Singer and now they know you're on your way and what happened to a quiet creeping up?' The Druid gasped in air with a rasping noise.

Pan looked at him curiously. 'Should you be blue?' he asked. 'I thought it was just the Britons, Boudicca, Cunobelinus, that crowd, that painted themselves blue.'

Gwyddion patted his own chest and held up a finger. 'Just a bit breathless, Lord,' he said, the pink returning to his lips. 'But I had to get out my question so I could know the answer.'

Pan looked thoughtful, an unusual expression for him, but he was on a steep learning curve these days.

'Lord?'

'Yes,' said Pan, ruefully, trying for cute and almost succeeding. 'But,' he brightened up, 'they don't know when I'll be there. They don't know what I'll be looking like. So we could still creep up.' He smiled triumphantly. They had a Plan.

'Yes,' Gwyddion sounded doubtful. 'But won't they be expecting the unexpected?'

'Is Oberon their king?'

'Yes.'

'Well, not too bright as I recall.'

'Puck's bright.'

'True.'

'Benedict's bright?'

'Who?'

'Lord of Unseelie?'

'Oh, him. Yes, bright, I'll grant you that. So sharp he'll cut himself one day, that one.'

'Titania's bright.'

'Who's that?'

'Oberon's Queen. She brought us Back.'

'From where?'

Gwyddion groaned. He looked at the god, standing there on the edge of the river, kingcups, bulrushes, watercress making a footstool, pussy willow and catkins his crown. 'Shall we sit?' he said, suiting the action to the words. He patted the grass at his side. 'How far back do you want to go?'

The god stepped out of the reeds and, folding his goat-legs elegantly to one side, said, 'How about from when you shovelled the earth over me, Druid. With particular emphasis on why you lot let the Mortals get so many, let the water get so dirty, let the air smell so foul, let my creatures get so few. Hmmm?'

'Are you sitting comfortably?' asked the Druid.

'Not really.' Pan reached round behind him and pulled out his pipes, which had been digging into his leg. He wriggled into position again. 'Yes, that's better.' Then he frowned. 'Got any wine?'

'No. Sorry.' Gwyddion reached under his robe. 'I've got this can of Coke.'

Pan wrinkled his nose. 'I don't think I'd like it.'

'It's Diet.'

'No.'

'It's Lemon.'

'Did I say no?'

'Sorry.'

'Got any cake?'

'No.'

'Ale?'

'No.'

'Maidens?'

'No. Look, can we get on with this. We've got a lot of years to cover.'

Pan looked mutinous. He clicked his fingers. A white cloth, spread with roast meats, fruit, wine, ale, cake, loaves and olives glistening with oil appeared on the starlit grass. Another click and a beautiful girl sat opposite them, poised to serve the food.

'That's better.'

'Comfy now?'

The god gave a happy wriggle and took a huge bite of cake and a huge handful of giggling maiden. 'Yes,' he said, spraying crumbs.

'Good. Then we'll begin.'

Chapter Thirty Five

The Singer sat on the bank outside Titania's bower. He avoided, quite naturally, the shrivelled bit which carried the shape of Annis. Titania, Oberon and the others gathered round. James had conjured up a buffet table from somewhere and was dispensing drinks, a cloth over his arm. Even Benedict was surprised at this development. But James, like Annis, was starstruck. Members of his family, years ago, had run off to join the circus, and no wonder. Some of them had, after all, two or even sometimes more heads. They were in demand. He kept presenting his good side, as he rather poignantly considered it, to Taliesin, and kept his voice low and melodious. The entire effect was rather startling and he didn't have too many customers. The goblins were there of course; it would take more than a mad-looking bogle leaving hairs in the glasses to put them off their drink.

'So,' the Singer slapped his knees. He communicated best through song and starting this conversation was hard. 'You're back, then.'

'Yes,' snapped Benedict. 'With no thanks to you.'

Titania shushed him. 'It is true, dear . . . can I really call you Al?'

He nodded.

'Well, Al, it is true we could have done with it at the time, but we managed, didn't we?' She favoured everyone with a smile, much copied since the Return by Oscar-nominated starlets, but never equalled. 'And you're here now.'

Despite being a bit of a Druid-of-the-world, Taliesin felt himself growing rather hot. He was definitely out of practice with Faerie women, though he had had his moments. He smiled back at her.

There was a crash. Oberon was out of his tree again. He stood up, shimmering slightly in the firefly dark.

'Now we've all made friends,' he said, acidly, 'do you think we could get on with the plans. You remember?' He looked wound the group. 'Plans? Stopping Pan? Making everything how It was before. Not Before, I don't mean. Before. Ordinary before. The before that came after Before, but before now. Last week, or whenever.' He looked from face to face, willing them to understand.

Titania skimmed over to him and pulled him into the group, whispering in his ear. He was wringing his hands, which didn't look terribly kingly. She didn't want the more impressionable Faeries to see. 'Hush, Lord,' she said, in that soothing voice reserved by the condescender for use on the condescendee.

'Don't hush me.' He shook off her hand. 'Don't hush me. It's all right for you. You weren't his right-hand man. You didn't . . . do the stuff I did with him. You've never really seen what he's like when he wants something. I can feel him calling me.'

'That's a good trick,' muttered Tiny to Freckles, who laughed so that champagne came out of his nose.

Without looking round, Oberon flicked his hair and a toadstool, a vivid green and a bit slimy suddenly took Tiny's place in the glade. A champagne flute clattered to the ground and broke on the second bounce.

Freckles looked round frantically, looking for the trick.

'Tine?' he squeaked, swivelling his whole body, since his neck wasn't really made for craning. 'Tine? Where are you?' He glared up at Oberon, who took no notice. Freckles, stiff legged with anger, marched up to his king. 'I suppose you fink vat's funny, dontcha?' he asked.

'I suppose you think that's fanny *what*?' Oberon asked, bending at the waist so he was nose to noisome nose with

Freckles.

'I suppose you fink vat's funny . . . you cruel bastard,' cried Freckles. 'He was my friend. He was *Tine*! I fought you loved us.'

Oberon glared down, his beautiful eyes sliding from side to side under Freckles' piggy glare. Everyone and thing held their breath. The Oberon suddenly swept Freckles up in his arms, wiping his tears on the creature's jerkin. 'I do love you!' He squeezed him to his chest, hiding every part of the goblin in his velvet and leather clad arms, except the little kicking legs. The kicking grew weaker and stopped.

Puck decided it was time to step in.

'Sire?'

Oberon continued to hug the goblin to his chest.

'Sire? Could you let go? I don't think he can breathe?'

'Eh?' Oberon sniffed and looked up.

Puck gestured to the clutched goblin and Oberon released his arms hurriedly. Freckles fell to the ground, where the landing knocked some air into his lungs. He hugged Oberon's ankles in relief.

'Fank you, Sire,' he managed to husk.

'Tiny?' Puck asked his king, pointing to the toadstool.

Oberon clicked his fingers and Tiny stood there, a bit bewildered and wondering where his champagne had gone. Briefly, he considered giving up drink. Freckles rushed over and hugged him hard. There's nothing like seeing your best friend turned into a green toadstool for making you realise how much you love him.

Oberon sat down with Taliesin on the bank. He was quivering. 'You see,' he said quietly. 'I'm not myself. That wasn't high spirits. That wasn't playing poker when the queen's not looking.' Titania raised an ironic eyebrow. 'That was mischief, cruel mischief and I did it with no thought to the consequences. That's what Pan is doing to me. You all heard him. He's on his way.' He bowed his head onto his knees.

Puck spoke for everyone. 'We must get the spell ready,' he said.

'Spell?' Taliesin asked.

'We've been planning a spell,' Mab said. Well, she was

supposed to be co-ordinator. It was time they let her get a bit of co-ordinating done.

Taliesin hutched up a bit and patted the grass next to him. Blushing, she sat down.

'Everyone has something to be in charge of,' she said. 'Puck is animal, Oberon is vegetable, Leanne is mineral. Benedict is water, Gwyddion is earth, Phoebe is air.'

The Singer waggled his fingers in a friendly way as each name was mentioned. Then he counted on his fingers, long and (lender, at home on any instrument, but not So good with figures. 'Isn't there one missing?'

'Yes,' Mab said. 'Fire is missing. Apparently, Moira, who was in charge of fire the first time, didn't do a very good job, so Annis says.'

'And Annis should know.' The Singer winked at the hag, who looked away. 'But we need fire now, I should have thought. Otherwise there'll just be a gap. I can just imagine the binding song. It won't scan as it is; Come on all you elements; Animal, come on; Vegetable, yeah; Mineral, o-ooh. Earth, come on now; Water, do your thing; Air, blow man blow; da da da da da da da da da da da. It will sound stupid.'

Oberon did a 'so what' face.

'But, more importantly,' Taliesin said, 'It won't work.'

Leanne stood up. 'James,' she said, in the kind of voice that automatically adds 'you're in trouble' to a name.

James polished a glass, round and round, round and round, nails squealing against the rim. He held it up to the dark sky and H firefly obligingly flew inside, to help him look for streaks. He shook the insect out, huffed on the glass and kept on polishing, looking everywhere but at Leanne.

'James!' This time, the voice didn't even bother with the bogle's ears. It went straight to the nerve endings in his spine and there was no gainsaying then.

'Yes?'

'Did I ask you to sort out fire?'

The bogle tried wide-eyed innocence. It didn't work. 'I don't think so.'

'I most certainly did.'

'Well, if you say so.' James tried a matey wink at a nearby

anything, but he seemed to be standing in the middle of a very empty space.

'I say so. Did you do it?'

Now the bogle tried abject. This worked better, as he spent so much more time on the practice. 'I didn't know what you wanted me to do,' he whined. 'You didn't say what to do.'

'Did you think to ask?'

'You weren't here, Mistress.'

'Isp? Phone?'

An ingratiating smile.

'James? Do you remember the name of the cleaner at Benedict's penthouse?'

'No.'

Leanne sighed and turned to Oberon. 'You live there now. Do you remember her name?'

'Er . . .' Oberon wrinkled his lovely brow. He remembered a small creature, she was flickering in the comer of his mind.

'Oh, please!' Leanne couldn't believe them. Different species, but oh, so alike. 'Sally.'

'No, that's not it.'

'I'm not asking. I'm telling. Sally.'

'If you say so.'

'I do. Any idea what her other name is? Benedict?'

'Er . . . Smith?'

'No.'

'Jones.'

"No. She's not a Mortal, you dolts. She's a fire sprite. Sally Mander. Get it?'

'Oh,' said Oberon. 'You should have said. Er . . . I don't get it.'

Titania said, 'I think the young lady in question is a salamander, dear. A fire starter. Am I right, Leanne?'

'Finally! Yes, she's a salamander. Go fetch, James, there's a good bogle.' Leanne sat down and buried her face in her arms. They heard her mutter 'Men!' but no one was quite sure whether it was just exasperation or whether she wanted a takeaway.

Chapter Thirty Six

'And so,' Gwyddion said, leaning back and slapping his knees, 'that's more or less what's been happening.'

Pan was lying back on the grass, his pipe forgotten on his chest, one leg cocked over the other, silver hoof tapping the empty air in time to the tune only he could hear. After what seemed an age, long enough for glaciers to slide across a continent, calve and slip lethally into an icy sea, long enough for men to leave the trees and walk upright, long enough to get to the front of a queue in the post office, he opened his mouth to speak. Gwyddion leaned forward to hear the judgement of the great god Pan.

'Coo.'

'That's it?'

'It's a lot to take in.'

'Well, yes. But not all of it is that important, not to you. I just told it all for the sake of completeness. I may have got a few things in the wrong order.'

'Yes, I thought you might have done. I'm not a numbers deity, as you probably know, but I was expecting the mortal kings to come in the order I, II, III, like that.'

Gwyddion flapped a dismissive hand. 'Like I said. Just for completeness, really.'

The god heaved a sigh. 'It all seems to have happened so fast.'

'You should have been there, Lord. Some bits were quite slow. George III for instance. I thought he'd never go.'

'I mean, all this . . . what did you call it?'

'Err . . .?'

'This. This smelly air. No birds to speak of.'

'Pollution.'

'That's the word. When did it start?'

'Extinction isn't all because of pollution. Do you remember the bit about the dodo?'

'I may have dropped off. Remind me. I was always rather fond of dodos. Friendly little chaps, on the whole.'

'Exactly. So friendly, they would walk up to the sailors who bashed their heads in.'

'Why?'

'For food? For fun?'

'That's not Fun.'

"No. Then the passenger pigeon. They were wiped out in less than a generation, by hunters. The last one died all by itself in a zoo.'

'I know how it feels.'

'Lord?'

'Well,' Pan waved his arm expansively and somehow managed to encompass the world, not just the tiny bit they were in. 'Well, I'm archaic, aren't I? Forgotten. They managed very well without me.'

Gwyddion felt a surge of pity and quelled it. He didn't feel it was quite the thing, somehow, to feel sorry for this marvellous being, who could change seasons when he turned in his sleep, who could be tall as the sky or as small as a snail on the thorn. And yet, because he was so marvellous and beautiful, so full of Life, somehow his loneliness was hard to bear, even as an onlooker.

'We all missed you, Lord. Whenever the first crocus popped out, or a cuckoo sang, I always thought of you.'

The god turned his head and lit up the dawn with his smile. 'Did you really, Druid?'

'Yes.' That was the truth. It was what he thought that he had best not share.

'Tell me again about the poets.'

'Poets have never forgotten you.'

'Really? Tell me a poem about me.'

'Umm, I can't remember one at the moment, I'm afraid.' Like all brains terrified on a primeval level, only one thought was in Gwyddion's head. Robert Browning – and what a bore he was, with his fluffy wife and fluffy dog – had written 'The Dead Pan', and that was all he could remember. He fought the thought.

'All right, Druid. You've done very well to remember this much.'

'Pan is dead,' muttered Gwyddion. 'The great Pan is dead.'

'Pardon?'

'Nothing, nothing.' Gwyddion bared his teeth; it wasn't a smile. He had just had to get it out of his system.

'I suppose the Singer had poems as well?' There was only one answer to this question, but Gwyddion got it wrong.

'Loads.'

The silence was enough.

'Well, not *loads*. Not really *loads*. But some.'

'For example?'

Gwyddion hedged. 'Well, he wrote a lot of his own, of course.'

'He always was a bit of a bighead.'

'True. And a few by other people, about what he was doing at the time.'

'Such as?'

'Well, for a while he thought it was amusing to charm animals.'

'What, snakes and things. I remember that.'

"No, that wasn't him. No, he did rats and bats and stuff. Then, one time, in Germany it was, he lost his temper and took some children into a mountain. He had to stop after that.'

'What did they call him then?'

'The Pied Piper.'

'Piper?' Pan's voice echoed round the countryside, thick with anger. 'Piper? He couldn't even leave my instrument alone. Piper?' The god leapt to his feet, fists clenched at his sides.

'Only because a guitar, harp, whatever is difficult to carry dancing along.'

'Dancing? *I* do the dancing. *I* do the piping. Oh, he's going to be sorry.'

'But . . .' Gwyddion was cowering in the dawn-cast shadow of a Pan grown higher than the trees. 'We thought you . . .'

'Were dead. Oh, yes, I heard what was in your head, Druid.

"And that dismal cry rose slowly, and sank slowly through the air,
  Full of spirit's melancholy, and eternity's despair!
  And they heard the words it's said – Pan is dead!
  Great Pan is dead! Pan,
  Pan is dead!"'

'I didn't think I knew that much of the poem,' cri Gwyddion. 'It's not what we thought, no. It's just a poem!'

'Well,' Pan's face was suddenly pressed against Gwyddion's, 'Well, little Druid. As you see, you were wrong. While all this history was happening above my head, while my birds were: dying, while my animals were leaving this little island, while the' Mortals were breeding like flies and messing up my woods, my water, my earth with their nasty leavings, while you were letting; all this happen, Druid, I was only asleep. But now, I'm awake, properly awake. My eyes are open at last.' He straightened up, and up, and up. He opened his mouth and roared. 'Pan is back. Tremble, Mortals. Tremble, Faerie. Tremble.' He reached down and snatched up the quivering Druid. 'Let's go.'

'But . . . but, I thought we were going to surprise them?' Gwyddion tried one last time.

Pan stood up, thirty feet tall, golden pelt gleaming, skin shining in the sun as it crept over the horizon. He shook his head and his wolfish teeth flashed as he opened his mouth to laugh. Then he spoke to the Druid, quietly. 'If this won't surprise them, Druid, then I truly am too late.' Then, tossing the Druid up and down thoughtfully in his hand, as if hefting his weight before tossing him overarm as far as the eye could see,

Pan stepped over the trees along the riverbank and set off for Titania's glade.

Chapter Thirty Seven

Phoebe was lying between crisp white sheets, curled warmly in the curve of a beautiful, loving body. She turned her head to look closer in the faint light coming through the gauze curtains, blowing in a summer breeze through an open window. From outside, she could just hear the first, faint sounds of a market being set up, wares were being shouted in a language it took her her a moment to recognize. She craned her neck a little more. A beautiful face, surrounded by golden curls. A faint smile gilded the lips and the eyes opened, cornflower blue between lids like a moth's wing, new hatched on a dewy morning. The lips opened. The Fair Sidhe – for it was surely a Fair Sidhe – spoke.

'Phoebe,' he grated. 'Phoebe, my collar wasn't starched yesterday. My egg was cold. My sandwich was stale. The children were noisy. These sheets are crumpled. Phoebe. Phoebe. Phoebe.'

'Phoebe?'

She woke up, drenched in sweat. She seemed to be lying on grass.

'Thomas?'

'No, Phoebe. It's me. Puck. You were dreaming.'

She sat up quickly and hugged the elf till his pips

squeaked.

'Oh, Puck. It was horrible. Thomas – he was so lovely, when we met. But he turned, in my dream . . . I thought I was back there . . .'

'Sshh,' Puck stroked her hair. 'It's all right. You're here, with us.'

'The children!' She looked round, wild-eyed.

'Mab has taken them to the village. Don't worry. She has a friend, a Mortal, who will look after them. It might get a bit rough round here shortly and we thought . . .'

'You took them without asking?' She was aghast.

'We didn't want to upset them. Or you.'

She leapt to her feet. 'I must go to them. They'll miss me.'

'Of course they will.' It was the Queen. She sat down and gestured to Phoebe to join her. 'They are such lovely children,' said Titania. 'So bright. So pretty.'

'Oh, yes,' Phoebe sat down again, eager to extol the virtues of her perfect, her lovely, her unique children. 'Undine is so forward at school. Of course, Thomas is very strict about homework and such, but . . .'

The Queen looked up at Puck and sent him on his way with a toss of the head. He took the hint, gratefully. Mortal children had never really been his cup of tea and hearing their mothers whittering was if anything worse than the children themselves. He wandered off across the clearing. At first sight, nothing much had changed. Oberon, it was true, was sleeping in the branches of a nearby tree, but the tree was doing its best and he looked quite at ease, a languid fall of velvet and leather, only slightly marred by the two goblins snoring in his lap. Benedict and Leanne were in conference, squatting awkwardly around a felled tree, trying to pretend it was a conference table. James had gone on a fire fay hunt, after several false starts involving lack of address; a sudden headache and please, please don't make me go, I'll get lost I know I will and Pan is coming. Mab was in the village with the children. Of Taliesin there was no immediate sign, but Annis was on patrol outside Titania's bower, so presumably he was in there.

Puck raised his head. Bacon. He went in search of breakfast.

The goblins, except Freckles and Tiny, who, still feeling a bit trembly, were the ones sleeping on Oberon's chest, had built a small fire on the edge of the wood and were doing a classic fry-up, grease, eggs (to Bill's disgust), fried bread, black pudding, sausage, mushrooms (gathered in happier times by Gwyddion and so, rather suspect) and, naturally, bacon. In a saucepan on another fire, was an orange lump of congealed nastiness, which once rejoiced in the name of baked beans. They had gone so hard and sticky, a portion was now a slice. Even so, the crowd around their makeshift canteen was large and growing. At the back stood the squirrel. He waved at Puck and raised his plate at him.

'It's good,' the squirrel mouthed over the noise of chewing and Hazel's querulous demands for a fully vegetarian menu.

Puck made his way round the assembled Faerie and joined the rodent.

'Hello,' he said when he reached its side. 'You look well.'

'Well, well, yes, I suppose I do,' the squirrel smiled, its teeth very much in evidence.

'You were a bit down when we met last.'

'You too.'

'You seem brighter.'

'You don't.'

Puck was not inclined to answer. He looked at the squirrel more closely. 'You just look . . . I don't know. Glossier. Sleeker, somehow.'

A delicate female cough came from behind his shoulder. He turned.

Another squirrel stood there, coyly playing with the end of her tail.

'Are you going to introduce us, dear?' she said, nudging the first squirrel in the ribs.

'Of course. Darling, this is Puck. Robin Goodfellow, you know.'

'Charmed,' said the squirrel. She nudged the other one

again.'

'What?'

She gestured, a species-wide movement that said 'And . . .?'

'Oh, sorry. Yes. This is the wife.'

'Delighted,' said Puck.

The lady-squirrel sighed. Civilization was slow to come in the squirrel world, and she knew they couldn't run before they could walk. She smiled toothily at Puck. 'Sorry Ay can't stay,' she said, in what would, in a Mortal, be a telephone voice. 'Ay'm building a new dray.' She lowered her eyes and her voice. 'We're expecting.'

'How lovely,' Puck said. 'Well, nice to have met you.'

She skipped away, her six-foot bulk making the ground shake.

No one spoke for a moment. Then, Puck said, 'So. Expecting?'

Probably the squirrel blushed. 'Well, you know how it is. Women, eh?'

'Indeed. Women.' Babies again. Children were everywhere. Once he had his eye in, Puck could see the signs wherever he looked. Goblins holding hands. Hazel was nuzzling rather more closely than usual to a very attractive bush. Looking over his shoulder, he was not surprised to see that even Benedict and Leanne were sitting much more closely together than necessary. Titania had left Phoebe and was standing under Oberon's tree, calling seductively up into the branches. Annis was still on guard over Taliesin. Phoebe was coming his way. He dived into the crowd and gave his attention to a bacon sandwich.

Pan was getting nearer, oh yes. He was definitely getting nearer.

Chapter Thirty Eight

Gwyddion was finding it hard to think. His whole mind was taken up with trying not to be sick. The fear of being thrown away absentmindedly had abated a little, once he realised that Pan didn't Intend to dispense with his services just yet. He tried to go floppy. I le tried to fly away, but he was caught there, like some giant yo-yo, Ht the god's command.

That they were making progress was obvious. With legs nearly fifteen feet long and a bounding goat's stride, the miles were being eaten up. But even Pan's long legs couldn't step over houses and he wasn't comfortable too near power lines, telephone masts and similar. Like Oberon, he got a raging headache when he was near waves of that length, so the route was tending to be a bit circuitous.

Not only were inanimate things slowing Pan down. Flocks of birds wheeled in the sky around his head, settling on his shoulders. Butterflies fluttered like the sky's curtains in front of the god, making him laugh for joy as he walked through them, making them scatter.

'That tickles.'

Gwyddion, spitting out wings and powdery scales, tried to laugh too.

Mortals came flocking out of their houses to watch them pass. As the news spread, lines of cars began to converge on their likely route and Pan had to step gingerly among them. Not that he was particularly bothered about the welfare of the puny life below his knees, but he had found out the hard way that it really hurt to step on a car. It was hard, it was sharp and, deep in its heart, it was hot. There had been a brief stop while Gwyddion took an aerial out of Pan's hoof.

Before too many miles had swept beneath the Lord of Misrule's loping stride their way was almost completely blocked.

The smell from the petrol fumes was appalling, even twenty-five feet up in the air it made Pan's nose wrinkle.

'Can't they *smell* it?' he asked Gwyddion in disbelief.

'When they first got cars and such, they smelt it then. But they seemed to prefer it to the piles of horse shit which had filled the roads before. Now, they buy the stuff for their rose bushes.'

'They *buy* horse shit?'

'By the bag. Then they spread it on the ground and say "Hmmm. Smell the country."'

'They haven't thought of going out into the country?'

'Oh yes, they do that.' The Druid gave him a knowing look.

'In one of these hot boxes?'

'The same.'

Pan looked helplessly around his feet. 'I can't get past.'

Gwyddion saw his chance. 'Shrink down, Lord. Then we can just walk past.'

'No. Too slow.'

'We don't even have to do that. We could fly.'

'I don't trust you.'

'You don't trust me? I can see why not. But I promise I won't trick you. I think we need an end to this. I have a suspicion I'm allergic to all these plants being out at once. Oak. Mistletoe. Mushrooms. Oh, and a few well-chosen herbs. That's flora enough for me. Not to mention the animals.'

'There's nothing here that shouldn't be,' Pan said, sounding hurt.

'Wild boar. Wolves. Bear.'

'They were around when I was here last.'

'All right then. But unicorns.'

'Yes. They were around.'

'I never saw one.'

'Nor did I. I was never near enough virgins, I suppose.'

'Well, never for long, anyway.'

The god smiled, reflectively.

'Come on, let's go down there, just behind that stand of trees. I will carry you the rest of the way.'

''Promise.'

Yes.'

'Cross your heart and hope to die.'

'Yes.' The way Gwyddion saw it, the die bit came in both ways.

Pan looked down at the stream of honking, smelly cars. He looked ahead of him into the cloudless blue sky. Somewhere, over that horizon, the Singer was waiting. And good old Oberon. All the lads. Puck, as well. He was homesick for the Old, Old Days. He put Gwyddion down carefully and shrank down to a more manageable seven foot.

'Smaller,' Gwyddion said. 'I'm not a heavy goods Druid, you know.'

'Smaller?'

'More than that. Bit more. Bit more.'

'I'm not going any less than this.'

'That will do then. Hop aboard.'

Pan skipped onto Gwyddion's back and put his arms round his neck and his legs tightly round his waist, being careful not to hurt him. This was a newly connected synapse in his brain and he quite liked it.

Gwyddion closed his eyes and soared into the air.

'Are we going, Druid, or are we going to stand here all day?' asked a testy voice in his ear.

Gwyddion looked down and was mildly surprised to find his feet still on the ground. He tried again, this time gritting his teeth for extra lift. Still nothing.

'I think perhaps you're still a bit heavy,' he said, apologetically.

'You flew with me before and I was bigger than this.'

'Well, I can't fly with you now.'

'Wait a minute. I jumped on your back last time. When you were already airborne. Let's try that.'

The first few tries were not any too successful. Somehow, doing it in cold blood wasn't as easy as taking the Druid by surprise. Pan took a few falls which would have had the goblins rolling in the aisles before they both decided to stop and think things through.

'Perhaps if I just do it when you're not looking,' Pan suggested finally.

'What?'

'You know, try and escape, like you did before, and I'll catch you.'

'Oh, I don't know . . .'

'Go on. Give it a try, Druid.'

'All right, then.'

Gwyddion stood around, looking unconcerned.

'Well,' said Pan. 'When are you going to escape?'

'If I told you that, it wouldn't be a surprise, would it?'

'We haven't got all day. I've worked myself up now, to giving the Singer a good hiding. I'm going off the boil.'

'Even so, I have to choose my moment.'

Pan suddenly roared, 'Just do it!'

Gwyddion jumped in fear and, before he knew it, Pan was aboard and they were flying over the trees.

'There.' The Lord of Misrule was smug. 'I said that would work, didn't I? Now, straight to where the others are, Druid, if you please. And don't spare the centaurs.'

'Pardon?'

'Don't worry. As a joke I can see that it has probably had its day. Just get me there. No funny stuff. I'm having a snooze. Wake me up when we're there.'

And so Gwyddion flew, round in circles occasionally, as the god slipped sideways in his sleep, upside down now and then, but always in the general direction of the glade. He sent frantic messages ahead, but telepathy was hard with what felt like a ton of god on his back. He sighed. He wished now he'd hung on to the owl. It might have been useful.

'Are we there yet?' Pan woke up suddenly and nearly fell off.

'No, not yet. I'll tell you when we're there.'

'Oh. Something woke me.'

'It was an airplane, Lord.'

'Eeugh. I can still smell it. Will they miss these things, Druid, do you think?'

'Miss them, Lord?' Gwyddion felt that familiar creeping in his bowel that had become a constant companion since he was snatched from the air only hours ago by the God of Confusion.

'When I have destroyed them all.'

'Ah ha!' Even Gwyddion could tell that wasn't a laugh, but Pan didn't seem to notice.

He nuzzled down among Gwyddion's robes, and his voice got quieter. 'Yes,' he muttered. 'First the Singer. Then Oberon. Then a few drinks. A few girls. Then, clean the place up.' He went quiet, then, 'Lots more birds. Lots more of everything. Except them. Mortals and their horrible smelly machines and dirty habits.'

Gwyddion held his breath and concentrated on the flying. A snore from behind him told him the god was asleep again. He rose higher to see the horizon better. They would be back soon. A plane went over.

'Hmmphh.' Pan gripped tightly as he awoke. 'Are we there yet?'

Chapter Thirty Nine

Taliesin was in Titania's bower, as Puck had guessed. The Queen had graciously given him her bed. He didn't look like the kind of Druid who had slept on a grassy bank lately. He was also not the kind of rock star who got up while the day was still dawning. Or morning. Or lunchtime. So he was still burrowed deep in the covers, gossamer, starlight, petals and web all clumped together over his curled up form.

Titania gently shook his shoulder. 'Al,' she whispered in his ear. 'Time to get up.'

'What time's that?' came from under the covers.

Titania straightened up, puzzled. 'I have no idea,' she said. 'I don't really do clocks. I could go and blow on a dandelion if you're desperate. It's just . . . time.'

He sat up, tousled and bleary. Ten million fans would have given their right arms to be here, now. Titania smiled down at him and he squinted in the light which poured in through the open doorway and outlined her loveliness in a halo of gold dust motes, or were they flower faeries, floating around her.

He rubbed his eyes. 'Mornin'.'

'Good morning, Singer.' She pulled back the covers smartly and pulled them back again. 'Oh, sorry.'

'Perhaps you could pass me my trousers,' he said, holding out an arm. Keeping her back turned, she passed him his clothes.

What a sweetie, he thought to himself. A few old-fashioned values back in the world had to be good.

Well, well, she thought to herself. Why does he think I can only see in front of me? He's been away a long time.

His clothes safely on, she turned round and offered him her arm.

'Shall we?' she said.

'Why not,' he said. 'It'll be good to see the morning, for once in a while.'

Oberon was still in his tree. Everyone had started calling it The King's Tree, the capital letters implied even from the dumbest goblin. The dwarves, naturally, never called it that. To them it was The Welching, Stuck-up, No-Better-Than-He-Should-Be Git's Tree, but the meaning was the same. He was still cradling his goblins, who were beginning to tire of his relentless affection. They had smelt the bacon and it was getting close to lunchtime as far as they could tell. Their little stomachs rumbled and Tiny had a mouth like a birdcage. He needed a drink. But no. Here they sat, trapped on the king's lap, being clutched every now and again as he remembered how much he loved them.

He felt happier off the ground, although he knew it was making no difference. He had played the scene in his head so often, he was almost word perfect. He would be standing in the middle of the glade, looking beautiful and rather svelte. An adoring crowd of assorted Faerie and the odd Mortal after an autograph would be gathered round. He would have just made a stunningly witty rejoinder and the glade was a-ring with merry laughter. Then, the sun would darken. He would look to his . . . thing, where his autograph hand was, right, that was it . . . and Pan would be standing there, poised to strike, pawing with his goat feet on the ground, eyes evil beneath his matted hair. He would have a club in one hand and be dragging a girl by the hair with the other. He would speak his name . . .

'Oberon?'

That's right, Oberon. He would say it and the king would approach him, feet dragging in the dust, weeping fans clinging to the hem of his garment.

'Oberon.'

He would be powerless to resist.

'Oberon. Will you stop squeezing those poor goblins and get down out of that tree this minute.'

Startled, he looked down. Titania stood on the moss at the base of his tree. She looked beautiful when she was angry, he thought. Which meant, since he could hardly bear to look at her luminescent loveliness, she was well annoyed right now. He tossed the goblins to one side, much to their relief and jumped down to land, light as a feather, beside her.

'Ow.'

'Ow.'

'My Lord,' said the Queen. 'Will you never remember that goblins can't fly?'

Oberon whirled round. He had hurt his lads again. How could he be so thoughtless? But the goblins were ready for him this time. No more hugging. No more squeezing. They were off to where a few rashers of bacon were cremating over the embers at the edge of the wood.

Titania sighed and, leaning over, stroked his hair. The ebony curls were springy as wood shavings, soft as silk. The perfume, musk and lily, filled the air as they stood there, deep in the love which not everyone understood. He put one finger to her lips, and she kissed it lightly.

'Come on,' she whispered. 'We're nearly there. Everyone's back now, except James and I'm sure he'll be here soon. He only had to find Sally.'

'She's a tricky one,' said Oberon.

'Really, Lord,' said Titania, on her considerable dignity. 'Had our fingers burnt, have we?'

'Certainly not.'

'Oh, not your fingers. What then?'

'Nothing. You were there. I couldn't even remember her name.'

'Not always a problem for you, Lord, is it?' said a catty

voice.

'Leanne,' smiled the Queen. 'Have you done your planning with Benedict?"

'Yes. We have everything in place. We're just waiting for James.'

'And Gwyddion, of course.'

'Of course. But since your people and my people failed to find hair nor hide of him, I think we must expect the worst. Anyway,' Leanne tossed her hair in Oberon's direction and was disappointed to see a total lack of reaction. In fact, the king was standing there, one hand wound tightly in Titania's gown and the other to his mouth, where he was occupied in chewing his nails. 'Anyway, we can do without him now the Singer is here.'

'True. But we're not just doing a binding with song, are we?' Titania tried to move off and was brought up short. She unwound Oberon's hand from her dress.

'No, all the elements will be used as well. Plus, the Singer is well versed in totemic lore, so Puck will be able to perfect his list of animals we need, although, he seems to be rather fixated on squirrels at the moment.'

'They are a bit big around here,' said Puck, as he passed by with an armful of mixed vegetation. 'I could do with a hand, Lord, if it's not too much trouble. I have my animals to gather, if you could get on with the plants.'

'Hmm?'

'Plants, Sire. If you could gather the plants?'

Oberon looked puzzled. Titania smiled at Puck and said brightly, 'The King and I will gather the plants together, Puck. He's a little upset at the moment. Not himself.' She peered at the elf. 'How are you, by the way?'

'Surprisingly well,' said Puck, and meant it. He wasn't feeling the Panic that Oberon was, although he knew that if he didn't keep busy it would sneak up and bite him on the bum. So he was scurrying about, with ivy one minute, a toad the next. Busy, busy, that's the way.

'Well, leave that, then, and we'll sort it.' She clapped her hands and a swarm of flower faeries came over and hung above her head, as she gave out instructions. She looked at

Leanne, who was still trying to attract the king's attention. Do you have something to collect, Leanne? Rocks, or something?'

'Erm, I'm done, really. I've had the dwarves on to it. Hard working little chaps. A bit stringy.'

'Well.' There was no answer to that, really. 'That's nice. So, we'll see you later, then.'

No one moved.

Yes. Later, ciao.'

Eventually, they wandered away, Titania leading Oberon by the hand, Leanne to go in search of Benedict. The last she had seen of him, he had been wandering around with a teaspoon, looking for water to collect. Somehow, she imagined the quantities would have to be bigger. She just had to make him see that.

Annis was crouching at the edge of the glade. She wanted an overview and here was the best place. Her black old heart was fluttering in her chest. She put her hand in amongst her rags and took out a pigeon. Absentmindedly, she let it go. But no, it must be her heart; the fluttering was still there.

Over to her left, Puck was standing, scratching his head. He was looking around for the toad, which had definitely been there five minutes ago. Annis burped gently and smiled.

Ahead of her, Titania and Oberon walked gently to and fro, the pile of flora growing despite the fact they were doing nothing. 'Cheats,' thought Annis.

Leanne was arguing with Benedict over near the edge of the wood. She was trying to take something out of his hand, and he was not letting her. Like a couple of bairns, thought Annis, not unfondly. Benedict was something of a favourite, if she could be said to favour anything at all.

That stupid airy-faerie was floating around in the treetops with gossamer bags, catching the four winds. 'She might as well try to catch a fart in a colander,' muttered Annis. She chuckled. In fact, she could oblige. Toads always gave her wind.

A dark spot, glittering round the edges, was approaching from the East. That had to be James. Better late than never.

She could hear the Singer tuning up behind her. Her heart gave another lurch, but he wasn't the cause of its flutterings.

Of Gwyddion there was as yet no sign.

And, on the breeze, faint, so faint that only she could smell it, there was a hint of musk, of reed beds, of wine, warm skin, crushed grass, honey.

Pan.

Chapter Forty

James had flown off eventually, far from happy. Butler he may be, errand boy he definitely was not. He muttered under his breath, a bogleish mantra few would have understood. Had there been an observer, high among the wispy clouds across the moon, his expression would have been enough to make words unnecessary. James was very annoyed, as well as being rather nervous. As far as he could see, he couldn't win this one. He had been given an address and instructions how to get there. The Elder had thoughtfully written it down for him. James had taken to the air with the map in his paw – somehow, what with an unexpected crosswind and an attention span to rival a goldfish, he had let go and the map had spun eddying away. So, finding Sally was not going to be easy, in fact, impossible. James began to sink into despair, something a Scottish bogle, far from hearth and home found easy. It was close to his natural state. He tried a little howl and felt a bit better.

Below on the ground, children hid their heads under the covers. Nervous spinsters suddenly found it essential to check the far recesses of the cupboard under the stairs and joggers out for an invigorating run dived for cover.

In her semi-detached in Willesden, Sally Mander, part time

cleaner and full-time fire fay, put down the phone. Leanne had been quite specific. She was needed on an important mission. James would be coming for her, so be sure to be ready. No packing necessary, but make sure she was easy to find. Well, that was no problem. She popped out into the back garden and, with a flick of a finger, lit a bonfire. Soon, acrid smoke from wet leaves filled the air, but at the bottom the fire burned hot and red. Done and dusted, she thought, as she went inside to pack just a few bits. James couldn't miss that.

Next door to Sally's humble home, the evening was following its normal course. Mrs Blewitt had served a nourishing meal to Mr Blewitt, who was now sitting in his favourite chair with a mug of Ovaltine on the small table placed solicitously by his side by his good lady. He was watching the news. Everything seemed very odd lately, and he feared that the standard of journalism was not what it was. There seemed to be no serious attempt to address the larger issue. All they could talk about was thirty foot freaks stopping traffic on the M5, temperatures of 25 degrees in Basildon, minus four in Guildford, at the same time and orchids growing out of the statue of Eros in Piccadilly Circus. He checked his watch, which showed the time, including the twenty four hour clock, to which he adhered with confusing tenacity, and the date. No. It wasn't April 1st. He switched off the television in disgust. There was only comedy on the other channels and Mr Blewitt didn't do comedy. And Channel Five was something that, as far as he could see, only happened to other people.

He settled back in his chair and shook out his newspaper. More nonsense, but it would fill the time until he went up the stairs to Bedfordshire. Then, his nostrils wrinkling, he sniffed the air.

'Beryl,' he called. 'Beryl!'

Mrs Blewitt rushed into the room. It wasn't like Mr Blewitt to raise his voice and he always made a point of not interrupting her while she was washing up, ever since the incident with his mother's soup tureen.

'Whatever is it, dear?'

'Smell anything?'

Mrs Blewitt sniffed tentatively. 'Burning?'

'Yes, burning. That young madam next door has got a bonfire going. At this hour.' Pausing only to put on his Wellingtons, his gardening anorak, his gardening hat and his gardening gloves, he grabbed his watering can and stormed outside. Soon, Sally's beacon was a smouldering mass on the lawn and Mr Blewitt, with the glow engendered by a job well done, was back inside, shaking out his newspaper.

Meanwhile, Sally was humming quietly to herself as she popped a few necessaries into a bag. This wasn't strictly necessary of course, but she had been passing as Mortal for so long and frankly rather enjoying it, that she was in the habit. She had discovered fairly early on that travelling with no luggage and yet appearing every morning in a completely different outfit, based mainly around red, yellow and orange, with accessories in charcoal grey, worried Mortals. So, she packed a bag.

After a while, she began to worry about James. Surely, even a dumb bogle could see her beacon. She glanced out of her back-bedroom window and stifled a scream. Her fire had gone out. Her fire had gone out! That just didn't happen to Sally. Her fires never went out. She rushed down the stairs and into the garden. As she thought! Big footprints, lots of water, a smug feeling in the air. Blewitt! She wrinkled her brow in the direction of his back door and stared hard.

To her great satisfaction, after very few seconds the door flew open and a burning *Telegraph* was thrown out. Mrs Blewitt was screaming.

Sally dusted her palms together in satisfaction and turned away to relight her fire. The noise didn't seem to be getting any less from next door. In fact, someone else seemed to be howling as well. She looked around, trying to get an angle on the sound. Wait a minute – it was overhead. She looked up.

Across the moon flew a figure to chill any heart. James!

And here was she, caught with her fire out. What a disgrace! Choosing another place that wasn't so wet and trampled, she quickly lit another fire, hot and red. She called to James above the crackle of the flames, but he didn't seem to hear her. He flew on, lost in his own misery.

Above all this domestic upheaval, James flew on unheeding. In his mind he was already running the home movie of what Leanne would do to him when he got back with no Sally. It wasn't pretty viewing, and he drew in a breath for another howl.

It was then that he heard his name being called, barely audible on the breeze. He looked all around, in that random way dogs have and as a consequence found himself flying upside down for several confusing seconds. As he spun in the air, he saw the flickering flames out of the corner of his eye, and when he had found it again, he saw a little figure dancing round the bonfire. Then, he heard her calling.

'James! James! It's Sally. James!'

'Sally!' he called. He had never been so glad to see anyone in his long life. He dived down towards the flames and soon was by her side. When she had worked for Benedict, back before, he had never taken much notice of her, except to examine, in his butlerly way, the edges of mantelpieces and underneath rugs, to see if she had done her job correctly. But now, anyone looking, and that currently was a clandestine Mrs Blewitt, shaking behind her nets, would have thought she was his best friend.

'How do you want to ride?' he asked her.

'How would you prefer?' said Sally. She could fly a little herself, but only as sparks rise – randomly and for short distances. For any long journey, she needed help.

'I don't often have passengers.'

'Yes,' Sally said thoughtfully. 'I heard about that.'

James ignored her. 'If you just hang on tight, I suppose it will be all right.'

'OK.' Sally jumped lightly aboard. She seemed to weigh

nothing, and James took to the air as if she wasn't there, his heart as light as his burden.

Mrs Blewitt had been vaguely aware of the Return of Faerie, but only vaguely. Mr Blewitt only watched the BBC News and then if there was nothing upsetting. Mrs Blewitt was not encouraged to watch anything of a documentary nature, as her husband was of the opinion that female minds were not actually wired up to assimilate facts. He naturally did not include wildlife programmes in this, unless they involved sex, in which case the Blewitts would switch off and have a quiet game of Scrabble. The *Telegraph* was tacitly acknowledged as Mr Blewitt's personal property, except for the crossword, which Mr Blewitt would carefully clip out with Mrs Blewitt's embroidery scissors before storing for future use in a clear plastic wallet marked clearly 'crosswords'.

It was with a degree of shock then, that Mrs Blewitt watched the proceedings in Sally' garden. She stood back from the window, leaning her forehead on the cool tiles of the kitchen wall, trying to summon up a coherent description to tell Mr Blewitt, who was currently in the bathroom, putting Savlon on the burns from the spontaneous combustion of his newspaper.

She went up the stairs and tapped on the bathroom door. Mr Blewitt always locked the bathroom door, even for cleaning his teeth.

'Yes,' came Mr Blewitt's muffled voice.

'Dear . . .' Mrs Blewitt was finding the whole thing very trying.

The door opened. 'Beryl. I am in the bathroom,' Mr Blewitt said tersely. 'We do not interrupt ablutions of any kind, do we?'

'No, dear.'

'Well, what is it?' He stood four square in the doorway, Savlon drooling from the tube in his hand.

'I . . . I've just . . .' No, it was no good. There was no way to describe this. 'I just thought I would see if you were all right, dear.'

Mr Blewitt almost smiled. 'Thank you, dear. That was very thoughtful. Now, if you'll excuse me,' and he closed the door.

Mrs Blewitt went downstairs and sat down in Mr Blewitt's favourite chair. She switched on the television.

Chapter Forty One

As Annis watched from her vantage point, James landed in the middle of the glade. Sally leapt down, light
as a spark and was immediately surrounded by her
sisters of the house fay kind, catching up on the gossip.

James sauntered over to Leanne, a swagger to his hips, a
sardonic smile among the drool on his lips.

'Well done, James,' she said, keeping almost all of the
amazement out of her voice. 'Well done.'

The butler managed to stop his tail from wagging. He was
a mover and shaker now, and no mistake.

'Why did you take so long?'

James tossed an eyebrow in a bogle-of-the-world way.
'Well, you know these fays, Mistress,' he said. 'Had to pack
and such.'

'She has no luggage with her.' And indeed, Sally had left
her bag behind in the excitement of the moment.

'Er . . .' James looked behind him and saw she was right.
"No, but she had . . . things to do.'

'Ah.'

'Plus, she's heavy.'

'Rubbish, James.' Leanne was already turning on her heel.
'You got lost, didn't you?'

'Not lost, no.'

'What, then?'

'We came the pretty way.'

'Which would be . . .?'

James shrugged, a good trick for a bogle, who already wears his shoulders round his ears. 'Who can describe the pretty way?'

'Very poetic, James, I'm sure.' Then she smiled. "Never mind, you're here now. When you've had something to eat or drink or whatever, perhaps you can help Puck. He seems to be having difficulty keeping his fauna in check.'

'It's probably because of the goat-leg thing,' said James, sympathetically.

'No, James,' sighed the vampire. 'Fauna, as in animals.'

'Oh.' James shuffled his feet. 'Sorry.'

'Just do it, will you?' Leanne went off to look for Benedict, currently standing hopefully next to a weeping willow sprite, holding out his spoon.

The Singer was quite enjoying this morning thing. It was years since he had been an early riser and the novelty of the fresh air was spurring him to song. He wouldn't usually risk a note until after dark – he had been singing for over three thousand years and he knew by now what was good for his throat – but everything seemed to be singing, from the sap in the trees to the birds in their branches and he had to join in. Toes were tapping throughout the Faerie glade and he was happy.

His song told of his life, in all his guises, everyone and thing he had seen; Avalon, Atlantis, peace, war, wine, women . . . the inhumation of Pan. Everyone he had been; Taliesin, the first and greatest incarnation, True Thomas, Blondel, the Pied Piper. He hadn't always been a singer; sometimes he let his words sing by themselves without a tune other than in the heads of the listener; Kit Marlowe, Shelley, Brooke. His present body pleased him, and he'd never had such adulation. So, he thought with a sigh, if this was to be it, his swansong, going down in battle royal with Pan, it hadn't been a bad life. Although he had much more planned. Much more.

The strings sang a lingering chord and he put the guitar to

one side.

Annis was edgy. Everyone was getting on with their tasks in a way, but they were so . . . there was no other word but *Faerie*. Annis went right back, back before most of these Folk, good or ill, were even thought of, were even twinkles in their fathers' eyes, where appropriate. She had watched the netherworld, that other world that she belonged in, she had seen it grow and develop. When she was young, young and lovely as she had once been, there had been few indeed. She could fly, walk, dance the length and breadth of the country and hardly see anyone. She could smell things then – she inhaled nostalgically and had to close her eyes as the rush of blood to the head made everything spin – she could smell a Mortal at a hundred miles; she could smell out where the unicorns were hiding deep in the never-ending wood; she could smell the phoenix, sitting on its nest in the high places; but most of all, wherever he was, near or far, if his smell was so dilute that only one part of a million gulps of air contained one fragment of his smell – most of all, she could always smell Pan.

She had missed that, over the years. She missed the old reprobate, although she quite saw why they had to do what they did. History would have been so different if he had roamed all these years. In fact, she gave a chuckle, deep in her phlegmy throat, there wouldn't have been much history, with him around. Pan tended to take scribes out and hang them upside down from trees. What he did with their quills did not bear thinking about, in these enlightened days.

Her nostrils, full for so many years with traffic fumes, the smell of old apple cores and abandoned newspaper that always hung over park benches at night, the smell of a frightened pigeon doing what it did best, were beginning to work again. Nerve endings in her olfactory region were sparking into life for the first time in hundreds of years. The smell of the goat-foot hung over the land like an almost visible cloud.

She had to make them see that, if they planned to do anything at all, they had to do it *soon*. It was no good going at this thing half-cocked. She chuckled again to think of that phrase in the same brain that could smell Pan so strongly.

She struggled to her feet and decided to start with Puck. She was sorry she had eaten his toad, but it was ages since she had had one. Pigeon palls, after a while. Fast food – bad for you, she thought. Now, where was the lad? Oh yes, over there, struggling with that boar. Tricky things, your wild boar. And even in her younger days she had never managed to eat a whole one. Perhaps not Puck, then.

Titania and Oberon were prancing round the glade in full Royal style. A cluster of assorted Faerie were in their wake and Annis thought briefly of Richard Dadd, artist, loony and a great friend, who would have given his eye teeth to paint the scene. Greenstuff was piled up in the centre of the glade, under the general supervision of Hazel, who was ticking things off a kind of check list, written on a piece of bark which curled down from his hand.

'Mistletoe,' grunted a goblin, dumping a heap at the sprite's feet. ''Ere,' he nudged Hazel in what were probably his knees, 'Gi'us a kiss.'

Hazel looked at him in disdain. He sniffed and ticked ostentatiously. '*Viscum album*. Next.'

'Holly,' said a Mr Dobie, trying to put his bundle down and finding it was caught up in his coat. 'Ow.'

'*Ilex*,' said Hazel, reaching down and untangling the poor little creature. "Next.'

'Wue.' A small elf was somewhere under a pile of leaves.

'Wue?' asked Hazel, bemused.

'Yes, wue,' said the elf. 'You know wue. The herb. Wue.'

'How are you spelling that?' Hazel asked, looking on both sides of his list.

'Spell? I don't do spells. I'm an elf.'

Hazel bent down and smelt the leaves. 'Oh! Rue. I see. *Ruta graveolus*. Check. Next.'

'Love in idleness.' Mab stood there, holding out a tattered bundle of flowers.

"No,' said Hazel firmly. 'We don't need that. How many

times.'

'Oh dear,' said Mab. 'I'll go and see if the Singer wants it.' She turned to go.

Annis stopped her. 'Don't embarrass yourself, dearie,' she said. 'The Singer is up to all your tricks. He invented many of them himself.' She took the flowers from Mab and they withered instantly. Mab flounced off to do a bit of co-ordinating elsewhere.

Annis lurched off to look for Leanne and Benedict. She didn't trust Leanne on a personal level, but she was sure that she had either done or delegated her tasks. She was that sort of vampire. In fact, she could see her young self there sometimes. She sighed.

But Benedict was another kettle of fish. He wanted, yet didn't want, to be part of the plan. Just as, the first time, he had started the ball rolling and then stepped aside, to see it crush its way to the finale, gathering a lot more than moss in its path.

She heard raised voices and made her way slowly towards the sound.

'But,' Leanne was saying, 'you can't collect water drop by drop.'

"Yes, I can. I am doing, look.'

'But I can't help thinking this should be special water, not just stuff from old puddles and hollow logs.' Without turning round she said, 'Hello, Annis.'

'Hello, dearie,' said Annis. 'In fact, he's quite right to collect this old water. It's been around. It's seen life and that's what we need for this kind of binding spell.'

'It doesn't really matter,' Leanne said. 'It is a well-known scientific fact that every water molecule on earth has been through a dinosaur at some point in its existence. So it doesn't matter where he gets it from. It's all old.'

'But does Pan know that?' Annis asked her. 'I can't help thinking, probably not.' She peered up at Benedict with her good eye, which seemed to Leanne to be a little brighter and more with it than usual. And the smell wasn't quite so strong, though clearly discernible, especially down wind. 'Good boy,' she said, patting his arm. 'Keep up the good work.'

'Good boy!' Benedict exploded. 'I am Lord of Unseelie, King of the Dark Horde, Master of . . .'

'Whatever,' said Annis, flapping a hand as she walked away.

She looked up to the treetops. Phoebe was doing her stuff, and she wasn't climbing any trees to check her out. The fire fay she knew would do what was needed when called upon. No brain at all, poor darlings, but very good at striking matches. Gwyddion wasn't coming back, at least alone. Of that she was certain. She bent down and scooped up a handful of soil and put it in her pocket. A bit of insurance. So that was that, then.

She wandered through the glade, looking for peace, quiet and a patch of sunshine. She found the very spot, squatted down, tipped her hat over her eye and waited.

Chapter Forty Two

Gwyddion flew lower and lower and lower, circling round to mark time He had seen the woods surrounding the glade grow larger on the horizon over the last few minutes and he had a pressing need to put off the evil hour, because he had a terrible idea that the hour would be very evil indeed.

Pan had slept for most of the journey, occasionally jumping in his sleep and gripping the Druid's shoulder so hard that he could hardly fly straight. He had become strangely fond of the god over the past hours – but he and the others went back such a long way, that their memories could hardly be contained in one head. Flashes of their time together came and went, like lightning, illuminating things with acid clarity, but only for a moment. Filling Pan in on his missing time had been instructive to say the least, but it had made him quite sad. All those years and yet here he was, in the end, flying through the morning air with one choice in his future.

He either sold his passenger down the river, or he saw his friends become the god's victims, saw Mortals sent back to living in huts and grunting, as opposed to living in houses with all mod cons and grunting. He sighed. Not much of a choice, really, when all was said and done.

He had a more immediate problem now, though. How was he going to land, without waking Pan up? It had never been his strong suit, landing. He had always tended to be a reach the ground running sort of Druid. If anyone was around, he just had to hope that they weren't watching, as he often tripped over things in his diminishing flight – rocks, pebbles, twigs, the pattern in the carpet. But they were nearly there.

He ran the possibilities through his mind.

Possibility one. He would look round and Pan would be gone. The whole thing had been a particularly vivid dream. If only!

Possibility two. Pan would wake and say he had changed his mind and that he would just go along with whatever Gwyddion had planned. He could just go a day in Brighton, a cup of tea and a jumbo cod and chips, if that was all right. Hmm. Unlikely.

Possibility three. They would get to the glade, everything would be ready, with Faerie in the air holding gossamer ropes to bind the god; herbs, fauna, all the spells in place. Within minutes, the Lord of Confusion would be bound and ready for his burial. Gwyddion tacked a p.s. onto this possibility – that Pan would not turn in his bindings and stare the Druid right between the eyes, putting guilt into his brain which would last for eternity. Not very likely.

Possibility four. The god would wake up and . . .

'Why are we circling like this, Druid?' Pan snarled in his ear. 'Forgotten the way?'

'No, no, not at all,' stammered Gwyddion. 'Not at all, no.' He continued to circle.

'Forgotten how to land, then, perhaps?'

"No, no. I know how to land.' He still circled, fifty feet in the air.

'Then I have to think something else,' said the god. 'I have to think that you are trying not to reach the glade where all your friends are waiting – where they wait with spells and bindings.'

Gwyddion laughed nervously.

'There could be two reasons for your reluctance, Druid. One is that they are not ready.'

No reply from Gwyddion, who was beginning to feel a little giddy, what with the nerves and the tightness of his circle.

'Or, you don't want them to bind me.'

Still no reply.

'I confess to being rather touched, Druid, if that should turn out to be the case.'

Gwyddion landed in a heap and lay stunned for a minute beneath the sudden weight of Pan, who had been growing steadily in the last few turns, back to his preferred height of a tad under seven feet. He woke to find the god bending over him, stepping excitedly from hoof to cloven hoof.

'Is that it, Druid? Do you really not want them to bind me?'

Gwyddion sat up and the god backed off, rearing up above him, the sun glancing off his golden hair.

'I don't know what I want,' he said at last.

Pan sat down beside him, in a movement like golden syrup flowing. 'Were you ever a woman in a previous life?'

'I've only ever had this life.'

'Really? It's just that you seem to have difficulty making up your mind.'

Gwyddion thought of Leanne, Titania and, although she was not overtly female, Annis and wondered why Pan thought women didn't know what they wanted. But, he supposed, Pan had had a larger consumer base from which to make his judgement.

'There is no perfect outcome, Lord,' said Gwyddion at last.

'There never is,' said Pan.

'There is one that is almost perfect.'

'Which is?'

'That I go ahead and tell everyone that, although you're back, you've changed your ways, you won't hurt anyone, not even by accident, you're not at all angry over what they did and there's no need to bind you.

Pan looked confused. 'I'm sorry, Druid,' he said. 'I thought you said that there was an almost perfect solution.'

'Yes. That was it.'

'I see. Let me tell you my perfect, or almost perfect solution. I go to where those namby pamby faeries are waiting. I stamp and roar, I destroy their merry glade, I grab Oberon and Puck, take them off on my rout. I hunt, I wench, I drink. And they put up with it.' He stared at Gwyddion, waiting for his reaction. 'Something wrong, Druid?'

'There's nothing I can say, Lord. We aren't singing from the same rune book.'

Pan leaned back and laughed aloud. 'Of course we aren't, Druid. As far as I can see, one side is going to lose. I hope it will be them. They hope it will be me. It's only you who thinks we can all win.'

'No, we can't all win. But there is such a thing as a draw.'

"Not in my world, Druid. But, you've been good to me, by and large. You haven't had much choice, but you have carried me on your back. You have told me a tale to fill a long night. I will let you go ahead and warn them of my coming.'

Gwyddion sat up, amazed. 'You will?'

'Yes. But it's not as good as you seem to think. I will be in the woods. I will be listening to what you say. I will be peering, prying, planning. I will be getting ready for the showdown. This time, they won't catch me sleeping, wine addled and sated by beautiful women. This time, they will take on Pan in his glory, and we will have to see what the outcome will be.'

The Druid sprang to his feet. 'Let's get going,' he said, dashing back and forth in his excitement. 'Let's go.' He ran into the woods. He turned. 'Come on,' he gestured wildly in the direction of the trees.

'You're excited, Druid,' said Pan, almost fondly.

'Of course.' Something in the god's tone made him pause.

Pan chuckled and the woods rang. 'It's almost as if you wondered who would win. There can be only one winner, surely.'

'Yes?' Gwyddion whispered.

The god laughed again. He threw back his head and roared. Birds flew into the air in clouds and wheeled above his head. Deer rocketed out of the wood and almost flew across the open heath. The warming day seemed to hold its breath. The Lord of Misrule, the God of Confusion, The Shape Shifter opened his mouth and spoke. His voice rang round the countryside and bounced off the sky. Everywhere they heard it. In the glade they heard it.

'Pan!'

Chapter Forty Three

'**P**an!'
Down in the village, Undine and Padraig lifted their heads. They were colouring in at the kitchen table. Mab's neighbour was indeed kind and understanding – perhaps that went with the territory if you were Mab's neighbour. You were either kind and understanding, or you weren't her neighbour any more. She had had a lot of moving vans at the house next door in her time.

The woman – 'Call me Auntie' – was standing at the worktop, making a cake. So nice to have some kiddies around the place, although these two were a bit strange. A bit like Mab, to cut a long description short, as she had told her sister on the phone. She stopped in mid-mix and listened, but the sound did not come again.

'What was that, do you think?' she asked, trying, for the kiddies' sake, to keep the tremble from her voice.

'I don't know,' said Undine, slipping out of her chair and heading for the door.

'Where do you think you're going, young lady?' asked Auntie, wiping her hands on her apron and heading her off.

'Mummy. We want to be with Mummy.'

'Mummy's busy, dear. I'm sure Auntie Mab explained.'

'She's not my Auntie. You're not my Auntie.' Padraig started to wail. 'I want my Mummy.'

Auntie was nonplussed. The children had arrived with Mab early in the morning. Mab had explained that their mother was busy, and the children needed somewhere a bit more comfortable to sleep for a few nights, rather than the glade.

Auntie had sniffed disapprovingly. Like many of the locals, she wasn't quite sure what went on down there. And not knowing made her instantly suspect the worst. She had seen all that faerie stuff on the telly, and Titania was beautiful, you had to admit. And that Oberon – well! Auntie lived a quiet life, alone since her husband had disappeared with the temporary secretary and the proceeds of the Christmas Club over twenty years before. But she never missed one of Oberon's programmes and took the phone off the hook and drew the curtains, to enjoy it all the more.

So, she took the children in, the poor little mites, covered in bits of moss and goodness knew what else. She had bathed them, fed them and given them something to do. They didn't seem interested in the telly, so she had fished out a colouring book, bought for some visiting children long ago. And so they had all been engrossed, she with her cake, they with their crayons, until that terrible sound had ripped through the peaceful air.

Auntie was kind and understanding, but not too nimble. Undine shook her off and continued to make for the kitchen door. Padraig meanwhile, under cover of his wails, was making his way down the hall to the front. Auntie left him to do his worst – the lock on the front door was a deadlock, the chain was securely fastened, against the intruder she knew was always lurking outside to rush in, rape and pillage his only aim, as soon as her back was turned.

She grabbed the sleeve of Undine's jumper, but the little madam wriggled out of it like an eel. She was through the back door in a twinkling, but Auntie still had the advantage. Her garden was completely enclosed – on one side, Mab's side, a lovely rose-pink brick wall was currently swathed in unseasonal climbing roses, their heady scent filling the garden, their stout thorns deterring any attempt to get out that way. At the bottom of the garden was a hedge of tall Leylandii, and embedded in their heart, a barbed wire fence. On the non-Mab, non-tree side, off to her left, was a fence, tall as the wall, but too rickety to climb, too strong for a little girl to break through. Basically, the child was trapped.

Auntie looked down the hall. Padraig was staring up at the lock and Auntie knew he could be left safely while she fetched his sister in. Then, she decided, Mab was going to get a piece of her mind. She had said they were good children. As if bloodcurdling noises in the middle of the morning weren't enough, she had two delinquents to cope with.

She went out into the garden, in time to see Undine float serenely over the fence. She stifled a scream and clutched her throat. She was one of *them*. Mab hadn't told her that. She thought they were human children, or she would never have taken them in. You really couldn't be too careful.

Padraig! She ran down the hall to find the door swinging wide. The chain was broken, but the lock was undamaged. How did he do that? In fact, had she been there to see, it was the faerie way, although not every faerie, as Puck could attest, was as good as Padraig at clicking their fingers. And the words 'Open locks, whoever knocks' – where had he heard that? But faeries are born, not made, and the blood ran deep in Phoebe's children. They just needed a wakeup call from Pan to realise what they could do.

Auntie ran down her path and leaned anxiously on the gate. Down the road ran the two children, hand in hand. Their clothes seemed somehow more diaphanous, their hair more tendrilly, their skin dusted with gold and green. As she watched, a hand to her mouth, their feet left the road, and off they flew, becoming smaller, with distance and the upsurge of their faerie blood.

In seconds, they were tiny dots on the horizon, heading for the glade and their mother. And more danger than they could imagine.

'Pan!'

All movement stopped in Titania's glade.

Annis smiled a tiny smile of satisfaction. So – he was near. She could smell him. She could hear him. Soon she would see him. Touch him, perhaps. She sighed and her old heart leapt again.

James howled in reply. He couldn't help it. It was an instinct from before time. He tried to turn it into a cough, but no one was looking at him. They were all surrounded by their own little tunnel-visioned world of Panic.

At last, thought Oberon, watching with unexpected detachment as his Folk held their collective breath. At last they know how I've been feeling. A cold hand enfolding your heart, freezing your blood, making your breath come as and when it can. That feeling that your eyes are moving a fraction of a second slower than your head. Or faster. Everyone's voice coming from the bottom of a well. Through cotton wool. In a foreign language. And yet, despite the fear, the fluttering of a smile is on your lips, excitement is coursing through your veins. Soon, they would catch up with him, where he sat now, on the crest of the wave of trepidation he had been riding for several sunsets now. And when the wave broke, as it had for him with that echoing cry, they will rush down its side, fear left behind and a strange calm taking its place. Up in his tree, he lay back and waited, like a rabbit at peace in the thrall of a stoat.

Up high above the treetops, Phoebe had almost seen the sound before she heard it. The topmost branches had bent like grass with the force of the noise and when it finally broke, she was tumbled head over heels back to the ground. She fought back against it but it was too strong. As she touched down, she was running, back towards the village, to her children, all thought of collecting the four winds forgotten, as Pandemonium ran at her heels.

Puck thought his heart had stopped. Seconds after the shock wave had passed through his body and left him quivering like a plucked string, he wondered if it had been a noise at all, or just a vibration in the air, set at exactly the right wavelength to make his body reach just the right side of the point of total disintegration.

But no, as his eyelids stopped quivering and his vision cleared, he could see that everyone had heard it. Goblins, especially the sheep, were running aimlessly about, making whatever noise was appropriate to their putative species; the Mr Dobies, moving faster than their usual zimmer-led pace, had gathered together and had quietly formed up in twos, hand in trembling hand, waiting to be told what to do. Some of the tree-sprites had lost a few leaves, but otherwise they had bent with the blast, except the oak-sprite, who was being tended to by a bevy of flower-faeries, some of them a little dishevelled in the petal department themselves. The dwarves, looking truculently over their shoulders, were disappearing, in single file and high dudgeon, down into one of their many tunnel-openings. They had obviously decided that this wasn't their fight. Puck made a mental note to sort out some other Folk to dig. His thoughts turned naturally to James. He knew he was around – no one else could howl like that.

Leanne, unexpectedly unnerved, clung to Benedict and made him drop his spoon. It didn't matter. He had watched in amazement as the water he had collected in it from a near-by puddle had risen at the start of the cry, into a tiny tsunami, throwing itself in micro-wrath over the handle and back into the puddle. He had been working on automatic for some while. He was not used to feeling like he was feeling. He, Lord of Unseelie, King of all dark things, the master of bats across the moon, the tingle down the back of the neck, the snicker in the dark alley, was scared out of his wits. So, he left his wits at the back of his head and carried on collecting his water. He sighed and bent to the puddle.

Titania scanned the glade. She had no concept of time as Mortals understood it, but she knew that what they had re-maining was short. The Singer, her first thought, was still sitting on the bank outside her bower. His fingers were idle on the strings and his lips were parted. He was listening, but not just with his ears. His whole body had become a receiving device and he looked as though he didn't like what it heard.

Looking round, she quickly accounted for air, water, min-eral, animal, vegetable. Earth was absent, but she knew about that. Where was fire? She tuned out what she didn't need, goblins, elves, disappearing dwarves, quivering aspen, broken oak, Puck, Annis, all the rest until she found what she was looking for.

A little group of house fays were gathered at the centre of the clearing, some bending down and others standing, head bowed. She skimmed over to them. They parted as she approached.

'Oh, Mistress,' cried a small brownie, clutching her skirt. 'It's Sally.'

'What happened?'

'I think that loud wind must have blown her out.'

Titania leaned down and took the cold hand of the fire fay. Her red hair was grey and lifeless, not springing joyously from her head as it had before. Usually, a fire fay's touch was hot and dry, but Sally's skin was clammy to the touch, whilst still feeling strangely brittle. The skin of her face was dusty and white.

'Sally?' Titania said quietly. 'Sally, can you hear me?'

The little face, pointed like a flame, turned in her direction.

'Mistress?' she gave a little cough and the smell of phosphorus came on her breath. 'That wind took me by surprise.'

As she spoke, small sparks played in her eyes.

Titania leaned nearer. As she did so, her breath made the sparks glow brighter. But then they seemed to die all the sooner. The queen became aware of a shadow on her back.

'She's not gone,' croaked Annis.

'Annis . . . I think she has.' Titania bowed her head and a silver tear dropped onto Sally's arm, with a tiny sizzle.

'She'll be gone soon enough if you get her soaking wet,' said the hag. 'You,' she pointed to the nearest house brownie, 'go and get some paper.'

'Paper? Here? What do we need paper for?'

'We had all those maps and things,' volunteered Tiny, who had wandered over trying to look brave. He had nearly been trampled by some maddened sheep when he tried to join the goblins, so he was keeping well out of it.

'The thquirrel took thothe.' Thydney had come up behind

Tiny.

'Keep him away,' Annis cried. 'She'll be wet through if you let him near her.'

Thydney backed away, looking hurt.

'I'm sure Annis didn't mean to be personal, dear,' said Titania, who nevertheless kept her distance. This was one of her favourite gowns and just because it was the end of the world didn't mean you had to look scruffy. 'What squirrel?'

'That great big one. The lady one. She'th building a netht. She took all the pageth.'

'What else can we use then?' Titania asked the group at large.

'Hurry up, whatever you use,' Annis said. She was fanning Sally lightly with a pigeon feather she kept in her hair for luck. The sparks were lively, but few.

'I know,' Tiny said, and careered off across the glade. They saw him suddenly shin up a tree sprite and heard a cry of pain. Then he was running back, a length of papery bark blowing behind him like a banner.

'Clever lad,' said Annis, impressed. She tore strips of the bark and laid them under Sally's head like a pillow. Then, she arranged a few more across her face. 'Don't panic, dearie,' she said. 'Time enough for that soon. Keep your eyes open and you'll soon be right as rain.'

'Well,' said Tiny. 'Not rain, or you'll be back to square one.'

'Don't push it, goblin,' grated Annis. 'I haven't had my elevenses yet.'

As the faeries watched, patches of black appeared on the bark mask. Then, small holes appeared in the patches, edged with grey, then tiny sparks danced around their rims. A small flame burst up now and then. Everyone blew gently down at the recumbent fay. Titania wished that Annis and the goblins would leave the blowing to those whose breath didn't smell like the bottom of a pond, but this was no time to be picky.

With a sudden soft puff of heat, Sally's bark crown caught fire and she was alight again. The crowd gathered round her backed off as she jumped to her feet, her whole being aflame. She passed her hands down her body, from her head to her toes and she settled down to a glow, as if of a fire see through frosted glass, from a great distance. But they could still feel the heat.

She followed Annis as she made her slow, halting exit from the group. She put a hand on her arm to stop her and was momentarily surprised by the strength she felt there. The hag stopped and turned.

'Thank you for what you did,' said Sally softly.

'Don't get mushy, faerie,' said Annis harshly. 'I was just doing what had to be done. Fire let us down last time. We needed you.'

'How can I thank you?'

'Well, perhaps, when all this is over, if you see someone who is cold, lying on a bench or in a doorway, just give them a bit of your warmth. You've got some to spare.'

'Might it be you?'

Annis looked into the fire fay's eyes, deep into the twinkling, amber pools. Sally could hardly bear her look but held it as-best she could. Annis' single eye, floating usually in random circles and hard to catch, was burning with a light to rival Sally's own. It bored like a laser. Sally gasped and stepped back. Annis dropped her stare and turned to creep back to her chosen spot.

'No,' Sally heard her mutter. 'I don't expect it will be me.'

Chapter Forty Four

As Pan's cry died away, Gwyddion gingerly took his hands away from his ears.

'I wish you would warn me before you do that kind of thing,' he whined. 'It really hurts.'

'That's the idea,' said Pan, not unkindly. 'I am making the point that I am, when all is said and done, the great Pan. And not dead, either.'

"No, I can tell that,' Gwyddion said, shaking his head. 'It feels as if my brain has come loose. I'm sure it's upside down in my head.'

'So?' Pan nudged him in the ribs. He was feeling good. The birds had begun to sing again in the silence, albeit a little tentatively. The deer, fear forgotten, were cropping the grass as if nothing had happened. A pheasant strutted across the short heath grass on the edge of the trees and called its harsh call. Pan whipped out his pipe and answered, short, low barks on his lowest reed. The pheasant looked up startled and, seeing no other cock, bobbed his head and flew away. Pan kept his pipe to his lips and bubbled back to the birds thronging above him, a thrush song, followed by the waterfall of a blackbird. A wren's chattering scold called a crowd of the pugnacious little birds out of a nearby yew. A piercing four note call made Gwyddion wince.

'Oh, no. Not an owl.' As if on cue, a barn owl floated, silent and pearl white as a feather, out of the trees and landed on Gwyddion's head.

Pan fell backwards laughing. 'It suits you, Druid,' he chortled.

'Droll, Lord. Very droll.' Gwyddion started towards the trees. The owl stayed put. Testing Pan's sense of humour was never a good idea and Gwyddion turned before he disappeared into the wood. 'I won't look very dignified will I, turning up with an owl on my head?'

Pan, who had already forgotten all about him, turned at the sound of his voice and went off into paroxysms of laughter all over again.

'Lord? Please?'

Pan waved an arm and the owl flew off into the wood.

'It's not going to wait for me, is it?'

'Of course not,' Pan said, wiping his eyes with the back of his hand. "No, of course not.' He gave a sniff and a small cough and sat up, looking grave. 'This is important, Druid. Off you go, now, to tell the others. I'm right behind you.'

'Right.' Gwyddion squared his shoulders and walked into the trees. Pan sat on the grass, covering his mouth like a schoolboy, stifling his giggles. He heard crashing in the undergrowth and an enraged Gwyddion stormed out onto the heath again, the owl firmly on his head.

'Sorry, Druid.' The god rolled about this time, with the exquisiteness of the joke. He waved the owl away. It flew off, a bit annoyed in its own right. It was all right for the Druid to talk dignified. How dignified did an owl look, perched on a tatty smelly Druid, that's what he would like to know.

'Thank you. I'll see you later, then.'

'Yes. Though I may see you first.'

Gwyddion gave Pan a nervous look and dived back into the trees.

'Don't forget,' muttered Pan, 'the Singer isn't the only shape shifter around here. Oh, no.'

He let Gwyddion get a start on him, then, in one bound, full of the joy of life, the promise of confusion to his enemies, his muscles bunched in a tacit display of power, he was on his feet. He pranced on the spot in time to the sweet music in his head and then whistled to the nearest doe, grazing unconcernedly in the gorse.

She came over to him, her innocent eyes held by his. He put a hand on her velvet head and raised her muzzle so he could look into her head, through the gateway of her luminous pupils. He took a breath, and suddenly was gone.

The doe opened her mouth. Pan's voice said, 'It's show time,' and he steered the doe towards the trees.

Slowly, the glade calmed down. Oberon stayed in his tree, Hazel carried on his ticking off on his list, Leanne and Benedict ambled round the perimeter, armed with a silver cup and an increasingly slimy spoon. Puck and James had an impressive collection of animals; the boar had been giving trouble, but less so now that the wolf was in line, and the bear, leaning casually up against Oberon's tree, had made all the fauna suddenly rather well-behaved. Titania was sitting with the Singer and Annis in the shade. Phoebe had arrived back from her hysterical flight to the village to find her children playing 'Find the Lady' with Freckles. She was currently shaking them and hugging them by turns, with the hugs just slightly in the ascendancy.

It was a peaceful scene, taken over all. A sheep goblin would now and again have a funny turn and would have to be slapped. Some of the more aggressive faerie were queuing up to take advantage of this stress-busting necessity. The hum of bees in the clover around Titania's bower underscored the rhythm of the afternoon as it wore on. Voices grew drowsy, the sun rose high in the sky, flowers bloomed and died at a glance from Annis. The air grew heavy with scented promise of the end of the world. Eyelids drooped and lips smiled as they foresaw life with Pan. How bad could it be? He wasn't so bad . . .

Gwyddion burst onto this idyllic scene like a bad smell. His journey with Pan had left him' dishevelled, to say the least of it. His hair, usually sleekly plaited at the temples and brushed till it shone like a silver waterfall down his back was standing out madly in all directions. It held so many twigs and leaves that the owl had felt quite at home there, during its two brief stays. His robe, once so white it was hard to look at was now streaked with all kinds of unmentionable stains. The house fays tutted to see it and the faeries of the laundry fairly itched to get it in the suds. A tidemark just above his knees bore testimony to Pan's natural love of riverbanks. The dropped food from their hurried picnic was still lodged in the robes many creases and folds. The back was still caught up somehow in the Druid's complicated underwear. Pan had noticed it from the first but found it too amusing to mention.

In his flight through the wood, Gwyddion had picked up fresh brambles, mostly in his beard, and he was picking leaf mould out of his teeth as he lurched into the sunlight.

A sheep goblin screamed, and was immediately slapped by Elder, who had had enough.

Oberon cowered on his branch. It was Titania who swept forward regally, hand extended in friendship for this tattered thing.

'Welcome,' she said, to my . . .' she stopped and peered at the tattered thing. 'Gwyddion? Is that you?'

He spat out a final piece of loam. 'Yes, Mistress, it's me.' Titania turned to the gathering crowd. 'It's Gwyddion,' she called. 'He's all right.'

'Are you sure, Mistress?' Puck asked, looking closely. 'He looks as if he's been run over.'

"Not quite,' Gwyddion said. 'But close, lad, very close.' He put a hand to the back of his head, trying to tidy himself up a bit for the queen. It came away covered in owl shit and he wiped it on the side of his robe. It would make no difference to the general effect.

'Where have you been? 'Titania asked, as she and Puck helped him to a fallen log.

'I've been . . . all over, Mistress.'

'All over?' the queen felt a nudge in her back and turned. 'Thank you, Annis,' she said, is full queen mode. You could have cut her regality with a spoon. 'Thank you for your help earlier, but we're all right here.'

Annis trundled on her way, brushing the queen aside. She pressed her nose to the quailing Druid and inhaled deeply. She nodded and chuckled.

'He's been with Pan,' she announced.

The crowd stepped back ore pace.

'Gwyddion!' said Titania, shocked. 'Are you a spy?'

'No! No, of course I'm not a spy. I would have said in a minute, if this disgusting old hag hadn't pushed her way in. How she can smell anything, I fail to see. My nostrils have closed up just having her near me for a minute.'

'Strikes me,' Oberon had risked land to saunter over, his veneer of calm still in place, 'strikes me that if I had been with Pan, I would have shouted it out straight away, as soon as I was clear of the trees.'

'No, no. You don't understand! I've come to tell you . . .'

Oberon's patience could stand no more stretching. His horns hurt and he had spent a nasty few moments earlier when they got caught in a branch as he flew up to his favourite perch. He had hung there like an exotic fruit until Titania had untangled him. 'Strikes me,' he continued, 'that I would have been so glad to see all my friends, that I would have run straight into the glade and told them what I had been doing. Not have to have it dragged out of me.'

"No. Not dragged. I would have said. Please! You've got to listen to me. I've been with Pan for long enough to know he's not all bad . . .'

Annis grinned. She had been expecting this. She looked around, her eye as keen as an eagle's, hidden under her matted hair.

'Lock him up!' shouted Oberon, striking a pose and pointing randomly into the trees.

Puck looked wildly around 'In what, Lord?' he asked finally.

'Something. I don't know. Wasn't Myrddion locked up in a tree or something?'

'Yes,' the Singer had come up behind the king and was looking with interest at Gwyddion. 'But that was done by the nymph Nimue and he allowed her to do it for love. I can't see any nymphs here, except that very young one over there,' he pointed at Undine, who hid nervously behind her mother, 'and I can't imagine any other denizen of wood or field fancying him at the moment. Can you?'

Gwyddion looked at his feet and noticed for the first time he only had one sandal. Taliesin stepped forward and took his arm.

'Oberon, I'll look after him. Is that good enough?'

Oberon glowered. Just like those Druids to stick together. If he wasn't careful, they'd have him bound and trussed like a chicken and under a hill. He'd keep an eye on them.

Titania spoke for her Lord. 'Yes, Taliesin, that would be wonderful. Take him to my bower. Someone will be along,' she gestured over her head to some of her faerie, 'to help you tidy him up. Give him something to eat and drink, although perhaps he's not hungry; he seems to have a sausage roll sticking out of his robe. Just a drink, then, and you can let us know when he's feeling more like himself.' She clapped her hands. 'Shoo, shoo,' she said to her crowding Folk. 'Nothing to see here. I'm sure you're all busy. Off you go.'

The crowd melted slowly away, but with much head turning as Gwyddion was led off. There were little clumps of gossip forming all around the glade. Rumour was spreading almost visibly, like smoke across the grass.

Puck went back to counting his animals. He was pleased to see that James had managed to capture a milk-white doe; he hadn't thought he had it in him.

As Puck went along the row, mentally ticking off his acquisitions, the doe turned its head. Annis was standing near, staring reflectively through her hair. The doe looked back and then, when it was sure, gave her a wink.

Chapter Forty Five

Gwyddion stood on the threshold of Titania's bower but seemed reluctant to enter.

Taliesin gave him a gentle push in the small of his back. 'In you go,' he said. 'Let's get you tidied up a bit.'

Gwyddion gestured to the beautiful room, much larger on the inside that out, not so much decorated as evolved out of the colour of rose petals, the sheen on a new conker as it bursts on the woodland floor, the scent of grass, buttercups and clean skin. He then gestured to his own appearance and Taliesin had to admit there was a serious dichotomy.

Nevertheless, Titania had told him to take Gwyddion there, and so he would. He looked around for a seat stout enough to take a man's weight and found none. In the end, he spread a rug on the bed and Gwyddion sat there, looking sheepish.

There was a small cough from the doorway and a small knot of faerie stood there, brushes and combs at the ready, damp cloths steaming lightly in bowls and a brilliant white robe folded and ironed, all ready to spruce a Druid up.

'Come in,' Taliesin cried. 'Come in and get on with your job. I'll be back later,' he said to Gwyddion, 'with food if you want and something to drink. Anything you fancy?'

"No wine,' Gwyddion said weakly. 'And nothing greasy. Nothing fried. No meat. No hunks of bread. No olives. No honey. No grapes. Did I say no wine? No mead. No . . .'

Taliesin crept away. If he had needed proof that Gwyddion had spent time with Pan, he had it now. Pan's diet had never been heavy on the green vegetables. Perhaps a nice salad would sort Gwyddion out. He set off towards the pile of vegetation that Hazel was picking though. He didn't expect lettuce, since it had never struck him as being particularly magical, and cucumber was even more unlikely. But there might be a few herbs that weren't too bitter that might pass muster. Parsley, perhaps. Sage. Rosemary and Thyme.

Leanne was starting to fret. She had spent so much time with Benedict and his water collection, she had given little time to her minerals. The dwarves seemed to have disappeared into one of their tunnels. She didn't like going underground, so following them was almost out of the question. She just hoped that they didn't know that.

She had put in an order for diamonds, for silver, for gold, silicon, to start with. Any mercury they might come across would be useful. She had always been fascinated by mercury, a liquid that was a metal – cool. She went to the edge of the tunnel and looked around, under rocks and branches, hoping to find a little pile of precious stones and metals, but none were to be found.

'Little buggers,' she said, stamping her foot. 'I knew I couldn't rely on them.'

'Problems?'

'Oh, Annis. You again?' Leanne sighed. She couldn't even summon up the energy to be nasty. She hadn't eaten, not really eaten in days and was getting testy.

'I say – problems?'

'Oh, you might say that,' said Leanne. 'I asked the dwarves to get me a few things and they haven't, that's all. It shouldn't be too hard to get what I need elsewhere.'

'What do you need?' asked the hag. 'Tell old Annis. I said I'd help you, didn't I?'

Leanne looked at her sharply. 'You did. But please remember that I am in charge. That was made quite clear at the time.'

'I'm old, dearie,' said Annis, remembering just in time to insert a quaver in her voice. 'I don't always remember.'

'Hmmm. Well, *I* am in charge of mineral.'

'If you say so. I don't recall the detail, of course,' Annis quivered, 'but when I was young, things had more power if they were hard won, delved with your own hands, dug with your own sweat. I don't think,' her voice grew stronger, 'that scaring a few dwarves into parting with some treasure really counts as difficult.'

'Well,' snapped Leanne. 'It clearly is difficult, since they haven't done it.'

'That's a little Zen, dearie,' said Annis, struggling over the spoil heap at the edge of the dwarves' tunnel. 'I think you ought to get down there and have a look around. They may have left some things as they went.'

Leanne shuddered. 'I don't do tunnels.'

'You'll be doing more than tunnels if we don't succeed in our task.'

'We?'

'That is, you, naturally.'

'Do I have to look down there?'

'Only way as far as I can see.'

Leanne braced herself and picked her way over the spoil heap and into the mouth of the tunnel, where she was immediately bent double. 'It's dark in here.'

'Well, it would be,' said Annis. 'It's underground.'

'Hah. Hah.' Leanne's voice had an eldritch echo, an effect she would have been grateful for had she been able to hear it from outside. 'Annis? Annis? How far in should I go? Annis?'

But the hag was gone, carrying a small bag of assorted gems, gold and silver she had found tucked on a ledge just inside the tunnel. She popped it into her pocket, along with the earth and the withered love-in-idleness. She chuckled. It was like taking candy from a baby.

Puck was trying to count his animals and it wasn't proving to be easy. For a start, he couldn't count, as such, and had to keep a tally on his fingers. Then, they kept moving about. The birds kept flying around, the herbivores were giving the carnivores a wide berth and the bees just didn't bear thinking about. Some of the birds were quite sweet, and no trouble, but the swan was a bit of a nuisance, rushing at faeries with no provocation, wings outstretched and hissing. It had trapped a Mr Dobie for some time in a hollow tree, the poor little creature's cries drowned out by the thunder of wing-beats. He had had to speak firmly to the fox, which had been tracking Bill around the glade as the little goblin collected what it fondly thought were important bits of grass for his Lord. It wasn't so much that Bill was being impeded in an important task. It was more how stress affected him. Some of the more earth-bound faerie were beginning to complain.

So Puck stood in the centre of the clearing and tried to get it clear in his mind. The bear, stag, doe, wolf, ram and boar were easy. They were either there or not. You didn't have to turn a rock over to check. The hare and fox tended to blend a bit more, but where Bill was the fox could be found not far behind and the hare was dancing quietly to itself to the tune echoing round Freckles' earphones.

James wandered over.

'How's it going, Puck?' asked the butler, still rather full of himself after bringing Sally back.

'Oh, you know,' Puck spun round and round, trying to keep the bees in sight as they spiralled in the air, looking for a suitable branch to land on. 'Coming along.' He gave up on the bees. 'Good work on the doe, by the way.'

James looked confused but smiled ingratiatingly, showing his canines. 'No problem.'

'I think we have all the rest, although I can't put my hand on my toad.'

James sidled away a little.

'But I hope a frog will do instead. I've got one in that bucket over there.'

'Bucket?' a small disquiet knocked on the back of James' skull.

'Yes. It's over there, half full of rather dirty water, but the frog seems happy enough.'

But will the Master be happy, thought James, but decided to say nothing. Sufficient unto the day was the evil thereof, although James was usually all up for evil.

'Then there are the birds. I've gathered them together and I just have to hope they're in the trees somewhere.'

James looked round aimlessly. 'Probably.'

'Oh no!'

'What?'

'I've forgotten something.'

'What?'

'A dog.'

'*What?*'

'I need a dog.'

'Don't look at me.'

Puck advanced on James, looking like a Faerie who means business. 'What choice do I have?'

'Plenty. The village is full of dogs.'

'And you should know, I suppose.'

'All work and no play, you know . . .'

'It's too late to go and get one. I need you.'

'Let's do without the dog, eh, Puck, old friend?'

'Don't grovel, James. We need a dog. You're a dog. No contest.'

'Please,' whined James, pawing at Puck's chest and drooling. 'Please don't make me be the dog.'

'Don't be ridiculous,' said Puck, knocking the bogle away. 'You are a dog. I can't help that.'

'I am not so a dog,' James sulked. 'I'm a butler.'

'A dog.'

'A Personal Assistant.'

'A dog.'

'A bogle.' James bared his teeth horribly and growled.

'Annis?' Puck asked the hag as she hobbled past. 'Is James a dog?'

'Yes,' said Annis. 'Definitely a dog.'

'There you are,' said Puck. 'You're a dog. Get in line. You'll be between the Hawk and the Owl, assuming they turn up.'

James dropped to his knees and hugged Puck round the waist. Puck walked away, dragging him behind, legs bouncing in the dust.

"Now, where are those bees?"

A scream which could only come from the throat of the King of Faerie rang round the glade. The bees had found a bough to their liking at last. Unfortunately, Oberon had got there first.

'Ah! There they are.' Puck lurched off towards the King's Tree, James trailing behind like a furry train.

In the excitement, no one saw Annis snatch up the wren minding its own business on a nearby bush, and tuck it into her pocket, to take its chances with the gems, the withered herb and the dirt.

Chapter Forty Six

P hoebe had finally stopped scolding the children. She was very proud of them, deep down. She still felt, like mothers everywhere, that no matter how well they had done, if it wasn't at her specific instruction, they needed a good telling off.

Undine had snivelled for a bit, for the look of the thing. Padraig had stared her straight in the eye without even a wobble of the chin. She saw, in that moment, what Titania had seen – a boy after the Lord of Misrule's own heart, who would be scooped up in his merry rout, to be spat out later, with no faerie left in him, just the bitter husk that was his father's legacy.

She left them in the care of one of the house fays. Mab was elsewhere, spreading rumour as she went about, to all intents co-ordinating. But Phoebe couldn't help noticing that brows were more wrinkled, eyes were more anxious, when she had done her stuff. Too late to worry about that now. Let her dabble in confusion – the lord of it would be among them soon enough and then she would find what confusion *really* meant.

Phoebe caught an updraft of warm air and checked on her winds, carefully stored in the tallest tree, safe in dense gossamer bags, woven for her by some willing spiders. She had a feeling, black and heavy, deep in her inside, that someone down there on the ground was not to be trusted. She didn't know who it was, but she was keeping her air up here where it was safe. She lay at ease in a high branch and let the warm zephyr rock her to sleep.

In the shade of a bush, Undine and Padraig were playing jacks with the house fay. She loved looking after children and had spent many a happy year entertaining the offspring of cottagers and farmers' wives as the parents clawed a living from the land. She was a merry soul and the children's laughter could be heard all over the glade.

The shade grew darker.

'Phew,' said Padraig, holding his nose. 'Is that you, Undine?'

Before the outraged child could answer, the grated reply came from the other side of the bush.

'No, it's me I'm afraid, dearie.' Annis peeped through the branches. 'I can't help it. I'm old.'

'Can you play jacks?' asked Padraig. If the smell wasn't something he could tease his sister about, it ceased to interest him.

'I haven't tried for many a long year, young man,' said Annis. 'How is it done?'

'Well,' Padraig said. 'First, you have to get down on the ground, like this.'

The house fay jumped up and took the strain as Annis subsided like a ton of bricks to the floor.

'Thank you, dearie,' Annis said to the helpful creature. 'Could you do an old lady another favour?'

'Well . . .' the little faerie was dubious. Phoebe had impressed upon her how important it was that she watch the children carefully.

'They'll be all right with me,' Annis grated. 'Won't you, dears?'

Padraig giggled. He had been losing at jacks – a trembly old dear like this one would be easy to beat. 'We'll be all right,' he said. 'Don't worry, we won't run away.'

'Well, all right then,' said the faerie. 'What is it you want?'

'Just a glass of water, dear, if it's not too much trouble,' Annis said. 'But, I don't want to be a nuisance. Just get it from that bucket over there. It's not very clean but it's how I like it. Just mind out for the frog.'

The house fay gave her a funny look, but went off in search of a glass, anyway.

'Right,' said Annis. 'How do you play this game?'

'It's easy,' said Undine. 'You take these things in your hand, like this . . .'

'. . . and throw them up in the air and catch them, but on the back of your hand.'

'Picking the ball up as well,' said Undine.

Padraig whispered in his sister's ear.

'Oh, yes. Sorry. If that's not too hard for you.'

'Hmm, let me see.' Annis blew on the jacks in her hand, threw them up, grabbed the ball and caught the jacks in one impossible to detect movement. 'Like this?'

Undine and Padraig looked astonished. 'How did you get them in a row like that?' the little boy asked.

'It's easy,' said Annis. 'Watch.' She blew on the jacks again and threw them in the air. This time, they made up a rough 'a' on the back of her hand. 'That's A for Annis, my name,' she explained.

'Do U for Undine,' begged the girl.

"No,' said Padraig. 'P for Padraig.'

'P is quite hard,' said Annis. 'But U should be all right. Now,' she held out her clenched fist to Undine. 'Blow on them.'

The child looked at Annis withered fingers, clutching round the jacks. She had long, pointed talons and bits of stuff, black and rancid, were stuck down them. Feathers and long hairs were caught in the nail of the thumb, bent over the rest. She drew back.

'Come on, now. Don't be frightened. Just blow.'

Tentatively, the girl blew on Annis' hand. The jacks tossed up in the air and, while they were still falling, Annis was up off the ground and was hobbling away. Her hand was firmly in her pocket.

'How did she do that?' Padraig asked in astonishment.

Undine was also astonished, but mainly annoyed. The jacks had come down on the grass to spell out the letter P.

Annis hobbled away, Undine's breath safely stored in her

grease-lined, and therefore air-tight pocket, along with the dried herb, the soil, the gems and a wren rather woozy from the smell.

She did a little jig, under her skirts and away from prying eyes.

The house fay, coming towards her with the glass of brackish water, broke into a run.

'What have you done with the children?' she asked in a panic.

"Nothing, dearie. Nothing. They're where you left them. Is that my water? How kind.' She took the glass and the faerie was only too glad to be on her way, back to her charges.

Very deliberately, Annis poured the glass of water down the front of her clothes and shuddered as a few drops made their way through the many layers between the air and her skin.

She made her way back to her withered patch of grass and squatted, with elaborate wheezings and groanings. She settled hack, patting her pocket every now and then for reassurance and waited. She was good at waiting. She had had a lot of practice.

The milk white doe was having some trouble from an unexpected quarter. Pan wasn't used to being accosted – he was the one who made all the running, always had been. But the stag in Puck's menagerie was giving him serious attention. The god had tried a few girlish caracoles and leaps, but the great stupid thing had taken no notice. He had tried butting, but his delicate horns made no impression of the chunk of nerveless venison armouring the side of the enormous male.

The other animals looked on in amusement. Until the doe had turned up, the stag had been rather indiscriminate and several of the sheep goblins would never be the same again.

The doe tried one more kick, easily sidestepped by the stag, who had one thought in his minute mind. 'She's playing hard to get' was his mantra, and he played it to himself whenever anything that he had set his sights on, be it doe, horse, five-bar gate or tractor did not fall immediately for his charms. He had a lot of luck, but also a lot of rebuffs. But he shrugged them off with a skill only given to those with one lone brain cell.

'Look,' snarled Pan, turning on the stag. 'Go away.'

The stag looked down his nose. His inamoratae had never actually talked back before. He wasn't sure he liked it.

'I'm not a doe.'

Tchah. How stupid did this doe think he was? He tried again and got a head butt that made his antlers rattle.

'Get it into your thick skull. I'm in disguise.'

Whatever.

Pan sighed. Why did it have to be so difficult? He should just manifest himself, here and now, and just beat these faeries hollow. But, watching them was Fun, with more Fun later, if he was any judge. So, he dropped his shoulders and wandered off to graze in the safety of Annis' smell. The stag, whose eyesight wasn't very keen, would never find him there.

The hag looked up as the doe approached. She smiled. She winked.

Chapter Forty Seven

Gwyddion had polished up quite nicely. The faeries had many secrets up their tiny sleeves and his hair glowed like mercury down his back, his nails were polished, his beard was like silk. His robe was so white it almost hurt to look at it and he had on a pair of beautiful sandals, woven from rushes, for his feet. He wasn't so keen on the rushes; it made the Panic of the last hours all flood back, but they were comfortable, and it was kindly meant. He checked his horn, his sickle, his mistletoe, his pouch of herbal tobacco, his pipe, his disposable lighter . . . well, a Druid had to have some comforts.

Beside him, Taliesin looked quite ordinary. He was dressed to blend, to such a degree that he almost seemed to disappear when he stood still. Standing leaning on a tree, as he was now, he was dressed in brown, flecked with green. When he had been with Gwyddion in Titania's bower, he had seemed dressed in brightest white, with a hint of rose petal at the edges. The old Shape Shifter hadn't lost his touch.

Gwyddion stood on the bank on Titania's threshold. He clapped his hands. No one took the blindest bit of notice. He tried again. Still no response. He reached for his horn and raised it to his lips.

Taliesin, seeing this, was by his side in an instant. He had heard Gwyddion play the instrument before, and it wasn't an experience he wanted to repeat. He raised his voice slightly.

'Everyone!' The note rang out like a bell and every face, in every colour from white through to grey, via green and brown, turned to him. He gestured Oberon down from his tree, Titania from where she sat with her ladies and Puck from the head of his ragged line of animals to join him on the bank.

'Benedict!' Titania called. 'Could you come over here, please?'

'There's a frog in my water,' Benedict said crossly.

'Are you taking anything for it?' called a goblin amid much hilarity.

'Phoebe!' This was not so enthusiastic, but Titania knew she had to be there.

There was a shaking in a high branch and a bleary-eyed Phoebe stuck her head out.

'What?'

'Could you join us, please?' Titania trilled. 'It's time.'

'Already?' There was a rustling in the treetop as she loosened the bags looped over a branch, then she swooped down to the ground. 'Where are my children?'

'They're here, with me,' called the house fay. 'They're all right.'

'Leave the kiddies, dear,' patronised the queen. 'You have work to do.' She looked around. 'Where's Leanne?'

'Here.' Leanne stepped out from behind a nearby bush. She was beautiful of course, it was hard for her not to be, but she looked as if she had been pulled through a hedge backwards. Long streaks of chalk and dirt decorated her business suit, once so crisp and smart. Her tights were in shreds and a heel had come off one shoe.

'What happened to you?' Titania asked, aghast.

'Those rotten dwarves, they sold me down the river.'

'You look more as if you've been down a hole,' said Titania.

'Not literally the river,' Leanne said. 'I mean they were

supposed to leave me some stuff for the spell at the mouth of their tunnel and they didn't. So I went to look for it.'

'Any luck?'

"No. Nothing. Just worms and moles. Hardly enough for a canapé on one of those. But certainly no gems or similar.'

'Oh dear,' smiled Titania. It pleased her more than she would admit to see Leanne looking so dishevelled. If only Oberon was taking notice at present. But he just stood there, eyes flickering over the crowd, jumping as if bitten now and then, and then just as suddenly shaking his head and muttering to himself. She hoped he would be all right when all this was over. You heard such things.

The queen was basically kind and swept a regal hand towards Leanne. Her dirty clothes disappeared, to be replaced by a flowing gown in amber which suited her like a skin. Tiny, who had been watching as the change took place, swore he had seen a brief second when there were no clothes at all, but since the toadstool incident, he had been rather prone to exaggeration and so the others ignored it. Tiny just hugged the memory to him – he felt he might need something to console him in what lay ahead.

Leanne looked down at the overtly Faerie outfit.

'Oh, *please*!' she said, but stroked the fabric, smooth as baby's skin, warm as new milk, with her hand lingeringly all the same.

'You look lovely, Leanne,' the queen said, smiling. 'But do I understand you? You have no minerals?'

"No,' said Leanne, keeping her eyes on the ground. Benedict was looking smug, swinging his bucket slightly and smiling.

Titania reached into her hair and plucked out her coronet. She threw it across to Leanne in an arc of cold fire.

The vampire's arm shot out and caught it as it rushed by. Titania was beautiful, kind and wise, but no thrower.

Puck said, 'Mistress . . .?'

'Ssshh, Puck,' said the queen. 'It's only jewels.'

'Diamonds?' breathed Leanne.

The queen inclined her head.

'Silver?'

'Well,' the queen chuckled, 'platinum, but an easy mistake to make.'

'Gold?'

'Three colours.'

'Thank you,' Leanne held it up to the sun and the diamonds flared. 'Thank you.'

The queen looked expectant.

'Mistress.'

Titania bowed her head.

'Thank you, Leanne,' she smiled. She raised her head and called, 'Sally?'

'Here, Mistress.' The fire fay was back to her old self, twinkling red against Gwyddion's austere white and Oberon's brooding black.

'Then, we are all here,' said Titania.

'Oh, yes, that's right.' The mutter came from near Titania's feet. 'That's right. "We're all here". Why wait till the coordinator says we're all here? Why not just announce it, eh? Has anyone checked everything is all here? Oh, no. Just announce it, why don't you . . .'

'Mab?' said Titania, bending down. 'Is there something wrong?'

'Wrong? Oh no. Everything's just peachy.'

'Would you like to say a few words?'

'Please. Don't do me any favours.'

'I'd really love it if you would.'

Mab stood up and half turned to the crowd. 'Everything's ready,' she muttered. 'Take your places for the binding spell.'

🕸🕸🕸🕸

The doe bent her slender legs and sank down on the grass beside Annis.

'It's almost too easy, isn't it?' Pan said.

'Be gentle with them,' Annis asked.

'Why?'

'I shall miss them . . . would miss them, I mean, should anything happen. Particularly him.' She pointed at Benedict.

'He seems harmless enough. I might spare him.'

'And him,' she pointed again.

The doe shook her head.

"No, sorry. I have need of him. He can't be spared.'

Annis turned to look at the doe, glowing faintly with an inner light, there in her shady spot. Pan was right, women couldn't always make up their minds. He would have been annoyed to find that he had just clicked the last piece into place.

Like a continent, slowly, imperceptibly, Annis began her final move.

Chapter Forty Eight

Titania turned to the Singer. 'How do we begin?' she asked him out of the corner of her mouth.

'The order doesn't matter,' said Taliesin. 'But every section has to be complete and done with proper solemnity.' He looked across the glade, to where a group of rabbits, their concentration span outstayed by several minutes, gambolled in a furry ring, egged on by the hare, which had wandered away from the other animals. 'Do you think that is going to be possible?'

Titania followed his gaze. 'I see your point,' she said. 'I'll just have a word with Oberon. He's usually very good at this sort of thing.'

'Really?' said Taliesin politely. Oberon was standing on the bank, looking longingly at his tree. 'He isn't very at ease out of his tree, is he?'

'I beg your pardon?' the queen wheeled round. 'Oh, I see what you mean. Could we, perhaps, incorporate his tree?'

'Hmm. I don't see why not. He is in charge of vegetable, after all. Promise him that if you have to, but get him to have a word with everyone first. We really need one hundred percent co-operation.'

That sounded a lot to Titania and so she went over to the

king and put a gentle hand on his arm.

'Dearest Lord,' she breathed in his ear. 'Could you speak to our Folk? They are worried and restless, and we need them to attend to the proceedings if they are to work.'

Oberon shrugged and his curls bounced on his beautiful forehead. 'What's the point? Pan is here already, I can feel him. He is out there, pretending to be one of us. So it won't matter what I do, confusion will follow.'

'Don't be negative, dearest,' she said, laying it on with a trowel. 'I can't see anyone he might be. And you know I know *all* of my Folk.'

'He's hiding,' hissed Oberon. 'If he's hiding, how will you know who he is? What if he is a Mr Dobie? Don't tell me you can tell them apart.'

'Do you know,' she said. 'I'm beginning to think I can. There's one, I know this for a fact, who looks a bit like someone called Brad Pitt. Mab told me.'

'Huh. Mab. I think she might be him.'

'She might be him, Lord?'

'Well, perhaps not, but he's around here, I know it.'

'All the more reason, then, to speak out. Let him see you're not afraid.'

'But I am.'

'Show him you're not!'

Oberon leaned down and kissed the tip of her nose, a feather touch of a faerie kiss. He squared his shoulders and stepped forward. The crowd slowly came to order. Even the animals were listening. Especially the milk white doe.

'People!' Oberon raised both hands and slowly brought them down to his sides. 'A great task is ahead of us. As you all know, the great god Pan . . .'

The doe nodded, pleased.

'. . . is among us again. I don't know how many of you were here when he was bound, many many Mortal years ago. But I can promise you that this time, he will be bound for ever.'

The doe sniggered.

'We have been gathering the stuff of spells and bindings, we have among us Taliesin, the Singer, to weave the spell with his music.'

The doe snorted. 'If you can call that music,' Pan muttered.

'What we need from you,' he paused and raked them with his stare, 'What we must have from you, is your total support. You must be quiet when quiet is called for, you must respond when the Singer asks you. But, most of all, keep calm. Don't be afraid. The God of Confusion, the Bringer of Mischief, the Shapeshifter, the Lord of Misrule will be amongst us in all his power, very soon. No matter what he does, what he may say, remember us, your King and Queen. Remember each other.' His voice dropped to just above a whisper. 'Remember Faerie.' He bowed his head and listened to the crowd. Nothing. Which was as it should be.

Taliesin leaned over and whispered to Puck, 'He's still got it. Tolkein himself,' and the Druid and the elf spat over their shoulders in unison, 'couldn't have put it better.'

Oberon spun round. 'Be quiet!' he roared. 'We are ready to begin!'

'Oops,' muttered Mab. 'Testy.'

'Crumbth,' Thydney sprayed in Bill's feathered ear. 'He'th croth.'

'Fit to be tied,' said Tiny.

'I thought that was Pan,' chortled Freckles and had to be sat on. The king had spoken. His Boys must obey.

Elsewhere, the crowd was largely silent. Even the Unseelie contingent were quiet; they had had years of going about their dubious business in peace and, while they approved of Pan in principle, in practice they had found he could queer their pitch. So they sat, stood or, in the more extreme cases, oozed, and waited for the ceremonies to begin.

Taliesin stepped down onto the level turf at the foot of the bank. He had spent his few leisure hours that morning trimming and cutting away at his guitar until it was just a frame with the twelve strings strung across the middle. He knew that Messrs Gibson would understand. A future of panpipe music was too much to contemplate. The Aeolian harp now hung in the King's Tree, catching the breeze. He waved a hand and a gentle chord thrummed through the clearing, calming the nerves of the gathered Seelie and Unseelie courts, soothing the brows of those that had them.

Chapter Forty Nine

Taliesin of the radiant brow, shape shifter and sooth-sayer, spoke to them, and his speech was song.

'Puck.' And Puck's key was C, crisp and jaunty.

'Announce your creatures, one by one, with name and purpose, as our totems rule.'

Puck stepped forward, dressed for the occasion in his favourite tight green. He cleared his throat and raised his arm, his hand extended like a perch.

'Blackbird,' he called.

From the deep wood that ringed the faerie clearing came a liquid song. Then, a blackbird, with a beak bright like the sun and yellow feet tucked up in its flight rocketed out from the leaves and swung down through the air to land on Puck's finger.

'*Druid Dhubh*,' sang Taliesin. 'He stands for a transition between realities and will help us take the god to his new reality beneath his hill.'

Titania leaned over and whispered to Leanne. 'Do we have a hill in mind?'

The vampire turned slightly and shrugged. Digging was not her business, not with what manicures cost these days.

The blackbird completed the phrase of its song – Taliesin would never interrupt a cadence – and flew off to perch on the roof of Titania's bower.

'Stag,' called Puck, and the monarch of the glen pranced

forward. Even though a deeply single minded animal, something of the occasion had rubbed off and he slowed as he approached Puck, raising and lowering his head so that those near to him could hear the swish of his antlers through the air.

'*Damh*,' sang the bard. 'For pride, independence and purification. To help us curb the pride of Pan before we bind him.'

'Hind,' called Puck, and held out his hand to the milk white doe.

The animal did not move.

'Don't tell me it's dead,' muttered Gwyddion. 'That's all we need.'

Puck raised his voice a notch. 'Hind!'

Annis nudged Pan's disguise with her toe.

'Oy. Ye're on.'

'Hmmph.' The doe woke up with a start and scrambled to her feet.

Puck stood there, hands on hips. The doe walked towards him, on her dainty tip-toe.

'*Eilid*,' sang Taliesin. 'For subtlety, which we must show, femininity and grace, to represent our queen.'

Titania smiled and waved.

'Good choice,' muttered Annis to herself, and smothered a laugh.

The stag had done his best to keep the mood going. But there was that pretty doe again. He stepped forward and Puck had to give him a clout. 'Stop that. Stand where you were told, you stupid thing.' He couldn't help looking at Oberon as he said it. It was a train of thought.

He turned away and called through his cupped hands. 'Tantivvy, tantivvy. The fox.' A golden stream of light slunk into the sunlight dappling the ground. The black tip of the fox's tail waved to and fro and one of the rabbits stifled a nervous laugh and was shushed. The animal licked its black nose and lay panting at Puck's feet.

'*Sionnach*,' the Druid crooned to the trembling animal. 'For diplomacy, cunning and wildness.'

The fox slunk round Puck's feet and settled down at the

hem of Leanne's dress. It felt inexplicably at home there and she, in turn, let it stay.

'The boar,' called Puck. The great truffling thing charged across the space and skidded to a halt at Puck's feet. The tusks gouged a deep divot in the turf as it turned just in time. The elf leapt in the air and hovered there, out of reach, while Taliesin announced the boar's true name and purpose.

'*Tore*. For the way of the warrior, for leadership. For direction.'

'He certainly made a beeline for Puck,' whispered Benedict to Gwyddion. 'I thought he was a goner there.'

But Puck was continuing. 'The hawk.'

A dot in the sky above hung over the crowd. It grew no bigger and Puck sighed.

'He's been trouble all day,' he muttered to Taliesin. 'Better announce him and let him stay where he is.'

'*Sealbhac*,' Taliesin sang. 'For nobility, which the god Pan has in great abundance.' The doe threw up her head suddenly and caught the stag a nasty one under the chin. 'For recollection and cleansing.'

'The dog.'

Nothing moved.

'*The dog*.' Puck repeated, then turned to the folk gathered on the bank. 'James, I can't believe you're doing this. Get down here.'

Benedict leaned forward. 'Down you go, James, there's a good butler.'

James looked into his master's face. He sighed and did as he was told.

'*Cù*,' sang Taliesin, and the harp echoed the sound. 'For loyalty.'

'You've got that right,' said James, as he slouched into his place in the line. 'Otherwise you lot could have whistled for my appearance.'

'Thank you, *dog*,' said Puck through gritted teeth. 'Owl,' he called.

'Oh, no,' said Gwyddion, trying to cover the top of his head.

'*Cailleach-ordhche*,' sang Taliesin, almost knotting his tonsils in the attempt. 'Detachment, wisdom and change.'

'It would be a change,' said Gwyddion to no one in particular, 'if that stupid bird sat anywhere but on my head.'

But it was not to be. The silent puff of moonlight swept over the treetops and landed without error on Gwyddion's polished hair.

Puck and Taliesin picked up the pace. The owl on Gwyddion's head threatened to unhinge the more unruly goblins. Freckles' face was an unwholesome pink in his attempt to stop himself from laughing. Taliesin, expert on crowds, knew they would be losing them soon, if they didn't hurry.

'Frog,' called Puck. With a soft lollop, the frog fell over the side of Benedict's bucket and bounced sluggishly over to Puck, who put it back in the bucket, much to Benedict's annoyance.

'*Losgaun*,' responded Taliesin. 'Hidden beauty, sensitivity and power.'

'Like me,' snorted Freckles, and had to be subdued all over again.

'Swan.'

'*Eala*. Soul, love and beauty.'

'And a broken leg,' muttered a disgruntled Mr Dobie from his wheelchair.

'Wolf.'

'*Faol*. Shadows.'

'Adder.'

'*Nathair*. Transformation.'

'And totem of accountants, presumably,' muttered Leanne to Mab, who sniggered.

'Ram,' said Puck, leaping into the air in plenty of time as the mad-eyed sheep rampaged into the clearing. He'd learned a lot form the boar. The goblins were strangely silent.

'*Rathe*. Sacrifice.'

'Hmphh,' muttered the doe, to the stag's surprise. 'That's what they think.'

'Hare.' The loony thing gambolled onto the turf at Puck's feet and immediately started cropping the grass.

'*Geàrr*,' sang the harp, echoing the Singer's voice. 'Totem of rebirth. Hold on, Puck. Why have we got a hare here? Is rebirth what we're after?'

Puck knitted his brow. 'Perhaps not.' He bent down and looked into the hare's liquid eye. 'Clear off.' The hare stayed put, chewing thoughtfully.

'Let's just ignore the hare,' suggested Titania. 'Time is pressing. It will be dark soon.'

'It will be dark when I say it will,' muttered Pan, under the doe's breath.

'Bee.'

'Just one?'

'Oh, all right then. Bees.'

The swarm detached itself from the branch of the King's Tree and took off over the roof of the bower, to lodge in a mighty oak behind. Had the bees been asked, that harp had been driving them mad. It was only their innate good manners which had kept them there until that moment.

'*Beach*, the swarm stands for community, organization and celebration.'

Annis couldn't resist a chuckle. What had any of those to do with today?

'Wren.' Puck called.

The little bird struggled in Annis' pocket and she held it down.

'Wren?' Puck called again. 'Anyone seen the wren?'

Everyone shook their heads, turned to their neighbour, pulled rueful faces.

"No,' the crowd answered.

Taliesin was on automatic pilot. '*Drui-en*,' he sang. 'For humility, cunning, god.'

'Ermmm,' Puck plucked the Druid's sleeve. 'It hasn't turned up.'

'Really?' the Singer asked. 'That's unusual. They're usually reliable. Oh, well, we've got plenty. We'll do without the wren.'

'Are you sure?'

'Yes, yes, we'll be fine.'

Annis smiled to herself. One down. Six to go.

Taliesin raised his arms and addressed the assembled

beasts and fowl. 'Oh, creatures of our totem, go back to your homes, burrow, grazing, perching. Let your spirits remain to guard us and guide us in our binding. Creatures of the land, birds of the air depart and do no harm.'

The harp sang in the tree as the creatures left the glade, leaving just trampled ground and other small tokens behind. Gwyddion prised the owl from his head and watched its silent flight with relief.

The doe wandered into the trees, watching out for the stag as it did so. As soon as it was out of sight of the watchers, it lowered its head. With a small pop, Pan stood there, in all his goat-legged glory. He patted the doe on the head.

'Thank you, for the lift,' he said. 'A tip, if I may. Watch that stag. He's got a one-track mind.'

'Oh, good,' thought the doe, as she tiptoed elegantly out of the wood.

Chapter Fifty

'I think that went well, don't you,' said Puck.

'Compared with?' asked the Singer.

'It went better than I thought it would, at any rate. I thought James would give us a lot more trouble, for example.'

'I worry about the wren.'

'You said it didn't matter.'

'Well, perhaps it won't.' The Singer raised his voice so that everyone could hear. 'And now, flora.' And Oberon's key was G major. Taliesin had decided that with the fragile state of some of the more hysterical denizens of faerie, perhaps the word vegetable in conjunction with the king might be bad stage policy.

A twittering broke out among the flower faeries and he had to hurriedly calm them down. "No, no, not you, Flora. Plants. Vegetable. You know what I mean.'

The flower faeries subsided, and the king stepped forward and stood there. 'I have woven a rope,' prompted Titania from behind him.

'I have woven a rope to bind the god Pan. It is made from . . .'

'Honeysuckle . . .'

'Honeysuckle and sweet . . .'

'Hops . . .'

'This is useless. I don't remember what's in the stupid

thing. Ask Hazel, he did the list.'

'But, Sire,' wheedled Taliesin. 'It must be you. Only you can give it the necessary gravitas.'

'Whatever. I'll tell you what. Hazel can say the names and I'll hold them up.'

Taliesin could see when he was beaten.

'Hazel, could you step this way?'

The tree sprite broke away from the small shrubbery in one corner and stepped elegantly through the crowd.

'Oh, Sire,' he said ingratiatingly, to Oberon. 'This is such an honour.'

'Of course it is,' Oberon grunted. 'Right. Let's get on with it.'

A host of faerie, dressed in their best, carried a swag of greenery, cunningly wrought with the help of many spiders, across the clearing and deposited it in a fragrant skein at Oberon's feet. He picked up the end of it and looked at Hazel.

'What's this, to start?'

'Honeysuckle, *lonicera*, Sire.'

'What he said.'

'Hop.'

'What?'

'Hop. *Humulus lupulus*, Sire.'

'Sorry. I thought you were ordering me about. Humus loopy, that.'

'*Aconitum volubile, calystegia hederacae, clematis eriostemon* . . .'

'I don't think this is working, do you?' Oberon said to Taliesin.

'Not very well, I have to say. Let me think for a moment.'

Oberon spent the time picking some petals from a flower and moodily crushing them in his fingers. The crowd began to mutter. The sky darkened as clouds began to gather in the west.

In the wood, leaning on a tree and cleaning out his nails with a rose thorn, Pan began to chuckle.

'I have it,' said Taliesin suddenly and gestured at the harp which began to play. 'If you can pass out the garland, Sire, until it is straight with no tangles, I think this might do.'

The bard stepped forward and began sing, starting low in his throat.

'I dreamed that, as I wandered by the way,
Bare Winter suddenly was changed to Spring,
And gentle odours led my steps astray,
Mixed with a sound of water's murmuring
Along a shelved bank of turf, which lay
Under a copse, and hardly dared to fling
Its green arms round the bosom of the stream, but kissed it
and then fled, as thou mightst in a dream.'

Oberon had got in a bit of a tangle, where some ivy had twisted around a piece of rowan further up the garland. Taliesin left the harp to its own devices, while he bent down to help. 'Ow.'

'Sorry, Hazel. What did I do?'

'That's one of one's fingers you've got there. It's not really meant to bend that way although one is, of course, extremely supple.'

'Of course.'

'Did you just make that up?' Oberon asked, as the harp played on.

'No. It's something I made earlier.'

'How earlier?'

'Oooh, several bodies ago.'

'It seems to fit our situation perfectly.'

'I'm not called the prophet for nothing, you know. Oh, hang on, the harp's been on that bridge for ages. Gotta go.'

He stood up and sang some more. And as he sang, the garland seemed almost to unravel itself.

'There grew pied windflowers and violets,
Daisies, those pearled Arcturi of the earth,
The constellated flower that never sets.'

Mab was entranced. 'How does he come up with them?' she sighed. 'It's beautiful.'

Titania was trying to tap her foot, but the metre was too complicated. She just listened to the words instead.

'And in the warm hedge grew lush eglantine,
Green cowbind and the moonlight coloured may,
And cherry blossoms and white cups, whose wine

Was the bright dew,'
'My favourite,' whispered Titania to Leanne.
'Yet drained not by the day;
And wild roses and ivy serpentine,
With its dark buds and leaves, wandering astray;
And flowers azure, black and streaked with gold,
Fairer than any wakened eyes behold.'
'Taliesin,' called Oberon. 'Talk about ivy serpentine all you like. It keeps getting in a tangle.'

'I've done now,' said the Singer. 'The next bit's about the river's edge and you know how Pan enjoys his water. Perhaps it would be better to leave it there.'

The harp brought the song to a close, and the smell of the flowers made the air drowsy and the storm clouds melted away under the perfume's spell.

Oberon held up the garland, perfect and untangled, white flowers winking in its green depths.

There was a scattered burst of polite applause. The Singer and the King both took their bows. Honours even.

Annis patted the dried up little bunch of love-in-idleness in her pocket. Two down and going well. Just five more to go.

In the wood, Pan scowled at the sky. Words! What had words to do with music. He blew a discord on his pipes, folded his arms, crossed his goat legs at the knee and sulked.

Chapter Fifty One

Leaving the garland spread carefully on the grass, Oberon returned to the bank, to be patted by Titania and ignored by everyone else. He had so nearly blown it.

'Mineral,' cried the bard, in F sharp minor. 'Leanne, step forward.'

Leanne, her faerie dress clinging more than when Titania had first fitted it, undulated to Taliesin's side. Her red hair fell across one eye and her sinuous form looked positively tempting.

'I have mineral here,' she said.

'What mineral have you?' asked Taliesin, waving to the crowd to repeat it.

'What mineral have you?' said the crowd, more or less.

'I have diamond, which is harder than all things, to bind the god Pan.'

'What other mineral have you?' the crowd raggedly asked.

'I have gold, most precious of all things, to bind the god Pan.'

'What other mineral have you?'

'I have platinum . . . which is . . . um, I wasn't expecting to have platinum.'

'Well,' Titania, jewellery connoisseur, stepped forward. 'Actually, platinum is harder and more precious than gold, so I suppose you could say that. Or, you could just say that it will wear gold out, but that isn't the point. I suppose . . ."

'Thank you, your majesty,' said Taliesin, trying to keep the audience together.

'I have platinum, which looks a bit like silver but isn't and is harder than gold.'

The audience were puzzled but piped up anyway.

'What other mineral have you?'

'Um . . . I think that's it.'

Puck sprang from his seat on the bank and smashed a glass at Leanne's feet.

'Careful, imbecile!'

'Silicon, for clarity of purpose,' Puck called to the crowd. 'What other mineral have you?'

Leanne muttered out of the corner of her mouth, 'Go on then, clever clogs. What other mineral have I?'

Puck bent down and retrieved a piece of burnt wood, relic of one of the goblins' fires.

'Carbon, for . . .'

'Had it.'

'What?'

'Carbon. Had it. A diamond is made of carbon.'

'How do you know that?'

'I ate a science student once. He was a bit gristly, but I like to begin with small talk and that was a bit of it.'

'Did you learn anything else?' asked Taliesin.

'Yes, as a matter of fact.' Leanne licked her lips and advanced on the Druid. 'I learned that blood has iron in it. That's a mineral, isn't it?'

'Only Mortal blood, surely?' the Singer said, backing away.

'Possibly. Possibly not. Are you ready to find out?' With an audible 'snick' her teeth sprang out, pointed and glinting in the sun. then, the sun went in as the clouds rolled back. A chill was in the air and the thunder rolled, sounding very like laughter.

'I think we'd better move on,' said Taliesin hastily, adjusting his clothing to his own comfort setting, after his mild mauling from the vampire.

'If that's the worst he gets from her, he'll be all right,' muttered Oberon to Benedict. Both faerie shared a knowing glance.

'Almost too easy,' whispered Annis to herself. 'Almost half-way and all is going very well.' She jingled the gemstones in her pocket. 'Very well indeed.'

'Well, that was a disaster,' thought Pan to himself with a chuckle. With the animals a worthy draw, the veg a definite win for Taliesin – Pan was never mealy-mouthed over some-one else's success; it was one of his better traits – this one had to count as a win for Pan, if only by default. Honours well and truly even, with earth, air, fire and water to go.

The world was in the bag.

Confusion rolled in on the clouds.

Mischief was in the air.

It was so close he could almost taste it.

"Nothing,' thought Pan to himself as he danced a little jig, "Nothing succeeds *quite* like success."

Chapter Fifty-Two

'I think that went quite well, don't you?' Leanne whispered to Mab as she resumed her place.

Mab grunted in a way Leanne didn't like, but there was no time for reprisals, as Taliesin was continuing.

'Earth, step forward,' he said. Gwyddion's key was D.

In the wood, Pan moved a little closer. Time for the Druid, time to see if his divided loyalties had come down on one side or another.

Gwyddion took his golden sickle from under his robe and it glinted in the few rays of sun still managing to force their way through the banking thunderheads off to the west.

He brought out a sprig of mistletoe and held it aloft, as Taliesin prepared the white cloth in which to catch it. He threw it into the air and it circled lazily above his head, landing finally in the outstretched linen.

He reached out with his left arm and with a flourish rolled back the sleeve. Bringing the golden sickle round above his head, he appeared to be about to slice off his own hand.

The crowd gasped, and held their breath.

But no. With lightning reflexes, he stopped the blade just as it hit the tip of his finger, and one perfect ruby drop of blood fell into the cloth. Gwyddion stood, head bowed, as Taliesin gathered up the corners and knotted them tightly. Then, he gave the bundle to Gwyddion, who threw it up into the air, catching it as it came down on the point of his sickle.

As the blade cut through the knot, the cloth fell open and a snow-white dove flew out, circling over the heads of the crowd with a piece of mistletoe in its beak.

Gwyddion bowed with a flourish and went back to his place.

The crowd were silent.

'Vat's *it?*' whispered Freckles to Tiny. "Vat's erf? I seen better on a street corner.'

'Well,' Tiny whispered back. 'I suppose they know what they're doing.' But he didn't sound very certain. Bill, who relied on Tiny to give the nod when to panic, began to cluck softly under his breath and peck randomly at the dust at their feet.

In the wood, Pan was doubled up with silent laughter. The squirrel, watching from his newly built drey further into the wood, sighed. He was glad now they had built this bigger place. From the way things were going, they were going to be stuck at six-foot-tall for a long, long time.

Taliesin watched Gwyddion go. He was a little puzzled by his colleague's behaviour. There had been much more than that when they had discussed it in Titania's bower. Fireworks had been ruled out early on as tacky, but somehow he didn't think one measly drop of blood could stand for sacrifice. Never mind. Air was next and this faerie had a lot to lose. When he wanted someone to rely on, give him a mother any time, he thought to himself. On reflection, his hadn't been up to much, but they had been different days.

He stepped forward.

'Air!' he sang, and the harp at least did him proud, with chords never heard before or meant to be heard again, in every key, sharp or flat, major and minor.

Phoebe had decided, especially after Gwyddion's lame performance, to give it all she'd got. She had primed a few hearth faeries, friend of mothers, in advance. They now stood at four corners of the glade, ready for the off. She herself had flown way up into the sky, above the clouds, to wait for her cue. Beyond the clouds to the west, she was disheartened to see more clouds, blacker than ever, with lightning playing in their depths and thunder muttering in voices just too muffled to understand the words. Phoebe gave a little shudder. Perhaps it was just as well she couldn't hear.

'Air!' Taliesin's voice came up through the levels of cloud and sun to where she waited. She let herself drop like a stone until she was feet above the ground and then slowed herself down, so that her dress billowed out and she landed like thistledown.

She stepped forward. Taliesin took up position by the harp, ready to turn it this way and that.

She gestured with one hand and called 'North Wind.'

The hearth fairy in the relevant corner undid the mouth of the bag she held and a wicked, icy, rollicking wind rushed out. It blew through the crowd, ruffling hair, bristles and, in a few examples, scales. Hats flew in the air, along with some of the smaller faerie, who held on, one to the other, in a long line, buffeted as the wind whirled past. It blew through the harp and a bluff, loud bass note sounded, underscored by wild waters crashing on rocky coasts. The snap of icicles falling from eaves were the percussion of the north wind's tune.

'Classy,' muttered Pan in his wood. 'Very classy. I always liked old Feeb. I'll see her all right later.' He rubbed his hands together in anticipation.

'South Wind!' called Phoebe over the North wind's noise.

The hearth fairy in the opposite corner undid her bag. A scent of grass meadows, lightly crushed by new born lambs' gambolling drifted over the heads of the crowd. The little skein of windswept faeries fell harmlessly to earth. The South wind passed with hardly any force; it went by with a hint of a warm sun kissing a peach skin. It trailed its fingers down necks and arms. It went on its way so softly, leaving just a hint of regret at a warm day's passing. Cow bells, bees, and song more beautiful than a bird ever sang accompanied the wind as she left the glade.

'Oh, Phoebe,' Pan said to the sky. 'I can hardly wait.'

'East Wind!'

And here Phoebe's downfall began. The hearth faerie holding the bag of East Wind opened it on cue. Sadly, so did the one in charge of the West. A bitter, mean-minded East wind flew across the glade, too lazy to go round so it just went through, cutting little creatures to the bone with cold. The crowd on the west side did better, with the warm wet west wind caressing them with hints of hot-pink sunsets and better times to come.

It was when they met in the middle that the trouble started. Whirlwinds sprang up, where the two temperatures came together. Small Seelie and Unseelie creatures flew into the air and some were sucked into the vortex and were next seen heading towards the village, whirling round with various debris, including, rather oddly, a farmhouse, small but perfect in every detail, which had appeared from nowhere. A faint cry of 'I don't think we're in Kansas anymore, Toto,' was heard as the tornado crested the hill, and then the silence fell.

The two courts assessed the damage. No one was seriously hurt, although lots of pride was bruised, and of course, the creatures caught up in the wind had yet to be accounted for. Phoebe looked around at the devastation and burst into tears. Taliesin stood nonplussed, holding the ruins of his Aeolian harp. He plucked a string, and it made a dismal 'thunk.'

Mab and Leanne were rolling as one, hysterical with laughter. The queen allowed herself a twitch at the corner of her mouth, and then tapped Mab with her toe.

'Sshh. This is serious.'

The two coughed and adjusted their dresses, wiping their eyes with the backs of their hands. Yes, it was serious. But, oh, how delicious, to see the high and mighty Phoebe brought so low.

A sound made them stop. Away in the wood, a stamping of hooves, hooves that could well be golden, silver shod. A clapping of hands, hands with long fingers, made to pipe and stroke and pinch and tease. A laugh, long and loud, a laugh to freeze a faerie's blood.

Pan.

Chapter Fifty Three

Taliesin stepped forward again. His heart was in his boots. He was basically an optimist, but by his reckoning the world of Faerie was trailing by rather a lot of points. Fire and water left to go. He was quite hopeful for the effects of fire. Sally was reliable and had been working on her part. Water – well, Benedict had been very quiet, and he had slopped a lot out of his bucket, not to mention what the frog had drunk.

'Fire,' he said and waved a languid hand at Sally – A major. 'Er . . . for purification,' he added, and went and sat down, his chin on his hand.

The glade was suddenly aglow. From every corner, cartwheels of fire appeared, skimming over the heads of the crowd. There were oohs and aahs from every side. Those with keen sight could see the little faerie or elf at the centre of the circle, spinning two little gouts of flame on the end of lengths of spiders' web, the centrifugal force keeping them in the air and moving them along at the same time.

Sally stood at the front, conducting them as they came, wave upon wave, to spin around her head. Then, at a signal from her, they formed a spinning cylinder which dropped over her head. When the little fliers spun off into the cooler air, she was left there, a column of flame which got bigger and wider and hotter and redder as they watched. Soon, it was too much and almost everyone turned their heads away.

It was because of this that no one saw Annis lean forward and light her pipe at the flame's edge. She leaned back contentedly, puffing away to keep the little glow red.

With a pop, Sally was back, the grass unscorched, leaving an imprint of her part of the binding on every retina.

Leaning on his tree, Pan kicked moodily at the mould at his feet. By his reckoning, that made them level, with just water to go. Benedict was a bit of an unknown quantity to Pan. He knew he was close to Man, he knew Annis wanted him left alone, but . . . could he risk letting him go ahead? What if his binding turned out to be strong? What if he could capture him, in a drop of water perhaps – it had been done. Some of his best friends had been stopped by water spells. He stroked his chin and thought.

Ahah! He had another Plan, another compromise. If the Unseelie Lord seemed to be doing all right, he would rampage into the glade, stamping, etc etc. Mayhem, rout, screaming, everything as planned. If he didn't seem to be doing so well, he would let him get on with it. He could make an absolute tit of himself and then he, Pan, could rampage into the glade, stamping and so on. Same outcome, but with the possibility of a few cheap laughs at someone else's expense. He moved nearer, creeping through the undergrowth until he was just a few trees in from the edge.

Sally had gone back to her place, the flush in her cheeks partly from the heat, partly from the pride. Fire had redeemed itself and if her part of the binding didn't hold, it was no fault of hers. She sat at Puck's feet and waited for Benedict to begin to do his stuff.

As someone who had been part of his household for years and years, she thought she knew him. Quiet, scholarly, very into machines, keyboards, phones, business deals and little else. The rest of the apartment might be full of fachans hiding in the wardrobes, water-demons behind the showercurtains and James' unspeakable snacks in the freezer, but she had always considered the Master the most civilised member of any Faerie court you cared to name. She wriggled into a more comfy position and hugged her knees, waiting

Taliesin was still fiddling with the ruins of his harp. He had planned a backdrop of watery cadences, the musical equivalent of a mountain stream, a rill running over the stones as it escaped the snowline. He had planned the deep throated roar of the weir, the tranquil depths of an unfathomable ocean, whale cries in the upper registers tying this binding, the last, to the first, the fauna. But it didn't look likely, with only two strings intact and the frame in ruins.

He turned to Benedict with a rueful expression on his face and shrugged. He hadn't wanted to let Benedict down. Despite the habits of his courtiers, he and Taliesin had always got along all right. A mutual detestation of bagpipes is a powerful glue in any friendship.

But Benedict had surprised him. He leapt down onto the smooth sward in front of the royal box, as he had come to think of it, his bucket replaced by a crystal goblet. Where it had come from, no one knew but the Unseelie Lord. In fact, he had found it on the Internet, and a confused TNT driver had arrived with it only just in time. Benedict had often found www.spells.r.us.unseelie.com/water/bindings to be a useful site, but he had never used them for anything this important. How could he have done – there had never *been* anything this important.

The wizard at the help desk had responded at once. The crystal goblet had been sourced within the hour, in the skeletal grasp of a long-dead king, in his barrow on a windswept Hebridean Isle. A team of goblins, with a few mining trows from uncharted Highland valleys, had soon burrowed down and were away on their toes before anything knew it was missing. Benedict, who had a tidy mind, felt a pang for archaeologists as yet un-degreed. They were going to be really confused. Especially when they found the mobile phone one of the goblins had left behind. But still, it was all in a good cause.

Annis sat up as straight as she could. Where in Pan's name

had the lad found that goblet. She remembered when it was buried, long centuries ago, where it could do no harm. How did he even know about it? Surely, an innocent cradle-song could not have lodged in his brain so well that he could unearth it now? But the evidence was in front of her. If he hadn't unearthed the memory, he had unearthed the cup. And that was bad. Really, really bad. For him. For her favourite son.

She leaned back into the shadows, her heart knocking in her breast, her whole body hurting with the pain her child must soon feel. A tear cut through the grime on her cheek and dripped onto her withered claw, clutched at her throat.

Her time had nearly come.

At the edge of the wood, Pan clenched his teeth in fury and stamped his golden hooves, in temper. The clouds were roiling overhead and the thunder nearly drowned out Taliesin's voice as he called to the spirits of water, a song without words that cut straight to the hindbrain and made everyone think they had their gills back.

Benedict held the crystal cup over his head and spread his wings with a clap that drowned the thunder.

Pan punched the air and the clouds burst. It didn't rain – the air was just suddenly full of water, water at its most painful, huge drops as big as a mortal fist and with as much power, bouncing the smaller faerie into the air and making the dust, turning quickly to mud, fountain up into the air, splashing every gossamer gown and staining everything.

Benedict called up into the sky, in an ancient tongue that set teeth on edge. The water poured into his cup, funnelling down from the sky and yet the cup was never filled. The cup changed colour, took on the blue of the ocean, the blue that no real water ever is. Rainbows formed around its rim and it was sparkling with the life of water new-minted in a spring newly-struck from the earth.

Sally looked into Benedict's face and hardly recognised her scholarly, silent boss. He had a radiance, a luminescence, a transparency she had never seen. Wait! A transparency? Then she realised that she could indeed see straight through him. His dark wings were turning into the multi-coloured spray at a waterfall's edge, his face was etched in a sheet of cool water under a willow's shade, his body was turning into a column of water, as if spouted up by the fall of an iceberg on a forgotten Antarctic shore. Benedict was water.

She screamed.

Pan stepped out of the wood.

Everyone screamed.

Then, the time for screaming seemed to be past and a terrible peace descended on the assembled courts of Faerie.

Into the glade stepped the great god Pan, Faunus, Aristaeus, Priapus – whatever name he chose to go by, he remained the Lord of Confusion and Misrule; Mischief hung about him like a cloak. The clouds had emptied into Benedict's crystal and an unearthly light, like sunlight underwater, bathed Pan as he tiptoes on his golden hooves towards the faerie kings and queen.

He had never looked so beautiful nor so terrible. His hair was flying out from his head, blown from the terrible energy from within. His skin slid over muscles so honed and toned over millennia of routing and dancing that not even a sleep of aeons could wither them. His goat legs flexed and stretched as he stepped carefully over the tiny folk at his feet. He had learnt in his few days of wakefulness that compassion was sometimes a good thing. Gwyddion would have been proud to think he had taught Pan something, however small and ultimately useless as a survival tool. His best feature was borne proudly, so extreme in this manifestation of excess that not even Leanne reacted. He had not learnt yet that less is indeed sometimes more. Silent, menacing, he stepped forward.

He smiled.

He brought his pipe to his lips.

He blew.

The smaller faeries hid their faces. Oberon stepped forward, pulled as though on a string. Benedict became less defined, not so much an Unseelie Lord in his prime, more a column of water, wavering and losing shape with each step from the goat-foot. Titania, Leanne and the others gripped the edges of their chairs. Puck and Phoebe clung to each other as the pipe began to charm them from their seats. Mab, unable to resist the call of mischief, crawled towards him on her belly. Padraig ran towards him laughing, arms outstretched and Freckles and Tiny were in his wake. The crowd began to divide. Those who were for. And those against. In other words, those who would live to tell the tale. And those who could not.

Pan's eyes glinted as he stepped forward, dainty as a cat, deadly as a cobra. His pipe was never silent; he seemed to be able to play with no breath, and why not. Breathing was optional to one such as he. The music kept Taliesin rooted to the spot, the first target in the Piper's sights.

He stepped nearer, and nearer.

Oberon's horns had sprouted fall and long now. His persona, the green man, Herne the Hunter, was in ascendancy and his Little Guys, his Lads, his Mates knew that they could now only be one thing – his prey.

Titania stood defiant surrounded by her handmaidens. She held Undine particularly tightly by the shoulder, to stop the little girl running after her brother. She, Titania, Queen of Faerie, would not be beaten by the great greasy thing. She had dragged her world back from the brink – it would take more than a smelly goat-legged barbarian to beat her. Oh yes! Her smile grew brittle, but she kept it in place.

Puck had lost his grip on Phoebe, who had run after Padraig. She was crouched with him now on the edge of Pan's path, arms round the child's waist, face buried in his bouncing curls. Even in Faerieland, genetics will out, and the child looked ready for the off; up for the rout wherever it took them. Puck sighed – he could see himself at that age, and it was not a sight to soothe his age-old eyes. He looked around for someone to hold, in what he thought were likely to be his final minutes. But there was no one.

Leanne and James were trying to get to Benedict, their shelter in any storm over the years. But he was unrecognisable now, a mass of water held together by willpower alone. A will that must soon break. James howled, but his voice was silenced by the relentless pipe.

Pan raised his pipes high, still blowing.

He danced a ghastly jig.

Dry lightning flashed from the sky, blinding every eye.

Chapter Fifty Four

When everyone's vision cleared, Annis was standing there.

No one had seen her move. She just was where before she was not. Pan took his pipe slowly from his mouth, but the music seemed to echo on in their heads.

He took one more step.

Annis did not flinch.

He spoke. 'Out of my way, woman. You have become old, no matter what you were once.'

Annis took the pipe out of her mouth and spat to one side. She put the pipe back in and clenched her teeth. "No,' she said, out of one corner of her mouth.

Pan leaned forward and roared. 'Out of my way!'

'I think I said no.'

Pan stamped. 'You're no Fun anymore, old woman. I shall crush you.'

'You made me a promise,' she said simply.

Heads snapped round to look at her with new respect. She had already talked to the god? When?

Pan shuffled his feet. 'I wasn't myself,' he muttered.

"No. You were a milk white doe, here in this glade. And you promised me you wouldn't hurt Benedict.'

'Who?' Pan looked puzzled.

Annis sighed. 'Lord of Unseelie. We've already gone through this.'

'Oh, yes. Well, what if I did?'

'As I remember, you were always good at keeping promises.'

'That was then. Before you trussed me up and buried me under a hill. All bets are off, I think.' He raked the crowd with his stare and all who could backed off a pace.

Annis, however, stepped forward. No shuffling now. She was more upright, her hair was pushed back from her face. She seemed to have two eyes, both looking in the same direction. Puck was struck by the fact that one was green and one was red. Where had he heard that before? And recently?

James' howl was getting louder now the music had begun to die away. 'Please,' he howled, in a spine-tingling key. 'My Master. Help him someone.'

Annis turned her head and then spun back to Pan.

She stepped forward and as she stepped, she grew. Her hair curled out down her back and the tendrils flew as if on a wind. Her skin grew soft and unlined, ruddy at the cheek. Her eyes grew clear. Her hand snaked out and caught Pan by the arm and she pulled him to her. Surprise made him clumsy and he stumbled into her arms.

She held him like a vice, one handed, while her other hand delved into the pocket of what had become a warrior-woman's battle dress.

She scattered the crumbs of soil on Pan.

'I bind you with the earth we tread on,' she hissed. 'Be bound by this and need no burying.'

Pan struggled and spat, as the bits of dirt got in his eyes and mouth.

'Let me go, woman,' he yelled, struggling to raise the pipe to his lips. 'I have unfinished business here.'

She opened her hand and the little puff of Undine's breath blew into his nostrils and made him sneeze.

'I bind you by the air we breathe,' she said, louder to be heard above the bogle's howling and the god's cries.

She scattered the smouldering contents of the pipe she held between her teeth around them in a circle.

'I bind you by the fire that we once shared, that warmed our children.'

'Typical!' screamed Pan. 'That's it, bring the children into it!'

'I bind you . . .' she stopped, feeling the front of her gown. In all the excitement, she hadn't noticed it had dried out. In an extraordinary piece of intelligence, on which he would dine for generations to come, should there be any, James soaked up some of his dwindling master in a hairy paw and ran across with it.

'Here, Mistress,' he panted. 'Use this.'

She looked down at him and his doggy heart swelled with pride.

She shook the drops onto the god's head, and he flinched.

'I bind you with the water that is our lifeblood.'

'Quite literally,' muttered Oberon. He could feel free will coursing through his veins. Mab had begun to sit up and look a little shamefaced. Phoebe had found the strength to carry Padraig back to Titania's side.

Annis pulled the little wren from her pocket and left it go. It fluttered in Pan's face, scolding as only that tiny bird can. It was crosser than it had ever been in its life and no seven-foot idiot with goat-feet was going to stop it venting its annoyance. A sputter of laughter crossed the glade.

'I bind you by the life you say you love. The life of wood and copse, of heath and vale.'

Pan snorted down his nostrils and shook his head. His struggling had grown less but Annis knew better than to weaken her grip.

'I bind you by the plants that clothe the land,' she said, crumbling the withered love-in-idleness in his eyes.

'I knew that would come in useful,' said Mab to anyone who would listen. Mab was not a faerie who could learn by experience and she would soon be as opinionated as ever.

'And I finally bind you by the gems and metals beneath our feet.' She scattered the contents of the dwarves' bag around them both.

Binding done, she put both arms round the god. Into his ear, she whispered. 'Come on now. Don't be angry. You know this is for the best. I know my time with Mortals is over. Why not spend the rest of eternity with me somewhere quiet?

Eh? You know it makes sense.'

He pulled back his lovely head and stared deep into her eyes. He sighed and leaned his forehead against hers. She was back, his lovely Anu, mother of (some at least) of his children. Chariot goddess, fearless in battle, a she-wolf in defence of her cub. She hadn't changed.

'All right,' he said, deep in his throat, out of range of Faerie hearing. Only Taliesin shook his head, as though his ear drums had come loose. 'But you'll have to loose me if I am to save . . . what did you say he was calling himself these days?'

'Benedict.'

'Benedict.'

'Oh, no. Just whistle. You know how to whistle don't you?'

Pan put his lips together and blew. There was a wet plop and Benedict sat there on the ground, damp but otherwise quite as usual. Leanne and James were all over him like a rash in seconds and he sat back, bemused but enjoying it.

'Thank you,' she breathed, and then whistled herself. A clip of hooves on gravel in one corner of the glade made heads turn. There, in the darkening evening, stood a chariot, pulled by . . . surely, it was just the shadows that made those horses look like centaurs.

Pan turned his head back to Anu. 'Oh,' he breathed, 'You remembered.'

She smiled and inclined her head.

'Shall we?'

'Let's.'

The two clambered aboard and the chariot turned in front of Titania's bower and clattered off into the wood.

Mab, romantic and joker, said wistfully to Freckles, who was dusting himself down at her side, 'I feel we should have put old boots or something on the back.'

Freckles patted her on the back and smiled, in his piggy way.

"Nuffink changes, Mab, does it?" he said, and went in search of his king.

Chapter Fifty Five

Puck woke up in a muck-sweat. For a start, where was he? And for another thing, who? Or what? His dream had been so vivid.

The sweat cooled on his brow and then grew colder still. His memory returned with a wrenching rush and he sat up, staring into the darkness. It hadn't been a dream. It had really happened. Or had it? His head hurt.

He groped his way out of bed and headed for the slightly brighter rectangle that marked the door and peeped out.

Titania's glade was empty of everyone and thing. It had been swept and tidied by some brownies the night before and now, in the pearly dawn light, there was no sign of fire, lightning strikes or other mayhem to be seen.

Tuning his hearing to its finest, Puck could detect snoring coming from one corner, signifying that the goblins were still asleep – hardly a surprise after what they had put away the night before, he thought with an inner laugh.

Soft breathing from Titania's bower, in several different sharps and flats, told him that the king had stayed over – so that was nice. The queen would like that.

Up in Oberon's favourite branch, a large unkempt shape resolved into the Lord of Unseelie, wrapped in his wings, sleeping stretched out in the arms of the oak. James slept beneath, whimpering occasionally in his sleep and being the bravest butler in the world, all over again. And also, Puck looked closer, a shapely leg was curled around the edge of one darkling wing. Leanne! Puck chuckled. So Pan had left something behind after all.

Mab had weaved her way back to the village late the night before, taking Padraig and Undine with her, with Taliesin by her side. And good luck to her, thought Puck. And to him, a small voice in his head added. Undine and Padraig were giving it another go with Auntie, until their mother was feeling better. She had had a bad fright. Puck looked round. Phoebe was nowhere to be seen and he wondered where she was. Not gone back to the dreadful Thomas, he hoped.

Gwyddion had flown off in the general direction of the West. He had had enough of magic, he said. He thought he might have another go at teaching. The hours were better, and the beer was cheaper. The owl was flying by his side and his going had been punctuated by his frantic shooing, and the owl's plaintive tuwhoo.

He carried on looking around the glade. A noise on the edge of the trees attracted his attention and he walked over. Two squirrels, of average size, were chasing each other up and down a tall beech. One of them came over and perched on Puck's shoulder, chattering madly in his ear. The other one stood at his feet, also chittering away, pointing into the trees.

He said, 'Sorry, Mr Squirrel, Mrs Squirrel. I expect you'll be glad to know I don't understand a word.'

Still making a squirrelly racket, they ran off into the wood. Their noise sounded almost like laughter. Pan smiled and turned back to the clearing, with thoughts of a few more minutes in bed.

His heart stopped with the sight that met his eyes.

Pan and Anu were there, standing hand in hand, glorious, golden, seven feet tall. Their centaurs – lady centaurs – pawed the ground beside them. As Puck watched, the door to Titania's bower opened and Oberon walked out, in a night-shirt of the finest linen, embroidered with ivy by the most dextrous faerie fingers. He walked up to the two and stood waiting.

Up in the tree, Benedict unfurled his wings. He put

Leanne tenderly on the branch and she didn't wake up. James jumped to his feet but was shushed as his Master touched down on the ground, folding his wings as he did so. James lay back down, head on his paws, tail slowly moving to and fro. The Unseelie Lord joined the three.

Then, Puck began to doubt the testimony of his eyes further. The two Lords stepped forward and hugged each other. Then Pan. Then Anu. Whispered words were exchanged that even Puck with his twenty-twenty hearing couldn't catch, nor was he meant to. It was private moment. Parents saying goodbye to their children. Well, as Pan said, ruffling Oberon's head where the horns had so recently been, not goodbye. More au revoir. Another coupla thousand years, they'd be gone in a flash. Anu, who had never been away, stroked her favourite's cheek. She blew a kiss at Oberon, and then the two were gone, the centaurs' hooves hardly making a sound on the raked ground. Puck watched them go.

When he turned round, Benedict was back on his branch and Titania's door was just closing. He shook his head and went back towards his guest room in the bole of a tree.

As he got there, the door opened. He watched in trepidation as it swung outwards, the gossamer curtain which hung inside the door billowing out as the warm air exited.

'Puck,' said Phoebe, holding a robe tight under her chin. 'What are you doing out there? You'll catch your death of cold.' She shivered dramatically. 'It's freezing.'

Puck looked around him. She was right. It was. Hoar frost hung on every twig, outlined every leaf. Each berry had a coat of glass. The grass was crackling with the breath of the freezing air. Nothing stirred, but one small snowdrop in the grass at his feet. He stared at it. It didn't move. No others joined it.

Puck whooped for joy. It was February!

He ran towards his doorway. 'I hope your feet are warm, Feeb,' he said. 'Because mine are as cold as ice.'

He paused in the doorway.

'Yes, as cold as ice.'